D1466526

LADY BLANCHE FARM
and
QUEEN ANNE'S LACE

Lady Blanche Farm
and
Queen Anne's Lace

*Two
full-length
novels
by*

FRANCES PARKINSON KEYES

LIVERIGHT PUBLISHING CORPORATION
NEW YORK

PREFACE

Some months ago, Mr. Arthur Pell of the Liveright Publishing Corporation paid me the compliment of asking me to write a brief preface to the new edition of my first two novels, *The Old Gray Homestead* and *The Career of David Noble*, which they have republished in attractive omnibook form. I was delighted to comply with his request for two reasons: first, because I realized that this new edition would meet the requirements of many faithful readers, who had been trying in vain to secure the earlier ones; and secondly, as I said in writing the desired preface, "because I have always felt a certain nostalgic affection for . . . *The Old Gray Homestead* and *The Career of David Noble*, perhaps because the setting of both is a village similar to the two in which I spent a great part of my early life and with which my inherited affiliation goes back nearly two hundred years."

Now that a similar request has been made in connection with the two novels which I wrote next—*Lady Blanche Farm* and *Queen Anne's Lace*—I feel I cannot do better than make a similar answer. The scene of *Lady Blanche*—written before *Queen Anne*, though published afterward—is again the village I called by the fictional name of Hamstead, while giving it the characteristics of the real New England villages which I have known so well and loved so much ever since my childhood. Anne, beginning her life in the same village, eventually leaves it for Washington—which is what I did myself. Indeed, a great many persons, when *Queen Anne* first made its appearance, were certain that the story was autobiographical; and though this conviction is a mistaken one, in so far as all but two chapters are concerned, certainly I never could have written it without the factual knowledge of our nation's capital and the feeling for it that I acquired as the young wife of a senator.

Blanche and Anne are New England girls, and though one goes further afield and attains greater heights of glory than the other, both personify the way of life in the region to which they belong, and embody its ideals. So again I will say, as I did in writing of Austin Gray and David Noble:

"The tradition and the heritage of New England are surely ones in which all of us, no matter what our places of birth, can partake; and it is my earnest hope that, through these two novels and in some slight way, I have succeeded in interpreting this heritage and this tradition, not only to New Englanders themselves, but to the rest of the country as well."

FRANCES PARKINSON KEYES

The Oxbow
Newbury, Vermont
October 1951

LADY BLANCHE FARM
and
QUEEN ANNE'S LACE

Lady Blanche Farm

A ROMANCE OF THE COMMONPLACE

TO

Catherine and Henry Deming

whose efficient, faithful and
devoted service has lightened my labors as a
housekeeper and facilitated my
progress as an author,

I DEDICATE THIS BOOK

with gratitude and affection

CHAPTER ONE

"I've swallowed," said Philip Starr to himself, "about two bushels of dust. Don't they ever oil their roads in Vermont, I wonder? And what I haven't swallowed is on the outside of me, gradually sifting in. I'm sure I can't make Burlington tonight anyway—it must be somewhere over on the other side of the map. For a small state, Vermont is about the largest—"

He interrupted his own train of thought by laughing aloud, and brought his motor to a stop beside the powdery highway which he had been mentally condemning.

"Irish, cropping out as usual," he said, grinning, as he locked the car, "or maybe I'm still dippy—typhoid bugs die hard. Anyway, I'm going to see if this brook doesn't wind far enough from the road somewhere soon for me to get into it, without being arrested in the process. I had no idea it got hot way up here in May."

He rolled under the barbed-wire fence, and scrambled into the underbrush of the woods that skirted the road. Never—never that he could remember—had he been in a place so utterly still. The little brook, slipping along over smooth stones, made hardly a sound. The sun, shining in through the evergreens, and the few slim birches, just beginning to leaf, among them, dappled the pine needles under his feet with splashes of light. There were ferns, half uncurled, jack-in-the-pulpits, pink lady-slippers, wake-robins; the quiet flowers that grow in quiet places. The crackling of dry branches, the twittering of a few birds were the only sounds.

Philip was right; the little brook, twisting and turning, wound farther and farther into the woods; it foamed into a tiny waterfall, widened to a small pool, narrowed, twisted, and fell again. The second fall was a higher one, the pool beyond it deep and placid and cool, and green as an emerald —ideal for a swim! But, pulling off his coat and jerking at his collar, the man stopped short and stared ahead of him, wondering if he were suddenly losing his senses.

On the edge of the pool, just beyond the waterfall—so close to it indeed, that its spray fell all about her—seated on a moss-covered boulder rising from the water, was a girl, her face turned from him, her white feet and ankles gleaming through the clear water of the brook. She had on a soft, short, close-fitting white garment, and her bare arms were raised above her head, half-covered with the masses of shining hair that fell about her like a golden cloud.

Philip had been whistling. He stopped, so abruptly that he choked. The girl, who had been unconscious of the approaching whistle, became vaguely aware of something different in her surroundings when it ceased. She shook her hair, dropped her arms, and turned around. Then after one startled second, in which Philip saw that her eyes were as blue as the shining sky which dappled the woods with its light, she smiled with entire friendliness.

"How do you do?" she asked pleasantly.

"I'm very well—that is, I'm not well at all. I've just had typhoid fever," Philip stammered. Then, thinking what an asinine thing that was to say, he went on, realizing all the time that he was not becoming less asinine, "That's why I'm here—trying to get better, you know."

"I see," said the girl, with the same serene pleasantness. "I'm sorry. Did you walk all the way from wherever you came, and is this the direct route to wherever you're going?"

Philip laughed. "No, I motored. I left Boston early this morning, but I got so tired and so dirty and so hot that I—"

"Left your motor by the side of the road, and followed the brook to take a swim. And now I'm here first, spoiling it all. What a pity! I'll go—"

"Oh, please don't! I don't think you're spoiling anything particularly," Philip stammered again, hoping that he was not staring at this vision of loveliness as hard as he felt that he was. "In fact you—you rather add—to the place—and I thought it was the prettiest place I had ever seen, anyway."

The girl put up her hands, and began drying her hair again. "Won't you sit down?" she asked after a short silence which she seemed to regard in no way as awkward. "You must be pretty tired."

Philip complied with this suggestion, feeling it to be an agreeable one, and, utterly at a loss as to what to say or do next, waited for the girl to make the next move. At last, as she continued to dry her hair in silence, he burst out, "Is one apt to run across—persons—like you—beside Vermont brooks?"

It was the girl's turn to laugh. "I don't know," she said. "I haven't seen many of them outside of Hamstead."

"Perhaps you're not a person at all? Perhaps you're a dryad —or a nymph—or something like that?"

"I wish I were," she said, and the least shadow of discontent seemed to have crept into her voice. "I don't remember much about dryads and nymphs—I always hated to study—but they had a pretty good time, didn't they? My cousin Mary knows all about them. She'd have her nose in a book half the time, if she didn't have so much else to do. She and Mother and Cousin Jane are all housecleaning today—that's why I ran away. I'd have had to help if I'd stayed at home. That's the way they always spend the whole month of May! And then in June, preserving begins and keeps up all the rest of the summer, and besides that, there's haying, and threshing, and corn-cutting! And by the time that's all over, it's Fall again and they begin the *Autumn cleaning!* You'd never believe there was so much in a house, until you got it all out in the front yard! And Paul is so lazy he never helps half as much as he might, and Mary has to stop right in the middle of everything and chase up the children, and Cousin Jane goes off to prayer-meeting, and Mrs. Elliott comes along and says, 'Well, that horsehair sofa is getting awful shabby, ain't it? I should think you'd get a new one'—and oh, it's all plenty bad enough to make anyone want to be a nymph and live in a brook, where life is just one perpetual bath, and there can't possibly be anything to houseclean!"

Philip threw back his head and roared, and after a minute, the girl laughed too.

"Well, if you're not a nymph, and you don't live in a brook, would you think I were awfully rude if I asked what your name is and where you live?"

"My name is Blanche Manning. I live on Lady Blanche Farm."

"Lady Blanche Farm!" echoed Philip. "What a pretty name!"

"Yes—there's quite a pretty story about it, too. Would you like to hear it?"

"Very much."

"All right—my hair's dry now. I'll go and dress and you can have your swim. I've got some lunch with me—where my clothes are—enough for two, I guess. I'll come back."

"Do you promise? Nymphs have a way of vanishing!"

"Of course I promise. I told you I wasn't a nymph. I'll sing out when I start back, and if you aren't ready, you can tell me not to come."

She slipped off the boulder, waded to the shore, and waved her hand. Then, a little, white graceful figure, she vanished among the trees on the opposite side of the brook.

It was more than half an hour later before he heard her returning. He had bathed and dressed hurriedly, and was sitting, greatly refreshed and tremendously hungry, but growing slightly impatient; his own temporary embarrassment having melted before her perfect naturalness, he was extremely anxious to have her return. At last she called:

"Hoo-oo-oo."

"Hoo-oo," he answered.

"What's *your* name?"

"Philip Starr."

"Well, Mr. Philip Starr, is it all right for me to come?"

"Yes, I've been ready ages. Do hurry."

She reappeared, still all in white. She did not, he noticed quickly, look very different now than when in the white bathing suit—of course he had by this time realized that this was what the slip had been. Wearing a simple white dress and white shoes, with her beautiful hair, braided and wound around her head and curling in little tendrils over her brow and ears, there was something almost uncannily fresh and young and sweet about her. She stopped on the bank, a forgotten difficulty suddenly occurring to her.

"We're on opposite sides."

"So we are! I never thought of that, either."

"We'll have to walk up a little way. There's a shallow place where I can get across on the stones—it's not far."

"I guess you've run away before. You seem to know the lay of the land pretty well."

"Oh, yes. Cousin Jane thinks Mother has let Paul and me both grow up awful shirkers. Only he just loafs, and I run."

"I see. Well, I'm surely glad you ran this time. Is Paul your brother?"

"Yes. He's twenty—the same age as my cousin Mary. They're sort of half-engaged. That is, Mary's wholly engaged to him, and he's about one-fourth engaged to her. That would even up to a half, wouldn't it? He's fond of her, but not nearly as fond of her as she is of him. He likes to have a good time with other girls too, and, for all Mary can see, there isn't another boy in the world except Paul. He's perfectly sure of her, and it makes him careless. I shouldn't like to be engaged that way."

"Don't worry, you won't be. How old are you?"

"Seventeen. It's a nice age."

"It certainly is. Are you going to be seventeen long?"

"Almost a year."

Philip Starr could not remember when he had laughed so

often. He leapt across the stepping stones, and took the box of lunch from Blanche.

"I meant to come over on your side."

"Of course. But I meant to help you across."

"I hadn't thought of that."

"Well, I had," said Philip abruptly, "I've been thinking of it for some minutes. It's a very pleasant thought to dwell on."

She looked at him with the same slightly startled expression as when she had first discovered him, but it faded again just as quickly. She put out both her hands and he swung her lightly across, so easily that she could hardly believe she was over.

"Now," she said, sitting down and leaning against a tree, "let's see what Mary has given me to eat."

"Oh—Mary knew you were running away?"

"Certainly. That's Mary all over. She puts up the lunch, and doesn't let anyone else find out until after I'm gone, and does my work as well as hers."

"Is she very plain?"

"*Plain!* No! What makes you think so?"

"People with that temperament usually are. And you said your brother—"

"Oh, Paul!" interrupted Blanche with contempt. "He doesn't know enough to appreciate her. He's ignorant about girls, though he sees a good deal of them. Now, I appreciate Mary, but I can't help imposing on her just the same. She's bigger than I am—taller and heavier both, and her eyes are gray instead of blue, and her hair's brown instead of yellow. She's got beautiful teeth, and the nicest smile—and she's smiling most of the time, whatever happens. And my! but she's a good cook! I simply can't learn to cook—everything always comes out either raw or burnt, or flat when it ought to puff, or puffed when it ought to be flat—or something! It fills me with a sort of helpless rage just to look at a cook-stove. It affects Paul the same way to look at a hay-field or a wood-pile. Mother thinks he's got heart trouble, so she doesn't urge him to work. He's got heart trouble all right, but not the kind she thinks— Well, here are lettuce sandwiches, and stuffed eggs, and sugared doughnuts. Oh, and two big pieces of angel cake! Aren't you hungry?"

For some minutes they ate in satisfied silence, dividing the contents of the box conscientiously into equal parts. There was a little folding cup tucked into the corner, and the girl filled it at the brook, drank, filled it again, and brought it, brimming and dripping with delicious coolness, to Philip.

"Do you mind if I smoke," he asked, when the last delicious crumb was gone, "while you tell me that story—about Lady Blanche Farm, you know?"

"Oh, yes—have you ever been in the Connecticut Valley before?"

"I'm sorry to say that I haven't."

"Well, it was mostly settled—around Hamstead, anyway— by men who came up the river from Massachusetts, not long before the Revolution. Then they left it for a while to go off and fight—we all belong to the Daughters of the American Revolution," she interrupted herself with a touch of pride. "They nearly all had big farms, and built big houses, and prospered; then they married each other's children, and have kept on living here ever since—the descendants have, I mean. We're nearly all cousins—third or fourth or fifth—in Hamstead. Cousin Jane had a cousin party once, and there were sixty-seven of us there, all cousins! It would be pleasant if it weren't so deadly dull. You can go out to ride over the hills, and at almost every house you pass, you'll see an old man puttering between the shed and the barn, and an old woman between the stove and the sink, or, if it's evening, both sitting on the front porch staring at nothing, just using up the time until they can die! In the village we have the D.A.R. meetings, and the Foreign Missionary Society, and the Annual Church Supper and Fair, and the Graduation from High School. Once in a long time we have a picnic or a dance, or go to the movies in Wallacetown. That's about all, and always the same people

—nice but tedious. You can't have many illusions or get up many thrills about someone you have known for five generations. That's why it's such a tremendous relief to meet someone I don't know at all."

Philip laughed again, aware that he was feeling strangely warm and comfortable inside at the inference that she might be having illusions or thrills about him.

"Thank you—where does Lady Blanche come in?"

"Oh, she came in right after the Revolution. My great-great-grandfather, Colonel Moses Manning, was a friend of Lafayette's. We've got some of the letters they wrote each other, framed, with his commission, in the Hamstead Library. He went back to France with Lafayette to visit him, and be presented at Court. Lady Blanche was a Countess who lived on the next estate. She was very young and lovely and sweet, and he fell in love with her."

"Peculiar man, wasn't he?" murmured Philip.

"Do you think so? Oh, you're laughing at me! You keep laughing all the time! You think I am awfully silly and countrified and—"

"You precious kid!" exclaimed Philip, sitting bolt upright in alarm; and then, as the startled look came into the blue eyes again, he went on very quickly and gently, "Excuse me. I didn't mean to be rude—or fresh. But I've been pretty sick, and it's a long time since I have laughed, or felt able to laugh. You don't know what meeting you, in this lovely place, has been like! I've taken on such a new lease of life this afternoon, that it bubbles over, that's all—do leases bubble, I wonder? Please go on about the little French Countess. Did she fall in love with him, too?"

"Oh, yes! Head over heels!"

"Nice for Moses," said Philip, his rising spirits asserting themselves again.

"Yes, wasn't it? At first sight, too! Just like a story!"

"Such things do happen."

"Yes, I suppose so," said the present Blanche, a trifle hurriedly, "—once in a great while, and ever so long ago, of course. So they were married, although her family wasn't very enthusiastic about her going across the sea to an unknown wilderness—but as all the rest of them were guillotined not long after, she was better off than they were, anyway. Of course Colonel Moses brought her to Hamstead to live. She had a fortune in her own right, and a wonderful trousseau— great boxes and chests of linen and lace and clothes and silver and jewels and books, and she had furniture sent too, from the château. And my great-great-grandfather built her a big brick house—the handsomest one anywhere around here— and—"

"It's a lovely story. What happened next?"

"The rest of it isn't so lovely. It's rather sad. The other farmers' wives in Hamstead didn't care for Lady Blanche. I think they were a little jealous of her because she was so much richer and more beautiful than they were, and she couldn't talk English well enough to make them understand that she wasn't haughty and cold, as they thought, but just as gentle and lonely and anxious to be friendly as she could be. So she made mistakes. The first time Moses took her to church—'meeting' the settlers called it then—they went to a long morning service, and took their dinner and ate sitting on the ground outside the meeting-house, visiting together, before they went back to the afternoon service. She wore a beautiful silk dress and jewels, just as she had when she went to Mass in the chapel in her own château in France. And the other women, who were all in homespun, wouldn't speak to her! She saw that she hadn't done right, so the next Sunday she went in homespun, too! But they couldn't forget that she had the silks at home, even if she didn't wear them!"

Philip's pipe had gone out. He was no longer laughing as he relighted it gravely.

"And—for a long time, she didn't have any children. That was considered almost a disgrace, in those days, it seems! Almost everyone had sixteen or seventeen! I was looking through the Town History the other day—it was raining hard, and I couldn't find anything else to do—and I came across a couple who had *twenty* and they named the twelfth one *Relief*—I should think it would have been anything but a relief, by that time! Well, Lady Blanche's husband was dreadfully disappointed; of course she was, too, but he didn't seem to think of that. He—he held it up as a reproach to her. And she grew more and more lonely and sad—"

The girl took the little folding cup in her hand, and began opening and shutting it. Then she carried it down to the brook again, and brought it back to Philip, overflowing.

"What was the end of the story?" he asked, gently, taking it from her.

"When she had been married about five years, she had twins —a boy and a girl. She wasn't strong, like most of the pioneer women. She died.

"Moses Manning never got over it," Blanche went on, after a long pause. "He didn't marry a second time, the way most of the settlers did, when their wives died—some of them three or four times! And he never called his place anything but Lady Blanche Farm, after that—it's never been called anything else, ever since. When the twins, Moses and Blanche, grew up, he built them each a house on his own place, and as the boy wanted to be a lawyer, he built a little office connected with the big brick house, for him. They both married—the children of other pioneers—and had large families, and inherited Lady Blanche's fortune, of course. The houses have never gone out of the family. Mother and Paul and I live in one—the big brick one—and Cousin Jane Manning, who's never married, in another, and Cousin Seth and his children in the third. Of course the fortune's been divided up so many times that it isn't very large any more, but it's enough to make us comfortable, and give us a good education, if we want it. Paul and I didn't 'specially, and Mary, who loves books, had to give up going to boarding school when she was almost ready for college, because her mother died, and there wasn't anyone else to look after her father and the little boys. Cousin Seth and Cousin Jane don't use awfully good English—Mother's terribly ashamed of them—but they could have gone off to school, too, if their parents had only thought of it, I guess—it wasn't a question of expense. And all the other families in Hamstead have kept on feeling that the Mannings are a little different—not as bad as if we were summer people, of course, but still different—from the rest of them. We wish they wouldn't—all except Mother—I think she rather likes it—but they do! And there's always one Blanche in each generation. There's a queer superstition about that—"

"What is it?"

"Oh, I can't tell you! You'd think it was awfully conceited and—fresh—and—"

"I wouldn't—I wouldn't—please—"

But the girl, laughing, shook her head, and got to her feet. "Have you any idea what time it is?" she asked.

Philip rose hastily. It was all he could do to keep from laying his hand on her shoulder, to stop what looked to him like impending flight.

"No, I haven't," he said. "I don't care what time it is. And I won't tease you to tell me about the superstition now, if you don't want to—that is, if you'll promise to tell me some other time. You—you'll do that, won't you?"

The girl hesitated, and, for the first time, blushed. The rosy color flooded her delicate face, disappearing in the golden curls that framed it. Then she smiled.

"Where were you thinking of going," she asked, "before you decided to have a swim and left your motor beside the road?"

"To Burlington, to visit some friends who have a big summer place near there. They happened to go early this season, and asked me to come and stay with them while I'm getting my strength back. But I can't get there tonight, now, can I?" he asked, the pleading in his voice becoming more and more apparent with every word he spoke.

"I don't believe you can, very well. I suppose you're not familiar with the roads?"

"Familiar! I'm not even on speaking terms with them! And there are hardly any guide-posts to introduce us!" he smiled, and, as he did so, he could see the lovely rosy color spreading over the girl's face again. "What's the name of the hotel in Hamstead?" he asked abruptly.

"There isn't any hotel. But probably—it's so late, and you've been ill, and everything—Mary would take you in."

"I don't want to intrude—"

"Mary wouldn't feel that you were intruding. Cousin Jane would think that there wasn't enough to eat in the house unless she had time to get a real company supper ready, and Mother wouldn't consider the house clean enough, and besides, Myra—that's our hired girl—doesn't approve of company. But Mary will make up an extra bed, and set another plate at the table, and fry a few more eggs—and that will be all there is to it! She'll be only too thankful to have the chance to make you comfortable. That is, that's the way I think she'll feel about it. At any rate, we better go down there and see!"

CHAPTER TWO

Lady Blanche farm lay a mile or so south of Hamstead, stretching on one side of the road back to the foothills of the Green Mountains, and on the other, in broad, sweeping meadows, straight down to the Connecticut River. Just beyond it rose a hill—almost a little mountain—covered with dark fir trees, their tips showing the delicate green of their new spring growth, silver and golden birches gleaming among them, young oaks and poplars quivering with fresh, feathery leaves. At the left, stood the two big houses, one of brick, with a small, semi-detached brick building—the lawyer Moses' office—the other of wood, white-painted and white-pillared, with a large flower garden, already as bright with color as a patch-work quilt, lying between them. Across the road was a smaller house, brick with a wooden ell, less true to line, and decidedly less prosperous in appearance. All three were shaded with great elms and maples, and flanked with lilac bushes laden with fragrant white and purple flowers and surrounded by wide lawns, though that of the smallest one, less smoothly mown and crisply edged than its opposite neighbors, would probably have deserved no more dignified designation than "yard"; while in the rear of all three were apple orchards, pink with blossoms.

As they came in sight of all this Philip Starr brought his motor to an abrupt stop, and turned to Blanche, who had unhesitatingly accepted his invitation to "help him find the farm," by riding back with him.

"Is that where you live?"

"Yes, the big brick house is ours. The big white one is Cousin Jane's. The one across the way is where Mary lives."

"Good Lord!"

"What's the matter?"

"Matter! It's the most beautiful place I ever saw in my life! You've got everything, mountains, river and valley! And the trees and flowers—and the houses themselves! I didn't tell you, did I—I'm an architect. I mean, that's my regular job. But on the side, I can't help dabbling in other things—sketching, modeling, carving—I was four years in Europe while I was growing up, and went back to Paris for a course at the Beaux Arts after I got through Harvard. And I've never—" his eyes turned from the landscape and swept over the face and figure of the girl beside him—"seen the Elysian Fields and one of the nymphs before!"

"It's pretty, but I don't see why you should think it's so remarkable. There are dozens of other places around here just as attractive—the Old Gray Homestead and the Big House, for instance. And it's so deadly dull!—Perhaps we had better hurry a little, or Mary may be through supper."

They stopped beside the least pretentious of the three houses, and walked up the cobblestone path. Here they encountered the only member of the Manning family who seemed, at that hour, to be visible and at leisure. On the huge granite slab that formed the front door-step, sat a small boy, who, in spite of the amount of his native soil with which his face and person were liberally encrusted, Philip saw at once to be of a singularly angelic cast of countenance. He was engaged in eating an enormous piece of lemon pie with his fingers.

"Hello, Moses," said Blanche. "Where's Mary?"

"She's putting Algernon to bed," replied the small boy, picking up and swallowing a portion of meringue which had eluded him and was sticking to the door-step, as he regarded the stranger with a thoughtful stare from a pair of dark-fringed, divinely blue eyes.

"Algernon!" exclaimed Philip, involuntarily.

"Yes," interposed Blanche, a trifle impatiently, "Cousin Laura—his mother, you know, that died—said she was so tired of the same old family names, that when he came along, she felt she'd simply got to have a change. She found that in a book called 'The Wicked Duke'; Algernon was the duke. It wasn't allowed in the Hamstead Library, but it was a great story, just the same.—Moses, you'll be deathly sick."

"I know it," responded Moses, with unruffled calm. "This is my second piece. But it'll be worth it. And Mary'll wipe it up—she always does."

"You're a horrid, disgusting little boy," said Blanche sternly. "I don't see how Mary has so much patience with you. I'd spank you. Come in, Mr. Starr, and I'll call Mary.—Mary!—M-A-R-Y—"

"Yes," floated down a voice from the upper story. "Coming, honey. Did you have a good time?"

"Yes, lovely. Hurry up—we've got company."

A door opened and shut quickly, there was the sound of swift footsteps coming across a hall, and a girl, with another golden-haired child—presumably the namesake of the wicked duke—in her arms, appeared at the head of the stairs. In a flash, Philip remembered and understood the quick resentment Blanche had shown when he asked her if her cousin were plain. For if Blanche were lovely, Mary was certainly beautiful, with the tall, superbly formed, quiet beauty of a Greek statue. And yet, it was not of a Greek statue that he almost instantly thought. The blue cotton dress that she had on, dulled and faded from frequent washing, had turned to the soft color in which the painters of the Middle Ages loved to clothe their Madonnas; the little boy, apparently snatched from his bath to answer Blanche's summons, was cuddled, pink and plump and sturdy against her shoulder. *Mary!* The coincidence of the name, too, seemed almost startling. What sort of a man could the indifferent Paul be, he wondered—and how many men in the whole world deserved anything like this!—The younger girl's explanation of his presence, which he had momentarily forgotten needed explanation, broke in upon his silent admiration.

"This is Mr. Philip Starr of Boston, Mary. I met him by the brook. He's an architect. He's been sick with typhoid fever, and is on his way to Burlington in a motor to make a visit while's he's getting strong, but he got lost. I told him I was sure you'd take him in for the night."

"I'm afraid I'm dreadfully intrusive," interrupted Philip, smiling up at Mary, but she in turn interrupted him.

"Of course not. Father and I'll both be awfully glad to have you. Will you put your motor in the shed while I get Algy tucked in? Blanche will take you. I'll be back in a minute, and show you where the guest-chamber and bathroom are."

She was already downstairs when they returned from the shed, bending over the guilty but contented Moses, whom she was endeavoring to rouse from the state of satisfied semi-coma into which he had sunk, to be bathed and put to bed in his turn.

"I'm afraid you won't have any dessert for supper," she said, laughing. "Moses seems to have cleaned out the pantry while I was busy with Algy. I'm not a very good housekeeper, or I'd manage some way to keep my eyes on both of them at once. But I can open a jar of preserves, and there are cookies. That is, I suppose there are. Did you eat the cookies, too, Moses?"

"Yes," said Moses, with a reminiscent sigh of pleasure.

"Well, then, we'll have just the preserves," said Mary cheerfully. "You go upstairs and turn on the water, Moses, I'll be there in just a minute— Hello, Paul!"

Her voice, soft already, softened perceptibly at the last words. Philip, turning quickly, saw a boy who seemed to be simply a larger and masculine replica of Blanche—there was an almost astonishing family resemblance between all these Mannings!—coming up the walk towards them.

"Hello," he said leisurely. "Hello, Blanche, you're going to catch it for running away. Hello—"

"This is Mr. Starr of Boston," put in Mary, quickly, repeating the somewhat scanty information which Blanche had been able to give her about him. "My cousin Paul, Mr. Starr—Blanche's brother."

"How do you do?" said Paul, without much enthusiasm. "Glad to see you—Mother's gone to bed with a sick headache —all used up after cleaning the North Parlor. And Myra wants to get off early to go to a temperance meeting. So I thought I better come over here for supper."

"Of course," agreed Mary warmly. "I'm sorry Cousin Violet is so tired—she ought not to try to do that kind of work. I'll run over later in the evening and rub her with alcohol. Will you show Mr. Starr where to go while I get Moses settled? Father isn't in from the barn yet, and if Hod wants to go to the temperance meeting with Myra he'll have the chores to finish up alone, so he may be late. Come, Moses."

She disappeared up the stairs again, her arm about the unrepentant culprit. Philip picked up his bag, which Paul had made no effort to take from him, and followed. Little as he knew of the customs of New England farmers, he thought it unlikely that there were many who looked like this one, or who were at leisure to appear in white flannels at six o'clock on a May evening. He resented both the boy's beauty and his clothes. Paul stopped at the open door of a small room and motioned him to enter.

"I hope you'll find this fairly decent," he said, depreciatingly. "Mary uses the best rooms for the family—thinks they have the first right to be comfortable—and none of the chambers in this house compares to ours and Cousin Jane's. And Mary's not much of a housekeeper—there's probably some dust about."

"I don't see any," said Philip, with perfect truthfulness, "and I think the room's charming. Yours must be wonderful, if they're prettier than this."

"Well, yes, I believe they are quite unusual. That's the bathroom at the end of the hall—there's only one."

"Thanks—have I time for a shave before supper?"

"I guess so—Mary'll wait for you anyway. But you'll probably find everything in a dreadful mess after the kids' baths."

"I shan't mind that."

The family was waiting for him when he went downstairs again. Blanche had gone home and changed her dress for another white one, softer and filmier than the one she had worn in the afternoon. Mary, apparently, had had no time to freshen up, and had simply tied a crisp apron of generous proportions over the faded blue gingham; while a tired-looking, elderly man, without a necktie and with a shabby coat slipped on over his khaki shirt and trousers, came forward to welcome Philip.

"Pleased to meet you," he said with the same unquestioning cordiality that Mary had shown. "Blanche has been tellin' us how she happened to find you and that you've been sick. I'm real sorry, but I guess our good Vermont air'll fix you up. Come and set down to supper. It's all ready—such as 'tis. I understand Moses has et up a good share of it."

There was, however, no scarcity of supper. There was, on the contrary, a good deal of it—two big slices of ham, with a quantity of clear, golden-brown gravy, fried eggs, baked potatoes, dandelion greens—"that I dug up in the back yard this afternoon," Mary said as she heaped his plate; hot biscuits and tea and the jar of strawberry preserves which Moses' delinquencies had forced her to open. Philip thought he had never been so hungry, that nothing had ever tasted so good—

"Want to smoke?" asked Paul at his elbow as they rose from the table.

Philip hesitated. He had not visited in many families where "they did their own work" but he had a vague feeling that he ought to offer to be useful.

"Don't we help with the dishes first?" he asked. "Those come next, don't they?"

"Mercy, don't you think of such a thing!" Seth exclaimed. "Mary'll have 'em done in no time, while I finish milkin'. You and Blanche and Paul go and set on the front porch and take it easy."

"I'm going to Wallacetown, to a show," said Paul briefly.

"Oh, *don't* tonight!"

Paul turned on his cousin impatiently. "What are you so down on Wallacetown for?" he asked crossly. "I've got all my plans made—I didn't know we were going to have company, did I? I'd have asked you to go with me, of course, only I knew you wouldn't care for it anyway, even if you weren't too busy—it'll be nine o'clock before you get the dishes done and the bread set and finish rubbing Mother's head." Then, seeing that Mary's face was still clouded, he added, more pleasantly and very persuasively, "Mary—you like me to have a good time, once in a while, don't you?"

"Of course I do. But—"

"Then say you hope I'll have it, like a good girl."

He slipped his arm around her, rubbing his head against hers, and kissing her cheek. She smiled, and returned his kiss.

"All right, run along," she said cheerfully. "Blanche, you can keep Mr. Starr amused, can't you?"

"Of course she can," said Philip hastily. But he stood still, looking at Mary with a slightly puzzled expression. Was it possible that Paul—*engaged*—he had the boy's sister's word for it—to this wonderful creature, was going to Wallacetown, wherever that might be, to a "show," his privilege to do so practically unquestioned, leaving her to wash dishes and make bread and soothe his mother's headache, and with a farewell that was certainly no more than cousinly, and hardly more than brotherly in its carelessness? To his chagrin, Mary seemed to guess what was passing in his mind.

"It's awfully dull on the farm for Blanche and Paul," she said, as she moved about, clearing the table. "I'm glad there's something amusing for him to go to. We don't often have a good show in Hamstead. And I'm glad that Blanche can have a pleasant evening with you. It's lovely on the porch—I believe there's a moon, isn't there? You can find your way out there all right, can't you?"

Customs of chaperonage in Hamstead are simple, not to say primitive. As a rule, however, they work out surprisingly well. Seth, coming in after dark from the barn, lighted the kitchen lamp, and read the *Wallacetown Bugle* and *Hoard's Dairyman*. Then he took off his shoes, and tiptoed up the stairs to bed. Mary, her dishes washed, and her bread, covered with a red tablecloth, set beside the kitchen stove to raise, crossed to the big brick house with a bottle of Florida water in her hand with which to rub Cousin Violet's head. When she returned, she went quietly in the back way. And Philip, going up to bed about eleven, found her in his room, turning down his bed, beside which she had just placed fresh water and a tiny vase of violets.

"I say, Miss Manning—may I speak to you for a minute?"

"Of course," answered Mary, making a neat triangle of the sheet and counterpane, and turning to him with a smile. "What is it?"

"Your cousin Blanche—she isn't engaged, too, is she?"

Mary flushed. "What makes you say 'too'?" she asked quietly.

"Why—she told me about you and her brother. I hope you won't think I'm fresh if I tell you I consider him awfully lucky."

"It's I that am lucky," returned Mary slowly. "Paul's the dearest boy in all the world, after you get to know him. I feel much older than he is, though as a matter of fact, we're almost exactly the same age. But—we're not exactly engaged. We're distant cousins, you know, and have been neighbors and great friends all our lives. We've a sort of an understanding—'keeping company' it's called, here in Hamstead. But—Paul isn't bound at all."

"Well, I should think he'd want to be," said Philip with visible admiration, looking at the girl again with an appreciation which was only saved from being a stare by its complete impersonality. "But now, about his sister? Has she got an 'understanding' or anything awkward like that with anybody?"

"No," said Mary, smiling. "She's very young yet, you know —barely seventeen. Why?"

"Because," Philip burst out, "I've fallen in love with her— head over heels. Of course I haven't told her so yet. But I think she's the loveliest—the most exquisite—oh, the—"

"Yes, I know," said Mary. "So you want—?"

"I'm twenty-four years old, and I'm a fairly decent sort," went on Philip, plunging as usual straight to his point. "I haven't any ancestral home like this—in fact, one of my ancestors was an Irish immigrant, and all of my family were very plain people—so plain that I don't know much about them—there weren't any town histories written about *them!* But we've always been honest, as far as I know, and we've prospered and risen in the world. I've lots of friends. I've inherited some money, and I'm earning more. I've got a pretty good job, for my age. I'm in Davis and Hamlin's office—"

"Gale Hamlin, the architect?"

"Why, yes! Do you know him?"

"I've—I've met him. His niece, Hannah Adams, was one of my classmates at boarding school. I used to visit her, sometimes, in Boston. But, since Mother died, I haven't had time to, of course—and there never seems to be a chance to ask her to come here. Gale Hamlin's her mother's younger brother —not so awfully old, you know—and he used to come to her house often. I thought he was splendid, and I know he's a 'big man' in his profession, of course! So you are in his office!"

"Yes," said Philip excitedly. "What tremendous luck! He can tell you all about me—Blanche's mother and brother, you know—and you, for that matter! There wouldn't be any very dark disclosures! And you will help me all you can with Blanche, won't you?"

Mary picked up her lamp. "I don't believe you'll need an awful lot of help with Blanche," she said, whimsically. "But

I'll say a few things to Cousin Violet that might make a difference. Good night."

"You *are* good! And you don't think I'm an awful chump going at things this way?"

"I think you're rather nice," said Mary, still whimsically—"if you must know!"

She was closing the door gently behind her, when Philip pulled it open again.

"Mary," he said, "I may call you Mary, mayn't I—tell me the superstition about Lady Blanche—about all the Blanche Mannings."

"Oh, it's nothing much—and Blanche seems to be living up to it all right."

"Do tell me! I'm awfully interested in—in everything about her, don't you see?"

"Well," said Mary, hesitating a little, "all the Blanches so far have fallen in love at first sight, and married strangers—and gone away from their own homes to live. They've had wonderful romances—not the plain, everyday kind of love affair that most of us get. Their husbands have adored them, and they've been rich and beautiful and—"

"Is that all of the story?"

"Is there anything," asked Mary, suddenly, "that I could tell you that would make you want her any less? Anything that would make you—afraid to try and get her?"

"Anything in the way of an old superstition, you mean? Good Lord, no!"

"Then," said Mary, "I think that's enough for tonight. And *good* enough for any night, too, isn't it? Especially for a man who has just said he was in love with Blanche—it ought to make you feel as if the suit were half-won already! Let me just make sure you've got enough blankets—it gets colder than you'd think, toward morning, in the Connecticut Valley. Good night."

CHAPTER THREE

Violet Manning was an extremely pretty woman with an infinite capacity for doing nothing. She had been the only child, much spoiled and petted, of a shopkeeper in White Water, the next village to Hamstead, who had stinted himself to give her "advantages," and had always "kept help" so that she should not roughen her delicate fingers or tire her slim little back. She was sent away to a would-be-but-didn't-quite-make-it fashionable boarding school, and acquired a veneer of culture, and a contempt for her parents, her neighbors, and her home-town, but not very much else. As the other girls at school did not consider her "quite our kind" she made no lasting friends among them. On her return to White Water, after she was "finished" at school, and had taken a three months' trip to Europe in a Raymond and Whitcomb tour, she might have been the belle of the countryside if she had only been as pleasant as she was pretty. But her would-be swains fell off, one by one, before the disdain of her manner; and it was with secret relief that, at the age of twenty-five, she accepted Martin Manning, and went to live on Lady Blanche Farm. She was careful to convey the impression, to him and to everyone else, that she was doing him a great favor to marry him, and he at least, believed her. A sturdy couple from "out-back"—Horace, or as he was more frequently called, "Hod" Evans and his wife Myra—were installed in the big brick house as "help." And Violet lay in bed late in the morning, and sat in the North Parlor—heretofore used only for weddings and funerals—embroidering centerpieces, and went to church on Sunday, dressed considerably better than anyone else in Hamstead. A woman with more brains would soon have been bored into activity by such an existence. But Violet was not bored. She was supremely satisfied at the easy and pleasant lines into which her life had fallen. If anything happened to disturb her serenity, she promptly had an attack of "nerves." In a less privileged person, her "nerves" would have been regarded as sheer ill-temper, but Violet's household trembled before her outbursts, and bowed down to them.

When she was a little over thirty, Martin, who still worshipped her blindly, died, leaving her with two small children, and enough money to live on comfortably, if simply. Black was very becoming to her. She looked divinely lovely in her widow's veil, which she did not discard for a long time. Every Sunday morning she went to church with Blanche and Paul at her side, her heavy black silk dress trailing down the aisle behind her. Every Sunday afternoon she went to the cemetery to place flowers on Martin's grave, taking the children. They hated the cemetery, and the weekly trips to it, but Violet cried when they told her so, and after that they accompanied her in silence. A good deal of family devotion has been caused by the fear of being made uncomfortable. Martin's birthday, and the anniversary of his death, were sacred dates, observed with fitting solemnity at Lady Blanche Farm. When the rôle of bereaved and sorrowing widow began to pall a little, and no one stepped forward to relieve her of it, Violet's laziness took refuge in that of the model housekeeper and devoted mother. She had not, she said with a regretful sigh, strength to exert herself beyond the demands that the large house and her boy and girl made upon her. Fortunately, with a contentment rare in New England, Myra and Hod stayed on; Myra ran the house to suit herself. Hod helped the hard-working and plodding Seth with the farm labor which Paul was supposed to be too delicate to perform, since an attack of scarlet fever, which had left him in a weakened condition, had given his mother the fixed idea that he had heart trouble. To be sure, Paul mowed the lawns and weeded the garden, but always under her careful supervision. He had been an unimaginative and amiable child, rather more silent and less sunny than Blanche, but extremely winning "when he was in the mood" as Hamstead put it. If an idea were presented to him, he thought it over carefully, even if he had few original ones, and usually worked it out to a satisfactory, if not brilliant, conclusion. His father understood him perfectly, and had he lived, would have supplied the initiative that the boy lacked, and stimulated his ambition. Violet did neither. He had inherited her inertia, from which she made no attempt to arouse him, as well as her plausibility, which excused his idleness even in the eyes of Hod and Cousin Seth. He went away to a near-by Seminary to school, and drifted half-way through a course at an Agricultural College; but he was not a natural student, and the farm ran along "well-enough" without his help. He was obstinate unless he was "handled right," and Violet did not make the effort to handle him at all. When, for no very clear reason, he stated that he had decided not to finish his course, she did not try to force him to do so. More through lack of vital interest than through viciousness, he became somewhat dissipated. Here, too, his father would have helped him, by talking with him intelligently and plainly. Violet merely excused him. There were some things, she said, that she couldn't, with modesty, discuss with him. This modern craze for frankness was disgusting. Boys always sowed wild oats for a time, and then settled down and married some nice girl, just as Paul was going to settle down by and by and marry dear Mary. There was no use worrying or making a vulgar fuss over what was coming out all right in the end, anyway. And meanwhile Blanche was such a comfort! Blanche had also inherited her mother's good looks, and the discontent which the latter had felt in her youth, but there was "more Manning" to her, as Hamstead said. Although she did not aspire to be useful, she at least aspired to do something. And she was a "nice girl"—friendly and sweet and unaffected—there was no denying that. And this was set down as greatly to her credit, "considering everything," said Hamstead, hinting delicately, when it might well have said, "considering her mother."

At ten o'clock in the morning following Philip's unceremonious arrival at Lady Blanche Farm, Violet was lying in bed with a new novel, still unopened, from the Hamstead Library beside her, when there was a brisk, if gentle, knock at the door, and Mary walked in.

"Oh, good morning, dear," said Violet pleasantly, rousing herself, "I've been wondering why you didn't come over. I thought you must be through your work by this time—there's never much to do, Sundays. Just take that breakfast tray downstairs, will you? Myra's getting ready to go to church, and seems to have forgotten it.—No, I thought it was raining too hard to attempt going myself. You know how easily I take cold. And then, I'm still exhausted after overdoing so yesterday. You have no idea what hard work it is, keeping this big house looking as it should. I could get along much more easily, but I can't live that way. My ideals are too high. The quieter I keep today, the better. I may be able to get around a little in a negligee tomorrow, if I'm careful."

"I'm sorry I couldn't get over earlier," said Mary, returning from her trip to the kitchen with the tray, "but I was up most of the night with Moses. He was deathly sick. I got delayed, seeing to him. But I guess he's coming around all right, now. I hope you'll feel enough better by noon to come over to dinner and meet Mr. Starr."

"Oh, my dear, I couldn't. I don't even feel equal to the effort of walking over to the bureau to comb my hair— Why, yes, if you feel like doing it—don't pull it.—So he didn't leave this morning?"

"No," answered Mary, brushing out the long soft curls to their full length, "it was raining so dreadfully hard that it didn't seem best for him to attempt it. It's cold, too, for May, and he's been sick, as I told you last night. He's telephoned his friends in Burlington not to expect him just yet. I've lighted a fire in the parlor, and he's making a water-color sketch of Blanche. It's going to be lovely. No wonder she's so pretty, Cousin Violet. I'm sure you've got the most beautiful hair in the whole world."

"Well, it *was* pretty, when I was your age, Mary, and I took more pains with it than you do with yours. Lately, you seem to twist yours up almost any way that's quick. Of course it was a great cross to me that mine turned white so prematurely."

"Oh, don't say that! It's even prettier now. If it had been gray, that would have been different! But this pure, dazzling white makes you look more than ever like a darling little Dresden china shepherdess! There!—Well, Mr. Starr'll be disappointed not to see you, he's so crazy over everything that's beautiful. I think he really ought to have been an artist, not 'on the side' as he says, but for his real profession, instead of being an architect. But of course there isn't usually as much money in it. He's with Davis and Hamlin—"

"Gale Hamlin?"

"Yes. He told me after I went home last night. It makes me feel as if we knew him quite well already. Of course a position with a firm like that is a pretty good guarantee of talent and character, as well as salary. And he must have money of his own besides. He's traveled all over the world."

At this moment, the conversation, which was becoming extremely interesting to Violet, was interrupted by the appearance of Miss Jane Manning, who entered somewhat brusquely, and without knocking. None of the famous "Manning looks" had fallen to her lot. She was probably one of the plainest women the Lord had ever made, certainly the plainest that He had seen fit to place in Hamstead. She was dressed in heavy black silk of excellent quality though unfashionable cut, and carried in her hand a Bible and a Sunday-School quarterly.

"Well, Violet— Well, Mary," she said abruptly, "aren't either of you goin' to church this mornin'?"

Violet murmured her excuses. Mary, who never either murmured or excused anything, stated her reasons plainly.

"I've got too much to do," she said, "with the children to look after, and dinner to get, and everything. I can't take a bit of comfort sitting half-listening to a sermon, while I'm wondering if Algy has fallen into the well, or what Moses has eaten this time. One day when I risked it last summer, he ate the raw green corn that I'd just brought up from the garden, and a piece of green blotting-paper that Father had just bought in Wallacetown. The combination of so much greenness was pretty bad."

Violet laughed, but Cousin Jane's expression became even more severe.

"That great boy ought to be goin' to Sabbath School himself," she said sternly, "instead of bein' left at home to get into mischief. I began to attend when I was three."

"I know," said Mary hurriedly, "but it isn't as if I didn't teach him myself. I tell him Bible stories, lots of them. He likes them, too. But I'm afraid he wouldn't be awfully good in church. I don't dare risk it."

"Well, I'll risk it then," said Cousin Jane. "You won't object to my takin' him with me and tryin' it, I suppose?"

"No-o," answered Mary, a little doubtfully. "Perhaps today would be a good time. He was pretty sick last night, so he isn't as lively as usual this morning. I'll send him down at twelve o'clock."

"What's this I hear," went on Cousin Jane, her mind, relieved on one score, promptly darting to another, "about your taking in some strange young man that Blanche picked up by the roadside? You ought to be ashamed of yourself, Violet, for letting that girl traipse around so! And I should think Seth would set his foot down! Any tramp that'll come along and ask for a meal you'll welcome, Mary."

"Oh, Mr. Starr isn't a tramp," replied Mary pleasantly, "he's quite an important person." And she repeated her biographical sketch of Philip's career with growing enthusiasm. Violet, too, was beginning to look more and more complacent. But Cousin Jane was not to be side-tracked.

"What do you know about his principles?" she asked without compromise. "Accordin' to your account, he's spent considerable time in France, and when that's been said, there ain't much more to add. We know what the French are like." This was entirely untrue, but Cousin Jane believed it to be so, and said it with a conviction that carried weight. "And I suppose you didn't ask if he was a church member—or *what* church. He may be a Unitarian or a Roman Catholic for all you know."

Mary, remembering that Mr. Starr was a Bostonian of Irish heredity, had an uneasy feeling that either of these surmises might be correct.

"Well, I'm sure he's a Christian, anyway, whatever denomination he belongs to—or even if he doesn't belong to any," she said warmly. "It sticks out all over him."

"Sticks out all over him! That's not a very reverent expression, Mary."

"Well, it does! He looks delicate, just now, of course, because he's been sick, but there's something awfully clean and wholesome about him. And he looks you straight in the face, and comes right to the point about things. He knows his own mind, and he laughs as if he didn't have a thing on his conscience, and he likes books and flowers and children; and if those aren't all good signs of a Christian, I don't know what are!"

"You don't know anything about religion at all," retorted Miss Manning. "I'm shocked to hear you speak so. Yes, I'll be over to dinner and see him for myself. I don't want to judge, of course, but I'm prepared for the worst— Where's Paul?"

The faculty that Cousin Jane had of ferreting out facts which the rest of the family would have been glad not to mention was distressing.

"Paul isn't well either, this morning," his mother said hastily. "He's in bed, too. He's really more delicate than any of you realize—if he gets the least bit over-tired, he has a dreadful headache, just as I do. He was out rather late last night. He said his friends pressed him to stay, he really didn't feel he could leave, though if he'd followed his own choice in the matter he'd have been in long before midnight. That reminds me, Mary, he called out to me just before you came in, that if you did come over, he wished you'd bring him up a pitcher of ice-water and a bowl of cracked ice. He hated to ask Myra to get it for him, because he knew she'd give him a temperance lecture. Not that he's been really *drinking*, of course, but naturally, young fellows like a glass of ale or so when they go out in the evening. You better go and get the ice for him now. And I'm awfully afraid you'll be late to church, Jane, if you don't hurry. I believe I'll get up after all. I'd hate to disappoint Mr. Starr if he really wants so much to meet me, and I'll make an effort to come over to dinner, Mary. I hope I shan't suffer for it afterwards. Turn on the water as you go by the bathroom, will you? And oh! Just get a couple of clean towels out of the linen closet. Be sure to take those with my own initials on them—you're so indifferent to refined little details like those!"

CHAPTER FOUR

The dinner which Mary stayed home from church to cook, was not an entire success, either in her eyes or in the eyes of anyone else who attended it, with the possible exception of Blanche and Philip.

In the first place, it was prepared somewhat hurriedly, and with a sore and grieving spirit—a combination of misfortunes which has proved disastrous to more pretentious banquets. Going into her cousin's room with the bowl of ice and pitcher of ice-water, Mary found Paul, clad in pale-blue pajamas, lying on his back in bed, his face lined and white, black rings about his closed eyes.

"Oh, here you are," he said, turning restlessly. "I've been wondering how much longer it would take you to get here. It'll save you quite a lot of steps when you come here to live, won't it?"

Even as unexacting a person as Mary could hardly be expected to feel flattered at so unromantic a reason for looking forward to marriage. But her cousin's face hurt her far more than his words. In spite of her wholesome freshness, she was by no means stupid. She knew perfectly well that "shows" in Wallacetown were apt to include other things "on the side," and she knew, too, that a drawn, mask-like pallor might be as certain an indication of dissipation as a puffy flush.

"Oh, Paul," she said reproachfully, "how can you?"

Paul sat up in bed, reaching for the ice-water. "How can I what?" he asked crossly.

"You know."

"I'm sure I don't. You're not very definite. Put some of that cracked ice in a handkerchief, will you, and wrap it around my head."

Mary complied in silence. Paul lay down again, and kept very still for some minutes, his tense expression gradually relaxing. Then he smiled, and put his arm around her.

"You're an awfully good girl, Mary," he said softly. "I don't know what I should do without you. Won't you give me a kiss? You haven't yet, this morning."

"Whom did you kiss last?" asked Mary in a hard voice.

"Why you, right after supper last night! Don't you remember? That is—" Mary's gray eyes were looking straight into his, and there was something in them which Paul found it impossible to meet. "Look here," he broke off angrily, "you are getting to be the greatest prude, do you know it? And an awfully suspicious, jealous one at that. Has a fellow got to be put through the third degree all the time, just because he gets engaged? If he has, I'm hanged if I think it's what it's cracked up to be."

"I'm sorry," said Mary steadily. "If I've misjudged you, I can only ask you to forgive me."

Again that straight look that was so hard to meet! Paul shifted his position.

"Well, I went to Wallacetown with Jack Weston—" he began.

"Jack Weston!" Mary's voice expressed her contempt.

"Yes—what have you got against him? He's never done you any harm, has he?—with Jack Weston and some of the White Water crowd—no one else from Hamstead."

"By 'some of the White Water crowd,' I don't suppose you mean our friends and relatives there, do you? You mean some of the girls and fellows that have just come to work in the new mill?"

"Well, what if I do? There's no harm in working in a mill, is there?"

"No—in fact, I think it's rather better to work in a mill than it is to loaf on a farm. Go on."

"I won't go on," said Paul, more angrily than he had spoken before. "You're enough to drive a fellow to drink—or worse—supposing I *had* done anything worse. But what does it amount to—kissing a pretty girl that you've had a lark with, when you say 'good-night'—anyway! It's only what she expects. It doesn't mean anything."

"It doesn't seem to—to you," replied Mary, very quietly.

"Oh, Lord! Why do you pick me up on everything I say? I mean, of course, it doesn't amount to anything *wrong*. Come back here—"

But Mary was gone, shutting the door behind her.

Outside the house, she hesitated, her lips quivering, her eyes full of tears. She couldn't—she couldn't—go home feeling the way she did, and start getting dinner. The village clock, striking eleven, decided her. Even in the midst of her unhappiness, she ran over what she still had to do before half-past one with a practical mind. Seth, who as one of the deacons, could not well miss the morning church service, had frozen and packed the ice-cream for her before he left the house. The two fowl which were later to appear as fricasseed chicken were boiling on the back of the stove over a slow fire. The asparagus was picked and cleaned and standing in a kettle of cold water ready to cook—not quite enough to go around, really, for it was still early for a "good mess," but with plenty of toast and a cream sauce, and reinforced by other vegetables, it would "do." The table was set. She could mash potatoes, and beat up a sponge cake, and make coffee all at the last moment. If she were home a little before twelve to get Moses into a clean suit for Sunday School, she would be there in plenty of time. Blanche had promised to "listen" for the little boys for a time, anyway— Undeterred by the rain, which was still gently falling, Mary walked up the road towards the little mountain which Philip had noticed the day before, and which he had since learned was part of the farm, and called in memory of the first Blanche, who had loved to go there, "Countess Hill."

It was very quiet on the mountain. Mary, walking up one of the wide, needle-strewn paths that led to the top, the soft rain hardly penetrating the thick trees, began, almost immediately, to find peace and what she wanted still more—time and space to think. There was a beautiful view from the top on fair days—the smooth, sloping meadows, the river, the New Hampshire mountains rising beyond the fields in the twin state beyond. Today the mountains were hidden with clouds, even the meadows veiled in mist. But Mary, sitting down on a big stone and looking out over them, was conscious of the feeling of joy and support that they always gave her. "I will lift up mine eyes unto the hills, from whence cometh my help—" the Bible verse passed through her mind. What did it matter if the hills were temporarily hidden—they were still there! And the meadows, too—"He maketh me to lie down in green pastures, He leadeth me beside the still waters—" Had the Shepherd boy of Bethlehem loved the fields where he herded his father's sheep, any more than she loved this Connecticut Valley? Her mother had loved it, too—the dead mother whose place she felt she was filling so poorly. She had also loved the Psalms—that was one reason why Mary knew them so well—she had learned them on rainy Sundays just like this one, standing beside her mother's chair. And on the simple gravestone in the Hamstead cemetery were engraved the lines that Laura Manning had loved best of all—the ones she had told Mary never to forget, no matter what else she forgot—"Yea, though I walk through the valley of the shadow of death, I will fear no evil. For Thou art with me. Thy rod, and Thy staff, they comfort me."

Wiping the tears from her eyes, Mary began to think resolutely about Paul. What should she do—what ought she to do? Break her engagement? How much, she asked herself, with a quick little quiver of pain, would he care if she did? Why was she always fated to make herself so unattractive to him, to be so tactless, when she was trying only to be fair and honest? A girl with less beauty and intellect, but with more wile

—she knew it only too well—could have held him in the hollow of her hand. And would either of them be any better off if she made what would be, to her, a heart-breaking sacrifice? In vain she admitted that neither her reason nor her instinct should allow her to love a man whom she did not respect or trust, not nearly as much as she already respected and trusted Philip Starr, who, twenty-four hours earlier had been a complete stranger to her. The fact remained that she did love Paul, with every fibre of her being, far more deeply, far more passionately, than she had ever let him see. She always had —she always would. She remembered how often, as little children, they had come up this hill together, to gather pine cones or pick blackberries; how they had ridden on hayloads and brought home big bunches of ox-eyed daisies and meadow-lilies to their mothers from the parts of the fields still untouched by the mowing-machine, and jumped in the hay after it had been put into the barn—only not right away, because, as her father always warned them, it must have time to "settle" first; how she had gone for the cows with him—little Blanche, as soon as she was big enough, tagging along behind them; how they had waded and sailed boats in the same brook where Philip and Blanche had met; how they had trudged off to school together, morning after morning, carrying their dinner in tin pails; how they had worked out their sums on the same slate in the evenings; how they had coasted down the long hills on the same sled, their arms around each other, and eaten "sugar on snow" out of the same pan at the "sugaring-off" parties in the early spring. . . .

Why should these little, childish things bind her now? What did they amount to? There was no romance, surely, in blackberries and slates! Romance was the sort of thing that was happening to Blanche, that had happened to all the Blanches. And yet, they *did* bind her. They had, all through those winters in her early teens when she went away to boarding school, through the summers of those same years when Paul seemed almost a little boy and she almost grown up, and temporarily finding less in common. That was the time, she remembered, when Paul had stopped kissing her, the shy awkwardness of adolescence getting the better of their long friendship. He had begun again when her mother's death had suddenly brought her back from school, three years ago now. He had kissed her first then, because he was so sorry for her— no one, knowing how she had loved her mother could have helped feeling sorry for Mary in those days, and besides, Paul was naturally sympathetic when there was any reason for sympathy obvious enough for him to discern it. And then, she was so pretty, so sweet, so plainly devoted to him—the boy would not have been human who would not have enjoyed kissing Mary, and, it may as well be admitted, the girl would have been even less so who would not have enjoyed kissing Paul when he was in the sweet and winning mood that was uppermost at that time. He had not actually even proposed to her. The kisses had changed a little in character, had become more frequent—some way, through embraces growing less cousinly and more loverlike they had reached "an understanding." It was not clear in the minds of either of them how or when. But from that faintly determined time, Paul had become all in all to Mary, and Mary had gradually become less than she was before to Paul.

She faced this fact resolutely. Paul did not love her as much as she loved him. Why—why? She almost cried it aloud. He was constantly failing her, not only by his whole idle, selfish life, but by follies such as he had committed the night before. Follies! There is little compromise of language in the speech of the average New Englander; he does not, as one writer has wittily put it, call a spade a silver trowel. The real name for such follies was sin, and Mary said it, even though she flinched in doing so. Sin! and how had she ever failed him— or anyone else—in thought or word or deed? Humble-minded as she was, she knew it had not been fair to take her out of school to keep house for her father and care for her little brothers, when Cousin Jane or Cousin Violet could have done it if they had been so disposed. Not that she hadn't been glad to do it—but just the same, it wasn't fair. It wasn't fair, either, that Cousin Violet with her small, grown-up family, should have a "hired girl" all the time, while she with the larger one, including two small children, and the extra hired men who came to work on the farm in haying and threshing time, should struggle along without "help" of any sort. With care, both the education and the "help" could have been managed as far as the expense involved was concerned—but it apparently had never occurred either to Seth or Jane Manning that part of the modest remnants of Lady Blanche's fortune might be used for Mary's benefit, and though this had occurred to her, she was too proud to suggest it.

Mary could not help knowing, too, that there were other men in the village who had been attracted to her, who would have been glad to make it plain that they were more than attracted, if she hadn't made it plain that no one in the world mattered to her except Paul. There was Thomas Gray, for instance, slow and plodding, but hard-working, kind and wholesome. And then—then there had been Gale Hamlin, the great architect, whose name Philip pronounced with an awe amounting almost to veneration. She had never told her family much about Hannah Adams' uncle. Her casual remarks about him had included little mention of his frequent calls at the Adams' house when she visited there, none at all of that last call, paid at the school when the news of her mother's death had come. . . .

The sharp note of a phœbe bird, singing beside her, brought Mary to the consciousness that she must have been dreaming a long time, and sent her hurrying down the hill, still undecided what she ought to do, but immeasurably, if vaguely, comforted and refreshed. Her first task on reaching the house was to thrust the reluctant Moses into stiff and spotless white, and start him down the road to church, a penny clutched in one hand, and an umbrella in the other. Then, having put Algy down for his nap, and glanced in upon

Blanche and Philip, who were still completely engrossed in the water-color sketch and each other, she slipped out of her wet garments, took a hot bath and dressed again in crisp, clean clothes, tied a big apron over her spotless Sunday dress, and began, a little breathlessly, to get dinner.

She need not have hurried, for everyone else was late, but as she had no means of knowing that they would be, she was both tired and ruffled when, at half-past one, she had a meal ready to serve which would have done credit to an older and more experienced cook. Violet was the first to appear, and Violet was "nervous." Mary knew it the instant she looked at her.

"Paul isn't coming to dinner," she said tartly. "You hurt his feelings very much this morning."

"*I* hurt *his* feelings!" exclaimed Mary, hotly. "Well, he certainly hurt mine!"

"He wouldn't have, if you hadn't been so unkind and unreasonable," accused Violet. "I can't think how you can act so, especially when the poor boy is ill. I should have asked nothing better than to sit beside him the whole morning, bathing his poor, aching head, if I'd only been equal to it. But then, of course, there's no love as devoted and self-sacrificing as a mother's! Though I felt the same way towards Martin. I didn't feel towards him at all the way you do to Paul. I couldn't have."

"No, I don't believe you could," said Mary, trying to control the grief and anger that seemed to be struggling for mastery in her voice. "I'm sorry he won't come—I'll take off his place. Won't you come in to the parlor now and meet Mr. Starr?"

While this meeting was taking place, very satisfactorily to both persons concerned in it, Seth Manning was sitting patiently in the family carryall outside the village church, waiting for his cousin, Jane, and his small son, Moses, to come out of Sunday School. Miss Manning, in common with her neighbors, saw nothing irreverent in using aisles and porch for a little informal visiting after the services were over, especially if some great occasion demanding their attention required it. And as just at this time Children's Sunday was looming large ahead of them, there was a good deal to consider.

"I'm just as nervous as I kin be about them new-fangled exercises Mis' Weston has chosen," Mrs. Elliott was confiding to Miss Manning. "Of course, seein' she's Chairman of the Committee on Entertainment, none of the rest of us could say a word, but it looks to me as if she'd bit off more'n she can chew. If Sylvia Gray was so's she could be around, I shouldn't worry none, but Land! have you heard? Sylvia's expectin' again, and she's real poorly. She ain't strong enough to have children so fast. I went and told her so the other day and what do you think she said? That she was real pleased, that she only hoped it would be *twins*, twin girls, so she'd have two of 'em, right off, to go with the two boys! She does beat everything!"

"I notice no one beats her, no matter how hard they try to get ahead of her," said Miss Manning, with some meaning. "I like her spunk, and she's making Austin Gray a good wife —she ain't near so frivolous as I thought she'd be when I first met her. Well, I hope the exercises will go off all right, I'm sure, though I feel doubtful about 'em, same as you say. And I hope and pray it won't be so cold the girls will all show goose-flesh in their short-sleeved dresses. I don't know why 'tis, but seems like just before Children's Sunday every year we have a spell of pipin' hot weather, and then the very night before, it turns so cold you need a furnace fire, and then the children look actually blue in their new muslins— Good mornin', Mis' Weston, how are you today?"

"Oh, I'm *well!* But I declare I was ashamed to come to church again in this old dress," Mrs. Weston replied, shaking hands limply. "Miss Sims promised to have my new one ready, and she disappointed me again, same as usual. That woman ain't got no idea of the truth. She can't help but get it done for Children's Day, though, less she lays in bed half the time."

"What you got? A new black silk?"

"No, I thought I'd like a change—something bright. It's a steel-gray poplin. I hope it ain't going to be too gaudy."

"Well, I hope not," replied Miss Manning, with doubtfulness. "It's fortunate that woman can sew better'n she can sing, and I kinder wish she'd stick to the sewin'. The choir'd be better off without her. That first anthem was flat from start to finish. And Molly plays the hymns too fast since she went to the Conservatory. Makes 'em sound real cheerful. The music in this church ain't what it used to be when I was young. . . . Come, Moses, I guess your father's ready by this time."

When at last the assembled family, with the exception of Paul, was ready to sit down to a repast by this time slightly overdone, Moses, whose patience, as Mary had foreseen, had been sorely tried at Sunday School, decided not to grace the occasion by his presence. His father, declaring that "they wouldn't have no nonsense," set him down in his chair with considerable firmness. But Moses, thus further outraged, lifted his voice and roared with such blood-curdling yells, that he was suffered to depart, it being deemed inadvisable to pursue discipline too far in the presence of a guest; and the small boy was soon heard stamping up the stairs, his voice echoing and re-echoing as he went.

"Ain't you goin' to ask a blessin', Seth?" inquired Cousin Jane grimly, when a door somewhere in the attic had banged, and quiet reigned again.

Seth was hampered by the desire to avoid trouble and to please everyone all the time. Violet had come to him just before they sat down, and urged him to omit this rite, for fear that Mr. Starr would think they were old-fashioned. He had agreed with her. But now he quailed before Jane's stern eye.

"For-what-we-are-about-to-receive-make-us-duly-thankful," he gulped, all in one breath, and was immediately conscious that now he had offended both his cousins, one by asking the blessing at all, and the other by his manner of doing it.

"Lemme give you some chicken, Mr. Starr," he said hastily, "which do you favor, light or dark?"

Before Philip could answer, Cousin Jane also asked a question.

"I suppose you're not a church member?" she said with dark conviction.

Philip smiled. "Oh, yes," he said. "My father was a Congregational minister. I hadn't told you that before, had I? . . . Dark, please, Mr. Manning."

"A Congregational minister!" exclaimed Cousin Jane in amazement, while the others sat staring at him in speechless relief at his tact in introducing so exemplary a relative into their ruffled midst. "Why, I understood Mary to say that one of your grandfathers . . ."

"—Was an Irish immigrant. Yes, he was—North of Ireland Protestant. Plumber, after he got to this country. Made lots of money when he got started to plumb—just hit the first wave in the fashion for bathrooms. He only had one child, and there was plenty of money to let him travel and study and prepare for the ministry—which was what he wanted to do— those queer freaks of heredity come sometimes, you know. He was minister for years of one of the largest Congregational churches in Massachusetts—until he died, in fact. As he wasn't dependent on his salary for support, he led a pretty pleasant as well as a very useful life. He—he was an awfully good sort for a fellow to have for a father. My mother came from Brookline, and *her* father was a florist, so she inherited money too —funeral harps, and bridal wreaths, and all that kind of thing are terribly profitable, you know. She was another only child. And I'm another," ended Philip, less cheerfully.

"Do you mean to say," asked Blanche, with unconcealed envy, "that you haven't a *cousin* in the world?"

"Not one. Nor parents nor grandparents. It isn't much fun."

"Blanche wouldn't agree with you," said Cousin Jane. But her mind was still too busy with Philip's unexpected and gratifying disclosures to dwell long on the shortcomings of

Blanche. "How come you not to go to church this morning, then?"

"Extenuating circumstances," answered Philip promptly, glancing at Blanche.

Cousin Jane's next remark was interrupted by a terrific clattering and banging in the room above them. Mary rose hastily, in the act of serving stewed tomatoes.

"That's only Algy," she said by way of explanation to Philip, "waking up from his nap."

"Good gracious!" exclaimed Philip, still considerably startled.

"I know. He's rather noisy about it. He takes the entire crib to pieces—bolts, screws, and everything. We can't find out how he does it, because he won't do it when there's anyone around. Then when the whole thing falls apart, he throws the sheets and blankets and mattress all over the room, and takes off his own clothes, and by the time I get there, he's sitting on the floor on the springs. He does it almost every day. I'll go and dress him and bring him down."

When Algy, still pink and warm with sleep, was settled in his high chair, the ice-cream was being served, and the fresh, feathery sponge-cake passed about. Both were delicious. There was a comfortable silence as everyone began to eat with renewed appreciation of Mary's talents as a cook, when the door of the dining-room began to open, inch by inch, and Moses reappeared on the threshold.

The recollection that there was to be ice-cream for dinner had proved too much for him. Wounded pride, which might have held out in the face of rhubarb pie or cottage pudding, had failed him entirely. He was ready and willing to ingratiate himself now even with his Cousin Jane. Unfortunately, before he had remembered the ice-cream, he had taken refuge under a discarded bedstead in the attic, lying on his stomach to howl until he could howl no more. And Mary, in the stress of other duties, had not yet "got around to houseclean the attic" that spring. The back of Moses' sailor suit was still immaculately white; but the front was covered with dust, and cobwebs half an inch thick mingled with an occasional muddy spot caused by his copious tears.

Brushing these off hastily, with a cheerfulness she was very far from feeling, his sister tied a large bib around his neck, partially concealing the wreckage, and sought to change the subject tactfully.

"Here's your ice-cream, dear," she said, pleasantly. "How did you get along in Sunday School? It's nice, isn't it, that you're such a big boy now you can go alone? You didn't lose your penny, did you?"

"I didn't exactly lose it," said Moses agreeably. "I ate it."

Mary shook her head to ward off the family storm she saw this announcement was about to bring forth.

"Why, you shouldn't have done that," she said brightly. "It might have choked you."

"Then I wouldn't have had to go to Sunday School," said Moses, still calmly.

This, too, Mary felt it wiser to disregard, especially as Moses seemed to be warming to his subject, and willing to talk without further prodding.

"Mr. Taylor asked me a lot of questions so's he could tell what class to put me in. He asked me to repeat the Lord's Prayer, and the Lord Is My Shepherd and the Blesseds."

"Yes, dear?"

"Well, I repeated 'em."

"I'm glad," said Mary, her relief growing. But she was relieved too soon.

"And then he began on the story of the Bible. He ast me about Cain and Abel and Jonah and the whale, and Saul."

"What did you tell him?"

"I couldn't tell him much about the whale. But I remembered Saul. He just raised Hell generally—and by golly, that's what I'm going to do if you ever send me to Sunday School again. I'm going to let loose, and I'm going to begin right now —to show what I can do. I . . ."

But before Moses could carry out his threat, the dinner party had ended abruptly.

CHAPTER FIVE

On Monday morning it was still raining—raining much too hard to attempt the unknown roads to Burlington which might be of clayish formation all the way and dangerously slippery. There was, Blanche added to this slander of the highways of her native state, to be one of Hamstead's infrequent dances in the town hall that evening. It was stupid for her tagging along with Paul and Mary, even when they were on good terms, and anyone could see that Paul was having one of his grouches. (Paul's "grouches" corresponded to his mother's "nerves.") And none of the boys in the village seemed to realize that she was old enough to be asked to go to parties by herself now . . .

"Well, thank the Lord for that," said Philip piously. "I'll stay, of course."

In the afternoon it cleared, and he went to Violet, hesitating a little, and asked if he might invite Blanche to go for a little ride with him.

"Why, *of course*," she said delightedly. "It'll be just the way to pass the time, after you've been cooped up for nearly two days. Take one of the roads out to West Hamstead. They're very pretty and quiet. I know our fine Vermont air is going to do you lots of good. You look better already than when you came."

"I feel better," said Philip. "Thanks awfully for letting me take Blanche. I'll be—I'll take good care of her."

The route which Violet had suggested was one which could easily be covered in two hours, with the old family horse, but no one seemed to think it worth a comment when Philip and Blanche, leaving the house a little before three, reappeared late for a six o'clock supper. They had come to a little lake—Silver Pond, Blanche called it—and found an old water-logged row-boat lying neglected beside it. They bailed out the water in it with a tin can, also found providentially near at hand, getting very splashed themselves in the process. Then they rowed about the lake for a time, and finally climbed a hill back of it, where, from the steps of an old, barn-like building set in the midst of a cemetery, they sat and admired the view.

"This used to be the Town Hall," Blanche explained to him, "where the town meetings were held, you know. Now we have them in the hall in Hamstead, where we're going to the party tonight. Father used to bring me riding out here with him when I was a little girl, and he told me that the cemetery was used to bury the victims of political quarrels in, and that there were always a good many, every year. Father used to love to joke—but I believed every word of it. It made me almost afraid to come by here, for fear an unexpected meeting might be going on. I asked him once which side of the hall the dead Republicans were on, and he said, on the right side, of course. And he told me to notice that there weren't half so many as were buried on the Democratic side—that the Republicans were always the better fighters!"

Philip laughed again. He had been laughing, off and on, all the afternoon, from sheer joy, and when Blanche told one of her little stories, with such perfect artlessness, he laughed more than ever.

"It seems to be absolutely peaceful here now," he said. "Let's not hurry away. I like it here."

"Well, we needn't, of course," replied Blanche, "if it wasn't for the dance."

"Oh, yes, the dance! Will you give me every other one?"

"I think that's rather many, perhaps, don't you?" asked Blanche, flushing a little.

"Oh, no, not at all! I wouldn't dream of asking for less. It isn't done."

"Now you're laughing at me again!"

Had any man, Philip wondered, ever found a girl so unspoiled, so utterly delicious? It was difficult for him to refrain from taking her into his arms then and there; and though somehow he managed to steel himself against doing this, he reached out for the little hand that lay lightly on the extremely narrow strip of wood that separated him from Blanche, and locked his hard, lean fingers with her soft pink ones. She made no effort to pull away. Indeed, the gentle pressure with which she responded to his hesitant overture, gave him the sensation of being entwined by the tendrils of *cordon d'amour*. Nothing that he had ever experienced in his life had awakened in him such a feeling of ecstasy. What tremendous—what undeserved—luck had been with him when he decided to take that swim!

"I am so glad you agree with me about the dances," he said, at last, rising reluctantly.

"But I didn't agree! Philip, how *can* you?"

Philip! She had already begun to forget to call him Mr. Starr. He had never known before what a wonderful name Philip was. The slow drive home was permeated with magic. The shabby reins lay slack over the dash-board of the buggy. The plodding old horse needed no guidance. Without knowing when or how he had begun to do so, Philip found that he was holding both Blanche's hands; he felt her golden head sink gently on his shoulder and rest there quiescent. The deepening dusk, enfolding them, seemed pregnant with the promise of still closer companionship, of more ardent embraces. But the prelude to these was perfect and complete in itself.

Neither the return to the farm, nor the family supper, nor the departure for the party to which Blanche had looked forward to eagerly, dispelled Philip's illusion of enchantment. Of course he got his dances. Many of the alternate ones he

danced with Mary. The little hall was decorated with apple-
blossoms and pine boughs, there was a table in one corner
with a big basin filled with grape-juice on it, and an "orchestra" of three pieces from Wallacetown furnished the music.
Philip had never been to a function in the least like it before.
There was "the White Water crowd" from the new mill there
—for country dances are public—but none of the girls, and
only Paul and Jack Weston among the men—paid the slightest attention to them. But Philip met some of the other Hamstead "young people" and liked them all—Dr. David Noble,
who had gone away as a boy, and achieved success and even
fame as a doctor, and had given it up, after all, to come back
and practise in Hamstead, was there with his beautiful French
wife. Austin Gray had his two unmarried sisters, Molly and
Katherine, with him, since his wife, Sylvia, was "not dancing
just then"; while the two Gray girls already married, Sally
and Ruth, were there with their husbands, Fred Elliott and
Frank French. The Congregational minister, Mr. Taylor,
though he did not dance, had brought his pretty daughter,
Elizabeth, who did. Jack Weston had a cousin from New York
with him, who had just come to board through the summer
with his mother. She was a little, dark creature, cheaply
pretty, her tiny piquant face painted and powdered, and still
more cheaply stylish, wearing a bright red dress, with only
velvet straps over her slim shoulders, and a V-cut bodice that
went almost down to her girdle in the back, and was not much
higher in the front.

"That girl doesn't look like your sort—like all the rest of
you," said Philip to Mary, when they were dancing together
for the third time, and he noticed how often her eyes were
turning in the direction of the pretty stranger.

"That's Rosalie King. She works in one of the big department stores in New York and has a fine position. But she's
been quite sick, so they've given her a long vacation, and I'm
sure she's earned it," said Mary kindly. "She hasn't been here
before, since she was a little girl. She's always had to shift for

herself, and she's as capable and self-reliant as she can be. Mrs. Weston's been looking forward all winter to having her come. I guess she'll liven us all up. Do—do you like her dress?"

"No," said Philip with the promptness that characterized all his speeches. "Do you?"

"No-o-o. But I thought that was the fashion now in New York, perhaps."

"In some parts of New York."

"Well, it doesn't look like Mrs. Noble's, or Sylvia Gray's dresses, and they always have lovely clothes. But we see the styles so seldom in Hamstead—"

"You don't think Blanche is likely to see much of her, do you?" asked Philip anxiously, his mind revolting at the thought of the precious bit of Dresden china he had found, coming into contact with a bit of cheap painted pottery.

"Why, yes! We're all friends and neighbors in Hamstead— most of us cousins, too, as Blanche has told you. If one of us has a guest—we don't very often—everyone else tries to make things pleasant for her. I know she went to the Taylors' to supper tonight. And—Paul seems to like her. He's danced with her quite a lot."

This was perfectly true. Paul had been visibly attracted to her from the first, and by the latter part of the evening his attentions were becoming extremely marked. It was plain to all that both he and Rosalie were enjoying themselves very much, and that under her tuition he was learning the "new dances" with which Hamstead was not as yet very familiar, and which shocked at least part of it a little. He left her side, however, to come and have the last waltz with Mary, according to Hamstead's unwritten law, and was more good-natured on the drive home than either his sister or his cousin could remember seeing him in a long time.

All of Lady Blanche Farm was sorry when Philip said good-by bright and early Tuesday morning. Blanche, to whom he had suggested a short walk through the orchard, lifted brimming eyes to his. He stooped and kissed the tears away from her lashes. Then he laid his cheek against hers.

"This isn't really good-by, you know," he whispered; and added softly, "sweetheart!"

Violet's farewell was likewise accompanied by tears, as well as by little pats and cooing sounds. A very small, very fine, lace-edged handkerchief, daintily manipulated, was a good deal in evidence. Mary packed a delicious lunch, and laid a neatly folded road map with Philip's route clearly marked in red pencil, on top of his suitcase. Even Cousin Jane remarked stiffly that perhaps he'd call in again some time.

"Yes, indeed, as soon as you'll let me," Philip responded, shaking hands vigorously.

"I guess you'd always be welcome, far as I know," she replied.

The day after his departure, the station agent called up Violet to tell her that there was a big box addressed to her, and marked perishable, express paid, waiting there. And, when it was promptly brought home by Seth and opened with some excitement, it was found to contain four five-pound boxes of candy, all exactly alike, but elaborately tied up with different colored ribbons. Blanche's ribbon of course was white, and her mother's violet, while Mary's was pale blue—none of which was surprising—but Cousin Jane's, to the amazement of all, was bright red! And under each bow of ribbon was slipped a card which read, "With kindest regards, and many thanks for my wonderful visit, from Philip Starr."

Suitors in Hamstead were not in the habit of bestowing confectionery in this wholesale fashion, not only on the object of their affections, but on all her family as well. And as Jane Manning had never had a suitor of her own, this was the first box of candy that had ever been given to her. She tried to conceal her pleased surprise as long as she was with the others. Then she carried the box home, very carefully, and put it on her bed-side table, near her Bible. It did not occur to her to open it. She drew up her rocker, and sat for a long time looking at it.

"No one but him would ever have remembered me," she said aloud, "at all, let alone sendin' me candy, at my age, and all tied up with red ribbon! . . . That nice boy!" she ended abruptly, and blew her nose hard.

The excitement aroused by the boxes of candy and the pleasant "bread-and-butter" letters which followed in their wake had hardly subsided when something even more thrilling happened. A beautiful limousine, beside which Philip's little Ford runabout could no more have stood comparison than could Cinderella's pumpkin with the fairy coach into which it was turned, driven by a slim young chauffeur, very smart in a uniform to match the car's upholstery, drew up in front of Seth Manning's door, and a tall, distinguished-looking man of early middle age got out and asked for Mary.

It was, unfortunately, Moses who answered the rap at the knocker. His mouth was full, as usual, of stolen sweets—he had eaten up almost the entire contents of Mary's box of candy—and he had no eye for style. He was not impressed by the appearance of the strange man. Moreover, his own appearance could hardly have warranted the hope that he might create a favorable impression himself. The day being warm, and Mary otherwise occupied, he had surreptitiously removed most of his clothing—in fact, everything except a pair of ankle ties, which had no connection with modesty and were retained simply because the hemp carpet in the front hall was rough.

"Hello," he said, pulling a piece of caramel out of his mouth, stretching it to its full length, and putting it back again.

"Er—hello," said the stranger, his face twitching slightly. "Does Miss Mary Manning live here?"

"Mary? Yes. She's out in the back garden, killing potato bugs . . . that way," said Moses, with a wave of the hand, indicating the direction which the stranger should take, having no mind himself to face Mary's probable comments on his costume—or rather, the lack of it—if he undertook to act as guide in person.

"Thank you very much," said the man, his mouth still twitching, walking off in the direction indicated.

Mary, hearing footsteps, straightened up quickly from the task over which she was bent, and turned a deep crimson.

"Mr. Hamlin!" she exclaimed, in great confusion. "Oh, you must excuse me! When did you come?"

"Just now, from Boston," he said, laughing and shaking hands. "I understand you are more cordial to guests from that locality than you once gave me to understand you were likely to be. I have had the pleasure of—er—meeting one of your small brothers, and he told me I should probably find you here. Aren't you glad to see me?"

"Moses! Oh, what dreadful thing was he doing this time? Yes, of course I am, but—"

"You didn't sound very enthusiastic about the prospect when I asked you once before if I might come. Do you remember?"

"Yes—but—" began Mary again, her flush growing deeper every minute.

"This time I came because Philip Starr asked me to. Naturally, I didn't tell him how glad I was of an excuse. He thinks I'm doing it entirely out of friendship to him—and, as a matter of fact, I *would* have been glad to do it entirely out of friendship to him—only, it's great luck, for me, that he happened to fall in love with your cousin. It'll get Hannah and me into touch with you again—Philip wants me to talk to Blanche's mother and brother about him—in my official capacity as his employer, on the score of his talents, his income, and his morals. He is a young man of unusual thoroughness, promptness and decision, as you may have gathered in your glimpse of him—qualities which, unfortunately, are not often found in one who is also an artist and an idealist. Moreover, he possesses, besides a deep love of beauty and a quite wonderful ability to interpret it, a very fine sense of honor. I had a special delivery letter from him yesterday morning. He seems to be in a tremendous hurry, but didn't think it right to press his suit until he had been more thoroughly introduced. I was instructed that as soon as this formality, through me, had been accomplished, I was to telegraph him at Burlington, and he would return here—unless, of course, it seemed absolutely hopeless for him to do so. In that case he thought he ought to wait until your cousin was a little older."

"Is there any reason why it should be hopeless?"

"None in the world."

"Then come over and meet Cousin Violet."

"All right," replied Gale Hamlin with twinkling eyes. "But remember that afterwards I'm coming back here to see you!"

Two days later, Philip stood in the white-paneled North Parlor of Violet Manning's house, waiting for Blanche to come down to him. The room was unlighted, and it was beginning to grow dark. The summer wind was blowing in through the open windows, and the air was sweet with the many flowers that stood about in clear glass bowls. Somewhere off in the lilac bushes a whip-poor-will was singing. . . .

The door opened and Blanche came in. Philip took a step towards her, and held out his arms. She walked straight into them.

"Lady Blanche—you little white flower—Oh, my *darling!*" was all he said, and covered her lifted face with his kisses.

CHAPTER SIX

Two Hamstead boys—Austin Gray and David Noble—had married heiresses, but in both cases the village had been cheated out of a wedding. For Sylvia Gray was a young widow with a ghastly experience in her first marriage behind her when she came there, twining herself into all their hearts, and her wedding to Austin was as quiet and simple as they could make it. And David Noble had married Jacqueline in France, on what was thought, at the time, to be her death-bed. Philip Starr would never have dreamed of considering his comfortable income a fortune. But it loomed large in the eyes of Lady Blanche Farm, and soon in those of all the country-side, for in the general rejoicing at the good luck which had befallen Blanche, it was augmented—consciously or unconsciously—by many persons. Violet herself was largely responsible for this. For once in her life, she threw off her inertia gladly, and went about among her neighbors scattering her good news as she went.

"Of course, Blanche is very young, and it breaks my heart to think of parting with her," she said, sighing and wiping away a few tears. "But I couldn't bring myself to stand in the way of the true happiness of one of my children for selfish reasons. That's never been my way. You know I've always given up everything to devote my whole life to them. She is just blissful—I never saw such ideal lovers in all my life. So different from those we usually see around here—either absolutely humdrum, or so coarse and vulgar it makes you shudder. Of course Blanche is too innocent about worldly things and too much in love to *think* of the material side at all, but

we older ones know that can't be overlooked altogether. Philip
can do everything for her. Yes, her ring is lovely, isn't it? Of
course you know plain solitaires are entirely gone by. You seldom see such pure, white diamonds. And he's given her a
pendant, too—a diamond star! Wasn't that a pretty thought,
and so clever! Philip is clever, unusually so. He says the name
she's going to have, Blanche Starr, is a poem just in itself. And
of course she'll have Countess Blanche's jewels, too—some of
those went to Seth's branch of the family, but Mary is going to
let Blanche have her share, and I think that's only fair, because of course she'll never need anything of the kind here.
No, Philip won't hear of a long engagement, so I'm going to
take Blanche to Boston right away, to buy her trousseau, and
see caterers and stationers and so on. I guess I can show his
fashionable friends that I know how things should be done,
even if I do live in the country!— They're going to California
on their wedding trip—of course Philip would have taken
Blanche to Europe if this tiresome war hadn't been going on.
Those foreigners are always cutting each other's throats,
aren't they? I'm thankful we're not in it, or likely to be. Philip
had been thinking of taking an officer's training course at
Plattsburgh, when he came down with typhoid, but of course
that's all given up now, and I'm glad of it, for I hate to think of
his getting mixed up with anything so shocking and brutal.
Yes, they're going to have an apartment in Brookline as soon
as they get back from their trip. Blanche is going to choose
it while we're down doing our shopping, and furnish it exactly as she likes. He says he's giving her *carte Blanche*—that's
just another of his jokes! Of course you wouldn't understand
it, not knowing French. I'm so relieved, now that I'm going to
have him for a son-in-law, that my parents gave me a refined
education. Yes—six rooms and a bath to start with, but of
course they can have a larger one whenever they need it.
Blanche is going to keep a maid, and have a motor, right from
the beginning. Of course, all Philip's friends—and he has thousands of them—will entertain for her and give her a beautiful

time. I've figured that she can't possibly get along without at
least two evening dresses, besides her wedding dress. I'm going to have electric lights put in the house. I've been meaning
to for some time, but it's such hard work, when you keep a
house the way I like mine, just doing the necessary things,
without having it torn up besides, that I've shrunk from it.
Now I feel I owe it to Blanche. We're thinking of buying a car
ourselves, too, right away. Paul's just crazy for one, and I don't
know any reason why we shouldn't have it. Jane doesn't begin to spend her income and she's glad to help a little at a
time like this; though of course I shouldn't dream of asking
her to, if she hadn't suggested it herself. You'd never believe
what a fancy she's taken to Philip. But then, she couldn't
very well help it. Philip is *charming*, and that's so rare in a
man! He calls her Cousin Jane already, and kisses her good-
night, and is so thoughtful and pleasant with her always. I
simply adore him myself. . . ."

There was not a single flaw in the crystal. Violet could purr
on for hours. In fact Hamstead grew a little tired of so much
perfection and so much purring.

"I call it puttin' on airs," said Mrs. Elliott to her friend, Mrs.
Gray. "So far as I kin see, Philip Starr *is* a nice young man,
and pleasant-spoken to everybody. But the Mannin's ain't any
better than the rest of us, and never was. To hear Violet run
on, you'd think they was of considerable more importance
than anyone else in Hamstead. Humph! Mary's had to work a
sight harder'n any girl around here, even the minister's
daughter, and there ain't a lazier, more worthless feller in the
whole township than Paul. Jane's face would stop a clock,
and Seth's so slow he wouldn't move any quicker if he was to
set on a hornet's nest. And, well, we all know what Violet is!
I'd like to know where all the money's comin' from for all these
fancy fixin's. Even if Jane is helpin' out, I guess there's some
limit to the foolishness she'd stand for—Jane's got sense, if she
ain't got looks. I bet they'll have to scrimp considerable after

the weddin's over. Maybe they're usin' capital. Hev you heard anyone say?"

Nevertheless, in spite of these expressions of disparagement, Mrs. Elliott and all Hamstead with her, flocked to see the trousseau, and then the presents, and, in early August, to the wedding. During the two months and a half that had elapsed since his first appearance there, Philip had spent every Sunday and holiday at Lady Blanche Farm, and, as Mrs. Elliott said, had been so "pleasant-spoken" that he had become cordially liked in the village, quite aside from the fact, that, as Blanche's fiancé, he was naturally an object of interest; and, in turn, he had come to have a very warm and real affection for many of his new friends and relatives. Only twice had his dream of perfect happiness been shaken; and he tried to dismiss both of these episodes from his mind as trivial.

Left alone for a time one rainy morning, he had decided to explore the little, abandoned law office. Violet had given him the key, telling him that it contained two lovely mantels, and other carved woodwork which he might like to see. Privately, he had been thinking what fun it would be to restore it, and put it in order for Blanche and himself to occupy when they came to Hamstead to visit. His investigations confirmed this opinion. It contained a cellar and two large, semicircular rooms, one above the other, and a small one with a little attic over it in the rear. The proportions were perfect, the neglected woodwork beautiful, the latches on the doors, even the great nails, of hand-wrought iron, the crane and kettle still hanging in the fireplace, all called forth Philip's admiration. The foundations were all as solid as the day they had been built. He sat down in one of the dilapidated chairs that had been left there, pulled up a shaky table, and drew plans and sketches. Under his swift pencil, the tiny place became transformed. There was the living room, bright with white paint and a landscape paper, and shining brasses, with Lady Blanche's portrait over the mantel, her desk in one corner, her harpsichord in another, and her gate-legged mahogany table in the center of the room; there was the chamber, with her four-posted bed —one of her hand-woven linen sheets serving for a counterpane—her bureau with its crystal lustres for Blanche, her low-boy for his own dressing table, her long gilt-framed mirror, and the sampler she had stitched, on the flowered walls instead of pictures. In striking contrast, the back of the house —a kitchen, a dining alcove, a bathroom, a small extra bedroom—should be thoroughly modern, containing much porcelain, nickel and linoleum. And of course there must be a little furnace and electric lights, but they'd use candles mostly, quantities of them, in glass and silver candlesticks. And, thinking of silver and glass, there must be quantities of that, too, as well as furniture, that they should have. Violet, to whom he had confided his plan, had told him *of course* he was welcome to anything—

He spent a long time over his pleasant task. Then, finding that Blanche, who had promised to join him there, was still nowhere in sight, he picked up some of the musty books lying on the table, and began to look through them.

They were mostly law books, with a few interesting marginal notes that the second Moses Manning had made; but Philip knew little or nothing about law, and did not understand them. The third volume that he opened, less bulky than the others, proved to be a county history, written by a local clergyman early in the nineteenth century. It was quaintly and gracefully worded, and the facts that it had to relate were in themselves valuable and inspiring. The Connecticut Valley had been settled by men of no slight caliber, and their subsequent Revolutionary record was noteworthy. Philip read on with increasing interest, which grew greater still when he reached that portion of the history devoted mainly to the Manning family. Here were Moses Manning's fine war service —the Lafayette letters—the journal and commissions—the trip to France—and here, too, was the Countess Blanche! The story of the great chests that came over the sea, and the silk gown

worn to "meeting"! And, at last, came the date of the twins'
birth, and, a few pages farther on, that of Lady Blanche's
death. But between these dates was something that Philip had
not yet heard.

". . . And the Lady Blanche, being very weak after her long
travail, was sorely spent, for she was a female elegantly
formed, but not sturdy, or of sound health. She lay in great
pain, and ever and anon she sank into a stupor from which
none could rouse her, nor did she regard my exhortations, or
the lamentations of her afflicted husband. But suddenly she
did raise herself in her bed, and did speak in a loud voice,
saying, 'Since I must die, neither shall any other woman in
this village who beareth twins survive her cruel labor; and
though I perish, there shall be, in every generation, a Blanche
Manning on this farm, who shall have not only my name, but
in whom my person shall also be seen again. And she shall
wed for love, being hotly wooed, even as I was wooed, by a
stranger. But because I have suffered, for all my love, in this
unfriendly, cold country, and because he who swore to love
me best has not saved me from anguish, but hath shown his
love to be but selfishness, since he hath failed me when I most
did need him—therefore, I say, she shall not love for long.
Within five years of her marriage either she or her husband
shall die, and die with the bitter knowledge that neither riches
nor passion nor high romance, nay, not even all three together,
suffice to make that great thing called love unless there be
other things, which my lover hath not given me, added unto
them. And, in the hour of their death, I will appear unto those
who die, and comfort them, for the manner of their passing
shall be lonely and grievous altogether."

"And thereat," went on the chronicler, "she lay back upon
her bed in peace, and did not speak again. And we marvelled
greatly that one so gentle should seek, in her last moments,
to lay a curse upon her innocent descendants."

Philip closed the book, shivering, and angry and ashamed
because he was shivering. That silly old superstition—what

did it amount to! But—had it amounted to anything? If not, why had neither Blanche nor Mary been willing to tell him the whole story of Lady Blanche? Had Blanche thought of it since she became engaged? Could she be worrying about it? He thought not—her perfect happiness had been too transparent to allow him to believe that for one minute. And indeed, even if she did know it, why should she be so foolish as to worry over anything like this? But he began, involuntarily, to recall the histories of other members of the Manning family. The Countess's girl-twin—the second Blanche—had married a Virginian, a classmate of her brother's at Harvard, who was shot, after they had had only a few radiant months together, in a duel with the man who had once been his best friend. The lawyer, Moses, had a daughter named Blanche, who went West in a prairie-schooner on her honeymoon, and was never heard of again after she passed the Alleghenies. And the lawyer's eldest son had a daughter who—but that story was too dreadful, and contained shame as well as tragedy; he could only guess at the truth of it, for it was seldom mentioned. Feeling as if his throat were being clutched, and as if he could not shake himself free of the hand that choked him, Philip sprang to his feet to see an apparition standing in the doorway.

Blanche also had been spending her time that rainy morning by making an excursion into the past. Her mother had felt it a good opportunity for them to go through some of the chests carefully stowed away in the attic in search of treasures to add to her trousseau and they had found a tiny iron-bound trunk, thrust far under the eaves and forgotten, full of the Countess's clothes; Blanche had carried them down to her bedroom and tried them on. They fitted her as if they had been made for her.

"Couldn't I keep one of them on, and surprise Philip?"

"I think it would be *lovely!* And you can do your hair like hers in the portrait, and wear that white brocade dress that she had it painted in—you'd be the living image of her!"

Accordingly, after a careful study of the famous picture, Blanche did her hair, with Violet's help, high on her head, powdered it, laced herself into the stiff, magnificent gown that had been the Countess's wedding dress, and went out to join Philip.

The startled, almost terrified cry that escaped him when he saw her, frightened her almost out of her senses. She ran to him, and put her arms around him, trembling too.

"What is it?" she exclaimed. "Oh, Philip! What's the matter?"

"Nothing—nothing . . . How lovely you look! . . . Are those some of the first Blanche's clothes?"

"Yes. Don't you think they're pretty?"

"Beautiful, darling. You—you're very like her, aren't you? Like her picture, of course, I mean."

"Yes—but I don't see why you seem so upset, even if I am. I thought it would please you to see me dressed up like this!"

Philip forced a laugh. "I'm not upset," he said pleasantly. "I've got bored to death, trying to read these old books while I was waiting for you, and I didn't hear you come in. . . . You startled me a little, that's all. You're—you're enough to startle any man, you're so lovely. I want a kiss—and I want to consult you about something. . . ." And then he told her of his scheme for fixing up the little office.

To his surprise, she did not respond to him with enthusiasm. At first she looked a little bored. Then, after a very brief and obvious effort at self-control, she interrupted him with a petulance which shocked him.

"For Heaven's sake, Philip! Don't you realize that I want to get away from Hamstead and *stay* away? If we fixed up this place, and put all that money into it, we'd have to *keep coming back to it!* That's the last thing on earth I want to do! I don't want an old-fashioned house, full of old-fashioned furniture, in an old-fashioned village! I want to live in a big city. I want a cute little modern apartment that fairly rustles with taffeta curtains and spreads, and rattles with china ornaments and has gilt chairs in the parlor and a painted bedroom set and curly maple in the dining room! I don't want a quiet existence; I want to give parties all the time—except when I am going out to them—little afternoon bridge parties and little evening theater parties—and heaps of dancing. We must get a Victrola right off. Then we can have two or three other couples in, once a week or so, and serve chicken salad and frozen pudding and coffee and pull up the rugs and—well, you know the sort of thing I mean. And I simply adore going to the movies and shopping around for lacy night-gowns and getting an ice cream soda in the middle of the morning, and having lunch at a tea-room. That's what I've done the few times I've been to town to visit. Why, Philip, I thought you were going to help me to *escape* from Lady Blanche Farm! I thought you *wanted* me to have a good time and pretty clothes, and heaps of new friends. . . ."

There was something almost grotesque about her, in spite of her loveliness, as she stood before him in her silvery brocade, clamoring for tawdry possessions and trifling pastimes. Philip had always vaguely sensed her desire for these things, her discontent, her restlessness; but he had never permitted the almost subconscious knowledge of it to mar his idyl. Now, the sudden dread lest the delicate fabric of his romance might be rent before his eyes, filled him with fear. But this fear was engulfed in the terrorized premonition which his research had aroused.

Somehow he steadied himself and managed to speak lightly. "I *do* want you to have a good time and party clothes and pleasant friends, darling," he said. "And you shall. We won't say anything more about this scheme of mine, since it doesn't appeal to you. It was only a fancy, anyway."

He drew her close to him, drugging himself, for the moment, with the delight of feeling her in his arms. But afterwards he sought out Mary.

Everyone always took stories of trouble to Mary, sure of help and understanding and comfort. The fact that it was ironing day, and that he found her, in the middle of a sultry afternoon, toiling away in a hot kitchen, and not sitting with folded hands in some secluded and restful spot, as comforters are traditionally supposed to be found, made no difference. He lifted a neat pile of handkerchiefs and napkins and towels off the chair nearest the ironing-board, and sat down. He could not bring himself to speak of Blanche's outburst, but he did speak of the ominous sense of foreboding which had been awakened by his perusal of Hastings' History and which had persisted ever since. Mary listened to his recital in silence, and without stopping her work: except for a moment to tie up Moses' finger, when he came in bleeding and roaring as the result of an encounter with his father's jack-knife, which Seth had carelessly left within his reach; and for such other slight interruptions as to find a cookie for Algy who—two hours having elapsed since dinner—was feeling the bitter pangs of hunger; to answer the telephone and promise to make an angel-cake and a cabbage salad for the forthcoming church fair; and a second time, after a slightly wistful glance at the clock, to decline an invitation from Sylvia Gray to come to supper, on the ground that she "really had a lot to do that afternoon." And when Philip had finished, she went to the stove for a hot iron, tested it with her hand, and began to press out Seth's overalls before she answered.

"You don't think we've kept this from you wilfully, do you?" she said, at length. "You know I asked you, right off, if there were anything that would make you want Blanche less, and you said no. And I'm sure that the reason she didn't tell you the whole story, that day by the brook, was simply because, as she said, you would think she was 'awfully conceited and fresh' if she inferred that she thought she was beautiful and likely to be loved at first sight by a handsome stranger. She doesn't read much, and she's probably forgotten part of the legend, anyway, even if she ever read it. It isn't given in the Town History—most of our early writers thought all superstitions inventions of the devil! I think the Reverend Hastings is

the only historian who mentions it, and that county history
has been in the office among the law-books, where Blanche
wouldn't be likely to see it. You—you wouldn't be so cruel as
to spoil her lovely happiness by telling her about it now,
would you?"

"Good Lord, Mary, you don't think I *want* to, do you? It
would just about kill me to give her up."

Mary glanced at Philip, and was aware of tears in his eyes.
"Then what do you mean?"

"I thought you might think—I think myself perhaps I ought
to—on her account, you know."

"On her account?" said Mary, stupidly.

"If there is any truth in a thing like that, isn't it my duty
to?"

"Why?"

"So—she could do something safer, of course."

Mary folded the overalls carefully. "There isn't anything
safer for a girl to do," she said in a low voice, "than to marry
the man she loves. If—if he loves her. No matter what happens
afterwards, she has something that lasts all her life—that no
one can take away from her—even if it's only a memory. And
if her life is the one that's short, what does that matter, if it's
full and perfect, and—complete?"

"I guess you're right," said Philip huskily. Then, still hesitating—"You don't suppose I think you're right just because
I *want* to, do you?"

"Did you ever think anything was right just for that reason?"

Philip searched his conscience. It is doubtful if many men,
searching as thoroughly, could have found so little for which
they needed to feel sorry.

"I don't believe so," he said at last, smiling at her.

Mary smiled back; and looking at her, but thinking of
Blanche, Philip felt that this episode was closed.

The second episode had nothing whatever to do with the
past, but a good deal to do with the present. Try as he might

—and he certainly did try—Philip could not succeed in liking Paul. What was worse, the more he saw of him, the less he liked him. He did not, to be sure, see much. The dislike, noticed, but carefully hushed up by Violet, seemed to be entirely mutual. And Paul was spending so much of his time, especially since the arrival of the new motor, in the society of Miss Rosalie King, that his family was favored less and less by his presence. Philip, who had marvelled at the way Mary bore Paul's shortcomings, and not only bore, but forgave them from the beginning, marvelled still more at the apparent indifference with which she bore his frank neglect.

But Mary was, as he was eventually to discover, far less indifferent than he had supposed, and knowing a little of the capacity for suffering that many silent and self-contained persons possess, the discovery disturbed him not a little. Next to Blanche, there was no one in the world for whom he cared as much as he already did for Mary. Had she been his sister, his feeling of admiration and affection could hardly have been stronger, and they were naturally thrown a great deal together. Going into Seth Manning's house one day on an errand, he first encountered Moses, who generally seemed to be on hand to receive visitors.

"Where's Mary?" inquired Philip.

"In her room," said Moses. "Say, Philip, I just seen a snake eatin' a toad out by the cellar door. He's got him about half et. Come along and see him."

Philip was not interested in snakes and toads. "In her room!" he echoed. It was so unusual for Mary to be "off duty" even for a few minutes, that the fact was alarming.

"Yes. Lyin' on the bed."

"Is she sick?"

"No. Cryin'. Hard," added Moses with emphasis.

"Do you know why?" pursued Philip.

"Paul," said Moses laconically.

Philip turned thoughtfully away. He was sleeping in the room adjoining Paul's on his brief visits at Lady Blanche

Farm, and he had some idea of the hours his future brother-in-law was keeping. After vacillating for a short time between his reluctance to meddle in other people's affairs and his distress at the thought of Mary's unhappiness, he waited up for him that night, and endeavored to have a talk with him.

The attempt was far from successful. Philip possessed more than the average amount of tact, and tried to put the question fairly and kindly. But Paul was enraged.

"You had better mind your own business," he shouted, so loudly that Philip feared Violet and Blanche might both be aroused. "I don't tell you how to manage things with my sister, do I? You've done just as you damned pleased about the whole affair, since the day you first struck the farm. And I'll thank you to let mine alone, too. I guess I know what I'm about!"

"I'm afraid you don't. That's just it," said Philip. "And I'm older than you, and have been about a bit more, and—"

"Oh, you're afraid I don't, are you? Well, I should worry," jeered Paul, who was picking up more or less New York slang. "We're a good little boy, aren't we? Never hit it up in all our lives! Well, run along to bed, that's the best place for one of your advanced years and experience—you must look out not to keep too late hours, or get your feet wet, or anything like that—might be fatal!" Then as Philip hesitated, Paul burst into oaths before which Philip, hitherto unacquainted with certain phrases of rural vocabulary, stood electrified for a moment, and then walked into his own room and closed the door.

And so the second episode, also, came to an abrupt end, and he strove to dismiss both from his mind.

The wedding day, which seemed to the impatient bridegroom so interminably slow in arriving, came at last—warm, clear and cloudless. The little white Congregational church, where all the Mannings had always worshipped, and where the marriage ceremony was performed, was decorated as it never had been before in the hundred and fifty years of its existence. Lady Blanche Farm was hung with Japanese lanterns from end to end, and the moon hung, too, like the largest and most glowing lantern of all, in the middle of a star-scattered sky. The Wallacetown "orchestra" played for dancing. A wedding supper, more sumptuous than any of which Hamstead had ever partaken, was spread on tables under huge awnings extending over the lawns, and two rooms were filled with presents which any bride might well have been proud to display and possess. Blanche, wearing the Countess's pearls, enveloped in a mist of white tulle and soft lace, looked more exquisite and fairy-like than ever. Mary, and Elizabeth Taylor, in sea-green chiffon, carrying huge bunches of lavender sweet-peas, were bridesmaids. Philip's friends—and they seemed to be legion—were there in full force, nor had Hamstead realized before how many Boston friends Mary had, too. Laura Manning's insistence that her daughter, whose fine mind she had recognized, should be sent away to the best school that could be found for her, had not been regarded with approval in Hamstead, where it was viewed as an unwarranted and unwarrantable extravagance; and Mary, quick to resent any slight to her beloved mother's judgment, had said little about the acquaintance she had made while she was there. Now, being human, she could not help feeling a little thrill of triumph at the plainly expressed pleasure that so many of Philip's friends showed at meeting her again. Gale Hamlin was there, with his sister and niece. Mr. Davis, the senior partner of the firm, had come, too, with his wife and sons; and many others. All Hamstead was there, of course, and most of White Water and some of Wallacetown; and all Hamstead included, that summer, pretty, painted Rosalie King, with her cousins, the Westons. . . .

Finally, Blanche and Philip drove off in their own motor, showered with rice and confetti, cheering and waving from their ribbon-bedecked car as they went. The guests remained a little longer to laugh and cry, and "talk it over." Then gradually they went home, motor-horns tooting, aged carryalls creaking, boys and girls singing as they walked arm in arm up the dusty road to the village. The Japanese lanterns went

out one by one. Jane crossed the lawn to her own house and
sat looking at her ribbon-tied candy-box for some minutes before she went to bed. Violet collapsed, in an orgy of satisfaction and tears, and Mary undressed her and made her a hot
drink with a bromide tablet melted in it, and pulled the shut-
ters of her room together, so that the sun should not waken
her too early the next day. And finally, coming out of her
cousin's room at two o'clock in the morning, after having made
her "as comfortable as could be expected"—to quote Violet's
own feeble whisper—she met Paul face to face in the hall.

He lurched towards her unsteadily. She had known, all day,
that he had had far too much to drink. There had been champagne, and a strong punch served at the wedding, for Violet
had had less fear of shocking some of her "narrow-minded"
neighbors, or of unnecessarily placing temptation in the way
of her son, than that Philip's Boston friends might think her
"countrified." And all the evening, Paul had been alternately
consuming first punch and then champagne and then punch
again. The results of his over-indulgence were all too obvious
in both his appearance and his manner. Mary looked at him
and her very soul revolted.

"How dare you!" she cried, "disgrace your sister's wedding-
day like this!"

Paul seemed hardly to hear her. But there was no doubt
that he saw her and that he found her very good to look at.
Philip had once said that Mary was lovely always, but that if
she ever got angry, she would be magnificent. Mary was very
angry now, so angry that she hardly knew that she was
wounded to the heart as well. She was, indeed, magnificent,
beautiful as Paul had never seen her, had never known she
could be. He threw his arms around her, and began to kiss
her violently on her neck, her cheeks, her lips. Mary tried to
struggle away from him, hot with fury, sick with shame and
disgust. He only held her closer. At last she succeeded in free-
ing one arm, and with all her might, struck him across the
mouth. Instead of sobering Paul, it stimulated his raging

senses to the point of frenzy. He confronted Mary with unleashed fury.

"You canting hypocrite!" he shouted, furiously, "moping around all summer, acting as if you were crazy to have me make love to you! And now going for me like a wild-cat when I try it! I guess I knew what I was doing when I let you alone! I guess I can get all the kisses I want without paying for them by being hit in the face! From now on, you can mope forever for all I care—but you won't have a chance to hit me again! I never asked you to marry me, anyhow—you've only pretended I did! I never wanted you at all! Why should I want a prude—or a shrew—or a jailor—for a wife? *You* wanted *me* —though you've tried to act so high and holy about it! And damn it, you almost got me! But I'm through with you now— *through*—do you hear? I'm *free!* And you'll never get me again after this!"

CHAPTER SEVEN

The lot in life of the girl who has been jilted is probably not very pleasant anywhere, but there is no place on earth where it is quite as hard as in a small country village. A generation or so earlier, the blighted maiden had usually sought refuge from the gossip that clattered about her by "going into a decline" and thus turned it into sympathy. But Mary was not made of the stuff that declines easily, in any generation. She went about her usual occupations, after Blanche's wedding and the storm that followed it, with her head held high, and her back straighter than ever. She got, of course, no credit for this. It was set down against her that she had never really cared for Paul, after all, or she "would feel it more." Almost in the same breath she was accused by someone else—or even by the same person—of having worn her heart upon her sleeve, for all to see.

"I ain't at all surprised," said Mrs. Elliott to her friend, Mrs. Gray. "Mary has set her eyes by Paul ever sence she wasn't bigger'n a minute, and no fellow likes to have a girl drop into his mouth like a ripe cherry—'specially when his mouth's kinder waterin' for wild grapes. Mary ain't the sort to set a feller crazy over her, anyway. She ain't got much ginger to her."

"Mary has to work real hard," replied Mrs. Gray doubtfully. "I guess she's pretty tired a good share of the time. She was lively enough when she was a youngster—until her mother died, come right down to it. And of course we ain't sure it was Paul's doin' that the engagement was broke. All we know is that 'tis."

"Oh, ain't we!" exclaimed Mrs. Elliott sarcastically. "Mary wouldn't ha' broke it till the cows come home. She'd ha' put up with all kinds of carryin' on, so long as she could keep him! And she couldn't at that. He's been chasin' all summer after that little hussy from New York . . ."

"Now Eliza! Sylvia says lots of people paint and powder, that it ain't a sign of real wickedness any longer, like we thought. She says she don't believe Rosalie realized Paul was engaged to Mary. Everybody 'sposed she knew, and so nobody told her, most likely—one of them cases where everyone's business is no one's business. She left right off, after Blanche's wedding! And it must ha' meant a lot to her to cut her vacation short—I don't believe she'd ha' done it without some real good reason. She was havin' an awful pleasant time here. Sylvia says that kind of a girl may be cheap, but they ain't vicious, and they are usually real good-hearted. She says they're just a type."

"A type!" snorted Mrs. Elliott. "Sylvia would find excuses for Judas Iscariot! How is she?"

"She's real poorly. I can see Austin's worried to death about her. My, but them two think the world of each other!" And the conversation drifted into other channels.

If village gossip was hard to bear, however, the family attitude was worse. Cousin Jane had a good deal to say about the inevitable fate of girls who ran after men who didn't want them, instead of attending their plain Christian duty. That, she said, had never been her way when *she* was young. Seth said very little, but his silent, dejected attitude made his daughter feel more than any unkind words could have done, that he felt she had disgraced him almost beyond utterance. It was hard for him to pass the plate in church, thinking over the old saying about ministers' sons and deacons' daughters. As for Violet, she became so violently "nervous" about the whole affair, that Mary dreaded to see her more than all the others put together. She never guessed that Paul was also suffering from his mother's "nerves."

"If you had the slightest consideration for me, you never would have let it happen," she lamented over and over again to her son. "My life is so full of grief and trouble that it takes a good deal of fortitude to bear it. Here is Blanche married—"

"You were tickled to death over that," muttered Paul.

"Paul! How can you be so vulgar! I tried to be cheerful, of course. But no one knows how I miss her. And Mary's money would have come in very handy, too."

"I didn't know Mary had any money."

"She will have, as soon as she's twenty-one, and that's very soon now. Laura had a little property of her own, and she left it all to Mary. I don't know as Mary knows it herself, but of course Seth will tell her soon, now. I always planned that you and Mary should be married on her twenty-first birthday. It seems to me there would have been such a beautiful sentiment about it."

But this was not the way Violet talked to Mary. She dwelt on the fact that the girl had not made herself "attractive enough" to Paul, that she was always neglecting to change her dress and tidy her hair, that she didn't join with him in those little pleasures that all young men like to "share with their fiancées."

"But Paul didn't expect to share them with me!" flared Mary, stung beyond endurance. "He didn't even *want* to! And I guess if you did all the cooking and cleaning and washing and ironing for four people, and took care of two children into the bargain, you wouldn't always look as nice as you do! Don't you suppose I'd like to take a bath every day, and spend twenty minutes fixing my hair in the morning, and again in the afternoon, and put on a nice, fresh, stylish dress that someone else had ironed, before supper? Don't you suppose I've longed to be comfortable and rested—and pretty whenever Paul saw me? I guess I'm just as human as any other girl, and I guess I know 'the way to do things' just as well as you do."

"Well, I should manage to do them then, and to look well at

the same time!" retorted Violet. "That's every woman's duty to herself."

"What about her duty to her family, if the two conflict?"

"Mercy, Mary, what a temper you have! No wonder Paul couldn't stand it! I'm sure I do my duty to my family, if any woman ever did, but I keep myself up, too. If you had more system about your housework you could get it done all right— it's all in the way you do it. And if you did that well, there might be a little more excuse for you. But I never set foot in your house that I don't see dust in it."

Violet felt that she had come out ahead in this tilt. Nevertheless, it "used her up" to have Mary so shockingly impertinent to her, as she said to Jane in telling her about it afterwards, and she did not attack her in this same way again. Instead, she brought Blanche's letters and read them to her. And listening to these accounts of Blanche's happiness was, to Mary, like having salt rubbed in a raw wound.

Blanche was blissful, Philip was perfect, they were divinely happy, no two persons had ever loved each other so much before. They had stayed in Boston for a few days before starting for California, because Philip thought Blanche was a little tired after the excitement of the wedding, and did not want her to undertake the journey until she was thoroughly rested. Then they had broken their trip at Chicago, stopping at the Blackstone—the most wonderful hotel!—and had gone to the theater, and shopping—not that she really needed anything so soon, of course, but just for fun, and the stores were so attractive, and Philip loved buying things for her—he meant that she should always have loads of pretty clothes. They had broken the trip again at the Grand Canyon and gone horseback riding on the trails. They had a drawing room all the way on the train, and dinner every night was just like a party, the dining room couldn't have been any prettier in a *palace*, and such delicious food! They were at Coronado Beach, and had a private sitting room, though they hardly used it at all, they were outdoors so much—Philip was teaching her to swim, and had hired a motor by the *week*. They were at Del Monte, trying to puzzle out the maze—the most fascinating thing! And she had never imagined anything so beautiful as the live-oak trees! And so on, and so on. Places and pastimes that had always been mere names, conjuring up visions of delight, to be sure, but never within the reach of "anyone we know," were becoming a matter of course to Blanche. Not that Mary begrudged her that—she had, from the beginning, rejoiced wholeheartedly in her cousin's happiness. But didn't she deserve a little happiness too? In the short glimpse of the world that she had had, she had seen enough of the easy, luxurious, lovely side of life to know that it is silly and ignorant to underestimate it—that it is scarcely human not to long for it. Mary was thoroughly human and she was very intelligent. She would have known how to squeeze not only enjoyment, but education, out of every drop of pleasure that she could have had. But this was not the worst of it. The man whom Blanche loved, *wanted* to lavish all these good things on her, while the man whom she, Mary, loved, had neglected and ignored her, and finally insulted her and cast her from him. Mary listened to Blanche's letters in silence, or said merely, "I'm glad she's having such a good time," in a low voice, but when Violet left her alone again, she always sat for a time clenching and unclenching her hands, dry little sobs of agony rising in her throat.

But hardest of all—harder than facing the village gossip, harder than facing Violet's complacence—was facing her own bruised pride, her own accusing conscience. Long ago—she knew it only too well—she should have told Paul that unless he mended his ways their engagement must end. She had evaded an issue which she should have met, salved a wound which should have been cauterized. She had been a coward. Because she feared losing Paul, she had compromised with right, and now she had lost him after all. She felt that she deserved her unhappiness, and this was more bitter than anything else except the way in which she had lost him. If Paul

had only told her squarely that he did not, after all, want to
marry her, but that he cared for her, as he always had, as a
neighbor, as a cousin, as a dear old friend—she could have
borne that. But the thought of the words he had spoken to
her in the hall that night after Blanche's wedding, the memory
of his heavy breath and violent kisses, branded her with
shame. She was cheapened, degraded in her own eyes, that
any man should have dared to behave so to her, and that was
infinitely worse than being cheapened and degraded in the
eyes of her family. Had she, after all, deserved that, too?

In all those dreadful weeks, Mary found only two sources
of comfort, besides the walks she took up Countess Hill to
gain solitude, and the prayers she managed, with shaken
faith, to say. The first of these sources was Sylvia Gray. She
was extremely fond of Mary, and usually saw a good deal of
her, but she was not well enough to do that now. The neigh-
borly visiting back and forth had been to a certain degree interrupted. But one afternoon, she telephoned that she was
"having a pretty good day," that Austin had gone off, and that
she wished Mary would bring her sewing and come over to
supper.

It was, as usual, hard for Mary to break away from her
family, but she spread out an appetizing cold supper on the
kitchen table, covered it carefully, left the kettle boiling for
Seth's evening cup of tea, and took the two little boys to the
barn for their father to watch while he was milking. Seth did
not altogether approve of this arrangement, but as usual, he
said little, and she promised to be back early—he was just to
pile up the dishes in the sink, she would wash them when
she got home and the boys could get along without baths for
once, even if they were dirty. She stopped a minute at the Old
Gray Homestead, where Mrs. Gray was sitting on her back
porch, feeling instinctively that this kindly woman had
spoken of her less harshly than most of her neighbors, and that
she did not need to shun her; then went down the shady road
that led to the little brick cottage where Sylvia and Austin

lived. On the way, she met the two little boys, Austin Junior and Peter, with their comfortable English nurse, going to see their grandmother—sturdy, rugged, black-eyed little chaps, one two and a half, the other barely a year old, and already almost comically like their father. Like most children, they were very fond of Mary, and hailed her approach with joy. She sighed a little, however, as she bent over them, thinking of her own little brothers, whom she had left, dirty and shabby, in the barnyard, while these two were so immaculate and well-cared for. She found her friend lying in the hammock on her deep and sheltered piazza, looking, as always, supremely lovely, but also very frail. The expression on Sylvia's face shook Mary for the first time from the thought of her own troubles.

"Sylvia! You're—you're not a bit well, are you?"

"I'm perfectly all right. But I'm afraid I shall be tempted to pinch the twins, very gently, of course, sometimes, to make up for all the trouble they've caused me. Just think, they'll be the first twins in Hamstead since the Countess Blanche's— only mine are going to be both girls!"

Mary shivered a little. "Why do you keep talking about having twins?" she asked. "You'll have just one, another boy."

"You wait and see! But I didn't send for you to talk about twins. I've got a new scheme, and I want to see what you think of it."

"The same thing that I think of all your schemes. They're wonderful."

"Well—now that David and Jacqueline have built that splendid Cottage Hospital, I think we've gone a long step forward in Hamstead. But after all, that only looks out for the people when they're sick or convalescent. I want to build something that will look out for them when they're well."

Mary dropped her sewing. "What do you mean?" she asked excitedly.

"Hamstead's the loveliest place in the world to live in," went on Sylvia, without apparent connection, "—that is, I think so. But I can imagine that I wouldn't have, when I was younger—especially if I'd been a boy. There isn't much to *do*."

"I see," said Mary, beginning to think that she did.

"And so, as long as there isn't, most boys try to find something. And what they find isn't always very good for them."

How much this kind, wise woman saw and understood and forgave! No wonder Austin worshiped her!

"I can't understand myself," Sylvia went on, "why more parents don't send their boys away to good, really first-class schools and colleges. There are lots who could afford it. Of course there are more who can't—I know what a grief it always was to father and mother Gray because they couldn't do things for their children. But some families—they don't seem to realize what a difference it would make, just at the age when it's perfectly natural and normal for a boy or girl to crave excitement and pleasure and activity and change. Books count for a great deal, but sometimes I think they're the very smallest part of what we call 'a good education'—unless, as in your case, books are one of the things you are craving. Of course I can't say all this to all the parents in Hamstead, and they wouldn't believe me—probably wouldn't even listen to me if I did—but there's something I can do, and I'm just going to do it. I'm a pretty good Episcopalian, but I believe just as many boys' souls have been saved by gymnasiums as by churches! And I want that nice new cousin of yours to start in on some plans for one as soon as he gets home from his wedding trip. I want it made suitable to use for dances, and I want a billiard-room, and a kitchen, and a swimming-pool in it, too. I want it kept open all the time, and I want big signs, 'Smoking allowed everywhere' placarded all over it, until everyone gets so used to the idea that it won't be necessary. I want . . ."

"Oh, Sylvia, no one in the world would have thought of this but you!"

"Did you ever hear," went on Sylvia again without apparent connection, "how wild Austin was when he was young?"

"I—yes, I have—"

"That was before I knew him. But he was twenty-seven when I came here. If I'd grown up with him, loving him all the time—as of course I should have, for I loved him as much as I possibly could from the first moment I ever set eyes on him and never could help showing it—I suppose it would have hurt me dreadfully—to have him wild, I mean. I suppose I would have either mistaken immaturity for viciousness and condemned him when he had really done nothing to condemn, or excused viciousness for immaturity and forgiven him when he should, some way, have been punished. Either would have been equally bad, and equally likely to happen. We don't judge clearly when we're unhappy. Of course it hurts Austin and me, a little, now, to think that he ever—slipped up at all. He and I have talked this plan over a good deal. He thinks it ought to help the fellows in Hamstead, some, anyway."

"But Austin," faltered Mary, "wasn't lazy. He worked hard, and he studied hard. He wasn't—"

"No, he wasn't lazy. He couldn't be. He'd have starved to death if he had been. Lots of energy is caused by necessity. And he had naturally a very quick, able mind, and a real love for books. Those are qualities that are no special credit to a man. I don't mean that I don't admire them—I do, tremendously—but they're more often natural than acquired. On the other hand, there are some men, without brilliant mentality, who are thoughtless and consequently selfish, or even cruel, but with a little help, they acquire the habit of thinking and see the error of their ways and mend them. Not always, of course—but sometimes. It's worth taking a chance on—to try to teach a man like that to think, I mean. Did you ever read 'Sesame and Lilies'?"

"Yes."

"Do you remember that poem by Coventry Patmore that Ruskin quotes,

'Ah, wasteful woman, she who may
On her own sweet self set the price,
Knowing man cannot choose but pay—
How she has cheapened Paradise!
How given for naught the priceless gift,
How spoiled the bread and spilt the wine,
Which, spent with due respective thrift,
Had made brutes men and men divine!'

"Isn't that what we're all tempted to do when we love a man—to walk straight into his arms, without knowing whether his arms are ready for us?"

"Or worthy?"

"If they're really ready, they will be worthy. That's just the point."

"I see," said Mary, very low indeed.

"And then," continued Sylvia, "Austin had ideals, always, even if he didn't live up to them. There's a tremendous difference between that and not having any ideals, not being able to see them yourself, and not having anyone care for you enough to give them to you. Austin's got a wonderful mother."

"So have your boys," said Mary, sobs rising in her throat. There was no more direct allusion to her trouble than that.

No one but Sylvia in all Hamstead would have been clever enough to see that nothing would comfort Mary so much as to be able to think a little more gently of Paul. Indeed, no one else considered that she deserved comfort or that this would be a legitimate means of giving it to her if she had. But this comfort, great though it was, did not last indefinitely. What Mary needed most of all was not to think, but to feel. After that talk with Sylvia, Mary found that she got through the days very well. But the nights seemed to grow harder and harder. Formerly, she had gone straight to sleep when she went to bed, because she was so tired. Now she was so utterly weary, mentally and spiritually as well as physically, that she could not sleep. And when she could not sleep, she cried—cried so violently that each morning found her more and more spent. No one, for a long time, saw her cry, and she was bitterly ashamed of the fact that she did it, even in secret, and still she could not help it. Her overwrought nerves, seeking some means of relief, found only this one, and they were, just then, stronger than her will-power. And at last something snapped, suddenly, and she broke down openly in the middle of the bedtime songs that she always sang to her little brothers.

She had had a long hard day, and it seemed as if evening and the chance to rest would never come. When, on top of everything else, the small boys showed no disposition to settle down promptly for the night, she began to feel as if her self-control were slipping from her like a cast-off garment.

"I want a drink of water," announced Algy, bouncing up and down on his mattress. "You've forgot to bring me my mug, Mary."

Silently Mary went to the bathroom, let the water run until it was cold, and brought the little white china cup painted with blue-birds to the child. He drained it at a gulp.

"More," he announced cheerfully, handing it back to her.

Mary filled the mug a second time, and as she did so, she could see the rest of the family, in the new automobile, starting for the performance of "The Merchant of Venice" at the annual Chautauqua entertainment at Wallacetown. She knew the play almost by heart, loved every word of it, had never seen it given, and even the little mediocre traveling company that was to play it, could, with her own knowledge of it, have given her a glimpse into fairyland if she could have heard it. And none of the others cared for Shakespeare, or were in the least familiar with him. They were simply going because it was "part of this year's program," because everyone else was going, because Paul welcomed any excuse to drive the car and Violet any excuse to be seen in it, and Jane and Seth any excuse to go to a play which could not, of course, be wicked, since it was "classic." No one had even suggested staying home with the children so that she could go.

"Can't I have a piece of candy?" was Algy's next question, as she reached the crib which stood by her bed. The experiment of having the two little boys in the same room had been tried and did not work, so Algy still slept beside her, and Moses in the adjoining room. "I ben a good boy all day, haven't I, Mary?"

"Yes, dear, pretty good. Where is your bag of lemon drops?"

"In my top bureau drawer. Bring it here, so's I can choose."

After he had chosen and the bag with its stickily shapeless contents which had once been lemon drops was replaced, Algy thought of something else.

"I didn't choose one for Moses."

The bag was brought back again, and another fragment carefully selected.

"I wish you'd stay with me for a while, Mary. I kinder think there's goin' to be a thunderstorm."

"No, dear, there isn't. But if there should be, I'll come right back."

"Well, I got a sorter pain in my leg."

"A sharp pain, or an ache?"

"No-o, just a regular pain. I think maybe it would feel better if you rubbed it for a while."

Mary uncovered the plump, brown legs and rubbed both briskly. "I've got to go now and hear Moses' prayers," she said at last, thinking that signs of drowsiness were finally beginning to be evident.

But Moses was not feeling devotional. He was constitutionally irreligious, and now that he attended kindergarten, the morning exercises at school seemed to him more than sufficient for his spiritual needs.

"I ain't a-goin' to say the Lord's Prayer tonight," he announced with decision. "I said it this mornin' at school. After this, I'll say it to you Saturdays and Sundays. I don't believe the Lord ever intended anyone to say that great long prayer

twicet the same day. But whether He did or not, I ain't a-goin'
to say it. I suppose He has some disappointments."

Mary did not feel equal to discussing theology.

"Very well, say 'Now I lay me.'"

"Now I lay me," began Moses without much fervor, "down
to sleep . . ." when a loud crash and a wail of distress came
from the next room.

"Oh, Mary, I've dropped my blue-bird cup! It's bro-o-
ken . . ."

Mary rushed to Algy's side and gathered him, dripping
wet, into her arms. On the floor, in a pool of water, lay the
beloved mug broken into fragments, while the crib, as well
as Algy himself, was deluged by its contents.

"Don't cry, darling! It's a shame, but Mary will buy you
another just like it, only prettier, maybe, the next time she
goes to Wallacetown. Hush, honey. Let Mary put you in bed
with Moses while she gets you dry pajamas and changes your
sheets and wipes up all the pieces so you won't cut your dear
little feet."

Comfort, fresh linen and more water all having been provided, Moses was urged to continue his devotions.

"I don't see why I should say, 'If I should die before I wake.'
I've said it and said it, and I ain't never died at all."

"Well, say just 'God bless' tonight, then."

"God bless Daddy and Mary and Algy," mumbled Moses
glibly, "and all my dear friends, and make me a good boy.
And bless Cousin Jane and Cousin Violet, and Blanche. You
needn't bother about Paul, he snitched my wood-chuck trap.
Amen. . . . Now sing me 'The Sugar Plum Tree,'" he com-
manded, climbing into bed and settling himself comfortably
on his pillow, prepared to take his ease while she did so.

Mary began it bravely enough. But the reference to Paul
was too much for her. Before she reached the Chocolate Cat
she found she could not go on.

"I'm afraid I can't finish 'The Sugar Plum Tree' tonight, darling," she said abruptly, bending over to kiss him; and in

spite of her, some hot tears fell down on his face. Then she fled from the room.

Algy, too little to sense her trouble, had already gone off to sleep contentedly. But Moses lay for a long time wide-eyed and pondering. He loved Mary as he loved no one else in the world, and Mary, plainly, was very unhappy. He tried to think of recent misdeeds that he himself had committed, but his slate was fairly clean. Such small blots as there were on it were not of the sort that would be likely to make her cry; he knew his sister well enough to be sure of that. Then he remembered that once before, early in the summer, he had caught her crying, and when he had pressed her, she had said she was worried over Paul. That was the time he had told Philip about it. Paul, thought Moses, was the last person *he* would worry about, recalling sundry grievances besides the "snitched" wood-chuck trap, which he cherished against his cousin. And Mary never mentioned Paul now—still that might be the trouble, just the same. It was too bad that Mary should cry over him, particularly when he deserved it so little, but if no one else would comfort her, Moses would. He sought about in his mind for the quickest and best means to this end.

Moses always slept with a small Canton-flannel dog named Spotty, to which he had been devoted from infancy. It had gone through numerous vicissitudes. More than once it had fallen in the brook, but Mary had always fished it out, and dried it in the oven. Several times it had been buried in the garden when Moses, in a cheerful frame of mind, had felt inclined to "play funeral." And one night he had ripped it open and devoured most of its lining—an experiment which had proved very disastrous to both. But Spotty still survived. His beady eyes glittered and his pink tongue shone in the dusk. Moses made a sudden resolve.

He hugged Spotty and kissed what remained of his nose. He gulped as he did it. Never, since he could remember, had he gone to sleep without first laying his head on the cher-

ished toy. Then he picked it up and pattered in to Mary's
room.

It was as he had expected. Mary was lying on her bed,
weeping. Moses held out his hand.

"Don't cry any more, please, Mary," he said softly. "I've
brought Spotty to sleep with you."

It was then that Mary realized that she had found a second
source of comfort in Moses. Most of her unhappiness had been
caused by selfishness. Moses was willing to make, for her, what
was to him a tremendous sacrifice. She drew the child, with
his little Canton-flannel dog still in his hand, into bed with
her and cried without restraint, holding him in her arms.
Moses lay solemn and silent, asking no questions, making no
overtures. But she could feel his sympathy in every curve of
his warm little body. Gradually she relaxed, a sense of peace,
of compensation, of contentment, stole over her. She fell
asleep, her cheek against her little brother's.

Things never seemed half so hard again.

Meanwhile, Paul, instead of rejoicing in his longed-for liberty, was finding it utterly "dull, flat, stale and unprofitable."

In the first place, living at close quarters with his mother's "nerves," unrelieved by Blanche's sunny presence or the ready escape to Mary's house which had always been open to him, was not a pleasant experience, as has already been hinted. But this was by no means all. For a day or two after his sister's wedding he was really ill. As soon as he was sufficiently recovered, however, he made his way, feeling very blithe and unshackled, to the Westons' to call on Rosalie. She kept him waiting for some time and when she finally appeared, she was not cordial, to say the least.

"I'm right in the midst of packing," she announced, without asking him to sit down and without even doing so herself. "I haven't much time to spare."

"Packing!" exclaimed Paul, aghast.

"I'm going back to New York on the midnight."

Paul strove to express his regret.

"Don't you go getting fresh with me!" said Miss King, crisply. "I'm not that kind and you needn't forget it, little one. . . . Why didn't you tell me you was engaged to that good-looking cousin of yours? My, but she's a looker!"

"I'm not engaged to her," said Paul shortly.

"Oh, she's thrown you over, has she?" jeered Rosalie. "Well, I should think she would. She can do a lot better than you, Little Boy Blue, even if you behaved yourself instead of hitting it up all summer like you've been doing. That Mr. Hamlin from Boston is sweet on her all right, and he's some swell,

believe me! He would dress her like she'd oughter be, too . . .
a perfect 38, that's the figure she's got. You don't often see it.
Put a French model on that girl and you couldn't touch her
on Fifth Avenue at any price. I'd like the fun of selling it to
her. I shouldn't think she'd have bothered this long with a
$13.95 marked down from $15, like you!"

"It was me that broke the engagement," said Paul, stiffly
and ungrammatically.

Rosalie stared at him speechlessly for a moment. But only
for a moment.

"So that's the kind of a bird you are, is it?" she inquired
with immeasurable scorn. "Well, I've got your waist measure
now, all right! I've heard a lot about 'ancestors' since I struck
this burg, and I don't deny that you've got something to be
proud of along that line. The men that came up here—to say
nothing of the women that came with 'em—and just got settled when the Revolutionary War broke out, and were willing
and glad to strike out again and fight for their country, and
to foot it way down to Harvard and Princeton to get an education, were sure all wool and a yard wide and then some.
But I guess if they could look up or down now, as the case
may be, and see their descendants wearing out the seats of
their trousers sitting on the post-office steps and saying what
they'd do if they was president, or standing on the curbstone
in Wallacetown thinking they're having the hell of a time
because they've got a couple too many drinks inside of them
and are talking to some skirt they wouldn't introduce to their
mother—I guess them old captains and judges and governors
would think the good old stock had run down to a pretty poor
line of goods! There are two or three real men in this town,
but I notice they don't play round much with weak sisters like
you and Jack. I got a fellah in New York—floorwalker on the
eighth—who doesn't know who his *father* was, let alone any
great-grands! And I've been kinder ashamed to tie up with
him on that account. But he's white clean through for all
that, believe me! If he could have your chance, my! what he'd

have done with it! A good home and money for an education
and a lady for a sweetheart! And you've turned up your ugly
nose at all of them—while he's had to climb out of the gutter
on his way to decency without a soul to help him. But he's
got there, all right. I've written Steve that if he still wants a
girl who's been fool enough to play round all summer with a
stupid rube that was another girl's beau, he can have her, and
he's telegraphed back prepaid that he'd be waiting in the
Grand Central right by the gate on Thursday, and that we'd
go and blow ourselves to a lunch at the Ritz together."

Rosalie having departed without further delay to smooth
things out with Steve, that episode seemed to be closed, and
Paul felt that he had reason to hope that it would be a long
time before anyone made him so thoroughly uncomfortable
again. But he was mistaken. The next person to treat him
harshly was Dr. Noble. Meeting the boy one day on the road,
down which Paul was wandering somewhat aimlessly, David
brought his motor to a stop and hailed him.

"Just the person I've been hoping to see," he remarked
pleasantly. "I wanted to speak to you about your fiancée. I'm
worried about her. I don't think she's looking at all well."

"If you mean my cousin, Mary Manning," said Paul with
forced dignity, "she isn't my fiancée." He felt uncertain, from
the doctor's even voice, whether he was actually unaware of
existing conditions, or merely pretending to be. He thought
the former unlikely.

"Oh," said David still pleasantly. "Well—of course that must
be a great disappointment to you, but perhaps it's all for the
best. You're younger than she is, aren't you?"

"We're almost exactly the same age. I'm six months older,
as a matter of fact," said Paul, swallowing hard.

"Two or three years *younger*, then, to all intents and purposes," said David cheerfully. "A girl is always older than a
boy at the same age, and Mary, poor child, had to grow up
early, while you're so—er—comfortably immature. Of course
your tastes wouldn't be particularly congenial with that dif-

ference between you, even—er—if they would be anyway.
Mary has such a fine mind. . . . Well, I must pass along the
good news to Thomas Gray the next time I see him, if he
hasn't heard it already. I believe he thought, with considerable regret, that you had the right of way in that quarter."

Paul glared. People seemed bent on reminding him that
Mary was not, after all, in the least dependent upon him for
masculine attentions. It hurt his pride.

"The war news isn't very good, is it?" went on David with
an abrupt change of subject. "Ever thought of enlisting in the
Foreign Legion?"

If the doctor had asked him if he had ever thought of cutting off his right hand, Paul could not have been more surprised. The war was still regarded in Hamstead, in spite of
the sinking of the *Lusitania,* with impatience, when it was
regarded at all.

"Lord, no!" Paul exclaimed now. "Why should I?"

"Why, you're exactly the sort of chap for it! I should think
you'd have been over there long ago! No ties of any kind,
independent income, fine constitution—"

"Farmers can't be spared," quoted Paul hurriedly, recalling
statistics he had happened to read in some newspaper. "It
takes five men in the field to keep one at the front."

"Especially when they spend as much time in the field as
you do," murmured David. "Yes, of course, you feel the farm
a great responsibility."

"And I've got heart trouble," went on Paul, growing very
red and writhing more and more at David's pleasant voice.

"Hard luck! But are you sure? Been examined lately? Well,
come up to the house some evening and let me look you over.
Or I'll run in and see you, if you don't feel equal to walking up
—of course it's almost a quarter of a mile. Some evening soon.
I'm going across myself, very shortly, as a member of one of
the Harvard Medical Units. We'll be connected with the British Army. Jacqueline's going to take up some branch of Red
Cross work—nursing, probably. Being a Frenchwoman by

birth will of course be a great advantage to her—cut lots of red tape. It isn't as if—we had any children," ended David a little wistfully. "I'm sure Austin Gray would have done something long ago if it hadn't been for Sylvia. Naturally any man that's fortunate enough to get a family like that makes it his first consideration as long as he can. Well, good-by."

Paul began to feel very sorry for himself. Public opinion, which he had at first thought to be wholly on his side, seemed to be gradually, but none the less surely, swinging the other way. If the older women still chattered against Mary, the younger ones spoke differently, and none of them would have anything to do with him. They didn't care to risk being jilted, they were apt to remind him sarcastically, if he so much as ventured to ask them to go motoring with him. If Mary Manning didn't suit him, why, he needed a girl made to order or there wouldn't be the least hope of his being pleased. He led an unappreciated existence, after twenty-one petted years. As for the men, he thought they were actually beginning to go out of their way to be disagreeable to him and pleasant to Mary. She was made the belle of every gathering to which she had either the leisure or the inclination to go, and when she discovered this, she began to go more than she had in several years. And, since Mary would not speak to him, he was not included in many of the invitations that were issued. He found himself virtually ostracized in Hamstead, and neither White Water nor Wallacetown, though he tried them both, seemed to furnish either lasting stimulation or lasting solace. The "mill crowd" was merely noisy. It was not really thrilling. He discovered, as many another man has discovered with resentment, the deadly dullness with which dissipation is permeated and which eventually reveals itself ruthlessly.

Driven at last to desperation by loneliness and boredom, he decided to go to Mary and ask to be reinstated in her favor. This seemed easy enough when he first thought of it, but the more he reflected, the more he saw that it might be rather difficult. He had treated Mary somewhat shabbily, he admitted. She was having a very good time without him—he was forced to admit that too—and there was really no special reason why she should ever crave his society. He started on his errand of reconciliation several times, only to turn back, feeling that his stomach was caving in uncomfortably for some reason, and that it might be better to wait a few days longer. At last, having spent a Saturday evening at home when everyone else under thirty in town had gone off on a picnic, returning in the highest spirits at midnight—Mary was with the Grays and laughing and singing when they dropped her at the front door—he took his courage, what there was of it, in his hands, and sought her out. He found her, late that Sunday afternoon in Indian summer, sitting in the fragrant orchard reading a book, a rather solid looking book. Most of Hamstead read only the daily papers—or rather, one favorite daily paper, and the *Wallacetown Weekly Bugle*—and novels, when it read at all. Paul himself confined his literary attentions chiefly to the sporting pages. He had never excelled in any sport himself, but that did not matter. Mary, however, liked "all sorts of queer things"—that is to say, biographies, histories and even poetry. As Seth had taken the two little boys to spend Sunday with a relative in White Water, she seemed to be indulging one of these peculiar tastes quite comfortably and free from interruption, and she was, Paul thought, looking unusually fresh and contented and attractive, seated in a low rocker among the trees, dressed in white, the sunshine falling on her hair.

"Hullo," he said, advancing towards her firmly, though inwardly quaking.

Mary did not appear to hear him.

"Hullo," he said again, perspiring freely.

"Hullo," said Mary quietly, without looking up.

It was the first time she had spoken to him since Blanche's wedding, almost two months before. Paul's heart gave a queer exhibition of acrobatic powers, as if it were turning somersaults all the way from his throat to his stomach, and then

began to thump—to thump so vigorously that he feared
it might be audible. He was pleased, and he was beyond all
reasonable measure excited. His collar began to wilt and he
mopped his brow.

"Have a good time last night?" he inquired carelessly.

"Yes. Did you?"

Paul choked, and fumbled with his tie. He could not understand why Mary should ask such a tactless question, when she
knew perfectly well— He decided to be magnanimous, and ig-
nore it.

"What are you reading?" he asked.

" 'The Life of Charles Francis Adams.' "

"Do you like it?"

"Very much. Haven't you read it?"

Another tactless question! Mary's voice expressed only polite surprise, yet she was well aware that he never read things
of that sort. Again he decided to change the subject slightly.

"Any relation to your friend Hannah?"

"I suppose they may be distantly connected. The name
'Adams' in Massachusetts is almost as important as the name
'Manning' in Vermont. Both good old families, and large. But
of course, both inevitably contain some failures."

The top of Paul's collar was rapidly sinking to the level of
his collar button. Mary went on reading.

"I thought I'd come over for a little while," he murmured
desperately.

Mary turned a page.

"Nice day, isn't it?"

"Lovely."

"Warm for the time of the year, too."

"And likely to grow warmer any minute," replied Mary, her
eyes still on her book.

Paul could feel even the back of his neck growing red. Still
he persisted.

"Blanche is back in Brookline. Mother had a letter from her

last night. She's thinking of leaving me and going down to pay her a little visit."

"I should think it would be a very pleasant change for her."

Something in Mary's tone made Paul look at her more carefully. The painful flush at the back of his neck spread all over him. He could feel the cold perspiration dropping down his spine. There was no possible doubt of it—*Mary was laughing!* She had been ever since he entered the orchard! At first she had done it quietly and he had not noticed it, but now she was actually rocking back and forth with merriment! In fact, she closed her book at last, looked him full in the face and gave a delighted squeal which rapidly changed into peal after peal of enjoyment.

Paul turned his back on her and strode away. Though unfamiliar with the quotation, he had, in substance, pictured Mary sitting like patience on a monument smiling down at grief. Apparently she was doing nothing of the sort. She missed him so little and was getting along so well without him, that when he went to her and tried to "make up," she felt she could afford to laugh at him! Well, he wasn't to be trifled with like that! He'd show her! Angrily he brushed away two big tears of resentment and hurt pride that were trickling down his flushed cheeks. The action, the last on earth which he would have wished observed, did not pass unseen. Moses, who had returned from his outing, was blocking his path, though Paul had not noticed him before.

"Cry-baby!" chanted the small boy, putting his thumb to his nose in the undignified but expressive manner natural to his age and sex. "Cry-baby, want a rattle to shake and can't reach it! C-r-y—b-a-b-y!"

This was so near the truth as to be doubly galling. Infuriated, Paul thrust him aside and marched on. In the safe seclusion of his bedroom he brushed his rumpled hair and changed his collar, then sat down to cool off and think things over. He'd show Mary . . . He dwelt for a few minutes on this agreeable thought. But show her what? That had not occurred to him at first. What was there to show her? And supposing he could think up something, would she consent to be shown? His recent interview with her, the mere thought of which caused him to grow hot again, did not furnish material for much hope of exhibition. Mary, after all, held all the high cards. His only chance, so to speak, was to lead through weakness up to strength. It would not be an easy or a pleasant thing to do, and Paul hated everything that was not easy and pleasant. But his pride, if nothing else, told him that it would be better than leaving the game unfinished, even if he lost. His common sense told him that if he did not finish it, he would have smaller hope than ever of another game with Mary. And he wanted to play with her. . . .

Having reached this conclusion, of which there was no possible doubt, neither comfortably nor rapidly, he decided to act upon it at once. He pelted down the stairs, slammed the front door behind him and fairly rushed to the orchard. Mary was still reading.

"Look here, Mary," he burst out, "I'm—I'm—sorry I—I acted as I did the night of Blanche's wedding. In fact, I'm—I'm just as ashamed of it as I can be. I'd give anything if you'd—overlook it."

"Overlook it!" flamed Mary.

"That was the wrong word," floundered Paul. "I meant, of course, I want to ask you to—forgive me. To—to be friends with me, if you won't be anything else—"

"Anything else!"

"Oh, of course, I knew you wouldn't be anything again after—after that! But I can't seem to say what I'm trying to. You know what I mean, though. Please, Mary—" and he held out his hand.

The girl closed her book, rose, and came towards him, looking at him with that clear and direct gaze that was so hard to meet—that he had, indeed, often found it impossible to meet. But this time, though he flinched, he looked at her squarely.

"Please," he said again. "I never would have done it if I hadn't been drunk."

She drew back a little. "You speak as if that were an excuse," she said evenly.

"Why of course it's an excuse!"

"Of course it isn't. It was—disgraceful, to do what you did, but it was even more disgraceful to get into a condition that would allow you to do it."

Paul had honestly not considered the matter in this light before.

"Well, I guess it was," he said, flushing. "I'll try not to get—into such a condition again. I *am* sorry. Honestly, I am. Won't you shake hands with me and forgive me?"

"I wouldn't touch you with a ten-foot pole. I certainly won't forgive you."

"Don't you believe me?"

"Yes, I believe you're sorry now, because you're having a horrid time. But if I forgave you and you began to have a good time again, you would forget all about being sorry and do the same thing right over again."

"I wouldn't—I swear I wouldn't."

"You're not going to have the chance. I must go in now and get supper."

"Well—won't you at least speak to me when you see me and—and so on—as long as I do behave?"

"Yes," said Mary over her shoulder. "I'll do that, if you just *happen* to see me. I won't if you try to like this, again."

And with this small concession, Paul was obliged to be satisfied. Or rather, he strove to be satisfied and was not. Mary was amazingly pretty, prettier than Blanche, far and away prettier than Rosalie King or any of the girls who worked in the mill at White Water. Why hadn't he noticed that before? And she had "pep"—oceans of it! How could he possibly have thought that she was tame? She was—well, she was *nice*. It made you feel good just to be with her, some way. If he only *could* be with her— But he *couldn't*. She had always been so easy of access, and now—now he couldn't get to her at all. And besides, she had been right about him. He had not only acted like a fool, but like a blackguard. He deserved his fate. That was the last conclusion that Paul reached, and the effect that it had upon him was more sobering than anything that had happened to him in all his life. He bowed under it, hurt and cowed and a little frightened. Then he pulled himself together, still wincing, and began to try to build together again, a stone at a time, the foundation for that happiness which he had destroyed.

CHAPTER NINE

When the ice is once broken after a quarrel between two persons who know each other well, it seldom freezes over again. This is, perhaps fortunately, true no matter what the new relation they bear to each other may be, or if one of them is much more to blame than the other. Paul was wise enough to guess that his cause would be hurt rather than helped if, immediately after his encounter with Mary in the orchard, he "happened" to see her too often. But he nodded to her when he caught sight of her at a distance, and she nodded back. If he, instead of Seth or Hod, went to the village to do the errands and get the mail, he brought the newspapers and packages into the kitchen, instead of depositing them on the shed steps, as had recently been his custom, and if Mary was in the room, he spoke to her and she answered him. He did not, to be sure, venture on more than "Hullo," or "Good morning" at first. But after a week or so he remarked that there had been a hard frost the night before, and that the post-office was being shingled. This daring attempt at conversation having left him unscathed and even unattacked, he risked stopping a moment, the next day, to warm his chilled fingers over the stove and get a drink of water at the sink. And summoning more and more courage with each new success, he finally appeared one evening after supper and asked Mary if she would lend him something to read. His motives in doing this were somewhat mixed. Now that he was shunning Wallacetown for purposes of amusement as rigorously as if it had been infected with the bubonic plague, and hastening back if he were obliged to go there on errands, for fear Mary might hear of the trip and misunderstand his reasons for going, he found time hanging rather heavily on his hands and was so at a loss for something to do that even reading occurred to him as a possible pastime. It was true that there were very few books in his mother's house, but he felt that the desire to improve his mind might be one which would appeal to Mary and cause him to find some slight favor in her sight. Most of all, however, he welcomed any excuse which could be construed as sufficiently reasonable to give him a few words with her.

She held the door half-open without inviting him to enter as he made his request, and the corners of her mouth twitched. He had the uncomfortable feeling that she saw through him perfectly.

"Would you like the 'Autobiography of Charles Francis Adams'?" she asked.

He looked at her miserably. "You know I couldn't make head nor tail of it," he said, in the voice of a prisoner at the bar who pleads for justice though he knows he deserves no mercy. "I'm not clever like you."

"You're thorough, when you take the trouble to be. Thoroughness helps in reading."

"All right, give it to me."

Mary vanished, leaving him on the doorstep, closing the door behind her. She was gone at least fifteen minutes. Paul, well aware that she was deriving as much amusement from making fun of him as she had in the orchard, stood his ground. When at last she reappeared, she had an unformidable looking volume in her hand.

"This is Rex Beach's 'Heart of the Sunset,'" she said demurely. "It took me a little while to find it, but I think you may like it better. If you decide you want Charles Francis after all, come back and get it."

"Well, your cordial invitation is a bribe worth considering," retorted Paul. Then, rather frightened at his daring, he blushed scarlet. Nevertheless he looked straight at her, smiled, and lifted his cap. "Thanks very much for this," he said.

"Good night," and turning, he walked whistling down the path.

Inevitably, a few evenings later, he brought the book back, having, to his intense surprise, thoroughly enjoyed it. Seth had gone to prayer-meeting, and Mary was putting the children to bed upstairs and did not hear his knock. After hesitating a minute, he went into the living room, put the volume down on the table, and began to look at the others that were lying upon it. There was a somewhat motley collection, for Mary, from her cradle up, had read everything she could lay her hands on, from Mother Goose to Madame Bovary. He chanced on a novel of Zane Grey's, glanced down the first two or three pages, and then, genuinely interested, sat down and began to read, entirely forgetting his awkward position as an unwelcome guest. When Mary entered, half an hour later, carrying a huge mending basket piled high with sewing, he started guiltily to his feet and stammered his excuses.

"That's all right," said Mary, tranquilly. "Why don't you read aloud to me while I sew? I've only just begun that story myself, and I hated to put it down."

"Do you honestly mean that?"

"If you would honestly like to. You might poke up the fire a little before you start in."

Seth, coming home from prayer-meeting an hour later, opened the door that led from the kitchen into the living room, and stared ahead of him for a minute, his jaw dropping. Neither his daughter nor his cousin saw or heard him; both were entirely absorbed. He closed the door gently behind him, and tiptoed across the floor to the back stairs.

"Great Godfrey!" he ejaculated to himself. "If anyone had told me Paul would ha' set down to pass the evenin' readin' a book, I should ha' let 'em know what I thought of their powers of guessin'. And ef anyone had added that he'd try to read it aloud to Mary, I should ha' said he'd get his eyes scratched out before he'd called out the title. And there she is, mendin' socks, peaceful as a kitten, same as her mother used to do when I was a young feller and went to call on her. Why, the very mention of Paul's name has ben like wavin' a red flag in the face of a bull all the fall! Women is sure strange critters. Wal, I guess it warn't just the time for me to butt in, anyways. Great Godfrey!"

It was not until the tall clock in the corner struck eleven that Mary either spoke or stirred. Then she rose, gathering up her piles of neatly folded and mended clothes.

"You must go home," she said. "It's getting late. That's a good story, isn't it?"

"Fine! Could—could we have some more tomorrow night?"

"I've promised to go to White Water with the Taylors. There's going to be a concert."

"Well, the next night, then."

"That's Sunday. I generally go to church Sunday evenings, now. Father listens for the boys."

"The service is over early."

"Yes, but Thomas walks home with me and comes in for a little while. You can come too, of course, if you'd enjoy it, but we couldn't read."

This did not sound especially attractive to Paul. Nevertheless, with his new-born caution, and in his gratitude for the unexpected favor he had just received, he decided not to say so.

"Well, perhaps I will. And thanks awfully for letting me stay tonight. I've had a fine time. May I take the book home with me?"

"Certainly—would you like a glass of milk and a doughnut before you go? I made fresh ones today."

"Um-m-m! *Would* I?"

They went into the kitchen, sat down beside the table with the red cloth on it, and talked over the story as they ate. They did not agree as to the probable outcome. A friendly argument ensued. When Paul finally got up and pushed back his chair, they were both laughing, and Mary, with a sudden gesture, snatched the book from him.

"You shan't find out which of us is right before I do!" she exclaimed. "You had better come over Monday night and read aloud some more. I promise not to look into it myself before then. Good night."

"Good night," said Paul, briefly and happily. And held out his hand.

The spirit of the evening had been so entirely friendly, so comfortable, so intimate, that it was not until Mary had put her hand in his that she remembered her statement of a few weeks earlier about a ten-foot pole, though Paul had by no means forgotten it. And when, growing crimson, she tried to pull her hand away, she found she could not.

"Good night," he said again, pleasantly and firmly, and gripping hard.

For a moment Mary struggled to free herself. Then she met his eyes. The first lesson in Paul's new course of education had been to learn to look Mary in the face, and, as she had said, Paul was thorough. Now he found the reward far greater than the slow and painful effort had been. Mary's eyes were well worth meeting squarely. In turn, the expression that the girl saw in her cousin's was so full of newborn humility and penitence, and yet so clearly determined to deserve, and claim, the right on which he was insisting, that she could not well see it and remain untouched. She stopped struggling and returned his pressure.

"Good night, Paul," she said softly. "I've had a good time, too," and smiled.

But if the homely commonplaces of intimacy can generally be relied upon to heal wounds safely, if slowly, a common fear or grief, with one swift stroke can strike out even the memory of them, at least temporarily. Violet, having fixed a date for her visit with Blanche, decided to go to New York for a few days' shopping first. She had no intention, she said, with a slight flutter of "nerves," when Paul, who had been giving some painful attention to the subject, pointed out to her that the state of their finances was still low after his sister's wedding and that such trips and shopping were expensive, of looking "countrified" when she first went to stay at her new son-in-law's home, and to meet her daughter's new friends.

"If you had shown any consideration of me at all, we wouldn't have been so straitened!" she sobbed.

"Why, I never urged you to spend all that money."

"Don't argue with me! You know it always prostrates me to have vulgar quarrels going on. As if this wretched affair with Mary hadn't ended every hope of our having her money! And then you try to put the blame on me and accuse me of—"

"Well, I've played Mary so many dirty, mean tricks that I suppose it's natural you should think I'd use her money to pay our silly debts. I probably would have—the way things were going. But I haven't accused you of anything. I only said—"

"Oh, I know what you said, but it makes all the difference *how* a thing is said, and the *meaning* back of the saying counts still more! I suppose you'll refuse to drive me to the midnight train, next!"

Paul did not, of course, refuse to do anything of the sort. To tell the truth, he was almost glad to see his mother go. Her indolence, her extravagance, her selfishness, seemed so appalling to him just then, that he found them increasingly difficult to live with, and none the less so because he thought he saw all these qualities reflected and magnified in his own character. It was also becoming clear to him that he must either earn more—or rather earn something—or spend less, if they were to get out of debt, and that he could put considerable time to advantage in figuring out how he was to do this. He began his reflections in this direction on his way home after taking her to the station. An unusually heavy snowstorm, such as seldom visits the Connecticut Valley as early as November, had obliged him to drive the old family horse, instead of using the new motor, and having plowed through snowy roads still only half-broken through, for a seemingly interminable length of time, it was two o'clock in the morning when he reached home. There was, he happened to notice, a light in Mary's room. When he had put the horse up and was going from the barn to the house, he saw that it was still burning, and heard her voice at the telephone through an open window. Seth and Jane were both away, attending a Sunday-School Convention which had opened the day before, and was to last half the week. Mary, it flashed through his mind, was therefore alone with the two little boys, and something was certainly wrong. He went up close to the house and called.

"Mary! Mary! M-A-R-Y, is anything the matter? Can I help?"

He was more frightened than before at the agonized voice that answered him.

"Yes—YES—Oh, thank God you've come!"

He pushed open the front door and bounded up the stairs. Mary, dressed in a long blue wrapper, her heavy hair hanging in braids down her back, was bending over the bed. And on the bed lay Algy, gasping and writhing, and then lying deathly still.

"He's got convulsions," Mary managed to say in a stifled voice. "I'm doing what I can for him, but I haven't been able to do much alone. I can't leave him a second. He might choke to death if I did."

"What am I to do first?"

"Start the kitchen fire. We'll get him into a hot bath."

Paul vanished without another word. In an incredibly short time, he was back again.

"What next?"

"See if you can get hold of a doctor. I tried, but Central was so slow in answering I didn't dare . . . Oh—Oh—" for the livid child was choking again.

There was no resident physician at the little Cottage Hospital. Dr. Noble, the head surgeon, lived at home. After what seemed like endless waiting, Paul got his house.

"David's with Sylvia Gray," he said a minute later, turning with a white face from the telephone. "She's very ill."

"Try Dr. Wells then."

There was another long wait, and then again Paul faced the despair in Mary's eyes. "He's gone there too, it's—it's a desperate case. Shall I call him up, there?"

"Yes—no— Oh, Paul, you know what the trouble is there! It's two lives, maybe, against one!"

"He might at least be able to tell us what to do."

"You'll have to try White Water—Wallacetown—any place you can think of."

Again Paul tried, running down between calls to pile more fuel on the fire. One doctor was sick himself. Two had gone away to attend a medical congress. A fourth, twenty miles away, appealed to as a last resort, merely offered advice the substance of which Mary knew already and didn't know how he could get there—"the roads aren't broken through down this way."

"We've got to face it alone," said Mary at last.

Paul knew that it was in that moment that his selfish and idle boyhood died and that the potential manhood in him came to life.

"We've got to face it together, Mary," he said.

It was eight o'clock in the gray November morning when David Noble finally came to them. On the hearth the dying fire was flickering in the cold light. In front of it stood a tub of water, long since grown cold too, and the room was strewn with a tea-kettle and several pitchers, soiled towels, un-emptied basins—all the necessary, unlovely things that make the horror of illness grotesque and revolting as well as tragic. On the threshold of the door leading into his own room, stood Moses, still in his night-clothes, Spotty clutched in his arms, munching a doughnut and looking at the scene before him with dumb, uncomprehending anxiety. Mary was sitting in a large rocker, with Algy, a little gray shadow of the rosy child of the day before, clasped in her arms. She seemed hardly to hear the doctor come in. But Paul, a glass of brandy-and-water in his hand, rose from his knees beside his cousin's chair.

"Algy was all right when he went to bed last night," he stated, briefly. "He woke up in convulsions at midnight. I was passing about two o'clock and saw Mary's light. She was all alone with him till then. We've done the best we could."

David raised the child's eyelids to look at the pupils and felt his pulse while Paul was speaking. He bent over, listening intently to the little heart. Then he raised his head.

"You've saved his life," he said, with equal brevity.

A few minutes later, in the blessed sense of security that had come over her, Mary asked for Sylvia.

"She didn't get her twins, of course?" she asked, almost lightly. "She's talked of nothing else for months."

David's face contracted, and Mary noticed for the first time that he looked strangely old and very, very tired.

"Yes," he said huskily. "She did. Twin girls, just what she wanted. And—she's taken one of them back to Heaven with her."

CHAPTER TEN

The tragedy of Sylvia Gray's death shook Hamstead to its very foundations. Men and women met and asked each other, falteringly, if it were really so. Austin was almost crazed with grief. Nothing—nobody—had the slightest power to soften the stunning blow that had prostrated him. He sat immovable by the bed where Sylvia lay, her dark hair falling softly about her delicate face just as he had loved to see it when she was alive, the tiny, perfect little creature who had died with her, lying still on her quiet breast, the heavy scent of flowers filling the room. Even David, who had always had more influence over him than anyone else except Sylvia herself, could not move him.

"This won't bring her back, Austin, you know," he said, at last, as gently as ever, but more firmly. "And—and she would have been the last to—to want you to take it like this. Her courage never faltered through anything."

Austin neither answered nor moved.

"We must think what to do for the other baby. You've got her, you know, and the two little boys."

"I don't want to think of the baby."

"It isn't the baby's fault," said David, still more gently, divining what was passing in Austin's mind.

"No—but it's mine! She wasn't strong enough for this! You said yourself, when the second boy came so soon after the first, that—that she shouldn't have another for a long time."

"Yes." David chose his words carefully. "But, Austin—you came first, with Sylvia, just as she did with you. She told me something I've never forgotten. She was so brave that it was hard to get her to admit, ever, that she felt ill—that everything wasn't all right. But once she said to me, 'David, if anything *should* go wrong, be sure to tell Austin, afterwards, that there wasn't one minute in our life together that I would have had different—that there's no price too great to pay for perfect happiness.' She meant it. How many men's wives do you think can say that?—Mine can't," he ended, his voice breaking.

Next to Austin himself, there was no one, perhaps, in the whole village, to whom the loss of Sylvia came as such a horrible shock as to Mary. Algy was still very ill. The fear that the child would yet die, in spite of her fight for his life, grew a thousand times larger now that Sylvia's death had brought the Valley of the Shadow so close to her. Until we actually see its somber light, we are apt to think of it as something terrible but remote, touching others but never ourselves. Then suddenly we find that we are walking down its paths.

Mary did not close her eyes, nor stir from her little brother's side for three days and nights. And all that time, beside the actuality of the stricken child that she saw there, she visualized the picture of Sylvia and one little baby—of Austin and the other. And she thought—involuntarily, but constantly—of Lady Blanche's dying curse and its reiterating fulfillment. Who could dare to say that it was merely an idle and powerless superstition? Whom would it strike next? She thought of Blanche, seemingly so secure in her radiant happiness, and trembled until her teeth chattered. The first time that Paul saw her again after the night of the double tragedy—that long night through which they had fought for the sick child together—he felt that he would gladly have given ten years of his life if he had not thrown away his right to take her in his arms and kiss away the tears and bring a little color into her white cheeks and a smile to her drawn lips. As it was, he could only venture to lay one of his hands on the two that lay so tightly clenched in her lap, and put the other gently on her shoulder.

"Don't," was all he could think of to say, all, that is, that he dared to say, his own lips quivering. "Don't, Mary," and was thankful when she did not repulse him, but clung to him, sobbing, while he stroked her soft hair.

Paul was suffering too, suffering not only with the shock of it all, when nothing in his easy, careless life had ever shocked him before, but with the revelation of truths that he had never sensed, with the facing of problems he had never solved nor tried to solve. The way that Austin loved Sylvia—was *that* the way men cared for women? The way that Mary loved Algy—was *that* the way women cared for children? Passion that was all love, love that was all self-sacrifice—what had that to do with careless sensuality, or equally careless affection? When, for the second time, David Noble sought him out, he found that the boy had already started to find him.

"What can I do to help?" Paul asked abruptly.

"There isn't much. Your Cousin Jane is proving a tower of strength to Mary by relieving her of the burden of ordinary daily grind. We men never stop to think that meals have to be cooked and dishes washed and fires built, no matter who lives or dies, do we? And even your mother and Myra—I beg your pardon, what I meant was, everyone is trying to help Mary now. And no one in God's world can help Austin."

"Then what were you looking for me for?"

"I wanted to tell you that I thought you did darned well the night that kid almost slipped through Mary's fingers. He would have, if you hadn't been there. And also—to give you a message from Sylvia. She seemed to have a good deal of faith in you."

"Why?"

"Lord knows—I don't," replied David with brutal frankness. "Unless because she always had faith in everybody. I had a rather long talk with her about a week before she—went —and one of the things she said to me was, 'Tell Paul Manning not to stop fighting to get Mary back, if he has to die doing it.'"

"How—how am I to go about it?"

"I should think it might be rather difficult," said David dryly. "I confess it's hard for me to see the justice of a Divine Providence that snatches Sylvia from Austin who worshiped the ground she walked on, and lets you treat Mary like—"

Something in Paul's face stopped him abruptly. "Well, I suppose Providence sees a good many things we ignorant mortals don't," he ended.

"Yes," said Paul slowly, "I guess It does. Do you remember saying to me a while ago that as long as a man had a woman like Sylvia, of course he'd make her his first consideration as long as he could? Maybe the time had come for Austin to make something else his first consideration. Maybe he's needed a lot more in France than he realized. Perhaps it took a—a tragedy like that to show him how much he *was* needed."

For a moment David stared silently at the boy. He was too surprised at such conclusions reached from such a source to give utterance to speech of any sort.

"I think you're right," he said at last. "But Austin isn't the only one, you know, who's needed in France just now."

"I know," said Paul. "I've been thinking that over, too— what you said about the Foreign Legion. I'll be up tomorrow night to have you look me over."

"Good for you! About eight? I shall be off myself pretty soon, now. I waited before signing up until—after Sylvia's time, because Austin begged me to do so. Now I keep thinking that if I'd gone when I first planned, maybe someone else would have done better for her."

"No one could have," said Paul, decidedly. "You'd know that, if you weren't shaky over the whole thing, same as the rest of us. Whether I go to the war or not, there's no reason why I shouldn't go to work if there's nothing the matter with my heart, is there?"

"Good Lord, no! Has that just occurred to you? You think about as rapidly as a turtle walks, Paul!"

"I know it," Paul winced. He was so thoroughly convinced

of his own ignorance and stupidity now that he was growing a little sensitive about being reminded of it all the time. "But isn't there a story," he added slowly, "about a turtle who kept on walking a long time—and finally won a race?"

"There is—a darned good story, too! Well, I'll see you to-morrow night! Meanwhile, there are probably lots of little things you can find to do for Mary, if you really want to!"

As David drove away, he found he could not get Paul and his unexpected sentiments out of his mind. "That boy was a nice little chap," he reflected, "unusually nice, as long as his father lived. Thoughtful, too, though he never said much. Darned if I don't believe Sylvia was right about him, as usual. The phase that he's been passing through has been pretty unattractive, Lord knows, but it may have been just a phase. If only he hadn't lost Mary— But if he hadn't, he never would have started to think again—he was too lazy. Well, it's all beyond me. But there's one thing clear—I've got to stop flicking him in the raw. He's had enough of that for the present."

David's remark about the daily grind of housework gave Paul his first cue to helpfulness. Mary began to find the kitchen fire built and the teakettle boiling when she came downstairs in the morning, the wood-box filled, the furnace tended faithfully day and night, the porches and paths kept free from snow. On Monday mornings he appeared to empty wash-tubs and hang out clothes. He asked Seth, moreover, if there were any reason why some of the laundry—heavy sheets for instance—and things like that, should not be sent out, and when Seth agreed with him that it might be a good idea, "for a while, anyway," he found a hamper to hold them and drove off with it in the back of the sleigh. At his instigation, Myra agreed to do all the baking for both houses until "things got straightened out." Violet undertook the mending, and Jane actually gave up a meeting of the Foreign Missionary Society to finish the weekly sweeping. And when, in spite of all this relief, Mary paid for her long strain and quietly crumpled up in a heap on the floor one afternoon when Algy was out of

danger, and Sylvia's grave was hidden with snow, Paul picked
her up and laid her on her bed, loosening her dress and taking
off her shoes as he called for help. Jane, fortunately, was in
the house and undressed her while he went downstairs to telephone for Dr. Wells and to get a hot-water bottle and a hot
stimulant ready. They had always, from childhood, gone in
and out of each other's rooms entirely without self-conscious-
ness, and neither felt any now. Paul helped out in any way
he could, whether it was in bringing up trays for Mary or
washing the dishes downstairs. And when he saw that it was
her inability to care for the boys that was worrying her more
than anything else, he turned his attention mainly to them. It
would have been hard to discover anyone more stupid and
awkward in dealing with a little child than Paul was, but he
did what he could. He could, for instance, read aloud to Algy
as the little chap grew better. He became familiar with the
Tale of Benjamin Bunny and the Adventures of Johnny
Chuck. When nothing seemed to taste good to the small invalid, he went to Watertown and found a bread-and-milk
set of bowl, pitcher and saucer, decorated with a juvenile
football game so alluring that broths and gruels went down
Algy's throat from it as if by magic. He whittled out wooden
toys with his jack-knife, sitting where Algy could see him do
it. He bought a letter board and made Algy chase the P
around with the A, just as Algy was going to chase Paul
around when he was well again. Moses, hitherto on very
strained relations with his big cousin, took to hanging around
the room and going to the post-office and general store with
Paul to do the errands every morning, and tagging at his heels
when he walked about the farm. Paul did better than he
realized and his reward was greater than he expected. The
first time that the children fell upon him, almost simultaneously, with hugs and kisses, was when he came in with two
small wooden snow shovels—"to use when Algy was out-doors
again, in no time now." As he hugged and kissed them in re-

turn, his embarrassment was equaled only by the inner glow of contentment that permeated his being.

He wrapped Algy in a blanket, and sat down with him in the big rocker, while Moses shoveled imaginary drifts into the fireplace and Spotty stood on guard against "any wild animals that might come in." Mary, up again for the first time, came in to find them thus occupied, Algy just dozing off. The inner glow of contentment changed to a leaping flame as Paul looked at her and saw the expression of surprise and gratitude on her pale face.

"You're awfully good to those children," she said softly, so as not to disturb Algy.

"They're great kids. I never knew before how much fun a kid is. I thought they were horrid little nuisances," returned Paul apologetically.

Mary sat down beside him. "Blanche and Philip are coming home for Christmas," she said. "Isn't that nice? We didn't have much of a Thanksgiving, for the first time I can remember on Lady Blanche Farm—things were at their very worst just then! Now Cousin Violet has a letter saying they'll surely be here the twenty-fourth, and of course she's perfectly delighted."

"That *is* good news! Got any more?"

"I don't know whether you'll call it good or not—but Austin Gray is going to France. I think that's much the best thing he can do, really. He says it's only a matter of months now before the United States will be in the war, too. Do you think that's so, Paul?"

"I'm afraid I haven't thought much about it."

"Well—he's going over as an ambulance driver, but he says he can get transferred to 'the real job' later on if we do. He was just here to see you. I went downstairs for a minute just as he came in, but I didn't know you were here, so he didn't wait. He asked me to invite you to go to New York with him, after Christmas. He'll be there for a fortnight, at least, making final arrangements."

"New York!"

"Yes. Wouldn't you like to go? I thought you were crazy to get away from Hamstead."

"I'm not quite so crazy as I used to be."

"No, you're getting fairly sane!" said Mary with a little laugh that made his heart leap, "and—just as kind and thoughtful as you can be. But you ought to go. It'll be wonderful for you! And I'm sure you'd be a comfort to Austin, too. He must think so, or he wouldn't have asked you. I'm afraid he misses David a good deal. Paul—it seems as if there really were a war, now that they're both going to be in it, doesn't there? I didn't half sense it before—just as I didn't think much about death until Sylvia died. It shows how awfully selfish I am."

"Yes," said Paul, smiling and shifting Algy's position a little. "That is just the way I should describe you—awfully selfish. Probably the most selfish member of the family. I don't see how the rest of us put up with you."

Something in his voice seemed to startle Mary a little. She rose abruptly.

"You'll go, won't you, Paul?" she asked.

"Yes, of course. Especially if you think I'd better. Mary, wait a minute—" but she was gone.

After that, for the first time since they had "made up," Paul saw that she was avoiding him again. The fact gave him fresh food for thought. She was willing to be his cousin, his friend, his companion. She was grateful far beyond his deserving for the little he had been able to do to serve her. She had forgiven him freely for all he had done to hurt her. But more than that she could not and would not do and be.

Paul was now, for the first time in his life, deeply in love, and perhaps for that reason, daily going deeper—going deepest of all because he felt it to be absolutely hopeless. Well, he must hide it as best he could. That startled look must not come into Mary's eyes again. He must accept the bitter knowledge that she regarded his love as something to fear, as part of his just punishment. When Blanche and Philip arrived, he took Blanche's statements of what she thought of him—it was the first time she had seen him since the engagement had been broken—so quietly that she was frightened.

"He didn't argue with me at all," she said, telling Philip about it afterwards. "Or interrupt me once. And when I got through calling him every hard name I could think of, he said, 'I'm sorry, but that's all too true for me to dispute it with you' and walked out of the room."

Philip was less surprised than she had expected. He had been watching his brother-in-law closely and had come to the conclusion that he had either misjudged the boy at first, or that the latter had improved somewhat during the last few months.

"Let Paul alone, honey," he said. "He looks to me like a man who is working out his own salvation."

"Working!"

"Well, thinking it out, then. And Paul does do some work— a good deal more than he used to do. He went to see David Noble before David went away and found that there was nothing whatever the matter with his heart, and since then he's been trying to strike his gait. I'm not picking him as a winner in a three-mile race, but at least he isn't out at pasture any more. Don't nag him."

Philip had almost added, "He gets enough of that from his mother—" but stopped himself just in time. He, at any rate, had not changed. He made no tactless mistakes, he hurt no one's feelings, he radiated good cheer and happiness wherever he went. Hamstead, secretly pining to see the bride and groom, refrained from "calling" for fear that such an attention would make Violet "more set up than ever." But Blanche and Philip did not wait for anyone to call. They called themselves, with entire friendliness. Then, heartily, Hamstead welcomed them. Yes, Philip was just the same, it said. His first popularity was plainly going to bear the test of time. And though Blanche was "some different," older, better dressed, more poised, she was "pleasant as ever." "It seems real good to have her back, even if it ain't but for a few days," Hamstead said. "How much do you suppose them furs of hers cost?"

Paul, with the rest of the village, was glad to have his sister and brother-in-law at home; glad not only because he was fond of them, but because it was easier, in their presence, to keep from saying the things he was longing to say to Mary— to keep, as he was longing still more, from touching her. It was not until, quietly, but happily, they were all celebrating Christmas at Cousin Jane's together, that he saw her shrink away from him a little again. Time, mercifully, softens every-thing—lover's quarrels and children's sufferings and even the thought of the Valley of the Shadow. Austin was finding his solution. Algy, thin but thriving, was in his high chair at the table once more. Philip and Blanche, radiantly happy, were with them again and had brought such a complete and satis-factory assortment of presents for everybody, from Hod to Cousin Jane, as had never been seen on the farm before. After dinner, while the two little boys took their naps, Violet went to lie down, Seth to smoke his pipe—it was not, in Jane's house, as in his own, permissible to do this anywhere—and Cousin Jane to help Myra, loaned for the occasion, with the dishes. The four young people were left alone together. And, as the door closed behind the last retreating elder, Philip suddenly snatched up Blanche and kissed her, announcing that he was so full of joy and dinner mixed, that he'd got to let off steam, some way, that very minute. And Blanche, curling up in his arms like a contented kitten, smiled and kissed him back. They settled down in the big winged chair before the fire together—

Over their unconscious heads, Paul looked at Mary. They could not possibly see him. Their backs, amply protected by the big chair, were towards the rest of the room. He crossed to where she stood, and the expression on his face was unmis-takable. Before he could speak, she fled from the room.

This time, unencumbered by a sleeping child, Paul went

after her. She had almost reached the stairs. He stepped in front of her.

"See here, Mary," he said, "I can stand almost anything you want to do or say and I know I deserve it. But please don't look at me that way. I can't stand it."

"Well, don't look at *me* the way you did then."

"I'll try not to. I'm trying not to, all the time. I only thought—it's Christmas Day—that perhaps you could, just once—I won't ask you again for a long time. . . ."

It is unfortunately true that many naturally sweet-tempered women, if they are also clever, take refuge, when they are hurt or frightened, in flippancy or sarcasm. It is to be hoped that they do not know how deeply they can wound with these weapons. But whether they do or not, Mary was no exception to this rule.

"Why should you care about it so much?" she quoted scathingly, "'a kiss doesn't mean anything.'"

Paul stepped to one side, leaving the passage upstairs clear for her. She went by him swiftly, her head up. Then, on the landing, she turned and came still more swiftly down.

"That wasn't fair," she said. "Please forgive me, Paul."

"No," he said slowly. "It wasn't fair, and it wasn't kind of you to remind me of it. But what I said was true. There *are* some kisses that don't mean anything in almost every fellow's life. They drink too much sometimes, too. I'm sorry, but it's so. But that doesn't mean they're hopeless drunkards and—degenerates. There hasn't been anything to drink, or any of that kind of kisses for me in a long time. You know that, and you know why, too. And you ought to know that it would mean more than anything in the world to me if I could kiss you again."

Paul had learned a good many valuable lessons in the last months. Mary learned one now. The boy was humble, but he was not abject. He was penitent over his past mistakes, but he was not morbid about them. If he had a right to demand nothing else from her, he deserved and demanded, at least, fair play and respect.

"When you go to New York—" she began.

"You'll let me kiss you good-bye?"

This was not at all what Mary had intended to say. She hesitated a minute, and then, in spite of herself, she nodded. Then she leaned forward and touched his cheek with her lips, so lightly that it seemed merely as if a flower had brushed it.

"The telephone is ringing," she said, over her shoulder and left him to answer it as she fled.

It was the station agent. There was, he said, a big box of flowers at the station, "same as had come pretty frequent lately, for Mary."

"I'll come right down and get them," said Paul blithely.

"Wal," replied the agent, who had known them both since they were children, "you needn't sound so tickled about it. They're from Boston," and he gave an audible chuckle.

"I don't care," Paul shouted back. "Merry Christmas, Sol!" He was indeed too happy at that moment to care whether a dozen men in Boston each sent Mary a dozen American Beauties. And she, that evening, was so much gayer than Philip had ever seen her, that he could not help speaking about it to Blanche as soon as they were alone together again.

"I didn't know Mary had so much pep," he said. "She was just as funny all the evening as she could be."

"Oh, Mary used to be awfully lively. She was a perfect case in school. I think that was really one reason Cousin Laura sent her away. Jack Weston used to sit in front of her and you know how slovenly and untidy he always is. And one day she leaned forward and wrote, 'Better change it' in crayon on the back of his dirty collar."

Philip roared with appreciation. There was nothing he liked better than to get Blanche started on stories about Hamstead, past or present.

"Tell me some more," he urged.

"Well, there was a long, lean principal here then—a man—and a little bit of a wizened-up old maid for his assistant. His name was Arthur Simmons Betts and hers was Ellen Maria Tibbetts. The class was just beginning plane geometry and had to put examples, triangles and squares and things, you know, on the blackboard. And one day Mary labeled her triangle with their initials and began to explain her problem, 'if the legs of ASB equal the legs of EMT—'"

Philip rocked back and forth, emitting hoarse sounds of joy.

"Of course she got an awful call-down for it. We all thought she'd be expelled or at least suspended for it, but that didn't depress her a bit. We used to have a closing hymn every afternoon and the pupils took turns in choosing it. It was Mary's turn that day, and she chose, 'I'm nearer my Father's house tonight than ever I was before'—"

"I wonder if she and Paul are really going to make up, after all?" asked Philip, wiping his eyes.

"Oh, I hope not—even if he is my brother! You wouldn't want her to marry him now that she's got such a splendid chance!"

"Splendid chance!"

"Yes. Of getting Mr. Hamlin. Why, if she took Paul, even if he was good enough for her, which of course he isn't, she'd be buried in Hamstead all the rest of her life!"

Philip preferred to think of Blanche as a "blithe spirit," as the nymph he had found beside a crystal brook. But there were times when he was forced to admit, or evade admitting, that there were, after all, traces of a somewhat material little human being about her. He reluctantly did so now.

"Well, I shouldn't mind being buried in Hamstead, with someone I loved," he said. "What do you say about starting in to fix up the little law-office for ourselves this spring after all? I know you didn't care much for the idea when I first suggested it. But I'd enjoy the work immensely, and I can probably get off for a month next summer."

"Oh, Philip, couldn't we go somewhere else? There's plenty of time for that! And I've never spent a summer out of Hamstead in my life! I'm crazy to see Bar Harbor or Newport."

"All right, honey, just as you prefer," he said quietly.

He left Hamstead with the growing certainty that Paul and Mary were "really making up." Violet shared this certainty and ran up several new bills on the strength of it. Mary came in and out of her house again as if nothing had ever happened. She helped with the preparations for Paul's departure for New York, with energy and interest. Neither Violet nor Myra had much skill with either the needle or the iron; Mary could do wonders with both. She embroidered and laundered a dozen new handkerchiefs, mended neglected socks and shirts, sponged and pressed coats and trousers and finally even packed Paul's suitcase with fresh piles of clothing. Austin had decided to go by way of Boston and they were therefore leaving on the morning train instead of the midnight. And when Paul came downstairs ready to start, he found Mary, and not Seth, waiting in the little old sleigh, to take him to the station.

She had, as Violet often remarked, "no style to her," and this morning she had even less than usual. It was bitterly cold, and she had on an old fur coat of her mother's, worn and shabby and out-of-date, a knitted hood of red wool, and red wool mittens. But Paul thought he had never seen her look half so lovely. The frosty air made her cheeks glow like roses and her eyes were as sparkling as the winter sunshine. She had seemed, since Christmas, so much less tired than for a long time, so much like his old playmate, his old sweetheart.

There was a long stretch of road with no houses on it between Lady Blanche Farm and the village. Mary drove, and they rode along, talking of trivial things, laughing often, until they had almost reached the end of it. Then Paul put his arm around her and laid his hand over hers.

"You promised me," he said softly.

Mary turned her face to his exactly as she might have done

ten years before. There was still much of the child's face there indeed—the same big, honest gray eyes and the same firm, rosy skin, the same little curls, escaping from under the red hood framing it. Paul had meant above everything else, that this embrace should be gentle, reverent even, and he did not for one minute forget this. But he had not reckoned on its proving so utterly impossible to keep all traces of the passion that was surging through him from his lips, and when he felt the cold, soft cheek growing suddenly warm beneath them, involuntarily he sought her mouth. Instead of drawing away from him, as he instantly feared she might do, she returned his kiss. For one heavenly moment they clung to each other. Then he bent over and kissed the little red mittens holding the reins.

"You dear girl," he murmured. "My own dear Mary—" and suddenly seeing tears in her eyes, he exclaimed, "I didn't hurt you, did I, darling? I wouldn't have, for the world!"

"No— Oh, no!"

"What is it then, sweetheart?"

"Hush! You mustn't call me that," she whispered. "I didn't realize, when I promised, that you wanted that kind of a kiss. I thought it was just for—for a proof that we were friends again—for always."

"We are friends again for always. And that's all I did expect. But of course this was the kind I wanted, even if—"

"It wasn't fair."

"I'm sorry. I didn't mean to, on my word of honor. But you kissed back!" he ended exultantly.

"I know I did. That's what wasn't fair. I—couldn't seem to help it. You were so—so—you meant it so!"

"I'm glad you see that now," he said quietly. But his heart was singing.

New York, to Paul, was not the glittering wonder that it is to most boys, seeing it at his age for the first time. It seemed to him so vast, so impersonal, so unfriendly, as to be almost formidable. No amount of splendor could make up for that, to him. He was essentially the product of a little village, happy and at ease only in the life of a small community. He went once or twice on sight-seeing tours, and to a few "shows" and roof-gardens. Nothing thrilled him at all. The vivid memory of the touch of Mary's lips, the thrill of that frosty kiss, still obliterated every other emotion. He finally went to the department store where he knew Rosalie King worked, and sought her out. He found her at the jewelry counter, dressed, as usual, in the height of fashion as she understood it, manicuring her nails during a pause in trade. She was not very cordial to him. Girls, Paul reflected, had inconveniently long memories for a fellow's shortcomings. But when he gave voice to his lonesomeness and depression, she warmed to him at once. Paul was by no means the only person whom Sylvia had sized up correctly.

"Homesick in New York! Well, if that ain't a scream! I s'pose you're pinin' for the bright lights of Hamstead—them two bright lights, one in front of the post-office and the other in front of the store!"

"I'm pining for Mary," he said shortly.

Rosalie patted her coiffure, and gave it a fleeting glance in a small mirror that she had produced from somewhere about her person.

"Let her rip," she said sympathetically.

Business was a little dull that morning. The popularity of the January sales was waning. Paul leaned over the counter and told his story, with the conspicuous omission of some of the most important parts. He told enough, however, for Rosalie to guess a good deal more and what she guessed moved her not a little. When he finished, she needed to re-powder her nose.

"Why don't you pick out something swell to take home to her?" she asked. "She likes blue, don't she? I got a bracelet here, with sapphires in it, that's classy down in the ground. When Mame comes back, so's I can go out to lunch, I want you to come up to the eighth and meet Steve. He's a regular feller. We'll all go out to Child's together."

Steve, in spite of his tall collar and frock coat, his sloping shoulders and slim waist, even in spite of his sleek hair and slightly receding chin, was also human and friendly. If Paul could not talk their language, he at least understood it. They not only lunched together, they arranged to spend Sunday together, also.

"We'll gather in a dame for you, too," said Steve, as they shook hands in parting.

"Like ducks we will," exclaimed Rosalie. "You ain't wise to this guy yet, Steve. I gotta put you on. We'll take him out to Harlem and show him one of them cute little flats you and I are thinkin' of takin' in the sweet by-an-by. They'll show him how to make life easy for a perfect lady that he's soft on. That's more the line of goods he's interested in just now."

In truth, "cute little flats," containing a living-room, bedroom, bath and kitchenette, "with all modern improvements," interested Paul far more than anything he had seen so far in New York. The houses at Lady Blanche Farm, like most of those in Hamstead during the last decade, had been equipped with bathrooms and furnaces and when at the time of Blanche's wedding, Violet had put electric lights in hers, Seth and Jane had done the same. But they had no set-tubs, no electrical labor-saving devices, no elaborate short-cuts to comfort and leisure. Paul began to wonder if he would not have done better to buy an electric washing-machine and a vacuum-cleaner than a sapphire bracelet. He asked Rosalie what she thought.

"Couldn't you get her both?"

Paul did some slow and careful calculating.

"I'm afraid not, just now," he said regretfully.

"Well, I'm not taking any bets, but I believe she'd like the bracelet. You could get her some electric curling tongs, anyway. They don't cost much."

"She doesn't need those," said Paul, thinking of the little curls under the red hood.

"Well, an electric flat-iron then.—How'd you like to go to a show?"

"*Sunday?*"

"Sure. This ain't Hamstead, little one. So long as you call it a sacred concert, illustrated, you can do almost anything in New York. There's going to be a swell picture at the Grand, right near here—'Hell's Agony,' the name of it is."

So they went, and two hours later he and Rosalie and Steve parted with much good will all around. And the next day Austin sailed, and Paul was free to go home again.

It was late in the evening when, after a long, cold journey, he reached the Hamstead station. He stopped to exchange a few friendly remarks with Sol Daniels, the agent, and then went around to the rear where Seth was waiting for him in the sleigh, and they were soon jingling along through heavy snow down the road to Lady Blanche Farm.

How still it was, how cold and white! How clean and open and friendly! Paul wondered that he had ever, for one single instant, imagined that he would prefer to live in a city, in that dreadful strangeness, that hurry and dirt and noise! Not that seeing New York hadn't been a wonderful experience, of course. But it was much more wonderful getting home after it, and it was going to be most wonderful of all telling Mary what he had seen, what he had felt, what he had divined—watching the light in the steady gray eyes, the expression on the changing mouth. And perhaps now—of course it wouldn't do to force the issue, even now, but perhaps—

"Is it too late to see Mary tonight?" he asked suddenly, feeling in his pocket to see if the sapphire bracelet was surely safe and thinking of the electric iron snugly stowed away in the corner of his suit case.

"Geddap, King," said Seth, addressing the wholly unregal creature that was taking them on their way. "What ails you,

Paul, ain't you ben listenin' to what I ben sayin' to you these last five minutes?"

"No," said Paul breathlessly. "I—I was thinking. She—she isn't sick, is she?"

"Well," said Seth slowly, "I guess she's ben sick—ailin', anyway—for some time, longer'n we realized. She's worked real hard ever since her mother died. Mary ain't one to shirk, of course, and not bein' experienced, it made it harder for her. Then she was considerable upset over that trouble you and she had in the summer. I guess we was all a little mite hard on her at the time. And she took Algy's fever and Sylvia's death a good deal to heart. Mary don't say much, and I never saw her cry or git 'nervous' like your Ma. But you remember she fainted dead away one time just after Algy begun to get better—sorter dropped in her tracks? She seemed to perk up again 'round Christmas, but danged if she didn't keel right over again the day after you left for Noo York. Now she's gone."

"Gone!" echoed Paul, an icy terror clutching at his heart. "You mean she's *dead?*"

"No, she ain't dead! Land, Paul, you must be gettin' nervous yourself. Geddap, King. She's gone to Boston, to visit that friend of hers, Hannah Adams, that's been teasin' her to come for so long. When Doc Wells said she's just got to hev a rest, or he wouldn't answer for the consequences, Mary give in. Moses and Algy and I hev moved over to Jane's to stay until she gets back. I ain't sayin' I like the change, but maybe it's all for the best. I kinder think that's what we oughter hev done in the first place, after Laura died, until Mary had finished her schoolin' and got her growth and strength. We could have managed the money end of it if I hadn't bought all them new cows that year. I guess a thoroughbred girl is worth more'n a thoroughbred herd, when you come right down to it. But Jane's doin' as well as she knows how by us now. She was considerable startled when she found Moses settin' in the front hall the other day, quiet as could be, tryin' to burn the fuzz off'n his stockings with a lighted match without settin' fire to the rest of him! Mary is used to little things like that, but Jane takes them hard. Yet she caters to them young ones more'n I'd believed she would ha' done. The other day she said to Algy, 'Are you doin' everything you want, dear?' and Algy says, 'No, I want to swear,' and he began, 'damn, devil, hell,' and so on, quicker'n you could say 'Jack Robinson.' Fortunately, I come along just then, and clapped my hand over his mouth before he got any further. Algy's ben out in the hay-fields some with the hired men and heard 'em talk, and you know their choice of words ain't always what you'd pick to have a Christian maiden-lady hear. However Jane'll get used to all such trifles if Mary stays away long enough. She says she don't see how Mary ever done so much work. We've had to get in Myra's niece from out back, to help her, and send the wash up to the steam laundry in Wallacetown besides, and buy bread once or twice, and still she's ben on the jump every minute, though the boys ain't ben sick and she don't read 'em half the stories or give 'em so many baths as Mary did. I guess Mary put a good deal of vitality into her job. Well, I give her Laura's money before she went, without any strings tied to it. It ain't much, but it's somethin', and if she wants to spend part of it, even the capital, jest havin' a good time, I shan't begrudge it to her."

"Do you think," asked Paul, choking a little, "that there was any other reason, that anything happened just before I left, that made Mary want to go away—besides just because she was tired?" And as he asked the question, the boy seemed to feel her face pressed against his, the ecstasy of that swift, passionate kiss that she returned, and to see the sudden tears in her eyes afterwards.

Seth considered this question carefully before he answered it. "Well," he said at length, "women's queer. I don't pretend to understand 'em. But Mary thought a lot of you, and you jilted her. That's the plain English of it, ain't it? She had to sit back and see Blanche marry a fine, rich, handsome feller that set his eyes by her, while she took the sneers of the whole village. I guess it hurt her a good deal, and it was a long while, as I don't need to tell you, before she could bring herself to speak to you again. But sence that night that Algy took sick, and you helped her out so good, she gradually got to be friends with you again. She was real grateful to you, and I guess she still likes you some, in spite of everything. Mary's like that. She don't change easy. She ain't off with the old love for the sake of gettin' on with the new, like some girls. And she could see that you was tryin' to do better. I want to give you credit for that myself, Paul. . . . I know it ain't so easy as it might be for a young feller to cut loose from his bad habits like I've seen you tryin' to do. But girls don't understand all them things, thank goodness, and then again, they forgive a darned sight easier'n they forget. Mary ain't harborin' what you done against you any more, but she ain't forgot that you done it, and she ain't certain you wouldn't do it again. She ain't said a word, but I got a sneakin' feelin' some way, that she'd begun to feel that you were thinkin' of tryin' to get back to the old footin' again, and you ain't the kind o' feller it's easy for a girl to say 'no' to, Paul, no matter what you want. You're good-lookin' and you're pleasant when you want ter be, and what beats both of them qualities, you got a way with you. . . . Wal, of course I don't want to pry, and I ain't askin' you no questions. . . ."

"I—I—had begun to hope that sometime—"

"Then," said Seth decidedly, "you're a bigger fool'n even I took you for, and that's sayin' a good deal. Mary made a mistake to let you get her easy before and to let you treat her neglectful after you did get her. She wouldn't make a mistake like that again, even if she wanted you, and I don't believe she does. Anyway, she don't trust you, and I'm dummed if I blame her. I look to see her be gone from here some time. And that ain't all."

Paul waited, his heart sinking lower than ever.

"I got a letter from Mr. Hamlin, the architect," said Seth,

"that was a considerable surprise to me. He says he asked Mary to marry him three years ago, when her mother died. And she turned him down because she thought Moses and Algy and me needed her, and because she was comin' home— to you. It shows she didn't have as much sense as she might hev, or she never would hev refused a man like that to stick to a boy like you. But I hope she's acquired a little sense. Anyway, he says he's glad to understand that conditions hev changed somewhat now and he wanted I should give my consent to try his luck again. *Consent!* Great Godfrey! I writ by return mail! Geddap, King!"

Late that night, when everyone else had gone to bed, Paul went out-doors and stood for a long time, looking towards the unlighted windows of the house across the road. Adam, facing the angel with the flaming sword which barred the gate into Eden, could have felt no surer that he had lost Paradise through his own wrong-doing than did this humbled and heart-sick boy.

CHAPTER ELEVEN

It was a bright morning in early May and the sun, streaming into the pretty living room, fell on Blanche's golden hair and turned the color of her delicate negligee from palest pink to rose. She was, her husband reflected, growing lovelier and lovelier with every month that passed. Just now, however, her face wore the expression of slight discontent which at first he had noticed only when she spoke of the dullness of Hamstead and which had left it altogether during the first radiant weeks of their marriage but which was now returning more and more frequently and far more plainly defined than he liked to see it.

"What's the matter, honey?"

"Nothing, except that I'm wishing I was a nymph again."

Philip laughed, and throwing down his Sunday paper, crossed over to the desk where Blanche had seated herself as soon as they had finished breakfast.

"The first time I heard you say that was because you wanted to get away from spring cleaning," he said lightly, "and the second, when you had to go to an intelligence office and engage a maid. The third time was when you tried in vain to crank the Ford on a cold day and I got home and found you nearly crying over it. What's the matter this time?"

"Bills," said Blanche briefly.

"Bills?" echoed Philip. "Why, I should think those were one of the last things that need trouble you. We've plenty of money to pay bills for all the things we really need. I thought they were all paid."

"I haven't shown them all to you. You bought me so many

new things the first of the winter, and these looked so huge, I was afraid to. I've kept putting it off."

"You silly child, hand them over—"

She gathered the fluttering sheets on the desk and gave them to him. Then, watching his face as he began to glance through them, she suddenly burst out, "I'm sure I've tried to be careful! We have only one maid, instead of three or four, and an apartment instead of a house, like almost everyone we know. And I really don't spend *anything* on clothes compared to the other young married women I've met this winter. And we don't go to the theater or entertain much, or—"

"I know, darling. It does seem to cost a lot, just to *live*. I didn't realize how much, beforehand. But after all, we had a lovely trip and we've been pretty comfortable and happy in this little apartment. It's a lot more than—" Philip realized that he had been very close to saying "than you had before you married me," but he bit back his words hastily and ended, "than lots of people have. And I can take care of all these all right. I've got money in a savings bank. But I guess we shall have to go a little slow for a while."

"Well, it's lucky we haven't had a baby! I don't know *what* you'd have said about bills then! And yet you've been perfectly crazy—"

Something about Philip's silence halted Blanche. She decided that it was wiser to change the subject.

"I had a letter from Paul last night," she said. "I meant to speak of it before. I guess he's rather fed up with Lady Blanche Farm, too. At any rate, he wants to come to Boston for a week or so and asks if it would be convenient for us to have him here."

Philip hesitated. He felt that the present state of his finances could ill permit him to give his brother-in-law the kind of a good time he would expect if he came to town. On the other hand, he was curious to see if the more favorable impressions which he had gained of the boy at Christmas time would prove to be lasting, and he could not, moreover, refuse such a request or even consent to it grudgingly without still further wounding Blanche's feelings.

"Of course, if Paul is coming to Boston, we must have him here," he said pleasantly. "When did he speak of coming?"

Paul appeared three days later, and Philip, with his usual fairmindedness, confessed to himself that the boy was still more changed, and though differently, it was certainly not for the worse. He seemed much older, much quieter, and decidedly preoccupied. It was very plain that he had something—perhaps several things—very much on his mind.

"Yes, of course I'd enjoy going to the theater," he said a trifle absently. "Thanks awfully. Or anything else you've planned. First of all, though, if you don't mind, I'd like to go and see Mary. I—I haven't heard from her at all, except indirectly, since before I went to New York. Do you think she's had a pleasant winter?"

"Pleasant winter!" exclaimed Blanche. "Why, she's had a wonderful time! The Adamses have one of the finest old houses in Boston, and know *hundreds* of the nicest people, and they and all their friends have entertained *continually* for her. Why, we're the merest plebeian suburbanites compared to Mary! And they've taken her on several trips, too— when she first came, straight off to Atlantic City for a 'rest cure' and later to New York to the opera and to cap the climax they went to Washington and stayed with Senator Field, a great friend of the Adamses, who has a perfect palace down there! She's packed these few months pretty full, I can tell you! And I must say she's a great success. I don't believe she'll turn her back on it all a second time in a hurry! Mary is nice, there's no denying that, and awfully clever, too, and you'd never believe the difference good-looking clothes have made in her appearance. She hasn't had many, but everything has been *just right*, color, style and all. She's learned to drive a motor, too, and taken the Red Cross First Aid and Home Nursing courses, and gone to morning lectures on Current Events—"

"And she's had time to rest and read," cut in Philip, "which I think has meant more to her than almost anything else. The first week she was here—before they took her off to Atlantic City—she was in bed most of the time. Then she began to go for a daily ride and to pick up generally. Mr. Hamlin's pretty attentive to her."

"Pretty attentive!" Blanche echoed her husband. "Why, he follows her like a shadow! Wasn't she queer not to tell us that he was after her before—and not to *accept* him? I don't see how she could have hesitated a minute!"

"I'm glad she's had a good time," was Paul's only comment at the end of these and similar disclosures. "I want to see her myself."

"Well, let's go to the theater tonight, as long as we have the tickets, and you can go there tomorrow afternoon."

There was an amusing farce running at the Park Square Theater and as the curtain went down after the first act and the lights came on, Blanche, wiping the tears of merriment from her eyes, gave Paul a sudden nudge.

"Look!" she whispered, "in the first box on the right!"

Paul turned in the direction indicated. The box contained six persons—a middle-aged man and woman, two younger men, one of them in khaki, and two girls. They were all good-looking and well-dressed, and all, unmistakably, having a "beautiful time." At the first glance, that was all Paul realized. Then it came over him that the two older persons were Mr. and Mrs. Adams, one of the younger men, Gale Hamlin, one of the girls Hannah Adams and the other—the one in white brocade, with the rose-colored velvet wrap flung over the back of her chair and the big bunch of orchids and lilies of the valley at her waist—was Mary Manning, whom he had last seen wearing a red knitted hood, and shabby little red wool mittens—

The theater seemed to be swaying, then everything blurred. He shut his eyes for a minute. When he opened them, the box was beginning to fill. Half a dozen extra men had joined

the party, one in navy blue, two more in khaki, adding to
its merriment. Hannah was entirely absorbed in the first
officer, but Mary seemed quite equal to handling the others.
Blanche kept whispering in his ear, as he watched.

"That blond man with glasses on, is Hannah's fiancé, Cap-
tain Merrill. They didn't intend to be married until fall, but
since he's in the army, they've put the wedding ahead six
months, now that war is declared. Mary's going to be maid-
of-honor, in Trinity Church, and wear pink and silver. She
isn't paying much attention to Mr. Hamlin, is she? Too busy
dividing up her favors! He isn't the only person who's crazy
over her, though I guess he has the best chance. Of course he
gave her those flowers. She has a fresh bouquet every morning
on her breakfast tray and another one at night, if she's going
anywhere, and of course she usually is. They're probably all
going to the Copley to dance after the play is over. I thought
Mr. and Mrs. Adams were too high-brow to come to a show
of this sort, but they certainly seem to be enjoying themselves. I guess they've unbent quite a little lately. Don't you
want to go up and speak to Mary?"

"Butt into a crowd like that? What do you take me for?"

"Well, don't snap my head off! You said you wanted to see
her!"

"I can see her all right from here."

"Well, *speak* to her then!"

"I'd have a fat chance of saying anything there now,
wouldn't I?"

"Well, don't have one of your 'grouches' about it—"

Philip hastened to interrupt the exchange of fraternal com-
pliments that seemed imminent. But Paul was, undeniably,
"grouchy" the rest of the evening and the following morning.
Immediately after lunch, provided with ample directions to
keep him from getting lost in the subway or confused among
the alphabetical side-streets, he left Blanche's apartment and
betook himself into town. Eventually he alighted from the
street-car at the designated corner, to find himself in front of

a florist's window. He hesitated a moment, then entered the shop.

"I want some flowers," he said, a little vaguely, "something pretty. For—for a lady."

"Certainly, sir. Orchids, two dollars apiece? American Beauties, fifteen a dozen? Or these gilt baskets, filled with white lilacs—just in—are very attractive. Twenty dollars for the smaller size, thirty for the larger ones."

Comparative wealth in Hamstead meant actual poverty in New York, Paul had discovered. In Boston, it meant, apparently, straitened circumstances at best. He fingered the slim wallet in his pocket nervously.

"Not any—nothing like those, I'm afraid."

The salesman appeared to lose interest. Paul thought he almost shrugged his shoulders.

"You haven't anything like—like what grows in a country garden, have you?"

"A few sweet-peas, you mean, or pansies?"

"Yes, and mignonette, and forget-me-nots."

"I could make you up an old-fashioned nosegay—"

"Yes, that's what I want."

When Paul took out his wallet to pay for the bouquet, he took out a little box, too, and writing on it in pencil in his curiously unformed and immature hand, "For Mary, with Paul's love," he slipped it in among the flowers which the salesman handed him. Then, thus armed, he turned towards Beacon Street.

His destination proved to be an enormous corner house of brownstone, on the water side. Its appearance instantly suggested age, wealth and exclusiveness. Paul, uncomfortable enough already, became decidedly more so as he rang the front-door bell. The appearance of the man-servant who answered the ring did not reassure him.

"Miss Manning is not at home, sir."

"Or Mrs. Adams? Or Miss Adams?"

"None of the ladies are in, sir."

"Could I wait? I want very much to see Miss Manning."
The butler seemed to hesitate.

"I'm her cousin, Paul Manning, from Vermont. I've—I've
come a long way—"

How silly that he should be pleading with this wooden-
faced automaton! He half regretted the words before they
were out of his mouth. But, as usual, he stood his ground.
And he was rewarded.

"I think Miss Manning would wish you to wait, sir. Will
you come to the library? I'll tell her you're here, directly she
gets in, sir—or Miss Adams, if she comes first, sir."

The library proved to be an enormous bay-windowed room
at the rear of the house, overlooking the Charles River, lined
with books to the ceiling and furnished in Cordova leather.
A bright wood fire burned under a marble mantel. There
were several crystal vases filled with long-stemmed roses,
photographs—many of them bearing well-known autographs
—in engraved silver frames, etchings and one or two beautiful
old paintings. The great center-table was almost covered with
magazines, laid in neat piles—French and English period-
icals as well as all the best American ones—and, at either
end, in bronze racks, a row of the latest books, history, biog-
raphy, science and fiction. Paul had never seen, hardly even
imagined, such a room before. The tiny apartment where
he had stayed with Austin in New York was luxurious and
complete, perfect in its own way, but it contained no space,
no atmosphere, no traditions. Paul was equally ill at ease in
either, but Mary, he knew, had "taken to" the aristocracy of
Boston as readily as Austin had "taken to" the plutocracy of
New York. Blanche was right—it was unlikely that Mary
would turn her back on it a second time. This was the kind of
house—for Mr. Hamlin's, he felt sure, would be very like his
sister's—that Mary could live in forever if she chose! Mary,
whose chance for "advantages" had been no better than his!
Mary, whom he had called a prude and a shrew and a jailor!
. . . He picked up some of the unfamiliar magazines, *L'Illus-*

tration, The Graphic, The Atlantic Monthly, and tried to read them. The clock on the mantel chimed and struck half past four. The butler reappeared and piled fresh wood on the fire.

"I doubt if Miss Manning will be in now, before tea-time, sir. Is there anything I could get you, sir? Some cigarettes, or a whiskey and soda?"

"No, thank you."

The door-bell rang several times, the postman, apparently, packages from department stores, callers who came and went. The telephone kept ringing, too, and was answered somewhere downstairs. The fire crackled a little with the new wood, blazed into brilliant colors and settled to a steady flame. The clock chimed and struck, and struck and chimed again. It was after five when he finally heard Mary's voice.

"Someone waiting to see me? Who is it, Judkins?"

"The gentleman said he was your cousin, Miss. I took him into the library."

There was a short silence.

"Thank you, Judkins."

"Shall I serve tea for you there, now, miss?"

"Please."

So they were to be alone—what he had hoped for so much! He heard her coming, lightly and quickly, up the stairs. Then she entered the room.

She was dressed in the dull blue color that she had always loved, a soft, flowing gown, a large, drooping hat, and Paul thought instantly of how Rosalie King had said Mary would look "if she only had the right clothes on." These were not the kind, he instinctively knew, that were hurriedly stitched together after the children were in bed at night, or painfully created by Miss Sims, the village dressmaker, from a "paper pattern." Neither were they made from materials bought at the Hamstead general store for twenty-five cents a yard or less. But the change in her was far greater than in apparel alone. He could see that now, even more clearly than at the theater the evening before. She was rested, she was happy, all of her gravity seemed to have left her. Her color was glowing pink and white, her eyes sparkling, her whole manner different. Paul had never seen a woman so beautiful, so vital, so full of promise.

"Paul! When did you come? I'm ever so glad to see you!"

"Just yesterday. I'm staying with Blanche."

"How nice! Isn't her apartment pretty? And isn't Philip— well, just almost too good to be true?"

"Yes. I guess he is true, though. Blanche is lucky."

Mary sat down, pulled off her white gloves and took off her hat. Her hair, dressed in an entirely new way, seemed brighter, more abundant, more wonderful than ever.

"Is everything all right at Lady Blanche Farm? Of course, or you wouldn't be here! Are you going to stay long?"

"Only a few days."

"We must try and make them pleasant for you. Hannah is giving a dinner for me tomorrow—I'm sure she'll want you to come. And we'll find an extra girl, too, of course—a pretty one, rather flirtatious. Would you rather have her fair or dark? And there are several good plays in town—"

"It's awfully kind of you. But I'd honestly rather not be asked to dinner. I—I came just for—for rather a special reason."

"Yes?" said Mary, still lightly. The silver tea-service had been brought in, and she was moving the delicate porcelain cups about. "Lemon or cream, Paul, and how many lumps of sugar? These muffins are good. Will you have those first, while they're hot, and cakes later, or both at once?"

"I'm going to enlist."

Mary, pouring tea, did not answer.

"I've—I've had a hell of a row with mother."

Mary handed him the cup. "You would, of course," she said quietly.

"Do you think I did wrong?"

"No—I don't think so. Tell me more about it."

"She's all right, physically, though she insists she's a nervous invalid. And she's all right financially, too, if she'll only be careful. We were in debt, rather, after Blanche's wedding, but I've paid that all up. I've used some capital of my own. Now she can keep Hod and Myra to work for her and have plenty of money left over for food and clothing and taxes and everything that I can think of—I've been over it all pretty carefully. She says there are lots of expenses, though, that I don't know about, things women just have to have. So I've told her she could have my share of our income, too, as long as I was gone. That's fair, isn't it, Mary?"

"I should think it was—perfectly fair. What branch of the service do you want to enter?"

"The Marines. If they can't get into a scrap on sea, perhaps they will on land."

"Yes—I suppose Cousin Violet, when she saw she couldn't stop your going, advised the Quartermaster's Department or something like that?"

"How did you guess? I felt there were lots of other men who could go into that, men with families, I mean, or who weren't all right physically. There's nothing the matter with my heart; I found that out from David Noble before he left. I've been doing more work since then. Cousin Seth and I have drawn a lot of lumber together. I've liked that. We've drawn ice, too. It's been a fine winter for teaming, lots of snow and still and cold, just as it was when—when you went away. It was David who first put the idea of going to war into my head. I've had plenty of time to think it over since, and I'm sure I'm doing the best thing. But I'm sorry to have quarreled with mother. Cousin Jane took her side, too, and your father. They quoted agricultural statistics to show how much I was needed at home, and 'Honor thy father and thy mother' and 'How sharper than a serpent's tooth' and things like that to me. No one seems to know there is a war, in Hamstead, hardly. I tried to make them see how I felt. I couldn't. I'd made up my mind to go, anyhow, but I hated going like that."

"Yes," said Mary. "It must have been hard. But I'm glad

you've been helping father and that you liked it. And I'm—I'm sorry, Paul."

"Sorry I'm going?"

"Oh, no. I'm glad you're going. Very glad. I hoped you would. I'm only sorry they couldn't see that you were right to go and that it made your going harder. I suppose it is hard enough, anyway."

Paul put down his cup and came and sat down beside her on the sofa. "Mary," he said, his voice trembling a little, "I haven't any right to ask, of course, but would you tell me?—Are you going to marry Mr. Hamlin?"

"No. I'm going home, very soon now. I've spent as much money as I ought to, just for pleasure. More, perhaps, for I've used some of my capital, and I'm not willing to accept favors beyond a certain point. I'll try to make them see your side, in Hamstead. I don't know whether I can, but I'll try. And that there is a war. And that they must wake up and help to win it, if they don't want to perish in it."

"Would—would you marry *me*?"

For a minute the girl did not answer. She sat looking into the fire and in spite of its bright reflection, Paul thought that some of the lovely color had suddenly left her face.

"I—I thought," he went on, taking courage at not being instantly repulsed, "that if you would—we could have just a week or so together before I enlist. We could go to some quiet little place by the sea—neither of us has ever done that. And while I am gone, I could—I could remember it—and look forward to coming back to you, *that way*, again."

Suddenly he knelt down, and half-buried his face in the soft folds of her dress. "Mary—I've been so lonely without you all winter. I've wanted to talk to you—about New York, and the farm and the war—about everything I was interested in and thinking over myself. I've wanted to see you working around the house in your blue dresses, and hear you singing to the kids. I've wanted to try to make some things easier and pleasanter for you. I never knew before that home, to me, meant—just you. Mary—I want you so—"

"I know," she said slowly. "I've known that, of course, since Christmas. That's why I went away. Because—you don't love me."

"I do, I do—I swear I do! I love you dearly. Oh, Mary, please, please—"

She drew away from him a little. "You think love is just that—'wanting,'" she said. "Wanting something you can't get. And throwing it away as worthless as soon as you've got it. If I married you, you would be happy that week. But the first little French peasant you met—"

"Mary!"

"Well, wouldn't you? Or at any rate, have I any reason to suppose—to know—that you wouldn't? You don't know what it means to love."

"I thought I did. But perhaps I don't—will you tell me?"

Mary hesitated. "I don't know that I can put it into words very well," she said at last. "It isn't something you talk about. It's something you feel—that you are. And I can only tell what it means—for a girl. I can't, of course, for a man. Perhaps they don't feel as much as we do, though they always say they feel more—"

She turned her head away for a minute, and then faced him. "I can't pretend I wouldn't like to live like this always," she said. "I love the country but I haven't any illusions about it. I know that Lady Blanche Farm—or any farm—means lots of hard work, lots of loneliness, lots of deprivation. I'd like to have a big, beautiful house in the city, and a 'swilomine' as Algy calls it, to ride around in, and books and music and pretty clothes, and trips, and the constant association with delightful people—and all the rest of it. And when a man whom you like very much, offers them all to you, and you realize that you could not only have everything you want yourself, but give your father rest and comfort in his old age, and your brothers a good education, and—and—you hesitate.

You can't help it. It is an awful temptation. Of course Gale
Hamlin is too tactful, and too—too square, to try to bribe
me. But it amounts to a bribe just the same. So I've tried to
love him, so that I—I could have all this. I thought I could,
perhaps. But I can't."

Mary glanced down at Paul, her lips quivering a little. He
was still on his knees before her, his eyes looking up into hers,
more steadily, this time, than she could look at him.

"Because," she went on, and her voice was very low, "you
feel when you love a man that it doesn't matter if he's so poor
he hasn't a shirt to his back, or so bad that you've got to
drag him out of the gutter, if you can only belong to him.
That you'd rather bake his bread, and sweep his room, and
wash his clothes, than sit on a throne of gold, beside anyone
else. That you want to share his poverty and his troubles
and make them easier if you can. That you want to turn to
him in your own sorrow and in your own joy. That you want
to marry him—to go to sleep every night in his arms, and the
first thing when you wake every morning, to feel his lips on
yours, kissing you before you begin your day's work together.
That you hope, in time, he'll be your children's father."

Paul rose from his knees and walked blindly over towards
the bay window. When he finally came back, his fresh young
face looked white and old.

"You didn't care for Gale Hamlin like that," he said, as if
he were scourging himself with every word he spoke, "so you
wouldn't marry him. You didn't want a man just because he
was rich and famous and good. And you didn't want just
the easy, pleasant things, like Blanche. You wanted the hard
part, too. That's—that's the way you cared *for me*."

"Yes," said Mary, unsteadily.

"And you don't any more."

It was not a question. Nevertheless, Mary answered it with
one.

"Do you think it likely?" she asked.

Paul bowed his head. "No," he said, "I don't think it's likely.

Of course I know it's impossible. It was insane of me to think for one minute that you could marry me now, after what I did to you, when you cared like that. I ask your forgiveness from the bottom of my heart, but I know I don't deserve it and I don't expect to get it. Good-bye."

After he had gone, Mary found the old-fashioned nosegay, with the sapphire bracelet tucked inside, which he had forgotten and which she had not noticed. And later in the spring, just before she went back to Hamstead, she received a limp, square letter, addressed in the same unformed handwriting that was on the jewelry box, on coarse tan-colored paper with a red triangle in the corner.

"Dear Mary," it said—

"I won't bother you by writing you again, but I can't start across without doing it this once.

"I do love you. I know you don't believe me and if you decide to marry Mr. Hamlin after all, I'll try to be glad because I know he deserves you—as much as any man can deserve you—and I don't, but I'll *make* you believe me when I get home. It would be silly of me to say I'll be more worthy of you then, for of course I'll never be worthy of you. But I'll make you believe me, anyway. And if I don't ever get home, please try hard to believe me without any more telling than just this. For I do. I do, with all my heart and soul. Perhaps I didn't before, but I do now.

"God bless you.

                    Yours always,

                                Paul."

It was snowing hard, but Mrs. Elliott, bundling herself up well and hanging her oldest chintz bag over her arm, closed the door of her spotless kitchen behind her and set out to go and "pass the afternoon" with her friend, Mrs. Gray. Hamstead, always quiet, was quieter than ever. The storm was not a violent one, with wind and sleet and drifting, but merely the silent laying of the white blanket that was to cover and protect the valley until warm weather came again. She met no one on the road. Hamstead was busy in those days, as well as quiet, and went about but little. As long as the war had been a far-distant thing—another "crazy quarrel among them throat-cuttin' foreigners"—it had stirred feeble interest and still feebler sympathy in most of the hearts in the Connecticut Valley and as it dawned gradually upon Hamstead's reluctant mind that the United States "was likely to be drawn into the horrid thing" it comforted itself with many good reasons why its own sons should not go—farmers were, of course, needed in the fields as much as soldiers in the trenches—men with families had their own responsibilities to think of first— an amazing number of cases of flatfeet and weak eyes and impaired general health were discovered. But gradually, almost imperceptibly, public sentiment changed. For the first time in the history of the village, Methodists and Congregationalists and persons who professed no faith at all, the "old families" who belonged to the D.A.R. and those from "out back" who belonged to nothing more exclusive than the Foreign Missionary Society, began to work together with a common interest, all petty differences forgotten. A white flag with a crimson cross in its center, hung proudly from the vestry window on two afternoons each week and all the women in the village met there together on those days to knit, to snip cloth into tiny pieces for "comfort pillows" and to twist trench candles. Even on the days when there were no meetings, they were not idle. They knitted at home or took their knitting with them to a friend's house.

Mrs. Elliott had seen Mrs. Gray watching her slow approach through the deep snow from the kitchen windows, and had waved a greeting. Now, as she mounted the porch, she shook her umbrella and stamped the snow from her over-shoes.

"No, I ain't a bit wet," she said, returning Mrs. Gray's hearty kiss. "I'm dressed real warm, underneath as well as on top—flannel, long-limbed and high-necked, same as I've always wore. I call them envelope chemises some women's affectin' nowadays a means of flyin' in the face of Providence. If we're goin' to set in the kitchen, I guess I won't lay off my over-shoes. If I keep 'em on my feet, it'll take 'em off my mind."

This point being satisfactorily settled, the two ladies sat down in rockers beside the stove and started work on their sleeveless sweaters, Mrs. Elliott, as usual, scarcely stopping for breath before she began her recital of the recent news of the neighborhood.

"Have you heard that old Mis' Hunter, up to White Water is married *again*? Mr. Taylor tried to reason with her, seein' he's buried four of her husbands already, but she said, as long as the Lord took 'em, she would. Shockin', ain't it?— How's the baby? I shouldn't have thought that Austin could have borne to go off and leave that little helpless creature, but it seems to be thrivin', don't it? I don't s'pose you have the least notion he'd want to marry again, not for a while, anyway. Yes, I knew he was real fond of Sylvia, but men are human. He might meet someone in France. I want to see his last letter. Writes you real regular, does he? And Thomas too?

I never thought Thomas would get made a sergeant so quick, did you? But then I s'pose there ain't much material to draw on down to Camp Devens. I'm always real pleased to hear about your boys, but I declare I steer clear of Violet Mannin' these days. You know how set she was against Paul goin' to war. But now she's got the biggest service flag in town and 'we are 100% subscribed' on her Liberty Loan card. I bet all she bought was $50 bonds, don't you? Be that as it may, mornin', noon and night she don't open her head except to talk about 'her hero.' Well, Paul Mannin' may be a hero, but if he is, I'm glad we don't get more of 'em around here. He—"

"I think it was kinder hard on Paul, goin' off the way he did," interposed Mrs. Gray. "All the drafted boys had so much done for 'em—balls and sermons and brass bands at the station and all that. Thomas has said more'n once, it made him feel cheap to accept it all, when Austin didn't have a thing of the kind done for him. The few that enlisted slunk away without hardly a kind word thrown after 'em. We thought they was half crazy to go. I blame myself a lot the way I acted."

"Well, I don't see as you've got any call to. It's well not to take up with a new notion until you've seen how it works on somebody else. I feel the same way about these new-fangled recipes. I never thought I'd live to see the day when there wouldn't be a barrel of white flour and a barrel of sugar settin' side by side in my pantry, but I ain't seen more'n a few pounds of either for quite a spell now. I'd have laid in a good stock of both if I'd only thought of it in time, but when I got round to order it, all I had handed out to me was some real sassy remarks about hoardin'. Hoardin' indeed! Why, I never thought of such a thing! Seems as if I was eatin' chicken feed a good share of the time now. It'll be a wonder if some of them mixtures don't land us in our coffins. I've been seized with sudden cramps several times lately, and I lay it to some 'substitute biscuits' I've et. And I hear we ain't goin' to have any coal, soon. All because of some Archduke that got choked—or was it shot?—by a crazy anarchist. Well, as I was sayin', Violet goes around with a letter of Paul's in her hand, and—"

"Does he write her regular?"

"Seems to. I can't make out that he's ben in any great danger yet, and I've questioned her close. Enjoyin' himself considerable, I should say. Them Mannin' children always just itched and hankered to get out of Hamstead and I shouldn't be a mite surprised if that itchin' and hankerin' didn't have somethin' to do with Paul's 'patriotism' and Blanche's 'romance.' And that brings me to my main piece of news—Philip Starr's number's been called and he's goin' to Devens this week. Blanche's comin' home for the present and I hear she's mad clear through."

"Oh, the poor child!"

"Poor child nothin'. I don't deny Blanche is pretty and pleasant, but there ain't nothin' very deep about her. I bet she's lookin' forward to comin' here with lots of good-lookin' clothes and new ideas and puttin' on airs with her old neighbors. Mary's got her faults, but I'll say this for her, she ain't near so high and mighty as the rest of the family. Blanche writes she took a course in makin' surgical dressin's and wants we should take that up in our Red Cross meetings. I hear she's got an 'instructor's certificate,' whatever that may be, and wears a long veil. I'd like to see myself bein' instructed by Blanche Mannin' with my head done up in a towel!— Have you seen the latest directions for sweaters? 'Stead of makin' them plain like these, you knit one row and purl the next, and have ribs on the shoulders. They don't take so much wool that way and they ain't so monotonous to make. Mis' Weston has finished her twelfth pair of socks—she can make her needles go just like lightnin'. She seems to miss Jack somethin' awful. I should think it would be a relief to her to have him gone. But some women don't realize their blessin's even when they're rammed down their throats— Well, I must start along home and make a mock veal loaf for me and Joe for supper. It's one of them new rules. I'll call you up in the mornin' and let you know how it comes out. Seems like I should be able to hear the real bossie mockin' me sure enough, when I stir up all them scraps and try to pretend they're good victuals. Clearin', ain't it? Well, this'll make nice sleighin' and that's one thing to be thankful for. It's lucky we got a few comforts left."

Mrs. Elliott was not entirely wrong in her guess that there were some compensations to Blanche's home-coming. These, however, were few and far between. Philip had longed to volunteer in the first days of the war and Blanche had been so bitterly opposed to it that he had given in to her wishes, trying not to let her see the bitter spiritual struggle and loss of self-esteem which it had cost him to do this. But when the draft came, there could be no question of evasion or hesitation. His little income, though it was not the fortune she had imagined it to be, would keep her comfortable, and there was no child. This, Blanche knew, had been a source of disappointment and grief to Philip while she had secretly rejoiced at "not being tied down right away." Now the fact that a baby might have kept him at home made her resentful that she did not have one.

It was out of the question for her to stay on in the little Brookline apartment alone, and there was nothing for her to do but to return, rebelliously, to Hamstead. Philip, with never-failing understanding and gentleness, saw how hard it was for her to do this, and insisting that it should hereafter be called "Carte Blanche" to perpetuate his joke, urged her again to amuse herself by having the little law-office renovated to suit the plans which he had made so long before. This time, the suggestion was a godsend. Blanche became genuinely interested and worked harder and more happily than she ever had done before in order to have the tiny home in perfect order for his first furlough. A heating plant and bathroom were installed, hardwood floors laid, paint and quaint wall papers put on the walls. The portrait of the Countess in her bridal finery hung over the mantel, her harpsichord stood in the corner, her bed was covered with the fine old homespun linen which she had brought from France. There was a merry little housewarming when Philip appeared, wearing his sergeant's uniform, for all Hamstead wanted to see him.

But after the last guest had departed, he lighted a fire in the wide, shallow fireplace of the big, soft-colored bedroom, and unfastened Blanche's party dress by candle-light as they stood before it. It had grown very cold outside, that still, white cold of the Connecticut Valley, and the many-paned windows were frosting over with delicate shapes. The man, looking towards them from the fire, suddenly shivered a little. They were so icy and sparkling, reflecting the frozen moonlight out there, that there was something of almost unearthly loveliness about them, something ghostly—

"Blanche," he said abruptly, "when you fixed up Carte Blanche, what did you do with those old law books that were here?"

Blanche was standing before the mirror, combing her hair. She did not even turn.

"They were so musty and shabby and dry-looking, I burned them up. Why, did you want them?"

"No. Did you burn them all?"

"Yes."

"Read any of them first?"

"No. I could tell by the looks that they were dull. Not what you and I wanted in our lovely home."

She walked across the room to him, her golden hair falling over her shoulders, her soft white dressing-gown flowing from her bare neck and arms in an unbroken line to the floor. Deliberately, she blew out the flickering candles, one after the other, and, in the dim fire-light, put her arms around his neck.

"It *is* lovely, isn't it?" she whispered.

Philip bent over her. There was something in her manner that had never been there before. Was she, too, feeling the mystery and power of the night? Had these last weeks of separation been teaching her, too—teaching her the lessons that for a time, it seemed as if he, for all his love, had failed to make clear to her? Was the dread which had been slowly growing through the spring and summer that his white star was to prove only a will-o'-the-wisp, to be taken from him after all?

"Yes, sweetheart, beautiful," he answered. "But I want you to know a story that was in one of those books you burned, just the same, if you don't already. I ought to have spoken of it to you before—"

As quietly as he could, he told her first of his reading of the legend and then of his talk with Mary about it afterwards.

"I can't pretend to explain it. But it seems to me the first Blanche didn't want to hurt any *person*, especially—that it isn't a curse in that sense—but to teach her descendants, if she could, what a terrible thing it is to be selfish. Sometimes I think it's the greatest sin in the world. Most of all, the selfishness that calls itself love. Occasionally mothers feel that kind of love for their sons, or children for their parents, or husbands for their wives—"

"You mean that is the kind that Colonel Moses felt for the Countess," said Blanche slowly, "and—and it's been so, straight through the family. That's the way mother cares for Paul. That's the way—that's the way I cared for you—once. But, oh, I don't any more!"

"That isn't the way I've cared for you," said Philip. "And do you know, there has never been any doctrine so easy for me to believe as the one of Atonement? Why, we see it verified all the time—the strong voluntarily assuming the burdens of the weak, the good voluntarily assuming the guilt of the wicked. The power comes from somewhere for them to do it. Perhaps, in this case, it's coming in some way we don't understand, through Lady Blanche to me. I'm not very strong, and I'm not very good. I don't think that for a minute. But I do love you with all my heart and soul. That—that makes more difference than anything else, I believe. That curse is never going beyond this generation, and you must tell me tonight, that you're glad—I ought to have gone to war when I first knew it was the right thing for me to do. We can't help that now. But you've got to say you're glad I'm going now—"

His arms tightened around her, his lips, meeting hers, lay for a long time against them.

"If only we had a son—"

"Whenever I think of Lady Blanche Farm," he went on, after a long silence, "I think of Mary and the mountain together—its strength and its beauty, its steadfastness and its peace. And I think of you and the brook—its freshness and fragrance and purity. It's shallow in places, it rushes into little falls, but where I found you, it widens to a deep pool, clear as crystal, a haven of refreshment and delight and—holiness. That's what you seem to me tonight—do you understand? Oh, my darling—"

CHAPTER THIRTEEN

And so the first winter of the war came to Hamstead, bringing nothing worse than preparing queer new foods made without much sugar or white flour and eating them in the kitchen, to save coal, and hanging service flags in the windows for boys who could still nearly all come home on furloughs, and knitting sleeveless sweaters while waiting for the mail to come in. The mail that brought letters from Jacqueline, nursing in a Convalescents' Home in Brittany; from David, operating in a field hospital directly behind the firing-lines; from Austin, driving his ambulance over shell-shot roads; from Paul, "somewhere in France" though not as yet, doing active fighting; from Jack and Thomas and Philip at Camp Devens—all as yet, unharmed and well. It brought, too, the first real interest in Liberty Bonds. The people in Hamstead had read about the First Loan in the papers. The second one they invested in themselves. Those who were too poor or too young to buy bonds began to buy Thrift Stamps. Moses Manning, who had always had a passion for drug-stores and counted that day lost whose low-descending sun had not seen him hanging over the counter of the one in Hamstead, and that day well-won when he could patronize the much larger one in Wallacetown, began to turn his back on all day suckers and ice-cream cones and even on chocolate sodas, in order to "get his card filled" at the post-office. He not only saved his own pennies. He made the reluctant and uncomprehending Algy save his, too.

"This here war, Algy," he said, more than once, prying a cherished coin loose from his brother's small clutching fingers, "has got to be won, if we don't never have a real feed again until it's over. But when it is, *Oh, gollies!*"

There was a ball, and a banquet, and "comfort kits" for all the boys. There were big boxfuls of angel cakes and sugared doughnuts and chocolate fudge, sent away by parcel post. There was the preparation of Christmas packages which were to vie in size and completeness with those sent from Burlington and Montpelier. There was the careful searching of the newspapers for accounts of the unsatisfactory conditions existing at Camp Devens . . .

Then, suddenly, the first blow fell.

A telegram came for Blanche.

And Sol Daniels, instead of telephoning it up to the house, as he had telephoned his chuckling messages about boxes of candy and flowers and wedding presents, so many times, wrote it down slowly with his stubby pencil, and locking up the station, walked down the road through the deep snow with it in his pocket, blowing his nose hard on his red bandana handkerchief as he went along.

To his intense relief, it was Mary, who was with her cousin a good deal in those days, who answered the knocker at Carte Blanche. Sol handed the grimy paper to her without a word as she opened the door, and cleared his throat.

"For Blanche?" asked Mary in a startled voice.

"Yes—it's a doggone shame. You better open it first, and then tell her what's in it."

"No—I want it myself, please."

Mary and Sol turned quickly. Blanche was standing on the tiny winding staircase, holding out her hand. She, too, had heard the knocker.

"I've been—been expecting it ever since Philip was home for his furlough. Take Sol in where it's warm, Mary, and give him some coffee. It was awfully kind of you, Sol, to bring it yourself."

"I'd a-rather ben licked then to a-brung it."

"I know—please."

She opened it slowly, almost carefully. It was from one of the doctors, and it was rather long. Philip had been stricken, very suddenly, with pneumonia. The case seemed to be a light one and he had preferred that she should not be told at once. But there had been an abrupt change for the worse —the entire illness had been a matter of only thirty-six hours. The doctor was obliged, with the deepest regret, to inform her . . . if she would telegraph her wishes, they would of course, be complied with insofar as possible—

The yellow sheet crackled in her hand. Every ray of color had left her face, and she leaned against the slender mahogany rail, gripping it hard. For a moment she shut her eyes, swaying, and Mary started towards her but she put out her hand as if to keep her back. Not even Mary could help her through this moment; she wanted to meet it alone. Then she came slowly down the stairs, and going to the window where the service flag hung, she took it down and stood for a long time with it in her arms, her lips quivering. At last she gathered it up, and crossing the room with it, she hung it, as if it had been an emblem of victory, over the portrait of the little French Countess. Then she faced her cousin and her old friend.

"I'll have a new one, with a gold star, in the window," she said quietly, "but that one belongs there. Can you have the express stopped at Hamstead for me, Sol?—You'll go with me, Mary, of course? Please tell Mother and Cousin Jane. I'd like to be alone a little while, I think— But I'll be ready to start in an hour."

There was no time to waste in "breaking the news gently." Mary found the two older women together and, without a single unnecessary word, told them what had happened. Violet, horribly stunned and shocked, broke into angry and rebellious grief which prostrated her completely. But when Jane had done all she could to relieve her and the frailer woman had recovered somewhat and they had taken the necessary steps to send Blanche and Mary to bring Philip home and to prepare Hamstead for its first military funeral, Jane went alone to her room and sat a long time, the tears rolling down her grim, plain face, the old candy-box tied with red ribbons which Philip had given her long before and which she had kept ever since on her bed-side table near her Bible, clasped in her hands.

"That nice, pleasant, happy boy," she said repeatedly, and added involuntarily, "and he *was* a real Christian, too, same as Mary said from the first."

Violet, when she had discarded her mourning for her husband, had laid it away in her attic with her usual exquisite neatness, and Mary, unlocking the trunk, brought down the things that Blanche needed and helped her put them on, just as she had helped her dress for her wedding, a year and a half before.

"If I had let him go when he wanted to, this wouldn't have happened."

That was the only complaint she made, the only grief which, so far, she seemed able to voice. But she said it over and over again, after she and Mary were on the train, and the door of the Pullman drawing-room had been closed, leaving them quiet and alone together.

"Hush, dear! He might have been killed in battle."

"No one else from Hamstead has been. And there'd have been some meaning—some compensation—a glory of achievement in that! This was just waste! Hundreds of boys are dying like that—when it could perfectly well have been avoided. They've been almost freezing to death in the camps all over the country."

"I know. I see how you feel. It's almost too tragic to bear. But I don't believe that anything Philip ever did was wasted, just the same."

"If Paul dies, at least it won't be this way."

"No."

"Oh, Mary, how could you let him go the way you did?

Supposing he never comes back, either—do you ever think of that?"

Did she ever think of it! Not long before, Mrs. Weston had handed her a letter that had just come from Rosalie King. She had married her floorwalker on a "hurry call" and they had had three days together before he "went across." Three days in a New York boarding house—there had been no time to prepare the little flat in Harlem. And that, she had learned, was to be all the honeymoon she would ever have. Mary, taking the letter from Mrs. Weston's limp hand, read it over twice. And she had refused "a week at some quiet place by the sea"—had denied Paul the chance of looking forward to coming back to her "that way." . . . Did she ever *think* of it!

"Yes, I think of it," she said slowly. "But I had to do what I did, just the same. Even if I'd known he was going to be killed. Paul didn't—didn't love me the way Philip loved you. And we mustn't think about him—about his not being safe. He was, you know, when your mother heard last."

"Yes—but there may be a telegram for her, too, any day. Mary—what do you think it all means? Why do the people who aren't needed, who aren't even wanted, live and live and live? While the ones like Philip—"

"Oh, I don't know—that's what I thought when Sylvia died—"

"Do you think that it's really punishment for selfishness—not just mine, but—"

"This whole war is a punishment of selfishness—and an atonement for it. Philip is—one of thousands—"

"But my part. That story coming true. And the certainty we both had that it was going to."

"I don't understand that either, of course. But I do know that some of the things we've always spoken of as 'supernatural' seem to occur much more frequently since the war, or else people are not so ashamed or so afraid to speak about them as they used to be. I believe the body and the spirit are in some way much more closely interwoven than we've realized. That's one reason why we must try so hard to make the one worthy of the other."

"I've always known they were closely interwoven in Philip. Oh, Mary, will—will he be much changed, do you think?"

He was not. He looked, indeed, so serene, so supremely happy, that Blanche, kneeling beside him, burst, for the first time, into healing tears. And the nurse who had taken care of him told her that he had suffered very little.

"It was all so quick," she said. "He simply wouldn't let us send for you, and we really didn't think it was necessary—until it was too late. He said you must be saved all the grief and care you could. He'd just had a letter—"

"He got it in time so that he could read it?" asked Blanche, with such a sudden leap of joy in her voice that Mary wondered instantly what had been in that special letter.

"Oh, yes. He was awfully happy over it, that was plain to see, and now that I've met you, Mrs. Starr, I don't wonder he wanted to save a lovely child like you from all the anxiety he could. He didn't suffer much, honestly. And just before he died—but I don't know as I ought to tell you—"

"You must—"

"Something strange happened."

"Yes," said Blanche breathlessly, looking from the nurse to Mary.

"He had been having some trouble with his breathing. He was unconscious for a little while, I thought, and delirious, off and on. Suddenly he opened his eyes and looked toward the foot of the bed, smiling as if he saw something there that pleased him. Then he turned to me and said, 'You did send for my wife, after all, didn't you?' I told him no, that we'd done just as he wanted about everything. He looked kind of puzzled and went on, 'But she's standing there with her arms stretched out, dressed all in white. She looks exactly as she did the last night we had together—*the first night I really found her.*'"

Blanche laid her cheek against the quiet hand lying on the spread.

"Go on," she said, after a moment.

"I was stupid enough to look there myself, for he kind of startled me. But of course there was nothing. So I shook my head, and said not to worry, that everything was all right. That's about all we can say, in such cases, you know. The puzzled expression faded, gradually, and he smiled again. I've had a good many patients, Mrs. Starr, but honest, I never had one with a smile like his—it went straight through you, some way—and then he spoke just as if he was talking to some-one."

"What did he say?"

"'So you've come, little Countess. But you mustn't ever come to anyone again. This must be the last time. And I'm not sorry. It's all been so perfect—so perfect, while it lasted.'— Do you know what flashed into my mind, I don't know why? There wasn't any real connection!—That line about a 'full, perfect, and sufficient sacrifice'—"

That was, blessedly, what it seemed to Blanche. Even in her first grief, she found, after all, the compensation, the "glory of achievement" that she thought she had been denied. She did not ask, she did not need, any longer, to understand. She needed only to feel, and as soon as her mental and physical exhaustion left her, to work.

She worked all the rest of the winter, and the next summer, and every woman in Hamstead worked with her. France, with its thousands of widows, was three thousand miles away, but Blanche was in their midst. Through her, they reached out and found those others—

When fall came, she was not working any longer, but the rest of Hamstead, thinking of her, worked harder than ever. For she was lying, very still and happy, in the big four-poster bed in the soft-colored chamber of Carte Blanche, with the golden, downy head of Philip Starr's son against her breast.

CHAPTER FOURTEEN

Moses and Algy Manning were coming home from school together, stopping frequently to dislodge stones from the thawing road and throw them into the brook, swollen to twice its usual size by the "spring freshet" and to gather the pussywillows growing beside it. They had, in three years grown noticeably taller and thinner, though just now they presented that chunky, shabby appearance peculiar to country children when they are well bundled up and which effectually conceals their true figures. They had also lost their golden curls, for they now went with Seth, once a month to Wallacetown for a "military haircut." Their faces, as usual, would have been improved by the ministrations of a handkerchief and a wash-cloth. But Gale Hamlin, who had been riding for some hours in his "swilomine" over roads that not infrequently caused him to strike the top of the car or skid into a ditch, leaned out of the window and hailed them with delight as he caught sight of them.

"Stop a minute, Morrison— Hello, you kids! Climb in here. Going home from school?"

"Yes," replied the two small boys together, accepting his invitation with alacrity, and seating themselves beside him without further waste of words.

"Getting along pretty well?"

"Fine," answered Moses. "Algy's in kindergarten. I'm in the second grade."

"Good for you! Can you write your name yet?"

"Write my name!" exclaimed Moses, with injured pride. "I kin write poems!"

Gale Hamlin coughed. "No, really?" he asked politely. "If you can, fame and fortune await you. Unfortunately, there are so many young gentlemen who only think they can. They can't, really."

"I'll show you," said Moses, who did not understand the greater part of this speech but felt it, on the whole, unimportant whether he did or not. Removing the cover from his dinner-pail, and depositing on the seat beside him two apple-cores, half a doughnut, a package of gum, a yard or so of twine, a jack-knife and a Second Reader, he finally pulled out a piece of blue paper on the outside of which was written in large letters, "Two Poimes. By M. Manning," and handed them to the doubting Thomas in triumph.

"Ther was a bee and—" read Gale,
"He sat on a tree and
He herd a sound
And he made a bownd
At the sound.
So that's all so call."

"Go on," said Moses, without false modesty.

"There was a workman
Who carried a can
And his name was Smiller
And he went to the miller
And sat on a piller
And thats all ther was herd
Of Mr. Smiller."

"You should try *The Atlantic Monthly*," said Gale, folding and returning the paper. "But if that isn't appreciative, there are several other magazines. I will give you a list, if you like, or I will undertake to place these for you myself, for a small commission."

"I guess so," said Moses, feeling again that he was missing the point somewhere. "I showed 'em to Mary and she laughed and told me to take 'em to school and let my teacher see 'em."

"How is Mary?"

"Well, she looks kinder peaked. Was you thinkin' of comin' to say good-bye to her?"

"Something of that sort. Why?"

"Because," replied Moses, "I wouldn't, if I was you. Thomas Gray tried it, and he wasn't suited at all. With the way she said good-bye, I mean."

"Moses and I were under the sofa, playing lion, only Mary and Thomas didn't know it," said Algy, in an illuminating aside.

"She shook hands, nice and polite, like she's taught us to do it," continued Moses. "I don't know what more was wanted. But there was something. He said so."

"Twice," volunteered Algy.

"And then he said, 'Mary, isn't there any chance for me at all?' and she said, 'No, I'm sorry, but there isn't.'"

"And Thomas," continued the faithful chorus, "said, 'Wasn't there ever any chance for anyone except Paul?' and Mary stiffened up and said, 'Paul threw his chance away.'"

"What happened next?" asked Gale, feeling very much as if he had been eavesdropping himself.

"Thomas spoke right up as if he was kinder mad. 'Well,' he said, 'are you goin' on rememberin' that all the rest of your life, 'stead of that he tried good and hard and *plenty* to *find* it again?'"

"Ah!" remarked Gale.

"And then Mary told him she couldn't discuss it with him. He was home just for a few hours, before he went to France. That was most a year ago. No one's tried it on her since."

"Suppose," said Gale, producing a crisp dollar bill, "that you boys go to Wallacetown with Morrison and have a spree? You might enjoy it and I—er—wouldn't run the risk of having any lions under the sofa while I was there!"

However unsatisfactory her farewells might be, Mary was nearly always delightful in her welcomes. She was very glad to see Gale Hamlin, and she did not attempt to disguise the fact. He told her a good deal of Boston news that pleased and interested her, while he drank the tea and ate the cookies that she brought him, before he asked her any questions, and the first ones he broached were more of a general than of a personal character.

"Hamstead is making quite a name for itself these days," he said at last, "with David Noble discovering a new anesthetic and Austin Gray winning the Croix de Guerre and even your village ne'er-do-well, Jack Weston, getting a lieutenant's commission. And—how is Mrs. Starr? I want to see her, too!"

"Oh, she's wonderful! So well, and so busy, and so happy with the baby! He's the loveliest little creature! Cousin Jane worships him, too—she's a different woman since he came! And Blanche is awfully generous about sharing him with her. Whenever she has to leave him, she gives Cousin Jane the first chance of taking care of him. Cousin Violet loves him too—more than she ever did her own children, I really think. You must see him before you go. He isn't like a Manning at all—he's the image of his father."

"I am very glad she has him. Does she have good news of her brother, too?"

"She doesn't have any."

Gale, smoking a cigarette, did not answer immediately.

"I'm sorry if I've made a stupid mistake," he said at last. "You didn't mention any bad news, the last time you were in Boston."

"No—I don't often talk about Paul."

"So I have observed," remarked Gale dryly.

Mary flared instantly. "Men are not fair to women," she said bitterly.

"I'm sorry to say that's often true. But it's no reason why women shouldn't be fair to men. Two wrongs never made a right, you know."

"Are you trying to tell me what is right for me to do?"

"I'm trying to tell you what is wrong. It would be wicked if you never married."

"*Wicked!*"

"*For you*—not for every woman."

"Why for me especially?"

"You ought to guess—remember, I've seen you in a house—how comfortable and beautiful and safe you make it. And I've seen you with men—I know how much charm you have, no matter how you try to hide it and how much power, no matter how little you choose to use it. And I've seen you with children —your patience and your wisdom and your loving kindness. Philip Starr has done wonderful things for the place—and the woman—he loved—by his death. But they're nothing to what you can do for the place and the man you may love—by your *life*—if you only will."

The girl rose suddenly and turned away from him. Gale crossed to her quickly, and put his hand on her shoulder.

"So you refused Thomas Gray?" he asked quietly.

"Yes—how did you know? There was never any question of Thomas."

"Or of me?"

"Yes, there was some question of you. I thought you knew that."

"Will—could you answer it any differently now?"

"No."

"Or ever, do you think?"

"No. I—I'm sure I never could."

"Then how are you going to answer Paul when he comes home?"

"Paul isn't ever coming home," said Mary steadily—so steadily, in fact, that a man who knew her less well than Gale Hamlin did would have been completely deceived by her tone.

"What happened, Mary?" he asked gently. "Please tell me."

"He was wounded last May," she said in a hard voice, "when the Marines first began to see active service. Not seri-

ously. The reports read 'Degree undetermined,' and for a few
weeks, while we didn't know how bad it was—Blanche took
it pretty hard. She and Paul were always very fond of each
other—more so than most brothers and sisters—though they
didn't show it much. She had had about all she could stand
already—that was before the baby came, you see. Cousin Violet had a letter, written by Paul himself in the hospital, that
came through very quickly, for a wonder, saying the wound
was just a scratch—that he'd be out again for the next 'big
scrap.'"

"Yes."

"He was. He was at Belleau Wood and Château-Thierry.
Then he was listed as 'Prisoner or Missing.' We haven't heard
since. That was nine months ago."

"Yes."

"There were very few Marines taken prisoner. I've read
somewhere that there were less than thirty, the first of September, and that those few were unconscious when they were
taken, either because they were so badly wounded, or because
they were made so, before they *could* be taken. We thought,
after the armistice was signed, we'd have some word."

"And you haven't?"

"No—not a syllable. We hope—I hope, anyway—that he was
killed. It would be much less horrible—than the other." Then
with a swift change of tone, she exclaimed, "Don't you ever
read the Casualty Lists yourself? You know what has been
happening to all the other Hamstead boys— Oh, I believe you
knew all the time, too!"

"Yes—I did. But I wanted you to tell me yourself. I've been
waiting, ever since last summer, to see if you wouldn't. I
wanted to know just how you felt about it."

"Do you know now?"

"I think I do—Mary, don't you ever bend?"

"Bend?"

"Yes—because if you don't, I'm afraid some day you're

going to break. You did, very nearly, you know, once before. You remember the old fable—

"I have been doing what I could," Gale went on, as Mary did not answer, "to locate your cousin ever since I found out the situation. I have—enough influence to make it easy for me, usually, to get information about anything I wish—"

"Oh, how kind—how very good of you!"

"But, so far, I haven't discovered anything. Now, however, I'm starting for Europe myself—almost immediately. Until now, at my age, and with my lack of training, it has seemed as if I could be most useful here. I am glad that at last there appear to be ways in which I can help over there—reconstruction, investigation—I don't need to tell you— There, my dear, there—"

He waited patiently for the storm to pass, stroking very gently the soft hair about the hidden face. He waited, it seemed to him, endlessly. For Mary was weeping with the abandonment, the utter hopelessness, that marks the ultimate despair of those strong souls whose fortitude enables them to restrain their grief until it reaches its culmination, and the shattering of whose spirit is all the more tragic because it is so sudden. Gale Hamlin's heart twisted in his breast at the sight of her unrestraint and the thought of her agony. He knew he was powerless to help her except by surrounding her with the sense of his infinite compassion, though, being human, he hoped that eventually she might reveal some consciousness of the comfort he had sought to give her, that she might, perhaps, eventually evince some sign of gratitude for it. But it was a long time before she raised her head, and as she did so, still far from composed, the door was flung unceremoniously open and Algy and Moses entered noisily, a liberal layer of molasses and chocolate added to the various other discolorations which Gale had observed on their faces a couple of hours earlier.

"The dollar's all spent," announced Moses, glancing from his sister to her caller suspiciously.

"Well," said Gale, with a slight sigh, "it lasted just about long enough. I rather wish, though, I had given you a dollar and a half!"

He turned toward the door, but Algy blocked his passage.

"Did she say good-bye to please you?" he demanded doubtfully.

Gale laughed. "To satisfy me, at all events," he said. "Will you take me over and introduce me to your new little cousin?"

Mrs. Elliott, who was "passing the afternoon" with Violet, saw him walk down the cobblestone path with a small boy on either side of him, from her point of vantage in the North Parlor window. Violet did not receive her callers in the kitchen, like Mrs. Gray. She did not consider it "select" to do so.

"Look here, Violet," called Mrs. Elliott excitedly, "if there ain't Mr. Hamlin comin' down Seth's front walk! He don't take 'no' for an answer very easy, does he?"

"No," said Violet, "and Mary doesn't say 'yes' very easily, either. I can't think what that girl's made of. She used to be always laughing and singing, but now-a-days she's so glum —except with the children—that you can hardly get a word out of her, and you can't ask her the most trivial question that she doesn't lose her temper. And she's never shown the *slightest feeling* about Paul! I should think she would have some sympathy for me, but it seems to mean nothing to her at all that my sad life is sadder than ever. I feel anyway, of course, that she is largely responsible for Paul's loss. Mary is clever, I'll say that for her, and she could have kept him here if she had only tried. I told her so, once, and what do you think she answered? That it was much better for him to lose his life than his soul!"

"Yes, she is real peculiar. Her mother was the same. She'd go a long time without hardly openin' her head, Laura Mannin' would, and then she'd up and take the bit in her teeth— like when she named Algy, and sent Mary off to school. I've always thought Mary some like her mother. But the menfolks do seem to like her—they never show much sense in their selections. Why, I never had an offer till I was most thirty!—Blanche don't seem to pindle none, does she?"

"No, she's actually *gained* since she's been nursing the baby, and she said the other day she'd never been happier in her life. I can't see what ails the girls in this generation. Rosalie King has come to visit Mrs. Weston again, and I can't see that she's changed at all. She doesn't even wear crepe—just plain black—and she says 'she should worry,' that she's 'hung on to her old job and got a raise at that' and that although she can't always buy the 'very latest' to wear, she's got a 'long way from September morn'—whatever she means by that! One of her usual vulgar expressions! And yet Mrs. Weston says she knows Rosalie thought the world of that man she married. She can't have, that's all—not in the way a woman of real refinement would have cared. Why, after Martin died, I refused all nourishment—except what was absolutely necessary, of course, to keep up my strength—and lay in a dark room for weeks and never dreamed of stirring out, even after that, except to go to church and to the cemetery. My heart was buried in the grave. I'm afraid Mary has been putting some of her queer ideas into Blanche's head, for when I asked her a little while ago if hers wasn't, she said no indeed, it was all with Philip!"

"Land! Where does she think Philip is?"

"She said in Heaven. And that Heaven was anywhere, if you could only see it."

Mrs. Elliott arose, and folded her work. "Them kind of notions give me the creeps," she said uneasily. "I must be goin'. I'm sure you'll get some let-up from all your troubles, Violet, but I'm forced to say I don't see no chance of it, with them two girls on your hands—one a widow-woman before she's twenty and the other cut and dried for an old maid! I'm glad I didn't have nothin' but a son, and him a real smart, level-headed man. He applied for exemption right off—with that

squint in his left eye, and a pindlin' family—the roads is awful
ain't they? I kinder think, though, that we're goin' to get an
early Spring. The frost has come outer the ground a good deal
today."

CHAPTER FIFTEEN

Hamstead had tossed aside its white blanket of snow, and after lying bleak and bare and brown for many weeks, had begun, gradually, to wreathe itself in scarves of delicate colors again, as it had when, three years earlier, Philip, walking through the quiet woods following the quiet brook, found Blanche beside the deep and silent pool.

Mary was sitting on top of Countess Hill, her chin resting on her hands, looking out over the meadows. It was one of those warm spring days, too clear to be described as hazy, when there is, nevertheless, a certain softness and mellowness in the atmosphere which renders everything almost divinely lovely. At the base of the hill, for miles and miles around it, lay the Connecticut Valley, green and gold, fair and fertile. Through it wound the river, sparkling blue in the sunshine. In the distance towered the mountains, some of them still capped with snow, which the sun, sinking behind the Vermont hills, on the other side, was turning to brilliant rose with its reflection. But none of the joyousness which had once flooded her being at the sight of the calm loveliness of the landscape enveloped her now. The valleys did not comfort her, the mountains gave her no strength. Mary was very tired this spring, and her weariness was enhanced by a sense of futility which bowed her down almost as much as by her sense of hopelessness. She thought of Blanche with constant self-disparagement and constant self-reproach. Blanche was doing so much now, so much that was big and splendid. Mary was doing nothing—nothing constructive, nothing that counted. And Blanche, though she had lost Philip, had had so much

love and joy before she lost him, and now she had their son;
while Mary had forfeited everything that Paul had meant to
her, and the ghost of her unconsummated love stalked constantly near her as she walked in loneliness and when she
tried to rest, it crouched beside her. She was not jealous of
her cousin. Only what *she* could do, what *she* possessed,
seemed as nothing in comparison to what Blanche did and
to what Blanche possessed. Mary was engulfed, not only by
grief, but by unfulfillment.

She sat very still, watching the changing light. Without
understanding why, and in spite of all her grief and weariness,
she felt that one of the great hours of her life had come. The
beauty and peace and promise of the country, which had
failed to console her, suddenly seemed to overcome her as no
inanimate things had ever overcome her before. She felt, like
an actual presence, the spirit of her puritan forefathers who
had turned this valley from a wilderness into a garden, who
had lived their simple faith as truly as they had professed it,
who had fought and died, when necessary, for an ideal. The
spirit of her ancestors? Was she not, she wondered precip-
itately, in the presence of something even much greater—the
spirit of the men she had known herself? She turned her head,
half-expecting to glimpse some heavenly vision, trembling—
But there was nothing to be heard, nothing to be seen, only
something wonderful to be felt. She bowed her head and
prayed.

It was a long time before she lifted it again. When she did,
Paul, bare-headed, dressed in khaki, was standing beside her.

She sprang to her feet, shaking all over, entirely unable to
speak. This man was not her cousin as she remembered him.
He was taller, thinner, paler, infinitely older and graver, all
the bloom and softness of his boyish beauty had gone. For a
moment she thought—it must be— She shut her eyes, swaying
and crying aloud, as she felt herself falling. Then suddenly
she was upheld by a strong arm, swung quickly around her

shoulder, a firm hand taking both her trembling ones in a warm and steady grasp.

"There, there," Paul was saying, as if he had been speaking to a little child, and patting her arm as he spoke. "It's all right. I didn't mean to frighten you like this. Don't, Mary. Don't cry so. Why, there is nothing to cry *about!* I'm all right. I'm *here!*"

She could not answer, she could not look up, she could not stop crying. The shock of her relief, with its violent termination of the strain of her despair, had swept away her last remnant of reserve. But Paul remained unshaken. He held her firmly and at last he bent over and rubbed his cheek against hers just as he had often done in the past.

"Can't we sit down and talk?" he asked, and drew her down beside him on the big rock, still holding her hand. Then seeing how utterly impossible it was for her to speak, he went on, "I got in on the four o'clock and walked straight up to the farm. I didn't let Mother know I was coming, for I thought, if I did, she'd have the minister, or a delegation from the D.A.R. or the Wallacetown band, or maybe all three, at the station to meet me. It never occurred to me that none of my letters from the other side telling her in a general way when to expect me, would have reached her. It ought to have, of course. The mail service has been so bad—"

"Tell me," said Mary, finding her voice at last.

"There isn't much to tell. You know what happened up to the time I was wounded. And the wound—the first one—didn't amount to anything. I was back at the front in no time. And then I was—hurt—again, before I was taken prisoner—"

"Go on."

"I was a prisoner several months, you see. I couldn't write then. Even after the armistice was signed, we weren't released right off. And then for a while, I wasn't well—"

"You mean you were starving."

"Well, I wasn't hungry, anyway!" said Paul, lightly. "But I'm all right now. And I'm *home.* You won't mind, will you, if

I don't tell you more than this, just now? We—the men who've been there—don't like to talk about it much."

"Are they true—the things we've heard about the German prisons?"

"Yes, I suppose they're true, as far as they go. I haven't read them myself, of course—" then realizing that she was trembling again from head to foot—"Look here," he said, "you mustn't take it like this. I'm all right now—honestly. Won't you say you're glad to see me? All the rest of the family has. Mother had hysterics, of course, but she was awfully glad, just the same. I couldn't help knowing that. And the kids swarmed all over me—it was great. Moses wanted me to show him how to kill Germans. We had a gory conflict on the front lawn and ended up with refreshments—a dozen packages of Peters' chocolate. And I kissed Cousin Jane on both cheeks, same as they do in France and she never quoted a thing at me. And Blanche—well of course Blanche and I both broke down a little. I couldn't help it, when I saw the poor little thing in her black dress, with that corking little chap in her arms. I didn't know, you see, about Philip—or little Philip. She let me take him in my arms, and he grinned at me—I didn't know before babies could grin as young as that! Friendly little beggar, isn't he? He clutched my finger with his hand when I stuck it out—great muscle, I should say, for his age! And he's so awfully pink and solid, isn't he? Well, then I went to the barn and found Cousin Seth milking. We've got some fine new stock, haven't we, since I went away? And we must get some more—I've all kinds of plans. I told him I'd be out to help him with the cows in the morning. He said I might find you up here."

The children had swarmed over him—he had found her father milking—the same little, commonplace things that had always bound them together! And now they were sitting on the old boulder, hand in hand, as they had done when they used to rest after picking blackberries—

"You're not strong," she said with a great effort, "and you've had this—this hard climb to reach me. I'm sorry."

For a moment Paul did not answer. Then he took the hand he held, and laid it against his lips.

"No, I'm not strong," he said huskily. "I know that. And I have had to climb—to climb a long way—to reach you. But I'm not sorry. I'm glad."

"Paul! You know I didn't mean it that way!"

"I know you didn't, dear, but I did. For it's true. But please tell me—aren't you glad I'm here, at last?"

"Yes," said Mary, very low indeed.

"Then, may I tell you—anything I want to?"

"Yes," she said again, lower still.

"Do you remember what you said to me—that day in Boston —about what loving really means?"

"Yes," said Mary a third time, though it was only a whisper now.

"Well—that's the way I love you. You were right—I didn't then. But I have learned to, since. A soldier isn't fighting all the time, you know. There are hours and hours—crossing on the transports—doing guard duty—and in—in prisons—when he can't do anything but think and think and think. And all I thought about was you. At first it was just a dreadful physical longing and raging grief because I hadn't got what I wanted. I'd felt so hopeful—so sure—that day I went to you in Boston, that I'd get my week—but all the time the things you'd said about how you loved me, kept hammering themselves into my stupid brain, making me see more and more clearly that, even then, I didn't care for you like that, or it wouldn't be my own disappointment I'd be thinking most about. It would be the way I'd treated you, from the time we were youngsters—taking all your loveliness and goodness for granted—and then throwing it away—"

He bowed his head. Mary put her arm around his shoulder.

"Don't, Paul," she said softly. "Don't speak of that, or even remember it any more. I've forgotten all about it."

"I haven't," he said between his teeth. "I never shall, I never can, unless—I can atone for it. I began to forget that I had lost you—and to wonder how—"

"How you could get me back?"

"Not even that—till afterwards. Only how I could make things up to you. Whether there was anything on earth I could do. You know it always takes me a long time to get things straight. The first thing I thought of wasn't the right one. I felt that perhaps if I did some dare-devil stunt, and got promoted, and won a medal, it would make you feel proud of me. But after a while I saw it would take something a good deal bigger than that to make me worthy to come to you and say I was sorry, whether you were proud of me or not. That I'd got to change *inside*. I'd reached that point by the time I got to prison, and then it was weeks and weeks before I could think at all. But when I could—it was what kept me clean—and sane—whatever they did to me—"

"What did they do to you?" asked Mary, brokenly.

"I'll tell you that some other time," he said briefly. "The rest I have to tell you now. I've waited a long time to do it. It's the only thing I've got to tell you. I haven't come home a 'hero' at all. I haven't any medals, I haven't even been promoted. I wasn't a bad soldier—there weren't any bad soldiers, that I saw—but I wasn't an especially good one—that is, there were so many lots better, that— But I *tried*. The war didn't 'make me over,' either. That is, I suppose it helped most of us a little, but it didn't 'create a new man of me' as the novels say— It was you, all the time—before the war, and during it, and now, most of all—that made me want to be a better man. And now I've come home to settle down in Hamstead, just a plain, ordinary farmer—not even a first-class one. It isn't in me to be anything better than that. But I love you—

"And there wasn't any 'pretty little French peasant,'" he said, after a long pause. And in that one simple sentence, Mary understood, though she could not answer, all that he was trying to tell her.

He misinterpreted her silence. He kissed her hand again, dropped it gently, and rose.

"It was wrong of me, maybe, to say all this to you—so soon," he said. "But I saw Mr. Hamlin just before I sailed for home. It seems he'd been trying to locate me, unsuccessfully, for a long time. He told me—that—that you hadn't changed your mind about him, and that he knew you never would. He told me, too, that he knew you'd refused Thomas Gray, though he only laughed when I asked him how he found that out. So I should have told you sooner or later, anyway, and I couldn't seem to make it later! Sylvia sent me a message once, by David—I didn't get it until after she died—telling me never to stop fighting for you, if I had to die fighting. I thought for a while, that I was going to die fighting—then in that German prison, I was afraid for a while that I wasn't even going to die *fighting*—that it was to be starving, rotting. Now I know I'm not going to die at all—not for a good many years, I mean— but I'm going to *live* fighting. Do you remember, when I was a little chap, how I used to stand in the front yard, whenever I wanted to see you, and simply holler, 'Come over, Mary, come over'? *And you always came!* I'm going right on calling for you now, until I've made you come again! I'll go down now, and see Mother—I promised her that I wouldn't be long. But we'll see each other, some way, right along, won't we, Mary?"

He was half-way down the hill when he felt her touch on his arm. He had not even heard her on the soft pine needles, coming up behind him. He turned quickly.

"What is it, dear?" he asked. "Is anything the matter?"

"No—yes—I haven't been honest."

"You haven't been honest!" echoed Paul in astonishment. "Why you're as honest as daylight! What do you mean?"

"When you went away—that day in Boston that you spoke of—"

"I'm afraid I don't understand."

"You said, 'You don't care that way any more.' And I—I asked you if you thought it was likely."

"Yes, dear. I knew it wasn't, of course, just as I told you. I knew it was impossible."

"I let you go away thinking that. I was afraid to let you think anything else, because I knew, though you 'wanted' me so much, you didn't really love me—then. I—I hoped you would, some day. It's nearly killed me ever since to think if you never came back, you wouldn't know—to remember that I didn't even kiss you good-bye. For I wasn't honest. I mean— it *was* possible—I mean, I did—"

Paul stood for a stupefied moment, staring at her. Then he cried aloud with joy.

"You care *now!*" he exclaimed. "*You have cared all the time!*" Then, as he tried, very gently, to take down the trembling hands with which she had suddenly covered her face, he realized that his own were shaking too.

"Mary," he said brokenly, "I won't, if you really don't want me to. But if you *do*—you won't make me wait any longer, will you? I've starved for *you*, too—"

"You won't ever have to starve again," said Mary with a great sob, and took down her hands herself.

Of course they went back up the hill, after a few minutes, and, sitting down again on the old boulder, told each other— with the frequent interruptions usual in such cases—all the things that had gone unsaid for two years.

"Did you ever find your bracelet?" Paul asked, at last.

"Of course. I've worn it ever since."

"Worn it?" he said, glancing down at her bare wrists.

"Yes, here."

She took his hand and laid it over her breast, and he could feel the little trinket, tucked under her dress, straight over her heart.

"I wish—I wish I'd known it was there, all this time. Would you take it out and let me put it on, now—where everyone can see it?" And when she had done so, he added huskily, "I'll have to get you a ring now, too, won't I?"

"Oh, no, please don't! This is my engagement present—I've always felt that way about it—I shouldn't want anything else!"

"I didn't say an *engagement* ring, did I? Lord! After I made such a mess of it once, you don't think I'm going to be *engaged* again, do you? I meant a *wedding* ring! How glad I am we don't live in New Hampshire where they have that inconvenient law about waiting five days after you apply for a license—"

"I'm glad, too," said Mary.

It was very late that evening, when Jane Manning, remembering that she had not "set back her chairs" against a possible storm—though there was not a cloud in the sky—went out on her piazza to "make sure everything was all right" for the night. Seth and the small boys had been there to supper with her, as nothing had been seen of Mary since early afternoon, and Moses and Algy always "cluttered things up considerable." Nothing had been seen of the newly-returned Paul for some hours, either—a fact over which Jane had tartly advised the fluttering Violet that she "didn't think she needed to worry none."

Jane stopped in the middle of her pleasant task and stood stock-still. The moon shone very clear and bright and on the wide granite door-step of her cousin's house opposite, she could see two persons—a man and a girl—standing very close together, their arms around each other. Then the man bent his head, and it was a long, long time before he lifted it again.

"Good night, sweetheart," she heard him say at last, and then saw him turn and come down the walk, his young face lighted with a radiance that did not seem to come wholly from the moon.

"Great Glory!" ejaculated Cousin Jane aloud, and without conscious profanity.

Paul heard her, stopped for a minute, and then walked rapidly toward her.

"Is that you, Cousin Jane," he called, "fixing up the piazza? Here, let me help you!" When complete order was restored, he blocked her entrance into the house for a minute, standing with his back against the door.

"Mary is going to marry me," he said, his voice ringing like a hallelujah, "right off. We're going away for a few weeks— till I get stronger, and she gets rested—to some quiet place by the sea. We've never, either of us, been to stay by the sea— And then we're coming back here to Lady Blanche Farm— coming home *together*. Oh, God, how happy I am!"

"I dunno's I blame ye," said Cousin Jane.

His mother's house was dark, and Paul did not feel sorry. In the morning, of course, she must be told, and Mary's father —but tonight!— However, when he noticed a faint light shining from the upper windows of Carte Blanche, he went close to the little building and called—

"Blanche! May I come up?"

"Yes—I've been hoping you would."

She was sitting in a low rocker, nursing her baby. He crossed the room softly, and sat down on a footstool beside her.

"Mary's going to marry you," she whispered.

"How did you know?"

"How could I help knowing, looking at you? I've seen that look in a man's face before."

"Oh, you poor little thing!"

"Hush! Don't speak that way! I don't feel like that about it! And I'm so thankful—so happy—that I've seen it in yours, too."

They sat for a long time together, after the sleeping baby had been laid back in his cradle. And meanwhile, the woman who had never had a lover went slowly up to her room, and sitting down in the old chair, slightly moved the box tied with red ribbons that lay on her bed-side table and took up the Bible that lay near it, to read in it, as always, before she went to bed. It fell open at the last chapter of Proverbs:

"Who can find a virtuous woman," read Cousin Jane, "for her price is far above rubies. The heart of her husband can safely trust in her— She will do him good and not evil all the days of her life— She seeketh wool and flax, and worketh willingly with her hands— She riseth also while it is yet dark, and giveth meat to her household— She reacheth forth her hands to the needy— Strength and honor are her clothing, and she shall rejoice in years to come— She looketh well to the ways of her household and eateth not of the bread of idleness. Her children arise up also and call her blessed. Her husband also, and he praiseth her. Give her the fruit of her hands and let her own works praise her in the gates."

The Bible slipped from her lap, unnoticed, and Cousin Jane sat for a long time with happy tears rolling down her cheeks.

"I suppose that woman in the Bible may have had her faults," she said aloud at last, "same as Mary has. I shouldn't be a mite surprised if she had a tongue and a temper and a backbone and didn't forgive and forget very easy, though Solomon doesn't mention it. Seems to me there's some likeness between the two. Mary's ben faithful to the trust her dead mother left her and denied herself to do for her father and her little brothers. She's ben strong and wise enough to say 'no' to a rich man she didn't love and turn the poor, weak, shiftless boy she did love into a fine creature that needn't be afraid to look his Maker in the face. And she hasn't shirked or nagged or complained or boasted while she's ben doin' it. She's kept herself sweet and lovely through it all. There may be better jobs for women to do than things like them, but if there is, I never heard of 'em, any more than Solomon seems to hev. We've ben worryin' considerable lately about the little Countess's curse, and I don't deny that it seems the Almighty gives strange powers to human bein's sometimes, even after they're dead. But for all that, I guess His blessin' is more powerful than anything else, jus' the same. And I guess, too, that as long as Mary stays here, that blessin' will rest on Lady Blanche Farm in the future, same as it has in the past."

Queen Anne's Lace

TO MY THREE SONS
HENRY, JOHN AND FRANCIS
WITH THEIR MOTHER'S LOVE

Contents

Prologue:

The Finished Design

Clarence Hathaway, who, as every one knew, was to be the next Ambassador to Great Britain if the President-elect had his way—and the President-elect was accustomed to having his way—emerged from the impressive doorway of his residence, and stood for a moment, slender cane hanging from slender wrist, sleek silk hat and spotless gray gloves in slender hand, sleek dark hair—slightly crisp, slightly gray, over the temples—uncovered, looking up and down Sixteenth Street, before he signified his consciousness that a gleaming Hispano Suiza waited before him, a chauffeur in maroon livery at the wheel, a footman similarly attired holding open the door.

He could hardly be blamed for pausing to survey the scene before him with satisfaction. It was a perfect spring morning of sparkling freshness, and a magnolia tree, top-heavy with bursting buds, gleamed pink against the grillwork of the basement windows; a small, vividly colored bird, perched on its topmost branch, was singing as if he would slit his throat; crocuses were pushing their way through the delicate green of the tiny lawn, fringed with daffodils, in front of the house; and from the marble balcony on the second story an American flag flew stiff in the breeze and shone in the sun. From the neighboring embassies and legations other flags were flying—French, Spanish, Swiss, Cuban, Polish—how glorious they looked, the tri-color, the crown, the cross, the bars, displayed in honor of the Stars and Stripes! Gravely, Hathaway saluted; there was nothing artificial, nothing self-conscious about the gesture; he had the elegance, the poise, the graciousness that made such an act seem natural and lovely; the chauffeur and footman, shaken from their stiff correctness, faced the American flag and saluted in their turn; Hathaway turning to them smiling.

"A fine day for the President, Jarvis—a great day for all of us!"

"Yes, indeed, sir; Squires and I 'ave been remarking it."

Hathaway nodded, smiled again, paused again, set one slim foot, shod in patent leather topped by a pearl-gray spat, on the step of his car.

"The Shoreham, Jarvis. We're stopping there for the Attorney-General-designate and his mother, and Governor and Mrs. Hildreth."

"Yes, sir. Very good, sir. It's a great honor for us to be taking them, as Squires and I 'ave been remarking, sir."

The dignitaries in question were already standing on the steps of the Shoreham as the Hispano Suiza slid to a silent stop in front of the hotel. Hathaway alighted and greeted them in turn.

"Good morning, Mrs. Griffin. Well, how does it feel to be the mother of a Cabinet-member? You've not kept Roy in very good order, but from now on—you must allow him no wild habits, mind! Mabel, you look as fresh as a May morning—or a March morning, I ought to say! *What* a day! Made to order, if one ever was! Made in Heaven, Anne would say— bless her heart!"

"I wonder how she is this morning?" The new Attorney-General, a thin, timid-looking man, quite evidently under the domination of his belligerent mother, spoke anxiously, and with a slight lisp, which his evident nervousness intensified.

"Oh, she's finely," announced Mabel Hildreth, settling herself comfortably in the corner of the car. Both the Governor and his wife bore unmistakable signs of long-continued rural prosperity, over which a slight veneer of recent official importance lay somewhat insecurely; but there was something very likeable about their rather round and florid faces, and Mrs. Hildreth retained traces of a girlish bloom which, though somewhat faded, must once have been very lovely. "Look out, George," she went on, "you'll get your coat-tails terribly crushed if you sit that way—and my, but you look hot already. Why can't you be like Clarence here? He never turns a hair, no matter what he has to dress up in— Well, Anne called me up herself at eight o'clock this morning—she says she's going to telephone her friends herself *always*—well, of course she won't—can't—but it's nice she feels that way about it. Her dresses are here *at last*— Mr. Goldenburg brought them over from New York, himself, on the midnight. And Anne says they're perfectly lovely."

"I haven't heard what she was to wear," interposed Mrs. Griffin eagerly.

"Why, *lace* of course! Venetian point, so old that it's fawn-color, combined with tan georgette and silk, this morning. Rose-point and white satin this evening. Neal wouldn't hear of anything less—"

"I don't quite see—" began Mrs. Griffin but the lively Mabel, who had the habit of interruption, broke in upon her.

"Oh, look at those beautiful horses—aren't they perfectly matched! And they're fawn-color, too! Are they—are they something special, Clarence?"

"Yes, indeed. It's the cavalry from Fort Meyer that acts as escort to the delegation going to the White House to meet the President."

"The President!" exclaimed the Griffins and the Hildreths together; and they sat quietly, awed to unaccustomed silence, which Hathaway made no attempt to break, as the car swung around the Treasury Building and sped down the cleared width of Pennsylvania Avenue, banked on either side with good-natured, orderly crowds. The official permit, displayed on the windshield, took it swiftly past the saluting guards at the Capitol; and here the host, as he guided his guests through the revolving doors, issued a few directions.

"You fellows join your respective colleagues now in the waiting-rooms—you're for the floor of the Senate, as of course you know. I'll take the ladies to the gallery, see them safely to the platform where they'll rejoin you after the exercises in the Chamber, and then find them after the President's address and look out for them during the parade. See *you* again for luncheon at the White House!"

The dingy old Chamber was filling fast as Hathaway and the two ladies took their places in the gallery. The balconies were, indeed, overcrowded already, only one vacant seat, in the front row of the Senators' gallery, apparently remaining unoccupied. On one side of this sat a lovely young girl, her golden curls uncovered; on the other a slim boy with ruffled hair and a wide, disarming smile, which he was bestowing impartially in response to greetings from every direction. They both caught sight of Hathaway, and waved to him enthusiastically, a welcome which he acknowledged with evident affection.

"Nancy and Junior are missing nothing," he whispered to Mabel Hildreth. "I shouldn't be surprised if they had been here for an hour already!"

Mabel nodded, her eyes on the Vice-President. This functionary was presiding for the last time, while final appointments were being made, Senators who were retaining their seats delivering eulogies upon Senators who had failed of reëlection, and the vanquished replying to these grandiose tributes. Hathaway called his companions' attention to the large clock under the press gallery and directly over the Vice-President's seat; and as they looked at it, they saw that its hands, which had stood at one minute of twelve, were turned back until these pointed at half-past eleven again.

"The new Congress begins at twelve," he told them, "by that clock. It doesn't matter what time it is outside. You may see the hands set back three times. This session can't end without all these little frills and furbelows."

At last the gavel descended. The Democratic Senators surged across the aisle, and took their places on the east side of the Chamber, with the Republican Senators and the Senators-elect, the visiting Governors, and the Cabinet members-designate. Mabel Hildreth, assisted by Hathaway, discovered her husband; Mrs. Griffin, without assistance, discovered her son. It was a supreme moment. The members of the House of Representatives, filing in, took their places behind the Senators on the east side, and behind the members of the retiring Cabinet and the Diplomatic Corps, gorgeous in gold braid, gold lace, gold medals, on the west side. The judges of the Supreme Court rustled forward, their black robes, voluminous as hoop skirts, billowing about them and the ranking military and naval officers who were placed near them. All these dignitaries made an impressive showing; but towards none of them did either of the two ladies allow their fascinated gaze to wander. Governor Hildreth and the Attorney-General-designate were, as far as they were concerned, the only two men on that crowded floor.

The Speaker of the House and the Vice-President-elect were, in turn, escorted to seats beside the Vice-President. The applause, which, though technically forbidden had rung out again and again unchecked, was quickly, voluntarily hushed; then it resounded again, echoing and reëchoing.

The President-elect had entered the Chamber, accompanied by an escort of three Senators and three Congressmen, and had taken his place in front of the raised platform where the Vice-President sat. And, when he had done so, he lifted his eyes to the Senators' gallery, just as a lady, with a soft full cloak partially covering a dress of heavy deep-cream lace, came down the aisle and took her place in the vacant seat between the golden-haired girl and the shaggy-haired boy. For a moment she sat with her head bent, her drooping hat with its delicate plumes concealing her face. ("She is praying," Hathaway said to himself, choking a little.) Then she looked up, and across the Chamber, meeting the President's eyes; seemed to steady herself; and, putting her arms around her children, rose with them to accept the tribute of applause which rocked the room. It came from every side; from the Senators' gallery and the Diplomatic gallery and the Press gallery; from Cabinet and Court and Congressmen. Not until she raised her ungloved right hand, with a gentle gesture which at one and the same time acknowledged and checked the outburst, did the tumult lessen. Then she gathered the folds of her cloak around her, and with complete composure, grace, and dignity, reseated herself. She had smiled, bowing, in every direction, she was still smiling—a smile very like her son's in its frankness, ingenuousness and charm, although a little more restrained; but, somehow, her eyes did not seem for an instant to have left the President's face.

"Neal told me that when he took his oath of office as Senator," Hathaway whispered, in a voice that shook, "he was almost overcome, when he looked up and saw Anne sitting in the gallery and—and found he could go on, after all. After that, he never came into the Chamber without instinctively looking up to see if she were here. He did it to-day—did you notice? . . . No woman ever had such a tribute in the Senate before. I wonder whether any ever will again."

His companions were only half listening to him. It did not matter. It did not matter, either, that the retiring Vice-President was making one of the most remarkable speeches that had ever been delivered in the Chamber, or that the new Vice-President, having been duly sworn in, was trying in vain to re-create the impression which his predecessor had made; that a message calling the Senate to special executive session was being read; that new Senators, repeating the same oath of office as the Vice-President, were "taking their seats." The President's own speech was the next thing that mattered; and after a long time—an eternity it seemed to Hathaway— suddenly, the Senate was adjourned, and the occupants of the galleries, hurrying to the doors, were rushing through the corridors and down the staircases. Steering his charges towards the stage, temporarily erected over the east steps of the Capitol, where the President was to take his oath and make his address, he turned them over to an officer, with hasty instructions that Mrs. Griffin should be taken to her place beside her son, and Mrs. Hildreth to her place beside her husband. Then he directed his own steps to the open space directly in front of the platform which had been roped off for the specially invited guests who had been in the Senate Chamber, but who did not have seats on the stage.

For the second time that day he paused and stood contemplating the scene before him, almost oblivious of the crowd that surged about him, before he took his seat. Far beyond the reserved space where he stood, over the park extending between the Capitol and the Congressional Library, was massed the waiting multitude, silent, calm, expectant. The wind which had whipped the embassy flags to tautness earlier in the day had died down; and the Stars and Stripes, standing between the Corinthian columns of the Capitol's façade, fell in quiet folds, as the rich draperies of some royal room might have fallen. The temporary stage had been designed by a master-mind, and executed by a master-hand; its harmony with the architecture of the Capitol was complete. Corinthian columns, replicas of those behind it, supported it; and on either side of them rose enormous vases, filled with scarlet carnations and snowy lilies. The national coat of arms, laurel-wreathed, surmounted the platform; and looped about it were long festoons of laurel, to which were fastened laurel-wreathed shields. The platform was crowded, and the sun shone full upon it; a shaft of this fell as if straight from heaven, upon the President's lifted face, as he emerged from the mass behind him, and stood revealed between the white columns, beside the black-robed justice.

"Anne will say that was another omen!" the thought flashed through Hathaway's mind, and instantly, as if by telepathy, he heard the man beside him saying, "Lord Almighty! *Did* you see that sun?" Hathaway glanced at the speaker—a stout, matter-of-fact looking person, certainly not the sort given to superstition. Then he looked up at the lady in fawn-color. She was sitting very close to the President now, the folds of her cloak falling softly about her slim form, her earnest eyes fixed on his face, as they had been in the Senate Chamber. He had taken the oath, the Justice had stepped back, and the President had begun his speech. He was talking about transient policies and about permanent peace, about the constitution and the World Court, about law and order, and economy and freedom. This was sane, able, conservative,— what had been expected of him. Gradually, a greater earnestness, a greater power, crept into his words; his strangely youthful, vibrant face became beautified, it glowed as if from some inner light; the impassioned eloquence which had first made him famous had never been so lambent before. He was speaking about America, about her heritage, about her future, about her place on earth. He visioned and revealed his country, personified as a steadfast figure, with never-failing courage and never-faltering faith, standing tranquil and mighty in the midst of dangers, or moving serenely and powerfully forward, a leader of enlightenment in a sorrow-stricken world.

"Lord Almighty!" exclaimed the stout person sitting beside Hathaway again, "I've always been patriotic, but no one ever made me feel this way about America before. I'll say we're going to have a great President—one of the greatest. He talks about the United States as if it were *real*, a person a—a woman. Like a man might talk about some one he was in love with—" Hathaway turned towards him.

"It is real," he said, "to the President. That's why he makes it seem real to you and me. You're right—he's making a great speech, one that will live. And the person who made all that real to him is his wife."

"Lord Almighty!" exclaimed the stout person for the third time. "You don't say so!" He leaned eagerly forward, as if fearing that he might lose a single one of the syllables which fell, clear as crystal, from the President's lips. He sat, breathless with admiration, mopping tears of honest emotion from his eyes, until the last sentence had been spoken, until after one lingering look towards the people beneath him, the President had turned, and with the lady in fawn-color beside him, had disappeared from the platform. Then the stranger spoke to Hathaway again.

"I'm from the West," he said, a trifle apologetically, instead of in the proud tones with which the average Westerner proclaims this fact, "so I'm not acquainted much here. My nephew—he's in Congress—got me this seat. I'll thank him to my dying day. Lord Almighty! What a speech! What a *man!* I hope you'll excuse me for asking, but from the way you spoke—do you know the President?"

"Yes," said Hathaway quietly, "I know him rather well. I'm—if you'll excuse me—on my way to lunch at the White House now, and I must find my motor and some friends of ours whom I've promised to take there with me after the parade."

The Westerner's chagrin at losing his newly found acquaintance was tempered by his excitement at the evident importance of this slim, sleek-haired, "dudish" personage. (Later, when the account of Clarence Hathaway's appointment to the Court of St. James, accompanied by his picture, was printed in every metropolitan daily in the United States, the Westerner's pride doubled and redoubled as he told his "home town" that he "knew the Ambassador.") He laid a detaining hand on Hathaway's sleeve.

"I don't want to keep you, of course," he said, apologetically, "but I want you should tell me just a word, before you go, about—about his wife. You said—"

Hathaway smiled, and shook his head. But he stopped for a moment before he moved away, the crowd closing in on him as he went.

"I couldn't tell you about her in a week," he said. "I couldn't tell you if I stayed here all day, trying. Nobody could tell the real story, as it ought to be told, about the part a woman has in her husband's career, from very humble beginning through long, hard, drab, uneventful years, and on to ultimate supremacy. It's a part very different from what's popularly supposed, a part not only misunderstood, but underestimated. Nobody could do such a story justice, though dozens of able biographies will be written about the President; but somebody ought to try. Not only because then the American people might appreciate—partly at least—their President's wife. But also because hundreds of women, who are longing to help their husbands, but feeling that they are failing to do so, would find consolation and encouragement in the story of Anne Chamberlain."

"Why don't you write the story yourself?" persisted the Westerner. "Or, if you can't do it yourself—I presume you're a busy man—why don't you find some one else who will? Some one you could trust to make a try at it, anyways. Lord Almighty, man! Don't fade away from me like that!"

For the Westerner found that he was speaking to the crowd in general, and not to one person in particular. He was also being looked at curiously, and he himself looked about in some bewilderment. He had agreed to meet his nephew in the latter's room at the House Office Building; from there they were going to see the parade together. It was late already and he ought to hurry.

"Just the same," he said to himself, as he scurried, panting, across the park, "I hope I put an idea into that slick-looking fellow's head, and I believe I *did*. I believe he heard me after *all*. I believe he'll get somebody to write that story!"

PART ONE

The Bobbin and the Thread

CHAPTER ONE

"Anne—Anne—where be ye?"

It was the third time the shrill, insistent call had penetrated to the hot little attic room. Twice the girl who heard it, unfastening her crumpled print dress and pulling out hairpins, had disregarded it. Now she jerked open the door and answered.

"I'm upstairs—undressing."

"Hev ye fed the hens?"

"Yes."

"Did ye fasten the gate after ye?"

"Yes."

"Hev ye put them clothes ter soak I told ye couldn't wait till next week ter be washed?"

"Yes."

"Well, don't ferget I want ye should wring 'em out the first thing in the mornin' and iron 'em after dinner."

"I won't."

"I ben lookin' at the string beans. I think there's enough ter start cannin'. Couldn't ye come down an' pick a few afore it gits dark?"

"Oh, *Mummer!* It's late now! I've barely time to get ready before George'll be here! I'll pick them to-morrow night."

There was a silence fraught with disapproval.

"Won't that do?"

"I s'pose so. Seems to me 'twould be a good thing to can 'em when they're fit, but I know that don't count none in your jedgement when you want to go to a dance."

Mrs. Chamberlain retreated with a sound of shuffling footsteps. She wore carpet-slippers in the evening to rest her feet, putting them on in the afternoon about the same time that she took her hair out of "crimpers"! Anne had seldom seen her mother tidy at both ends at once.

She bit her lip, and went on with her undressing, tossing her coarse cotton chemise, petticoat and stockings after her dress on the pine bedstead, covered with a dingy patchwork quilt, that was crowded under the eaves, and kicking her tattered shoes under it. The cheap little alarm clock, ticking away on the pine bureau, warned her that she must hurry. She snatched up the broken comb that lay beside it, and drew it through her tangled mass of yellow curls, with swift, impatient strokes, so that the snarls hissed and broke. Then, pulling it tautly away from her small ears into a tight flat knot on the top of her head, she fastened it securely, and filled the heavy, cracked white basin from the heavy, cracked white pitcher.

A sculptor would have used her as a model for a bathing nymph, with a delighted prayer of thanksgiving to Providence for giving him so perfect a subject. For she was slim and straight and supple, as exquisitely white-skinned as she was finely formed, except for the tan on soft forearm and softer neck. But to herself, she was simply a hot, tired girl, hastening to make herself clean and cool to go out with the young farmer whose place adjoined her father's, and whom both had long taken for granted she would eventually marry. She would have liked to feel, naturally, that she could make herself beautiful as well as clean and cool; but that seemed almost too much to hope. However, she did her best. She dusted herself with talcum powder from a highly colored can stamped in an "oriental design," and rubbed her neck with "rose perfume" from a still more highly colored bottle, decorated with a crimson flower which bloomed brightly on one side, and a pink ribbon which was tied around its neck. These toilet perquisites had been purchased, at the total expenditure of fifty cents which she could ill-afford to squander, on her latest trip to Wallacetown, and she knew they must be reserved for great occasions only, if she were to justify her extravagance to herself. But this really did seem a sufficiently great occasion. Then she put on her "best underclothes," made of lansdowne, embroidered—by herself—with sprays of forget-me-nots, and trimmed with crocheted lace which she had made herself; her one pair of silk stockings, originally white, but grown yellow from many washings, and carefully darned; two of the darns—one on the instep and one just above the heel—showed, but that could not be helped; black patent leather slippers, somewhat cracked and shapeless, came next; then a pink silk muslin dress, with a knot of black velvet on one shoulder, and a black velvet sash, made from an old "sacque" of her mother's, carefully steamed, pressed, and recut—she had read in the "Symposium of Styles"—which her friend Mabel Buck loaned her from time to time, since she could not afford to subscribe to a fashion magazine herself—that "a touch of black was always very Frenchy." Last of all, she loosened and rewound her hair, and added another knot of velvet to its shining coils.

"I'm glad I've got some flowers to wear," she said to herself, as she surveyed the results of her efforts in the small, blurred glass over the washstand. "I *will* have a *real* flower garden some day, even if Pupper and Mummer do think it's a waste of time and space. I know the sweet-peas are almost a failure, because I got them in so late, but I'm sure there are enough so that I can manage. I haven't picked them for three days on purpose."

She was down the steep narrow staircase in one swift rush of color and motion, across the kitchen, out of the rusty screen door half hanging on its hinges, and punctured by holes whose uneven edges curled shaggily back, over the scraggly yard to the still more scraggly garden. The one line of scanty sweet-pea vines, growing close beside the flourishing string-beans, was completely stripped of blossoms. Anne, holding her skirts carefully around her, dashed from the garden to the narrow front porch, where, their labors for the day ended, her parents and her two small brothers, Sol and Sam, were taking their ease in unwashed relaxation.

"Who picked my sweet-peas?" she demanded accusingly. "You all knew I was saving them for to-night, and they're gone."

"I picked 'em," announced Mrs. Chamberlain, rocking heavily. "I took 'em down to the cemetery an' put 'em on your Aunt Sarah's grave. They're settin' there now, in a preserve jar, side of some nasturtiums and candy-tuft Ella Wiley brought. They look real handsome. It's just three years ago today sense your Aunt Sarah passed away. I presume ye've ben so took up thinkin' about this dance ye're goin' to, ye ain't thought of the dead. Maybe ye'd like to go down and take 'em off the grave," she ended with supreme scorn.

"I would, if I had time," the girl burst out fiercely. "You knew how much I wanted them—and they're mine, anyway! I bought the seeds, and planted them, and I've tended them. They won't do Aunt Sarah any good, and they were all I had!"

Her mother remained entirely unmoved; clearly, the matter of the beans still rankled; but her father glimpsed something of the tragedy of her disappointment.

"Shucks, Nannie—what does a few flowers matter? Ye're the greatest hand to take on, over nothin'. If ye hev to hev flowers, there's some roses left still on that bush down the lane by the medder. They're kinder gone by, but I guess they'd answer. 'Twouldn't take ye long to run down there and see."

"Sol, you go! I'll get my skirts all dusty!"

"Hold 'em up an' ye won't. I can't pick flowers, roses leastwise. The pesky thorns stick inter me so, I get to hollerin' an' let go, an'—"

"Sam, won't *you?*"

Sam gave a deep groan, reminiscent of too much supper. "Them cucumbers I et don't seem to lay jest right," he objected graphically, "or mebbe 'twas the blueberry pie. The crust wuz kinder heavy. Yer pies ain't nothin' extra, Nan. I'd rather set still for a spell than go weed-chasin'. I ben workin' hard all day, anyway. I—"

"All right! You just wait till I ever help you with anything again! Either of you! You'll see—"

She was gone, a blur of pink and gold, past the chicken-yard, with its sagging wire, and the foul pig pen with its rotten trough; through the creaking gate to the malodorous barnyard, where half a dozen lean "grade" cows regarded her with dumb resentment. Then down the lane to the meadow where the grass, a poor crop which should have been mown a fortnight since, was still standing, sparse and dry. The rose bush clambered, prickly and parched, over a decaying fence. It was, as her father had said, not far. But Anne hated the white powder of dust on her shiny black shoes, the tiny beads of perspiration which, with her haste, gathered on her face; most of all she hated the laziness and indifference on the part of her family which had made her quest necessary.

"They might do something to help *me*, once in a while! But they never do, never! When I do all I can for them! It isn't fair—"

In her anger, she attacked the unoffending rosebush with more vehemence than caution, and pricked her finger. She whipped it swiftly to her mouth. But she was not quick enough; a drop of blood had fallen on her bodice, just above the waist-line.

"Now I've got to get something to cover *that*—and there aren't enough roses— Oh, what *shall* I do?"

"Why don't you take some of that white flower growin' on the other side of the fence, in the medder, and put it with yer roses? It's kinder large—that'll cover up yer spot."

Anne wheeled about. George Hildreth, who was to take her to the party, was standing beside her. His blond hair lay wet and sleek away from its uneven part, and his round, red, and rather flat face shone with soap and scrubbing. His blue eyes, usually somewhat vacant in expression, beamed in anticipation. He was dressed in his best, a garnet pin in his spotted tie, a monogram buckle on his belt, chocolate-colored shoes. Evidently he had arrived during her absence, and on being informed where she had gone, had welcomed the opportunity of greeting her apart from the gaze of the assembled family, and had followed her. Unconsciously, she had spoken aloud, and he had heard her.

"You look great anyway. I don't see why you should worry about flowers."

"Do you honestly think so?"

"Well, I guess I do!"

There was not the slightest doubt of the earnestness of George's admiration. Anne veered away from a more tangible proof of it.

"But those flowers *would* be pretty. Could you climb through the barbed wire and get me some, or would you hurt your clothes?"

George hesitated, torn between his desire to serve, and his consciousness of the twenty-nine-fifty, earned by the sweat of his brow, which he had so recently expended on his new "pepper and salt" suit—"the latest in collegiate apparel"—as he had been assured when he had bought it in Wallacetown, and which he was now wearing for the first time.

"Would it take too long to go round by the gate? We could let down the bars and go round inter the medder. We could both go."

"Oh, George, you're just like all the others! You never can do anything *quick!*"

"Now, Anne, don't get mad. I only thought—"

"Oh, I know what you thought—the same as I know what Pupper and Mummer and Sol and Sam think! You've got about as much action between you as Aunt Sarah!"

"Why, she's been dead three years—"

"I *know* it! That's what I *meant!* You can't even see *that!* —come on then, we'll go round by the gate."

"Honest, Anne"—

"For Heaven's sake, *come on!* Do you want to get to that party before they start playing 'Home Sweet Home'?"

"I don't care, Anne, so long as I can be with you."

He put his arm about her. She did not actually shake it off, but her lack of mental response to his caress was so marked that a physical withdrawal would really have been less chilling.

"Well, I do! I want to dance every dance! And then there won't be half enough!"

"I know you like to dance, Anne, and you know I always want you should have a good time, but—"

"Help me pick some of these flowers, then, so we can start."

For a moment they pulled away, silently, at the white blossoms. Then Anne laughed—laughed so joyously that George realized, with a bounding heart, that her vexation must be passing.

"Do you know the name of these flowers?"

"No—I never heard. I've seen 'em always, growin' in medders, an' along roadsides where the crops an' soil ain't none too good. They're kind of a pest, I s'pose—but they're pretty. They don't seem to belong, someway, with the dust and weeds and rocks. They're kinder like lace."

"That's what they're called—Queen Anne's Lace. It's funny, isn't it, my name, I mean, and wearing them, and finding them in a place like this, and not having anything else pretty—"

She held a spray up against her face, smiling as the soft white blossoms brushed her cheeks. Then she broke off the stems, and twisting them in the thorny roses, thrust them into her belt.

"I don't see nawthin' funny about it," said George stolidly, "but they look nice, the way you've fixed 'em. You're awful sweet, Anne—couldn't you give me a kiss before we start for the dance?"

CHAPTER TWO

George did not get his kiss, but as he had not expected it, he was not unduly disappointed. Anne was always "offish." She hated to be "pawed." She flung away from him impatiently, and started, on a run, back up the lane. George followed at a more leisurely pace, chewing a piece of grass as he went— at this rate, they would never be married—he was making no progress at all. And he wanted to marry Anne, very much. He grew warm all over, at the very thought of it. But he never seemed to be able to think of the move that would help his cause along.

When they were seated in his new top-buggy, with its slim, rubber-tired wheels, and were actually on their way into Hamstead, Anne relaxed a little, and they fell into casual and friendly conversation, without reference to his lover-like advances, which he made no further effort to resume. But with dogged perseverance he sought to win his point by other means.

"Are you pretty well through haying?" Anne asked noncommittally.

"Yes, Saturday night'll see it done."

"You've had good luck, haven't you?"

"Fine. And the oats and corn's comin' along great, too. I don't know as I ever had a better year. And my creamery check keeps a-mountin' and mountin' straight along."

Anne made no direct response to this boastful statement, with its hidden thrust at her father's lack of prosperity in dismal contrast to her suitor's abundance.

"I'm thinkin' some of throwin' out a bay-winder in the

dinin' room an' puttin' in a furnace. An' a bathroom. There's space for one beside the parlor-chamber."

"That would be nice, wouldn't it? Why don't you unbrick the fireplaces, too, and throw away the air-tights? Every one's doin' it down in Hamstead."

"Well, mebbe I will. It ain't a bad idea. The house needs paperin' an' paintin' too. It'll look real good when I get it all fixed up. I cal'late I could get all them improvements done by late fall."

Again Anne gave no sign that she had drawn the obvious conclusion.

"You aren't honestly figurin' on teachin' another winter, are ye?"

"I think I better. It's hard to get girls to come to these district schools 'out back.' And ten dollars a week helps out a good deal."

"It helps out yer *family*. I don't see that *you* get much outer it."

"Well, *somebody's* got to see that the taxes are paid, and that we don't starve, at least."

"Yes, and that somebody'll be you, just as long as you'll do it. There are two good husky young 'uns, and an able-bodied man an' woman just settin' back and lettin' ye."

"George! Don't you dare criticize my family!"

"I shall, too—if yer so dead set on teachin', ye could keep on after we was married. You could do all the housework there is in my house with one hand tied behind ye, convenient like it all is. And you could hev all the money ye earned to spend on yeself—clothes an' books an' a pianner."

He had scored at last. He saw it, and pressed his advantage.

"Ye've always wanted ter travel. We could take a real nice trip this fall. I could plan the work so's I could git away for a spell after the crops is all in, an' before the cows begin to freshen." George was suddenly conscious of a slight conversational indiscretion, and blushed; but Anne, apparently, had not noticed it. She was thinking about the trip, and George went on eagerly, "We could go to Niagara Falls, or Montreal, or Boston."

"Oh, George, everybody goes to those places. Everybody that can afford to."

"Well, where do you want to go?"

"To New York. And—and Washington."

George gulped with surprise. But he was game.

"All right. To New York and Washington."

"Especially Washington."

"Why on earth—"

"I don't know. But I'm crazy to see it. I think I'd like to live there."

"For Heaven's sake, Nan! Why you haven't a chance in the world, any more'n I have, of ever livin' anywhere but in West Hamstead."

"I know it. But I wish I had."

George saw his rosy dreams vanishing into thin mist. He sought to recapture them.

"But it'd be worth somethin' ter go. Mebbe we could go more'n once."

"Well—"

"Nan!"

"Let's talk about something else for a while."

"Oh, Nan, please—"

He leaned forward, laying his hand earnestly on her knee, trying to look into her eyes. She put her own hand over his, gave it a friendly pressure, and then shook her pink skirt free of it.

"I can't, George," she said with equal earnestness. "Honestly, I can't. I know how much you'd try to do for me, and I do like you. But it isn't enough."

"It's a lot more'n you've got now."

"I know—when I said it wasn't enough I didn't mean that I wouldn't be lots more comfortable than I've ever been before. I know I would. I meant that I somehow couldn't look at things the way you do. We're at swords' points half the time. And then I don't care enough."

"You just said you liked me."

"I do. But I don't love you. That is, I don't believe I do. I don't like to have you touch me, and I certainly never wanted to touch you. If a girl's in love with a man, I think she does."

George blushed again. Anne seemed to have less mental than physical reserve.

"That's a long way from feeling you'd be glad to marry a man. And it's further still from feeling as if you'd die if you couldn't."

"It—it would all come out all right, you'd see."

"It wouldn't. I couldn't make you happy."

"I'll take that risk."

"And I couldn't be happy myself. *I won't* take the risk."

"Won't you think it over some more?" asked George miserably. "You know how it's been with me, ever since we was kids. I'm a good provider. You shouldn't never lack nothin'. And I'd be a kind husband. We *would* be happy. If ye can't say yes, don't say no neither. Not for a while, any- ways. That's not askin' much of ye."

Anne hesitated. She had no wish to be needlessly unkind, and she was really fond of George. He was, as he said, not asking for much.

"All right," she said at length, "I won't say 'no' yet, if you won't pester me. And if you won't talk about it any more to-night— Have you heard what there's going to be for music at the dance?"

George settled back in the buggy with a sigh of mingled relief and triumph, slapping the reins over the horse's back as he did so.

"The Wallacetown Band's goin' to play," he replied. "Four pieces. I bet it'll be slick. I hear there's a number comin' down from there to go to it. Roy Griffin has got company. A feller he knew at college, named Neal Conrad, is visitin' him, so they're gettin' up a party. Conrad's come up from Hinsboro where he lives, in one of these new-fangled horseless carriages. I don't think much of them."

"Don't you? Where have you seen one?"

"I ain't seen one. But I've heard tell."

"In the postoffice, sitting around the air-tight with a lot of other mossbacks who never saw one either, I suppose," said Anne scornfully. "Oh, George! Don't you *see*? It's just as I said! We never look at things the same way! *I* believe that horseless carriages are going to be a great success, and revolutionize transportation."

"I do wish you wouldn't use all the long words there are in the dictionary like that. I can't keep track of what you really mean."

"I mean I think they're going to make a great change in travel, and work, and pleasure. I wish I had a chance to go out in one."

"Well," said George sarcastically, "mebbe Neal Conrad will ask ye to. Roy and him are comin' down to the dance in his. That's what I started to tell you."

The words were hardly out of his mouth before he repented them. He had put an idea in Anne's head that might much better have been left out of it. Of course, it was not probable that this city-dude would take any notice of her, but it was possible. He recalled that she knew Roy Griffin, just slightly, of course, but still well enough for him to ask her to dance. And Roy Griffin might introduce his friend, and then—Anne was so pretty, and so smart, and such a good dancer—he inwardly cursed his stupidity, and they drove on in silence.

The "ball" had not been in progress half an hour before his worst fears were realized. At first everything went well. The town hall in Hamstead was looking its best, decorated with festoons of colored crêpe paper, the electric-light globes hanging from the pressed-steel ceiling shielded with large crêpe paper flowers; big bunches of sweet-peas had been placed on the window sills, and on the table where the pressed-glass punch-bowl filled with grape-juice-lemonade and surrounded with paper cups was standing. The Wallacetown Band was grouped about the square piano near the stage, opposite the lemonade table, and was already beginning to "tune up" as they entered. George surveyed the scene with satisfaction. He had paid for their tickets, fifty cents apiece, while Anne withdrew to leave her knitted shawl in the dressing-room, and exchange a few joyous, whispered confidences with her best friend, Mabel Buck, who was waiting for her there; when she returned, he sat down beside her, to scrawl his initials at frequent intervals over her "program" with the small tasseled pencil attached to it. The first and last dances were his by unwritten law, of course, because he was her escort; but he wanted to secure as many as possible in between these before the Hamstead fellows, who had come to know her when she was going there to High School, butted in. He had to hurry. David Noble and Austin Gray were already crossing the floor in their direction, and others would follow close upon their heels.

"Don't take too many," whispered Anne, who was watching developments quite as carefully as he was, but with other ends in view, "you don't want to make the whole town think we're engaged."

"Why, of course I do! Every one knows we're keeping company! Now, Anne—"

"If you say another word about it to-night, I won't dance with you *at all*— Hello, Austin, hello, David, I'm awfully glad to see you— Yes, I've got most of them free. George, do give me back that program. Goodness, you've written your name all over it. Have you an eraser?"

"No," said George doggedly, not deigning so much as a nod towards the intruders.

"Then I'll have to get another program."

"I've an extra one," cheerfully volunteered Austin's younger brother, Thomas, who had joined the group. "That's right, let's start all over again. I want the Schottisch, Anne, there's no one dances it so good as you. Both numbers that are Schottisches, one before the intermission and one afterwards. And the Portland Fancy. And the second waltz— Hello, Roy."

"Hello yourself. Hello, Anne."

"Oh, Roy, I'm ever so glad to see you! It's ages since you've been down."

"I know. But I've been awfully busy. Say, what have you got for a feller?"

"There doesn't seem to be much left but a 'Paul Jones.'"

"Shucks! You'll get whistled away from me in about two seconds! Well, I'll take that, and how about the first extra?"

"Fine."

"I've got a friend here, I want him to meet you."

"I'd love to."

"I'll get him right away—"

But the Wallacetown Band had begun to play the strains of the opening waltz. Even Anne's independence of spirit did not permit her to question George's right to that, without an instant's delay. She rose, shaking down her skirts, and thrusting her program into her sash, slipped into his arms. But she smiled back at the deserted group over her shoulder. She was perfectly satisfied. Roy, she knew, would not forget.

CHAPTER THREE

The second dance was the "Paul Jones," and Roy came promptly to Anne's side as soon as the music for it began. Roy was not especially popular, either in Hamstead or in Wallacetown, where he was well known and to West Hamstead—"out back"—he never went, so, by repute, he was not popular there, but branded as "stuck up." He had gone to Harvard, and had graduated from the Law School there as well as completing his academic course with considerable success. He had spent a summer in Europe, and part of a winter in California. He was an only child, and had inherited a comfortable fortune from his father, a prosperous hardware dealer, who had been immensely proud of him, and had wanted him to have "advantages." It was owing to his father's death that he had returned to Wallacetown, and settled there to practice, in order that his mother, who was too old to be uprooted from her native element, need not be left alone. He was a good son, and a good citizen, and he was rapidly proving himself to be a good lawyer. But he was insignificant-looking, "pindling" the neighbors had always called him—slightly built and anemic, his glasses, shielding his near-sighted eyes, always hanging half way down over his nose. He lisped a little. Anne liked him, because he lent her books, and talked with her about the glimpses of the great world which he had had. And he liked Anne, recognizing her beauty and brains and spirit. But she did not stir his senses, and he felt himself slightly above her, though he was careful—more careful than he was toward many other persons—not to let her see this. The Chamberlains were a "shiftless lot" and the thrifty Griffins looked down upon all such. It did not occur to them that good could come out of Nazareth.

It was known in the village that Roy had made fashionable friends while he was away at college, but they seldom visited him, largely—though this was not known—because he seldom invited them. When they did come, it was only for a night or two, and he generally took them "up to the mountains" on a driving trip, so Wallacetown saw nothing of them. He lived quietly along from year to year, alone with his mother, who did all the housework, exquisitely and precisely. His law-office was in the ell of their house; by means of this arrangement Mrs. Griffin could always be sure that it was in perfect order, and that the clients were respectable.

Into this well-ordered household, Neal Conrad burst without warning. He was "motoring through" to see some wealthy clients of his own, who were spending the summer in the mountains, and "simply had to see good old Roy." The terrified horses who skitted wildly to one side of the dusty road at his approach were not more taken aback by his sudden appearance than were the Griffins. But when they recovered from the first shock of his unheralded arrival, and the further shock of the discovery that he intended to spend several days with them, they accepted his presence with a mild joy and a satisfaction that was by no means mild. Neal "had a way with him," and he "was making a name for himself." This important combination was difficult to resist; after he had gone, it would be agreeable to refer to him, casually but frequently, in conversation with the neighbors.

Roy had meant to tell Anne something about his guest as they twirled about together; but the whistle blew for the forming of the ring before they had had time to exchange a dozen words, and they immediately lost sight of each other in the maze of the "grand right and left." When the whistle blew for the second time, Anne found herself facing a stranger; sensed, instinctively, that it must be *the* stranger; and was caught up swiftly and swung into a quick-step without the exchange of a word.

It was only a minute, of course, before the man spoke to her. But in that minute she became crowdingly conscious of a number of strange sensations. He was so startlingly different from any of the men she knew. His hair-cut was different, and his collar, and his tie, the shape of his blue serge coat, the texture of his spotless white trousers. He had a square jaw and square shoulders; and he held her so easily, yet so firmly—so closely. He did not seem in the least concerned because they had never met, or at a loss to know how to talk to her.

"What fun this kind of a dance is! Gets every one acquainted, the very first thing—I'm Neal Conrad, a friend of Roy Griffin's—I'm visiting him."

"I—I thought you must be Neal Conrad."

"So you'd heard about me in Hamstead? Well, I *must* be getting famous!" They laughed together, and Neal's firm hold became still a little closer as he turned her around.

"I've known Roy a long time. He promised to introduce you to me."

"Well, I should hope so! I'd be terribly disappointed if he didn't."

"But there wasn't time before the party began," Anne went on, completing her sentence as she had intended before this astonishing person interrupted her.

"We must make up for lost time now then—darn it! There goes that whistle!"

"You said this kind of a dance was great fun!" exclaimed Anne, laughing again.

"Well, I've changed my mind. It's a darned poor kind of a dance. We were just getting nicely started—but I'll see you later."

The grand right and left had already begun again. They took their places in it tardily, and Anne, at least, self-consciously. It was accounted nothing short of a crime to hold it

up, and she knew it. George, as she approached him, showed
a face as black as a thunder-cloud. But her own conscience
ceased to trouble her when she saw that he was guilty of
trying to cheat, by going rapidly until he reached her, and
then signaling for the whistle. She quickened her own pace,
and sped by him without a glance. When the "Paul Jones"
finally ended, she was dancing with David Noble. She admitted that she was thirsty and turned with him to the lemonade table.

Neal Conrad meanwhile had sought out his host without
delay, and taken him impatiently aside.

"Who's that girl I danced with the first time the whistle
blew? I didn't even have time to get her name."

"How should I know? I wasn't watching you."

"Well, she said she'd known you a long time and that you
had promised to present me. I wish you'd hurry up and do
it."

"I've known all the girls here a long time, and I've promised
all of them that I'd introduce you to them. You're THE EVENT
of the evening."

"This girl," continued Neal, not in the least discouraged,
"had on an awful pink dress trimmed with black velvet bows,
and she'd been using cheap perfumery. But she danced like a
featherweight angel, and she was a raving, tearing beauty.
You don't often see a blonde with any pep, but she had it.
Now, do you know whom I mean?"

"I've known whom you meant all along," lisped Roy, enjoying his little joke. "It's Anne Chamberlain. She's over there
by the table now, drinking lemonade with David Noble."

"Come on," said Neal briefly.

The necessary formalities consumed very little time. At the
end of them, declining David's invitation to join in their refreshment, Neal asked to see Anne's program.

"I'm awfully sorry. It's all filled."

"Nonsense!"

"It is, really," she said, blushing. "Ask David."

"Anne's program is always filled," her partner corroborated.

"But I wish it wasn't," she added, blushing more deeply still.

There was not the slightest doubt of her sincerity. Neal regarded her with amusement.

"What shall we do about it?" he asked.

"I don't know."

"Well, I do. I'm going to ask the band to add two more extras. And they'll both be mine. Don't forget."

"I shan't," said Anne ecstatically. "But do you think the band will be willing to play them?"

"I think so. In fact, I'm perfectly sure of it. Then—what do you usually do during the intermission?"

"Why—I wait for it to be over."

"Of course. But where?"

"Right here," she replied with growing bewilderment.

"The worst place you could think of. Why don't you come and sit it out with me in my motor?"

"*Where?*"

"In my motor. The horseless carriage, you know."

Anne hesitated. Such a suggestion had certainly never been made in Hamstead before, because it was the first time that any one had stopped there with a horseless carriage. Therefore she had no precedent for either accepting or declining the invitation. But she knew perfectly well that local etiquette demanded she should refuse.

"Fine," said Neal heartily, quite as if she had given him a swiftly affirmative answer. "I'll come for you. Now I must go and speak to the band."

The first of the extras, which, without the slightest apparent difficulty, he succeeded in persuading the band to interpolate, came just before the intermission. It was a waltz —"The Beautiful Blue Danube." Anne had never heard it before, and when she asked Neal its name, he looked at her again with unconcealed amusement as he told her. It was then that she first noticed his eyes—gray-brown, almost yellow in certain lights, flecked with black, merry and warm and flashing, and at the same time oddly penetrating.

"It was written by quite a famous Austrian composer— Strauss. The best thing he ever did. Listen to it, don't talk, and *dance* it. If you've never waltzed to it before, you don't know what dancing can be."

She had never known before what dancing could be! That was true enough, whatever the music was, far truer than he guessed. Or did he guess? She hoped he did not—feared he did—then longed to tell him so herself. But she was speechless. A silence no less insidious than the sensuous strains of the singing melody bound her. She could not break it, not even when, at the last lingering bars, his encircling arm tightened for an instant and then relaxed its hold, and she felt his fingers on her bare elbow, guiding her lightly.

"Out this way. To the left, under those maple trees. Ought you to have brought a wrap?"

"No."

"Let me help you. The seat is rather high."

(What was the magic in those strong, white hands, so different from any hands that had ever touched her before?)

"Do you mind if I smoke?"

"No."

"Perhaps you'll join me?"

"Oh, no!"

"That wasn't fair. I knew you wouldn't. I only wanted to hear you say it."

"Why?"

"I don't know. But I like your voice. Where did you learn to use it so well?"

"I never learned at all. I've just kept trying— I've thought about it, I mean, and practiced by myself. And I love beautiful English. But I've never heard much."

"Where did you go to school?"

"In West Hamstead, at the district school until I was old

enough to go to High School. I teach the district school my-self now."

"And you went to High School—"

"Here in Hamstead. I lived with Mummer's Aunt Sarah. She was an old lady, a cripple. She was awfully good to me. She let me come and live with her and work for my board and go to school. If she hadn't I'd have had to go out as hired help when I was thirteen."

"Are—are your parents dead?"

"Oh, no. But they've never seemed to prosper. Pupper's had hard luck always, and Mummer isn't strong." Anne hesi-tated a moment, and then continued, in a burst of confidence, "I'm afraid you won't say anything about loving to hear me talk again, after hearing me call them Mummer and Pupper. But I did when I was a little girl, and when I learned that I ought to say Mamma and Papa, they wouldn't let me change. They thought I was trying to put on airs. I guess Roy Griffin is the only person around here who calls his mother 'Mamma.'"

"Did you think of 'Father' and 'Mother'?"

"Yes—but they didn't like that either."

"I see—so you've never been away from Hamstead?"

"Well, of course I go to Wallacetown. On errands. And once in a while to a show. And I've been down the valley as far as the state line once. That's the only time I was ever on a train."

"Wouldn't you like to go further away than that?"

"Wouldn't I like to? What do you suppose?"

"Well, I suppose you would. So why don't you? Why don't you let me come and take you for a nice long drive up through the mountains in my automobile?"

Anne was speechless. It was impossible—and yet it had hap-pened. For the first time in nearly an hour, she remembered the existence of George. And only because it would be such a satisfaction to tell him that his jeering prediction had come true. Then her heart smote her. George would be hurt, terribly hurt, by the mere knowledge that the invitation had been extended. If she accepted it, he would be stricken.

"I could come for you right after breakfast," Neal went on, "then we could stop in Wallacetown and pick up Mrs. Griffin and Roy. We could have lunch at some hotel. We could go a long way in a day, you've no idea. Then I'd bring you back in the evening."

"Oh, I can't, I can't!"

Neal flung away his cigarette, and looked at her curiously in the moonlight. There was real anguish in her voice.

"Well, don't take it that way, even if you can't. But why can't you?"

"You have no idea how much work there is for me to do at home. Mummer didn't like it to-night because I came away without starting the beans for canning. And there's extra washing to do this week."

"We could go on Sunday."

"*On Sunday?*"

"Yes, why not?"

"I don't believe you understand our ways. We never go anywhere on Sunday."

"Well, couldn't you, for once?"

"No—even if I thought it was right, I have to play the organ in church and teach my Sunday-school class, and—"

"Wouldn't somebody else do that for you, just once?"

"No one ever has."

"That's no sign no one ever would. You might ask."

She tried to shake herself free from the lure of his suggestion.

"I—George wouldn't like it at all if I did."

"Who is George?"

"George Hildreth. He lives on the next farm to ours."

"I see. Are you engaged to him?"

"No, but—"

"But he wants you to be?"

"Yes. I've known him for years. He brought me here to-night."

"Three cheers for George!" said Neal heartily. "I don't believe you really intend to marry him, though, do you?"

"No, but—"

"Then wouldn't it be a real kindness, in the end, to let him find that out right away?"

"Perhaps, but—"

"Do you know how many times you've said 'but' to me to-night?"

"No, but—"

They both laughed. It seemed, somehow, very easy for Anne to laugh with Neal Conrad. And in the course of her laugh she recovered herself somewhat.

"I may as well tell you. I couldn't possibly go with you to one of those big hotels. I haven't anything to wear."

She was afraid, then, that he was going to laugh at her instead of with her. But he did nothing of the sort. He regarded her with less amusement than before, and something very like tenderness.

"You don't need to dress up, you know. Haven't you a simple little serge suit of some sort? It's cool, motoring."

"No."

"And you couldn't get one?"

"No, I couldn't afford to buy one. And anyway, I wouldn't know what to buy. I wouldn't know what was suitable."

Neal saw that he was facing real heartbreak, frankly confessed. He veered away from it with consummate tact.

"Well, we could take a picnic lunch and eat it by the roadside. Then you could wear anything you happen to have. What you'd wear to church, as long as we're going on a Sunday. How would that do?"

"I don't believe it would do at all."

"Why not?"

"It just wouldn't."

A scraping and booming sound began to float through the

open windows of the town hall. Clearly, the band was preparing to recommence its ministrations. Neal's time was growing short. He leaned over, and took Anne's hand, which
somehow she could not seem to withdraw, and spoke to her
very earnestly.

"Look here—you're not refusing because you think I'm trying to be fresh, asking you to do this when I'd never met you
before?"

"No-o-o."

"For I'm not. If you'd rather, we won't say anything more
about the ride until I've called on you several times, and all
that. This is Thursday. I could come twice before Sunday,
anyway. To-morrow evening and Saturday evening. You're
willing I should come to call, aren't you?"

"Y-e-e-s."

"The only trouble is, I can only stay here a few days. I'm on
my vacation, but it's got to be a pretty short one. I'm a lawyer,
you know, in Hinsboro. Roy and I were classmates in college,
and through the law-school. We roomed together one year.
He'll tell you, or your family, anything you'd like to know
about me. I'm doing pretty well—quite well. But this is the
first vacation I've ever taken, and I can't afford to leave my
office too long now. I mustn't take any chances. I've worked
too hard, building up my practice, to let it slide. You see that,
don't you?"

"Yes."

"And before I go away, I'd like to see something of you—a
good deal of you."

Anne's heart had bounded from her fluttering breast to her
throat. She could not answer him. Inside the hall, the leader
of the band was beginning to call the numbers of the Portland Fancy. Thomas Gray would be hunting for her, and
George—

"Won't you please say you'll take that drive?"

It was no use. She could not struggle against his insistence.

She could not struggle against her own longing. Somehow she found her voice.

"All right," she said breathlessly. It was barely more than a whisper, but Neal, hearing it, knew that she would not change her mind. "Yes, I'll go."

CHAPTER FOUR

The motoring party took place, not without violent opposition from more quarters than one.

In the first place, neither Mrs. Griffin nor Roy was in the least enthusiastic about it. Neal broached the subject to his friend on the way home from the dance, and Roy objected to it with more vigor than Neal would have supposed him capable of displaying in regard to any subject.

"You asked Anne Chamberlain to go up to the mountains with you! Good Heavens, Neal, you don't know anything about the girl at all!"

"Well, suppose you tell me something."

"She comes from one of the most worthless families in the whole town."

"Well, she's come a long way then. You don't call *her* worthless, do you?"

"No, I rather like Anne."

"Good! I like her very much; and she's darned attractive."

"You must have seen plenty of good-looking girls."

"I have. And plenty of bright girls. And plenty of girls with lots of go to them. But I never saw one that combined all those qualities so thoroughly in one and the same person. I got her to tell me a little about herself. She said her father had had hard luck, and her mother wasn't strong."

"Hard luck! the kind of hard luck that comes from never doing any hard work! His farm is going to wrack and ruin, it's mortgaged, and he's head over heels in debt besides. His barns have never been painted, and it must be twenty years since his house has. As for Anne's mother being delicate—well, she weighs about three hundred and fifty pounds, and she may have heart disease or kidney trouble. I shouldn't be at all surprised. If Anne hadn't worked her fingers to the bone and taught school besides these last two years, I don't know how they'd have lived. There are two little brothers that have to be fed and covered—you couldn't call them clothed."

"And you think a girl with that much spunk isn't worth knowing?"

Roy stared at his friend with growing astonishment. Neal had not only been swiftly hit. He had been hit hard.

"I didn't say that she wasn't worth knowing. But—why, she doesn't even know how to dress!"

"She knows that she doesn't know. And that being the case, she'll learn. Give her time. She can't be much over twenty."

"She isn't quite that."

"Then you just wait and see what she'll look like by the time she's thirty! You don't object if I at least *ask* your mother to go with us?"

"You can ask her. But I know she'll refuse."

"Surely she wouldn't expect me to insult the girl by inviting her to go off on an all-day trip with me without a chaperon!"

"Good Lord, Neal! You don't need to invite her at all."

"But I have. And she's accepted."

"Then you both ought to be willing to take the consequences."

"Look here, Roy, I thought you were a friend of mine. You're not acting much like one."

Roy felt a pang of contrition. He was a gentle creature.

"I'm sorry, Neal. I shouldn't have spoken as I did. Anne's a nice girl. Every one admits that. I'd be as sorry as any one to see her get into trouble."

"It's inconceivable that she should get into trouble," said Neal icily.

"Yes, of course. What I meant was—go ahead and ask Mother. I'll say what I can to her, too."

"Thank you," said Neal, still coldly.

Because of his repentant spirit, Roy said even more to his mother than he had intended. But in spite of this intercession, Neal found her adamant when he first approached her.

"I couldn't think of it, Neal. It would make talk, going on a Sunday."

"It's the only day the poor girl *can* go. She works like a dog all the rest of the time."

"And I don't know her at all. It wouldn't seem natural starting off that way with a stranger."

"Why, I should think you'd like to get acquainted with her. She and Roy are such good friends."

Roy's mother looked at her guest for a moment with bewilderment, and then with growing terror. What was he suggesting? That her precious child, the only companion of her declining years—*Roy*—and one of *those Chamberlains!* It was unthinkable!

"I'm trying to cut him out. I thought perhaps you wouldn't mind. But of course—"

Neal went into his bedroom and shut the door carefully behind him. He stood looking at the neat bed with its starched, frilled, pillow-shams and stiff white spread, at the picture of the funeral wreath hanging above it, and the woven dog with the blue ribbon around its neck on the rug near by, and laughed. All is fair in love and war. He knew that he had won. When he emerged, Mrs. Griffin accosted him, and asked what he would like to take along for a lunch. She could make a veal-loaf, and she was quite a hand at an angel cake.

Anne, meanwhile, was having difficulties, too. She decided that it would be wiser to take the bull by the horns, and tell George about the invitation at once. They were no sooner settled in the rubber-tired buggy on their way back over the hills than she broached the subject.

"George," she said, "do you remember what you said to me on the way in? About Neal Conrad asking me to go out with him in his horseless carriage? Well, he has."

George gasped and then sputtered.

"The fresh city guy! I hope you give him all that wuz comin' to him."

"I told him I'd be pleased to go. You suggested it yourself! Why should I think you'd mind, after that?"

"You knew I was only jokin'."

"You weren't joking. You were jeering. Trying to get even with me because I'd said you were behind the times."

"Are you goin' just to get even with *me?*"

It would have been welcome tidings, she knew, if she had said she was. But she was too honest.

"Partly—a little. But mostly because I want to. I've never been to the mountains."

"I'll take you to the mountains."

"You've had plenty of chances to ask me, and you never did. It's too late now."

"Are you goin' off all alone with this feller?"

"Of course not. Mrs. Griffin and Roy are going too."

"Wal, you went outside an' set with him quite a spell, I noticed. Did he kiss you?"

"Of course not. He's a gentleman."

"He's a man," said George darkly.

"I think you're awfully vulgar and—and insulting. I don't believe he even thought of such a thing."

"You know darned well he did."

"Well, then, it's all the more credit to him because he didn't do it! It's more than you would have done, with the same chance!"

"You ain't comparin' me an' him, are you?"

"I am not. There's no comparison possible."

They were actually quarreling. The evening on which George had counted so much was turning out worse than a failure.

"I think you've acted real mean," he mumbled.

"I don't care if you do. If you say another word, finding fault, I'll jump out of this buggy and *walk* home!"

She meant what she said, and George knew it. There was

nothing to do but relapse into sullen silence. Not another word was spoken during the six-mile drive. They even parted without saying good-night.

It was after two when Anne slipped into bed. An hour later before she fell asleep. But she was up again at five, and by seven the "extra wash" was on the line, and she had started picking the beans. While they were cooking, she ironed. And when the dinner dishes were dried and stacked away, she asked her father if she might take the team and drive to Wallacetown.

"Land sakes, Anne, can't you never set still? I sh'd think you'd be glad to lay down an' take a nap, after bein' out all night, ef you've done up all the work yer ma wanted you sh'd do."

"I need to do some errands."

"I was kinder thinkin' of mowin' the medder this afternoon."

"Oh, Pupper, you *know* you weren't! It's no kind of a hayday!"

"I s'pose you think you know more 'bout farmin' then I do. That's just like a woman—wal, go ahead, ef yer so set on it."

She escaped before he could change his mind, without even waiting to put on a fresh dress. She could only pray that neither the Griffins nor Neal Conrad would see her in Wallacetown. It was half-past one already, and it would take her until nearly three to reach Wallacetown. The bank closed at that hour, and the bank was her first objective. She reached it barely in time, and presented herself at the cashier's window.

"I want to draw some money out of my savings-bank account," she said breathlessly.

The cashier, who had known her a long time, looked at her dumbfounded.

"You don't mean to say you're going to cut into that money your Aunt Sarah left you?" he asked without stirring.

"That's exactly what I mean. I want fifty dollars. If I don't spend it all, I'll bring part of it back."

"Why, Anne Chamberlain, you don't mean to tell me that you're going to take it out and *spend* it! When you haven't but three hundred altogether, counting interest."

"Oh, Tad, please hurry!"

Still protesting, he counted the notes into her hand—five crisp, new bills. She had never seen so much money, at once, in all her life before. She tucked it into her shabby little purse, thrilling at the crackling sound which it made. Then she sped down the street to Mr. Goldenburg's store, stopping to look into the window as she reached it. The display consisted mostly of hamburg edging and seersucker, which was being sold by the yard, at a reduction. But back of these attractive wares, three headless "dummies" stood, draped with white muslin dresses, and above them ran the legend, "Special Bargain Sale. Marked down to $9.98."

A white muslin dress had not been included in her calculations. But, as she looked at these, she suddenly saw herself clad in one, when Neal came to call that evening and the next —if he really did come. It was the kind of thing a girl ought to wear, under such circumstances, she saw instinctively, sheer and snowy; that the material was coarse, and the lace trimming coarser, did not matter. The crude color of her pink dress, the heaviness of the black bows that adorned it, seemed hopelessly hideous to her all at once. If she bought a white muslin dress, it would mean buying white shoes and stockings, too, and the right kind of a slip, but she felt too reckless to care—if necessary, she could draw out more money. She unlatched the shop-door, and walked in. By good luck, she encountered the proprietor himself, a kindly Jew who had been in Wallacetown only a few years, and who had prospered there.

"Vel, vel, if it ain't my liddle frent Anne Chamberlain! Vat can I do for you, my dear?"

"Oh, Mr. Goldenburg, I want to buy such a lot of things!

I've just drawn fifty dollars out of the bank, and I'm afraid it isn't enough. If I run short, will you trust me until I can go back and draw some more? The bank's closed for the day now."

"Vel, now, I tink I could. But you shouldn't take out your money, yust to spend, like this. You goin' to get married, *hein*? To dat flat-faced poy, George Hildreth?"

"No—it isn't like that at all." She hesitated, blushed, and finally decided to confide in the merchant. "Have—have you met Roy Griffin's friend, Neal Conrad?"

"I seen him. I know apout him. Dat's a smart young man."

"I met him at the dance in Hamstead last night. He—he invited me to go to the mountains with him and Roy and Mrs. Griffin in his horseless carriage. And—he said he might call to-night."

"Oh, is dat so? Vel, dat's anoder story, Anne. I'm real pleased to hear it. Don't you worry apoud your liddle savinks. You puy yust vad you need, and ven you pegin to teach school again digs fall, you pay me pack a liddle at a time, *hein*? I dake the fifdy dollars now an' the rest lader on."

"Mr. Goldenburg, you're as kind as—"

"Now, now—vat vas you tinkin' of virst?"

"A suit. A—a 'simple little serge suit,'" quoted Anne, "have you anything like that?"

"Of course I haf. Dark blue. Dat's vat you vant. Dvendy-fife dollars." He paused. "Id's geddin' on late in de summer. Ve'll say dvendy. An' a vide shirt-vaist to go mit-maype doo, so you could keeb nice an' clean. An' den you'll valk down to Miss Lynn's and puy vun liddle blue an' vide hat."

"Yes," breathed Anne, "that's it. But I must have some shoes to go with it from you first."

"Sure. Nice dan oxfords. An' silk stockings de same color. An' gloves."

"And—and could I try on one of those white dresses at the same time?"

An hour later, she was on her way home again, her new possessions tucked securely under the seat of the rickety buggy. She had spent seventy-five dollars. But she did not begrudge a cent of it. She was deliciously happy.

The family were already at supper when she slammed the kitchen door behind her. "Wal, here ye be at last," her mother said heavily, looking up from the cold pork and maple syrup she was eating. "I sh'd think you might have ben here to help me git supper."

"I left everything all ready."

"Ain't yer goin' ter set down?"

"No, I'm not hungry. I'm going in to dust the parlor, and then I'm going to dress."

"George must be comin' over," chortled Mr. Chamberlain, pouring his tea into his saucer, "I shouldn't be a mite surprised ef they wuz t' settle everything up ter-night."

Anne had decided that it would be wiser to say nothing about her new acquaintance until his arrival was imminent. There would not be much time, then, for explanations. Unfortunately, however, she ran too close to the wind. The disorder in the parlor was worse than she had expected. She had had no time to go in there that morning, and she had counted overmuch on its being kept sacred from intrusion, according to New England tradition. Aunt Sarah's haircloth set, her wax flowers under glass, her "Rogers group" and her wool carpet were all in there; so were the crayon portraits of Mr. and Mrs. Chamberlain, taken at the time of their marriage, a kaleidoscope, and a set of views of the White Mountain to be viewed through a double magnifying-glass, on a small teetering stand. Unfortunately, nothing was sacred to Sam and Sol, and their mother was too indolent to interfere with them. They had spent the showery afternoon looking at the kaleidoscope and the views, and chasing each other around the furniture. The pictures hung awry from jostling; the tidies on the backs of the chairs were disarranged; the photographs were scattered about; the carpet was tracked with mud; it took Anne some moments, in spite of the speed with which she worked, to put things to rights. She was not half dressed when she heard the chugging sound of the horseless carriage, and, from her window, saw it come to a noisy and violent stop in front of the house. There was nothing to do but leave the situation for Neal to manage, while she hurried as fast as she could into the new muslin dress. After all, he was probably entirely capable of managing it.

She did not overestimate his resourcefulness. Hat in hand, he advanced, smiling pleasantly, towards the porch where, as usual, the entire family, with the exception of Anne, was gathered.

"Good evening," he said with the utmost friendliness. "This is Mr. Chamberlain's house, isn't it? Is this Mr. Chamberlain? And Mrs. Chamberlain? And Sol and Sam?" He shook hands heartily all around. "I'm Neal Conrad, of Hinsboro. I'm visiting Roy Griffin in Wallacetown, and I had the pleasure of meeting Miss Chamberlain at the dance in Hamstead last night. So I ventured to come and call."

His cordiality and composure were contagious. Mr. and Mrs. Chamberlain spoke with one breath.

"Pleased ter meet yer. Won't yer sit down an' make yerself ter home?"

"Thanks, I'd be glad to—unless—unless the boys would like to come out and take a little spin with me first?"

Sol and Sam sprang to their feet simultaneously.

"Say, Pupper, kin we? Oh, Mummer, let us!"

"It's perfectly safe, I assure you. Perhaps you'll *all* come?"

Mr. and Mrs. Chamberlain exchanged glances, and Mr. Chamberlain sighed heavily. With obvious disappointment, her husband spoke for both.

"Thanks kindly. I guess me an' Mummer'll set here. We're kinder tired after a hard day's work, but the boys kin go, if they're a mind ter."

When, fifteen minutes later, the horseless carriage dashed into the yard again, discharging its owner and his guests, the latter beaming, their countenances smeared with chocolate, Anne was just coming out of the front door. It was so perfectly timed, that the hand of the Lord seemed to be in it. Perhaps it was. For something told Anne, who of course had overheard everything, to wait in her room after she finished dressing, until Neal's return. He advanced towards them all, without appearing to single her out.

"Well, we had a fine little ride—the first of many, I hope— Good evening, Miss Chamberlain, it's nice to see you again— I'll accept your invitation to sit down now, sir, if I may."

"It's cooler inside," said Anne.

"Oh, I don't mind the heat."

Apparently Neal had no intention of seeking the seclusion of the parlor. He did not seem in the least anxious to see her alone. Anne was puzzled and a little hurt. The conversation was general. Neal talked a good deal himself, to be sure, but he made the others talk, too. Even Mrs. Chamberlain stirred from her apathy to tell him about Aunt Sarah's last illness, while Mr. Chamberlain and the boys became enthusiastically loquacious. At the end of an hour, when Neal rose to go, they all urged him to stay a little longer.

"I'm awfully sorry, but I promised Mrs. Griffin I'd get back early. She's nervous about this car of mine. Imagines I've run over the side of one of your mountains if I'm gone long. However, I'll come again, if I may."

"Wal, thet's what I call a nice feller," remarked Mr. Chamberlain, as their guest, waving one hand high above his head, disappeared in a cloud of smelly dust. "Lots of good horse sense, and real smart an' pleasant, too. Why didn't ye tell us about him, Nan?"

"I didn't have time," said Anne, chokingly. Then, without another word, she dashed upstairs, and flung herself, still dressed, on her bed, crushing her fresh new finery. She was terribly tired, bitterly disappointed. Neal hadn't seen the parlor, the one presentable place she had in which to receive him, and which she had worked so hard to make tidy. He hadn't noticed the clothes on which she had squandered her savings. He hadn't said a word about their trip, or even made a definite reference to coming the next evening. Nothing had gone right. She buried her head in her limp and lumpy pillow, and stifled her sobs. And so she fell asleep.

She awoke rested, and consequently hopeful. Probably he would come again, and this time everything would be all right. She ironed out her dress, put sweet-peas in the parlor, baked and frosted an extra cake, made lemonade. Again the fates were against her. Neal appeared, as she had hoped, and was cordially welcomed—by Mr. and Mrs. Chamberlain, Sol and Sam. But George had arrived before him, and had taken possession of the parlor and of Anne.

She escaped, of course, long enough to greet Neal. But for a second time, he declined her invitation to come in.

"Mr. Hildreth would never forgive me," he said laughingly, "and I'm sure the boys want another ride. This time I shan't take no for an answer from your father and mother, either. Do come, Mrs. Chamberlain."

Anne's mother, who had been torn between her fear that he might not renew his invitation, and her hope that he would, rose with assumed reluctance.

"Wal, ef yer so dead set on it," she puffed, "mebbe I might as well. Jest a short ways. An' don't drive too fast. It would put me all of a tremble ef ye should."

They were gone. Anne fed George with the lemonade and cake. He devoured both with relish, and she sat dumbly beside him, only shaking her head when he urged her to join him, listening intently for the return of the motor.

At last it came. Every one was laughing, and Neal was coming up the scrubby walk with a small boy hanging on either hand. At the rickety gate he paused. Anne could see and hear him plainly.

"No, I don't believe I better come in," he was saying. "You know what I told you about Mrs. Griffin's nerves. I don't like to disturb her. But I've been wondering— She and Roy and I have decided to take a little ride through the mountains to-morrow, and I thought possibly you'd let your daughter come with us. We'd take good care of her. You've seen for yourselves that there really isn't anything to be afraid of in a horseless carriage. Would you have any objections?"

Again Mr. and Mrs. Chamberlain exchanged glances. "Why, no," said Mr. Chamberlain at length, when he thought he had understood his signals correctly, "I dunno's I would. I think 'twould be a real pleasant change for her. Don't you, Mummer?"

"Wal, I dunno's I've any objection either, ef Anne would like ter."

"Suppose we ask her."

Sol and Sam, preceding him, burst screaming into the parlor, too excited to brook delay.

"Say, Nan, what ye think? Mr. Conrad wants ye should go to the mountings with him! To-morrer! Gee, but yer lucky. Say, Nan, bring us home a balsam, will ye?"

Suddenly Anne saw it all—the tact, the skill, the kindness with which Neal had managed everything. And she had doubted him— Oh, how stupid, how wicked she had been! She went towards him, blinded with contrition, with gratitude, with joy.

"I've just been asking Mr. and Mrs. Chamberlain," he said blandly, "whether they would have any objections to your going to the mountains with the Griffins and me to-morrow—provided, of course, that you would like to go. They've been kind enough to give their consent. Would it be convenient if I came for you about nine?"

"Yes," said Anne.

She could not, to save her life, have said another word. She stood still watching the others as they swarmed about him, while he cranked the car and climbed into the high seat. Then she went back—to the parlor and George. There was one piece of cake left, and a little lukewarm lemonade at the bottom of the pitcher, swimming above undissolved sugar and a few seeds.

"I guess I *am* a little hungry and thirsty after all," she said gayly, "I'm going to finish these myself, if you don't mind."

CHAPTER FIVE

Anne was waiting for Neal in the yard when he appeared, promptly at nine, the following morning. He insisted on going to the porch and chatting with the family for a few minutes; then they started off. At first he was entirely occupied with gear-shifts and brakes; but soon he turned to her gayly.

"This is fine! You don't know how pleased I am!"

"It's fine for *me*. You've been simply wonderful, arranging it all, and making it look so easy when it was really hard."

"Oh, that was nothing— Did you get some one to play the organ and teach the Sunday-school class?"

"Yes."

"I thought you would— Do you mind if I tell you how nice you look?"

"Of course I don't mind. Why do people always ask you if you mind when they have something pleasant to say, and remark, 'I think you ought to know' when they're going to tell you something perfectly horrid?"

"I don't know. But they do, don't they?" Neal laughed. "Well, then, 'perhaps you won't mind' if I tell you, too, how lovely you were these last two evenings. You look just like a white rose in that muslin dress."

"Oh, do you really think so? I'm awfully glad! I bought it Friday, in Wallacetown, from Mr. Goldenburg. And these clothes, too. Was this what you meant by 'a simple little serge suit'?"

"Exactly. And the hat is corking, too—I've been doing some shopping myself. I've bought two of those new bottles that keep things hot or cold, whichever you like. Have you seen one?"

"No, but I've read about them in advertisements."

"Well, to-day you'll see them in action. We're going to have hot coffee and iced tea. Mrs. Griffin has put up a wonderful lunch; and it's a perfect day. I should say we were having good luck all around."

"Well, I should say we *were*."

The Griffins, armed with hampers, jars and wraps, were all ready to start when Neal and Anne reached Wallacetown; and Mrs. Griffin, taking in Anne's attractions with one swift glance while the introductions were going on, was not long in deciding that Roy must be rescued, at any cost. She insisted on sitting on the back seat with him, while Anne resumed her place beside Neal in front. And every time Roy leaned forward to speak to the girl, his mother called his attention to something by the roadside. Roy, thus besieged, soon abandoned all efforts at conversation; and Anne, apparently, forgot him entirely. Not once did she turn around, without being first addressed; for that matter, she did not talk much to Neal either. Her rapture at the sensation of swift motion, like imagined flying, her eager astonishment at the beauty of the scenery, her joy in being with Neal, were all too great for utterance. They reached the famous "gorges" in time to go through them before luncheon. Mrs. Griffin was sure the walk would be too much for her, and besides, she wanted to get things ready for their meal. So Roy dutifully remained behind to help her. Once or twice, hungrily, he took a stealthy glance at his watch, realizing that Anne and Neal were certainly not hurrying, that they must indeed have lost all track of time— At last they reappeared, flushed and laughing. Anne had taken off her coat, and Neal was carrying it over his arm; the delicate skin of her neck and arms showed pink and soft through the sheer white of her shirt waist; her hair was curling in moist tendrils around her face. Roy thought, miserably aware that it was now too late for the thought to do him any good, that he had never seen her look so pretty before—or else he had, stupidly never realized how pretty she was. She had brought back some little souvenirs—birch bark canoes, a balsam pillow, a red pennant, and was arguing that *she* ought to pay for them, that Neal simply mustn't spend so much for her; and Neal was insisting, teasingly, that this was his party.

Still contending, they sank down on the grass beside the Griffins. The contents of the magic bottles were tested and declared delicious; so were the veal loaf and the angel cake, and all the other goodies which Mrs. Griffin had cooked with such skill, and wrapped in paraffin paper with such exquisite care—stuffed eggs, chicken sandwiches, sugared doughnuts. At the end of the feast, Neal produced from a hiding-place in the car two large boxes of candy, one blue and one lavender, gayly festooned with ribbon; and while the ladies were opening these, with exclamations of surprise and delight, he lit a cigarette. Roy did not smoke; his mother did not approve of it.

After a lazy half-hour they removed all traces of their feast from the shady little nook, and Neal suggested that they should ride down to "the Lake" and row a little while.

"Oh, I'm terribly afraid of boats!" exclaimed Mrs. Griffin, shrinking back. "And Roy doesn't know how to row. I've always been afraid to have him learn, because he might drown. But you take Miss Chamberlain, Neal. We'll wait for you here. I might get a little nap."

The row took even longer than the walk, and it was late afternoon before they started on their way home; twilight when the Griffins were deposited at their front door, and Anne and Neal on their way back over the hills to West Hamstead. As it grew darker, the stars came out, softly and gently, and below them, in the river valley, the mist hung like a bridal veil. At the last mile, a great golden moon swung slowly into sight above the distant blue of the mountains. Neal brought the car to a stop, and spoke a little huskily.

"I've got to go away in the morning," he said, "I've stayed

longer than I should already. Of course I'm coming back. You know that. But I don't want to say good night yet. Couldn't we take a little walk somewhere together before I leave you at your house?"

Anne hesitated. He laid his hand over hers, as he had done on the night of the dance.

"Please," he said as he had said then, but in a voice which shook a little this time. And again she found herself powerless to refuse.

"We could let down the bars and go through this pasture to the lane that runs out to the meadow back of our barn. No one will see us. And it's very quiet and lovely there."

"Yes. That's it."

He helped her out of the car and opened the bars. Together they passed into the cool greenness of the pasture, dotted with little pointed fir trees, shadowy with the feathery elms and maples that bordered it, drenched with the heavy evening dew of midsummer. A whippoorwill was singing, unseen; but except for this, the air was freighted with warm, pregnant silence, sweet with the scent of the August fragrance.

"I'm afraid you'll stumble and hurt yourself, it's so dark where the moonlight doesn't strike. May I put my arm around you?"

"Yes."

They were in the lane now, near the rosebush with its sharp thorns and falling petals. Was it possible that it was only four nights before, Anne asked herself, that she had stood in this same place, which now seemed so mystically lovely, in rage and rebellion? In rage and rebellion, while now . . . Neal could feel her young body, quivering with rapture, beneath his encircling arm.

"What is it, Anne? Tell me!"

"I was only thinking . . . I came here, the night of the dance in Hamstead, to pick some flowers to wear to the party.

Mummer had taken the sweet-peas I was saving and put them on Aunt Sarah's grave. They were all I had."

"You poor child!"

"So Pupper suggested the rosebush. I got all hot and dusty, hurrying, and then I pricked my fingers . . . there weren't enough roses anyway. George followed me down here, and asked me why I didn't mix them with some of those flowers growing in the meadow."

"I noticed them at the dance, of course."

"Do you know what they're called?"

"Certainly I do—Queen Anne's Lace . . . by Jove!"

How quickly he had sensed the symbolism which had eluded George entirely! In the moonlight, she could see the expression of his face as he turned from her to the field of stirring grass studded with the fragile white flowers on their slender stems, and back to her again—the tightening of his mouth, the softening of his eyes. She caught her breath.

"It grows where the soil is very poor. The farmers think it's just a weed—an awful pest."

"Because they can't see how beautiful it is. Anne—Anne—my darling!"

His arms had tightened about her like bands of steel. He bent and laid his face against her hair, then suddenly, with a little cry, his lips brushed across her cheek, seeking her mouth, and found it already upturned to the hard, hot kisses which he pressed down on it. They clung to each other, two clean, passionate young creatures, fused in the white flame of their first great desire . . .

Neal was the first to recover himself. He drew away from Anne gently, with a caress that he might have given to a child. Then he took her face between his two hands.

"Look at me, Anne."

"I am looking."

"I didn't mean that this should happen—not for a long time yet. Not because I didn't love you—"

"I know you love me—"

"But because I didn't want to hurt or even startle you—"

"You haven't. I love *you*. It would have killed me, not being sure."

She thought he was going to take her in his arms again, to kiss her until it hurt, as he had before. Instead, he knelt down in the long grass, and bowed his head.

"Anne," he said, so softly that she could hardly hear him, "Anne, you are a queen—a queen in disguise, a fairy changeling perhaps, but a queen just the same. Will you help me earn the lace for you to wear?"

CHAPTER SIX

A little over a month later, Anne and Neal were married.

He did not allow their sudden betrothal to interfere with his plans. The following morning he started off in pursuit of his wealthy client. Four days later he returned, with the report of complete success in his venture.

"That meant five hundred dollars to me—to us—," he told Anne, "and we'll need it. You mustn't think of me as some kind of a fairy prince, even if you are a queen."

"I don't," said Anne, flushing.

"You do, too. You know you do. Bless you! But I'm not. I'd be willing to bet that George Hildreth's got twice as much salted away as I have, this very minute. Sure you don't want to change your mind?"

"Neal—I wish you wouldn't."

He saw that her love was so strange to her still, so sacred, that she could not jest about it.

"All right, dear, I won't. But we must talk over the practical side of things. Because I want to marry you right away."

"Yes. That's what I want, too."

"Anne, I wish you wouldn't," he mocked, lightly. "You have no idea how hard it is for me to behave when you speak to me like that. But we ought to straighten out a few important details first, as I said. . . . I've got a good practice, for a fellow my age, and it's growing. I'm earning a fair income. And I've saved something. Not an awful lot. I worked my way through college, and ran into debt, a little, while I was getting started. That's all cleaned up. We can begin clear, with something ahead and something behind us. But we've got to begin small.

I'm afraid you've been misled by the automobile. I got it second-hand from a man who owed me money and couldn't pay. And it's the best investment I ever made, since it brought me to you. I thought I'd try and rent a little place we could live in this winter, and we could look around together, after we were married, for something better. I'd like to buy or build a little house for our very own, right away. It's poor economy, in the long run, to pay rent."

"Yes. I see that."

"Shall I go ahead, as soon as I get back to Hinsboro, and see what I can find for temporary quarters then? Are you willing to leave that to me?"

"Of course I am. And I'll get ready, too. Clothes and linen. Of course I can't have much. But I've a little legacy from Aunt Sarah. I'd rather spend it on my trousseau than anything I can think of."

"Well, that's settled then. Now—where would you like to go for our honeymoon?"

"Anywhere, with you."

"What would you say to Washington?"

"Oh, Neal, how did you guess! I've longed and longed—"

"Well, so have I. So that's settled, too. And we won't stint on that trip, either. We'll have a good time— I don't believe I've told you—I'm tremendously interested in politics. Even more than in law. I'm a member of the City Council in Hinsboro now. Perhaps some day I can go further."

"Oh, *Neal!* I'm sure you can."

"Any one can be President, you know," he said teasingly. "*You* could."

"Well, perhaps I can be mayor. But we'll have a look at the White House anyhow. Maybe it won't appeal to you, and that would settle it," he laughed. Then, changing the subject abruptly, "Another thing we mustn't economize on is your ring."

"Honestly, I don't need an engagement ring. I shouldn't mind a bit—"

"Nonsense. Let me hold your hand a while, so I can measure your finger."

Neal's second visit was even briefer than his first. But in the course of it he had a long talk with his prospective parents-in-law, whom he found stunned but acquiescent—and then insisted in announcing the engagement in the *Wallacetown Bugle*. Having thus burned all his bridges behind him, he departed to tell his own father and mother of his impending plunge into matrimony.

He had adroitly contrived to avoid much discussion of the Conrads with Anne. He knew, all too well, how bitterly they were bound to oppose the match, but he hoped, as far as possible, to keep this knowledge from her. Mrs. Conrad came from one of the oldest families in the country, and she never forgot it or allowed any one else to forget it; she belonged not only to the Daughters of the American Revolution but to the Colonial Dames; to the Episcopal Church and the Wednesday Sewing Circle. She subscribed to the *Atlantic Monthly* and the *Boston Transcript*. All humanity, to her, was divided into two classes—those who were "refined" and those who were not; the display of all human emotion was to her "disgusting"; she was fond of the words, "good breeding," "culture and tradition." She lamented the passing of the standards of the days of her youth, so infinitely superior to those of more recent times, and doubted whether any girls were "nice" any longer. Her husband's standards were much like her own, and his sense of self-importance quite equal to hers, though, like herself, he depended largely on the past to establish his claim to distinction. He had never made much headway in his profession as an architect. Both were distinguished-looking, in a lean, cold way, which helped to maintain the impression which they were anxious to create. They had very little money, but they contrived to keep up appearances in a way that was almost uncanny. No one outside the family guessed the bitter, biting economies that went on inside the spreading house on the most select street in town. Their elder son, Arthur, an unmarried clergyman, and their widowed daughter, Harriet, lived with them, as well as Neal. By pooling their resources, in this way, their income went much further than it otherwise would have done. Harriet had very pronounced views, all Neal's decision of character without his charm. She believed, long ahead of the times, in prohibition and woman's suffrage. She also believed in the depravity of the Latin races, and all members of the Roman Catholic Church, and in the infallibility of the Conrad family. Her husband had committed suicide by jumping from a sixth story window while they were on their honeymoon.

When Neal burst in upon his family, they were already gathered around the one reading lamp in their living-room after their evening meal—they always referred to it as "dinner," but since there had been no guests, as indeed there seldom were, it had in reality been a very frugal supper. He kissed his mother and sister dutifully, but without enthusiasm, and told them, immediately, of the fat fee which he had captured in the course of his vacation, and the promise of further revenue from the same source. Then he told the rest of his story.

"I knew you'd think that was good news. But I've got some that's better yet. I'm going to be married."

There was a moment of ominous, horrified silence. Then a simultaneous exclamation.

"*Married! To whom?*"

"A girl named Anne Chamberlain."

"I don't know any one by that name," said Mrs. Conrad, endeavoring to recover herself somewhat.

"You wouldn't. I met her while I was gone. She lives in a little place called West Hamstead."

"My son—are you really telling us this in earnest?"

"I certainly am."

The Conrads exchanged terrified glances.

"Then I must ask you to explain yourself."

Neal's worst enemy could hardly accuse him of a lack of

eloquence, on any theme or on any occasion. And this time he outdid himself. The results, however, were even worse than he had feared.

"Do you expect us to admit this engagement if we are questioned?"

"Certainly. It's been announced in the *Wallacetown Bugle* already." He noticed his mother's shudder. "I shall see that it's in the *Hinsboro Times* to-morrow."

"And you expect us—your father and I, your brother and sister—to go to the wedding . . . to receive this—this—person."

"My *fiancée*. Very soon my wife. Of course."

"Perhaps you were thinking of bringing her here to live."

"I wouldn't be so cruel to her."

He had scored. His mother attempted to draw blood in her turn.

"Have you thought what the withdrawal of your contribution to the family expenses is going to mean to us in our old age?"

"Harriet and Arthur aren't so very aged. It wouldn't hurt either of them to get out and hustle a little, as I've had to do."

"Neal! do not degrade us—and yourself—with vulgarity! I suppose your language—and your conduct—are the result of your political associations. You should never have allowed yourself—a gentleman, by birth at least—to be drawn into them."

"Then why are you so proud of the fact that one of your great-great-grandfathers was a Colonial Governor? Politics are more decent now than they were then, by a long shot."

He got up suddenly, and stood with his hands on the back of his chair, facing them.

"Look here," he said abruptly, almost violently, "I've had a long drive, and I'm tired. I'm going to bed. But I'll tell you this much, and then we won't discuss the subject again. I'll continue my usual subscription to this household just as long as you're decent to Anne. Not a second longer. It may not be very aristocratic to bargain, but I notice that none of the rest of you seem to want to work, and I don't believe you want to go hungry. You better think it over."

There was no hint of this battle, however, or of his own victory, when he wrote to Anne. She took his letter out into the pasture when her day's work was over, to read and re-read, pressing it to her lips each time she did so.

"Dearest—darling—sweetheart—" it began.

"I can't find any name lovely enough and loving enough to tell you how I feel about you.

"I miss you so terribly that I'm doing everything I can to shorten our separation. I've found a little home for us. It's the upper story of a house belonging to a friend of mine—he's had it fixed up for a flat, to rent, with an entrance and stairway of its own. It's very small—just a living-room, bedroom, bath-room and kitchen, but we could manage in that for this winter, couldn't we? It's sunny and clean and new, he and his mother have never used that part of the house—and there's a gas stove and a set tub in the kitchen. The furniture's rather aw-ful—mission oak in the living-room and a brass bed, and so on, but I don't mind if you don't.

"I've been to a stationer's, and asked him to send you some samples of wedding-invitations. I thought perhaps it would be easier for me to attend to that than for you. Write me which you like best, and a list of your friends whom you want to in-vite, and I'll have the cards addressed and sent out from here.

"Do you think you can manage a church wedding? And is there a church parlor or something of the sort in which we could have a reception afterwards? Of course my family and some of my friends will want to come up, and I realize how little room there is in your house. But do just as you think best. I've asked Roy to be my best man. I think that's only fair, considering that he introduced us. Bless his heart! good old Roy! My brother Arthur would like to assist in the mar-riage ceremony, and I should like to have him, if that would be agreeable to your own minister and to you. And of course I want George Hildreth to be one of the ushers.

"I want you to have your ring to wear right away, so I'm going to forgo the joy of putting it on myself. It started to you by express this morning—a solitaire diamond in a Tiffany setting. I know my mother is sending you something, too, with a letter welcoming you into the family.

"I wish I could kiss you to-night, over and over again, as I did that time down by the rosebush, and feel you in my arms. But I will before long. And meanwhile you know that I love you with all my heart and soul, and that I am counting the days that must go by before you are my wife.

"NEAL."

Anne wrote back:

"Dearest Neal: The ring came this morning, and fits perfectly. I put it on right away, and have it on now. Of course it's the most beautiful thing I ever saw in my life. I never dreamed that I should ever have anything like it, and of course I shouldn't have had it, if it hadn't been for you.

"Your mother's letter came too, and a lovely brooch which she said had belonged to your great-grandmother, and which she had kept for your wife ever since you were a little boy. I put that on, too, though it looks strange with my percale dress. There is a big garnet in the center, then a row of pearls, then a row of turquoises, then an openwork design in gold. I suppose you've seen it. It's beautiful, too, but of course I like the ring best. I was very much surprised that your mother should give me a present. It was awfully kind of her.

"I've chosen the sample for a wedding-invitation that I like best, and I'm sending you a list of my friends' names. I shouldn't have known I ought to do this if you hadn't told me about it. There never has been a wedding in the little church here, but we can have ours there, if you wish. I'm afraid you'll be disappointed, for it's very bare and plain and small, but we'll do our best to make it as pretty as possible. Mr. Hains, our minister, would be pleased to have your brother Arthur take part in the ceremony.

"I think the little flat will be wonderful. I love mission furniture and brass beds.

"What do you think? Mr. and Mrs. Goldenburg have invited me to go to New York with them! Mr. Goldenburg takes a trip every year at this time to buy his fall stock, and he's going to help me make my money go a long way in getting my trousseau. I'm going to have a real wedding dress, and a veil, and orange blossoms. We're leaving Monday, so send your next letter to me at the Waldorf Astoria Hotel, New York City. I think we'll be gone a whole week. I simply can't believe it's true. Next to getting engaged to you, it's the most wonderful thing that ever happened to me.

"George feels terribly. He hardly looks at me when I meet him, and he won't speak to me at all. But Roy and his mother have been awfully kind. Mrs. Griffin has given me half a dozen teacups, and Roy has given me a set of Shakespeare in four volumes. I've put them on the parlor table where I can go and look at them often.

"I wish I could write letters like yours. Of course I can't. But just the same, you know how much I love you, and that I'm wishing all the same things that you are wishing, and counting the days, too.

"With a heartful of love,

"ANNE."

To Neal, the next few weeks represented a period of worrying over details, and surmounting difficulties. But to Anne, it was a month of enchantment. The drab, workaday world, was, after all, such a beautiful place, and the people in it so transcendently kind and generous. Her class at High School, and her Sunday-school class sent her wedding-presents—a silver pickle-fork, a cut glass "sugar and creamer"; Mabel Buck made her a set of crocheted mats; even George sent her a present—a huge lamp, hand painted in pink roses, on a gilt stand and with a fringed shade. Then the presents began to come in from Neal's friends and relatives, presents beyond anything she had ever imagined: a little chest of flat silver, smooth, shining knives and forks and spoons, six of each, a large silver bowl from the mayor of Hinsboro and his wife, a silver sandwich-plate from the City Council; a lemonade set from the mother and son whose house they were to share; innumerable pretty trifles from his classmates at college and his legal acquaintances that looked to her like priceless treasures. But, after all, no one gave her as much as the Goldenburgs, no one was quite so thoughtful. First, Mr. Goldenburg went through his old stock, and found appropriate wedding-raiment for Mr. and Mrs. Chamberlain, Sol and Sam: a "stylish stout" not quite so stylish, to be sure, as when it was laid in, three years before, but still undeniably stout enough for Mummer; a "gent's guaranteed two-thirds wool," that needed the guarantee to convince the doubtful, but Mr. Chamberlain was not inclined to be doubtful; two "schoolboys' special," so special as to have attained no great vogue, but beautiful to the eyes of Sol and Sam. Mr. Goldenburg let them have all these things on credit, though no one knew better than he the state of Mr. Chamberlain's finances. Then he went through his stock again, searching out bargains for Anne . . . she could have those towels just as well as not, there were imperfect threads in them, but they would look nice when she had embroidered them. Those handkerchiefs, those aprons, were badly soiled, but she could wash them out; that pleated wool skirt, those shoes and shirtwaists, were discontinued lines, but if they happened to fit her . . . he let her pay him for them, to save her pride, but they cost her next to nothing. After the invitation to go to New York was extended by Mrs. Goldenburg she lay awake all night, trembling with excitement; and when they were actually on their way, they all three put their heads together and made out a list of her household needs.

Half a dozen sheets, half a dozen pillow slips, a pair of blankets, a quilt, two spreads; two dozen bathroom towels— that would be plenty, with the odd ones Mr. Goldenburg let her have; one half dozen each glass and kitchen towels; three dozen napkins; three table cloths—"You won't use doze much; these new-fangled mats, d'oylies dey call dem, safes lots of vashing; put doze down, my tear." Then the clothes, more entrancing still; six nightgowns, six of each undergarment beside the "bridal set"; a kimono, two pairs of shoes, a dozen pairs of stockings, three gingham dresses for house wear; a dark blue silk for afternoon wear; a dark blue coat that would "fit in" both with that and with the serge suit already purchased, a hat to match; the wedding dress itself, white *crêpe de chine*—that was to serve, later on, for all occasions where "best" was required. "Oh, Mr. Goldenburg, I'll never be able to buy all that with three hundred dollars—you know that's all I have left." . . . "Yes, you vill, my tear, you'll see. An' I'm goin' to speak to some of my pizness frents apout you. One in de caterin pizness, he'll send you up a nice little lunch by express, one florist, ve'll talk to him apout de decorations for de church."

The visit to New York was one of rapture from the beginning to the end of the five days that it lasted. Anne had never been in a hotel before—had never seen an elevator, a menu card, a bell-boy or twin beds; she had never ridden in a subway, or attended a play in a theater. There was a bathroom of sorts in Mabel Buck's house and Anne had used the tin tub, bound with water-soaked wood, when she had visited Mabel, sharing the luxuries of the Buck family; but this was her first experience of white-tiled perfection with running hot water, and a tub of solid porcelain, for her own exclusive use— for Mrs. and Mrs. Goldenburg actually had a bathroom off their bedroom, too! She made mental notes of everything, gleaning fresh bits of knowledge from each new experience. How much this trip was doing to prepare her for the still more wonderful one to Washington with Neal! He was not going to find her ignorant, after all, of all the niceties of life which he knew, as she had feared. Only once was she cowed by a waiter or bewildered by finger-bowls or uncertain how to follow an usher. Mrs. Conrad would have shuddered at the thought of the Goldenburgs as social mentors, just as she would have thought a marriage hardly legal when the bride brought to it an outfit as meager as Anne's; but to the girl, both seemed more than adequate; they seemed almost God-given.

The Goldenburgs had lost a daughter, Rachel, who would have been just Anne's age if she had lived. Mrs. Goldenburg finally confided this to Anne, her beady eyes brimming, her plump hands twitching; and Anne in turn confided it to Neal when after a three weeks' absence he returned to West Hamstead, and stood amazed at all that had been accomplished while he was gone.

"So they're doing all this for me in her memory! Just think of it."

"I believe they're doing it partly in her memory, but largely because they love and admire you. The Jewish race appreciates qualities like yours. But anyway, they're doing it, whatever the reason is, and I shan't forget. Perhaps I can do them a good turn some day."

"Neal—would you mind very much—do you suppose it would be possible—for me to keep on teaching after we are married?"

"Of course I'd mind. I wouldn't hear of it for an instant. Whatever put such an idea into your head?"

"I don't see how my family is going to get along without what I'm earning," she faltered.

Neal did some swift calculating. His contribution to the expenses of his own family had been seventy-five dollars a month, nine hundred dollars a year. Of course, now that his board and laundry would no longer come out of that, what he gave them would be clear gain, except for his share in taxes and insurance; but he had made a bargain and he must stick to it. If he added this burden of Anne's to his own, they were going to be a good deal straitened in consequence; but that, as he saw it, was what he ought to do. They were in the same boat, as far as their dependents were concerned; and he intended to do the rowing.

"You've been earning ten dollars a week?"

"Yes."

"How many weeks are there in the school year?"

"Thirty-eight."

"Three hundred and eighty dollars—well, we'll manage to find that much some way. Don't you worry."

"You mean *you'll* send it?"

"Of course—why, Anne, darling, don't take it that way—"

For she was crying—shedding glad tears that sprang from a heart overflowing with gratitude and adoration.

"There, there—why, it isn't anything at all—I'll be earning so much a few years from now that I shan't even notice it. Then I'll pay off the mortgage on the farm, and your father can get a fresh start and—now, Anne . . ."

Neal's general satisfaction received only one setback: The revelation that the "organ" which Anne played in church was not an organ at all, as he understood the term, but a "reed organ." No bridal music worthy of the name could be achieved on such an inadequate instrument. But again, Anne's genius for making friends bore fruit. The leader of the Wallacetown band agreed to transport a square piano over the hills at his own expense and to play it himself on the all-important day, accompanied by a violinist and a 'cellist.

Mrs. Griffin, in an outburst of hospitality, offered to take the entire Conrad family into her house, and to entertain them throughout the period of their stay; and she proved so perfect a hostess, so thoroughly "refined" so far removed from anything that was "disgusting" that the Conrads' worst forebodings melted away at once, almost as the perfect biscuits and flaky pies she made melted in their mouths. She set a much better table than they could either afford or conceive. There was nothing to rouse their forebodings, either, when Anne appeared in the flesh to take supper at the Griffins' and be presented to them soon after their arrival. She was wearing her white muslin dress, and even Mrs. Conrad was forced to admit that there was nothing wrong with her appearance. The dress was cheap, of course, but it was suitable and it was becoming; and the girl's excellent figure and natural style set it off. There was no denying that she was good-looking—well, Neal might be forgiven for thinking her beautiful. Her skin and her teeth were both perfect. Those counted for more, really, than those great dark blue eyes with their fringed lashes, and the masses of soft golden hair. And her manner was not awkward at all, or bold; on the contrary, she was rather silent, a little shy, but perfectly polite, perfectly self-possessed. In the seclusion of their own apartments, afterwards, they confessed to each other that she was not so very dreadful, after all . . . though of course they did not say as much to Neal.

Their forebodings were not roused the next day either. The September morning dawned cold and crisp and clear, mellowing into golden warmth before noon. The drive over the hills, through silent, shady roads, with glimpses, at every clearing, of the blue-massed mountains in the distance, was beautiful enough to stir more senseless souls than theirs. The little church which was their destination stood high above the clustering houses around it, austerely white, strong in the simplicity of Puritanism. Inside, boughs of fir and spruce, mingled with boughs of maple and oak had been spread behind the pulpit and over the windows; sprays of roses were lifted in front of the green masses, and tied on the pews. A very unhappy-looking young man, with a hurt and puzzled expression on his kind, flat face, was waiting to receive them, to take them to their places in front, on the left; he seemed anxious that everything should be right, that they should be comfortable and pleased. The orchestra was playing the wedding march from Lohengrin very acceptably. The strange country minister, standing beside Arthur, had a fine head, something gothic and serene about it; Neal, paler than usual, but handsomer than ever, chin and shoulders squarer than

ever, came in with Roy, who was trembling visibly with nervousness, but correct to the last trifling detail of costume and
custom; Mabel Buck began her progress up the aisle. The
Bucks were well-to-do, and proud to have their daughter invited to take part in the wedding; her filmy, pale pink frock,
her wide lacy hat, left nothing to be desired in the attire of a
maid-of-honor; her costume had been selected from the latest
Altman catalogue, and did full justice to that establishment.

And then came the bride, a mist of tulle around her, a
coronal of delicate blossoms on her golden hair, a long sheaf
of them on her arm—Queen Anne's lace.

Ten minutes later they were all in the church parlor. Con-
gratulations were being received and kisses exchanged. The
wedding breakfast over which Mr. Goldenburg, resplendent
in frock coat and gray trousers, was presiding, left nothing to
be desired; it was in the same class with the roses, more of
which appeared on the tastefully laden table. His "pizness
frents" had done him proud. So, he reflected, had the girl
in whose future he had invested. He sized up the Conrad
family with one or two swift, appraising glances.

"Dey took on apout it when de poy told 'em, and now de're
disaboinded pecause dey can't fint more vault!" he muttered
shrewdly to himself. "Dey hat petter not make her unhappy,
dat liddle Anne! put even if dey do she'll come out on top,
yust de same, py and py. A great lady—twendy years from
now, maype—put a great lady, some day!"

But alone in her little attic room for the last time, no thought
of possible future greatness for herself entered Anne's head.
Her thoughts were all of Neal, who, in her mind, was so great
—so glorious—already, that nothing could magnify him in her
eyes. Mabel helped her change from her snowy bridal raiment
to the "simple little serge suit," enhanced with a new blouse
of matching blue and a new early fall hat. In the open fitted
bag—one of Neal's wedding gifts to her—was everything she
needed for that night—the lacy nightgown with its white ribbons, the pale blue kimono and bedroom slippers, fresh hand-

kerchiefs; her suit case and trunk were already locked and strapped. Her tiny new gold watch—Neal's other wedding gift—was ticking away at the end of its long fine chain, securely tucked in her belt. Neal was waiting for her outside, in the horseless carriage. They were to motor to a famous inn, nestled in the heart of the hills fifty miles south, and spend their first night there, lingering on for another day or two if it suited their fancy, then taking an express to New York which connected with a midnight train to Washington. A drawing-room was to be engaged as soon as they decided when they wanted to go. The horseless carriage would then be shipped by freight to Hinsboro. The careful plans for her comfort and happiness had all been perfected by Neal—

Anne closed her bag, and turned to kiss her friend.

"I'm not going to say good-by. We'll see each other often. My marriage isn't going to make any difference. After Neal and I get settled I want you to come and visit us. Neal says the living-room sofa makes into a sort of bed. Mabel—will you do one more thing for me?"

"Of course, honey-bunch."

"Take this bag down to Neal, and tell him I'll be there in just a minute."

Slightly surprised at being dismissed, but without objections, Mabel departed. Anne closed the door carefully behind her and locked it. Then swiftly, she knelt beside her bed.

"Oh, God," she prayed aloud, "please make me worthy of him! I don't know how to say it. I don't even know how to think it, but Neal is so wonderful, and good and great, that I *feel* he's going to rise to high places. Help me to go with him, show me the way. So that he won't leave me behind, so that we can be together always. For Christ's sake. Amen."

PART TWO

Knots and Tangles

CHAPTER SEVEN

Two weeks later, their wedding journey over, Neal and Anne began their homemaking together in the little four-room apartment in Hinsboro.

The trip to Washington had been everything that they both had dreamed of and hoped for and more. To a sophisticated traveler, the capital city in early September, emptied of official and resident society, and sizzling in the damp and sultry heat, is at its worst; but Anne and Neal were neither sophisticated nor traveled; and to them it seemed as beautiful as a vision of a white-pillared Paradise. They went through the Treasury Building and the Army and Navy Building, wearily but persistently; through the Corcoran Art Gallery, puzzled but eagerly. They went by boat down the Potomac to Mt. Vernon, and spent a day there, wandering through the mansion and garden, resting on the shady lawn overlooking the river; and they spent another day at Arlington and Alexandria, instead of trying to crowd all three into one expedition. They climbed to the top of the Washington monument, lingered before the picture of Pocahontas in the Rotunda of the Capitol, surveyed the beautiful chamber of the Supreme Court, sat for a few minutes in the vacant gallery of the House of Representatives. It was here that Neal gave voice to his only regret.

"If Congress were only in session! I'd like to see these fellows in action."

"You will some day."

"Yes, we'll come again."

They crossed the green park to the new Library of Con-

gress recently opened, glittering with mosaic, gorgeous with
Pompeian red—it was good to find that they could lunch
there, for hour after hour passed by, and still they had not
half seen it all, the endless corridors, the wide, shallow-
stepped staircases leading on and on to new wonders. They
were so tired when they reached the hotel that night, that
they could not study the map they had bought or read in
their guidebook about what they had seen that day and
intended to see the next, but tumbled off to bed like sleepy
children, the ruby-colored balloon which Neal had bought
for Anne, in sheer excess of joyousness, from an itinerant
vender, floating above their heads.

He bought her flowers, too, every day, from other itinerant venders, for they found these humble merchants sta-
tioned at almost every street-corner, at every park and circle;
Anne had always a small bunch to stick in her belt, a larger
one on the plush-covered table in the center of their room.
They walked up and down Pennsylvania Avenue, looking in
the windows of the small, cheap shops which disfigure its
fine length, purchasing "views" and other inexpensive souvenirs for themselves and their families; and when they had
walked until they could walk no longer, Neal hired an open
victoria by the hour, a sagging vehicle sadly drawn by a
sagging horse, guided by a sleepy negro, in shabby livery
that had seen better days; and in it they drove about the
city. Last of all, marveling at their temerity, they went to
the White House. It seemed almost too much to believe that
they could actually walk inside those strong iron gates, unquestioned, and into that shining mansion. Yet no one stopped
them. The uniformed attendant at the entrance regarded
them kindly. He was used to bridal couples and this pair
was an unusually attractive example of the species. He
smiled. Neal and Anne smiled back. Then they found themselves in the dim cool basement corridor where the portraits
of the Presidents' wives are hung, ladies smiling still, in their
pictured satins, as they did in bygone days; next in the small

square room where the china used in each administration, neatly ranged behind glass doors set them "choosing" the sets each liked best. From another smiling attendant they found that they were allowed to go upstairs; and there a guide awaited them. The day was torrid, and there were only a few other sightseers—some skinny, shabby, school-teachers, a prosperous-looking merchant from California— as he himself proclaimed—an elderly man and his wife "doing" Washington in two days—none, except themselves, Neal and Anne instinctively felt, atune to the simple beauty and serene dignity that surrounded them—the marble-floored hall, the high-paneled dining-room, the Red Room with its glimpses of the garden and lawns beyond, the tall windows, the empty, circular, Blue Room, the homelike, dainty Green Room with its white mantel, the dazzling chandeliers and mirrorlike parquetry of the East Room. They left in such a state of exaltation that Neal felt the day called for some special celebration to mark it. . . .

"Let's go and have dinner at the Shoreham to-night. That's the swell hotel here, I've heard. Shall we? Next time we come we'll be staying there."

Anne agreed, joyfully, and decided to wear her wedding-gown to their little feast. The dark blue silk, which had seemed so glorious a garment when she purchased it, was, she had already discovered, suitable only for sight-seeing. Even in the unostentatious dining-room of the Hotel Hamilton, where they were staying, it was not just "right" for evening wear; but having no other dress, except her white muslin, which she could not wash out herself here, and her wedding-dress, which she wanted so much to save, she had tried to make it "do," even though this meant she could not change, when she came in, hot and dusty, at the end of the day. It was much too warm to wear her suit, unless she took off the coat, and that, she had discovered wasn't "right" either. Ladies wore their coats, just as men did, when they were in tailored attire. Yes, certainly, she would have to wear the wedding-dress tonight. Then Neal, with that uncanny faculty of his for guessing what was in her mind suggested something else.

"But let's go shopping first. I want to have the fun of buying you a dress myself to *prove* I've got a right to."

"Neal, I don't need one, really—"

"Nonsense, of course you do. A pink dress. You had on a pink dress the first time I saw you."

"That hideous thing!"

"Well, this isn't going to be hideous, you'll see!"

It was not. It was frilly with ruffles, frothy with lace, a fairy frock. The saleswoman who waited on her outdid her own professional enthusiasm when she saw how Anne looked in it. And she showed the price ticket to Neal surreptitiously, that Anne's happiness might not be checked by the figures printed on it. It was, the saleswoman shrewdly suspected, far more expensive a dress than they had expected to buy. Neal noticed her strategy, but he paid for the dress unflinchingly, producing his billfold without an instant's hesitation, and drawing out quantities of crisp, clean notes as carelessly as if there were thousands more where those had come from. When the saleswoman saw this, she made a suggestion.

"Wouldn't Madam like a wrap to go with the dress? I have just the thing, marked very low, because it's so late in the season. The new fall goods are beginning to come in already. But this is just exactly as stylish, and such a bargain." Almost instantly she flung around Anne's shoulders a moss-green cloak, of soft-embroidered wool, satin-lined in a paler shade of the same color. The bride stood reflected in the tall glass before them like a rose surrounded by its leaves.

"Neal, you *mustn't*."

"Why, don't you *like* it?"

"Don't I *like* it?"

"Then I must." He counted out more clean, crisp bills carelessly. "Send that, with the dress, to Mrs. Neal Conrad,

Hotel Hamilton, please," he said to the saleswoman, "right away. Be sure it gets there in time for dinner."

"Wouldn't you like to open a charge account here?" inquired the capable person addressed, grasping the bills with one firm hand as she wrote "Rush" across the address with the other. "It could be arranged in an instant, I'm sure, at the office. Then any time Mrs. Conrad came in . . . or if you live in another city, I could send things on approval. She would only have to write. Mrs. Maple, my name is, and I'd be only too glad. It would be a real convenience to her, I'm sure."

"A very good idea—where is the office?"

Anne was still protesting when they finally left the smart little establishment into which they had unwittingly wandered—the outside had not "looked expensive." A little fur neckpiece to wear with the blue suit on cool days, and slippers and stockings to match the new frock had been added to the other purchases.

"Neal, you know we ought not to open charge accounts and do wild things like that. You told me yourself we must 'begin small.' And then you go to work and spend more on clothes for me in one hour than I've spent in nearly twenty years."

"I want you to have pretty clothes. You're so darned pretty yourself, and sweet, and good." It was all he could do to keep from kissing her on the street. "That client of mine up in the mountains—"

"Well?"

"Well, his next bill will be bigger than I meant to make it, that's all."

The little dinner began with a surprise. They were hardly seated in the rose and cream dining-room, at the Shoreham— the only hotel dining-room in Washington with real atmosphere, even when swathed in the linen covers of the off-season—when a very sleek-looking young man sprang up from a near-by table and hailed Neal with genuine, if correctly tempered enthusiasm.

"Neal Conrad! my dear fellow! where did you come from —and when—and why—at this time of the year? Not that it matters, so long as you've arrived!".

Explanations were immediately in order. Clarence Hathaway, a former classmate of Neal's at Harvard, had entered the diplomatic service immediately after his graduation. He had spent much of his boyhood in Europe, and this had fitted him admirably for his future work. He was already third secretary of legation at Madrid. Home now on leave, he was receiving certain important instructions from the State Department before sailing to resume his post. Hence his presence in Washington. Neal sought to congratulate him upon his success.

"Nonsense! What about yours! Making money hand over fist, so I hear, and causing hibernating Hinsboro all sorts of spasms with your political prowess; Governor or something, aren't you?"

"No," said Neal, laughing, "sit down and have dinner with us, won't you? This is Anne . . . my wife," he added, with a shade of difference in his voice, as Hathaway swung around, apologizing for his intrusion, swiftly solicitous.

"A bridal party! My dear Mrs. Conrad, what must you have thought of me, charging in on your exquisite solitude à deux like that? But I was so glad to see Neal in this God-forsaken place, and I hadn't heard . . . Did you send me cards? They would have missed me anyway, if you had, no doubt, I've been tearing around so. Newport, the Adirondacks, the North Shore . . . But you will let me be host, of course! . . . What kind of cocktails do you like, Mrs. Conrad?"

Fortunately, he did not wait for her to answer. Anne, blushing with bewilderment was looking to Neal for help, and he had not caught her signal.

"A clover-leaf, of course, and Neal and I will have martinis. Then some jellied bouillon, salmon mayonnaise, with cucumbers—birds—a Waldorf salad—baked Alaska pudding —champagne to celebrate this glad occasion, some liqueurs with the coffee. After dinner we'll go to the theater—not that there's much to see, but we'll see what there is— It's pretty dull, too, after Madrid—a wonderful city. I can hardly wait to get back there. Have you ever been to Spain, Mrs. Conrad? Well, you and Neal must run over soon—an enchanting country!"

Madrid! He suggested it as casually as George used to speak of driving her into Hamstead. But Neal took it calmly enough, or at least appeared to do so, and Anne steadied herself. She mustn't betray her nervousness, her provincialism, and embarrass Neal—Neal who was really twice as wonderful as this attractive stranger. Mr. Hathaway did not, after all, make many conversational demands upon her—it was only necessary that she should follow his dashing lead. And this, inwardly stumbling, but outwardly sure-footed she managed to do.

"I know a woman—a famous hostess here in Washington— who says that when she's one man short for a dinner she comes to the Shoreham for lunch, and invariably finds just the right person with whom to fill in, eating here. She says it saves a great drain upon her nervous resources. I'm in for a little of her luck, evidently."

"And so are we."

"That's sweet of you, Mrs. Conrad, sweet,—and very neat, too, wasn't it, Neal? Of course there's not much of any one here now. Over in the corner, all alone, is Madame Del Garde, the wife of the Portuguese Minister. They have a lovely summer place on the East Coast of Maryland. I spent my last week-end there. She must be in town for a few days' shopping. Stunning, isn't she?"

"Complete," murmured Anne, taking in the finished perfection of the dark, handsome woman's black satin evening dress, high comb, and white lace scarf.

"Complete, yes, that's the word exactly, complete! I must tell Madame Del Garde herself sometime, she'd like to hear that." His eyes wandered towards the diplomat's wife again, and he half rose, bowing in response to her smile of recognition. "And opposite the last window on the left, talking very hard together are the President's secretary, Mr. Taylor, and Senator Harriman of Nevada."

"The sheep-man?" asked Neal with interest.

"Yes— I wonder what ewe-lamb is going to be slaughtered now—but we mustn't talk scandal, must we, Mrs. Conrad?"

"No," said Anne serenely.

Hathaway glanced at her, in swift appraisement. She really meant it. Well, then—

"And opposite them, further on, are Shimera, the naval *attaché* of Japan, and his daughter. They're absolutely inseparable."

"It's so kind of you," murmured Anne, eating salmon for the first time in her life, "to tell us about all those interesting people. Isn't it, Neal?"

"You bet," said Neal enthusiastically. "Say, Hathaway— do you think the democrats mean to push Nerton in the next campaign?"

The two men plunged into politics; Neal was talking very frankly. He was thinking seriously, he said, of running for mayor, but it took so much money, and he wasn't sure the machine was friendly.

"Pshaw," said Hathaway. The salad was being served, and he produced a gold cigarette case, tendered it to Anne. She had been watching Madame Del Garde, and was prepared for this—nevertheless, she had made up her mind to decline.

"We don't, much, where I come from," she said easily.

"Of course not—please excuse a very stupid mistake!" He actually thought it was! Anne's heart beat high as the cultured, sophisticated voice trailed on, "I'm hoping to be made Minister, rather early in life, as such things go—that's the way my ambition lies. Confirm my appointment without a vulgar row, won't you, Neal, when you get to the Senate, which ought to be about the same time."

"Sure," said Neal heartily, and they all laughed again.

Later, while they were getting their hats before starting for the theater, he and Hathaway had a moment alone. And Hathaway asked a question.

"Where did you find her, Neal?"

"In a place called West Hamstead, Vermont, about two months ago. She taught the district school. She's the daughter of the village ne'er-do-weel."

"Are you in earnest?"

"Never more so."

Clarence Hathaway whistled softly. "Any more like her left behind?"

"There's no one," said Neal, "like her in the whole world."

Clarence whistled again. "I'm inclined to think you're right," he remarked. "However, I'm glad there's one. She'll do very well, as you said, in the Governor's mansion."

"I didn't say," protested Neal.

"Well, you better. *Allons, mon cher.*"

Still later, lying in the curve of Neal's arm, Anne thought it all over—the strange meeting, the stranger visions of new worlds to conquer which followed it. How many worlds were there, yet to be revealed to her? She had already glimpsed so many of which she had never dreamed, these last weeks. And now it was their last night in Washington, the last night of their honeymoon, and in the morning they would be going back to Hinsboro, to the little four-room apartment, to hard work and everyday existence. It was fun to joke, of course, about embassies and executive mansions, but, after all, it was only a joke—at least for the present. Yet, there seemed something about this encounter with Clarence Hathaway that was pregnant with meaning—with promise, with prophecy.

On the squat, substantial chair that stood by the tall window draped, correct hotel-fashion, in lace curtains and crimson velvet over-draperies, lay her moss-green cloak and her frilly pink dress, the long silk stockings fallen beside the little satin slippers that matched it. The rest of their baggage was packed, but these new treasures she had decided to leave out until morning, in order to be able to look at them once more in daylight. The latest bouquet that Neal had bought her—great warm, top-heavy roses—scented the silent room. He was asleep, or nearly so; and yet, asleep or awake, he encompassed her with his thoughtfulness, his solicitude, his love, of which the dress and the flowers were but the visible tokens. That—not future fame, but present happiness, was, after all, what counted.

He stirred slightly, kissed her drowsily, drew her more closely to him. Instantly, thrilling to his touch, she responded with an ardor that surpassed his own. So he had not been asleep after all. He wanted her. He needed her. He was all hers. She was as essential to him as he was to her. These were the glad thoughts which surged through her senses. Yet, before they really slept, he spoke to her again of Clarence Hathaway, whom she, in her rapture, had entirely forgotten.

"Attractive, isn't he, darling? And brilliant! I believe he'll prove a great diplomat, one of the greatest we have."

Anne resented, ever so slightly, this mental intrusion, just as she had resented—though she must be careful not to let Neal guess it—Hathaway's physical intrusion at dinner. "If only," she said gently, "he did not look quite so much as if he had been stroked."

It was a long time before she thought of Clarence Hathaway again; or Washington, except as a honeymoon memory.

When they reached Hinsboro, they had to begin, right away, to economize. They had spent more money than they expected. But that, Neal said with a laugh, was, of course, to be expected! And Anne laughed too, when he said it. But after he had gone to his office, she sat still, with a pencil and a piece of paper in her hand, and did sad little sums, before she even washed the breakfast dishes or made the bed.

It had sounded *huge*, the amount they could count on for housekeeping, when Neal first told her about it; and here it was melting away to nothing, in her careful hands, . . . just as those great blocks that the iceman brought melted away in her immaculate little refrigerator, so that she had to buy more—and more—and more. The steaks and the chops that reposed so juicily on that same ice melted away like- wise—in Neal's mouth, the instant he got home at night, starving hungry.

"My, but you're a good cook, honey—another helping, please, and lots of butter gravy—just floods of it, all around the baked potato. And stick a piece of bread in it too—'fish in the pan' we used to call that when I was a kid."

Two pounds of steak—porterhouse, Neal would listen to nothing less—four chops, one small fowl for boiling, one thick slice of ham—in less than a week he had devoured all this, with comparatively little help from her, though she had a healthy appetite. He drank two great cups of coffee, every morning, thick with double cream, ate cream on his cereal, whipped cream on the molded jellies and blancmanges that formed many of their week-day desserts, ice cream, which Anne made and froze herself, every Sunday. So there was the milkman to be reckoned with to no small tune, as well as the iceman and the butcher. Then Neal liked iced orange juice, the very first thing in the morning, before he sat down at the table. She took it into the bathroom, and he sipped it while he tubbed and shaved. The friendly Italian at the fruit-stall, just around the corner, found in her a steady and not too unremunerative a customer— And all the butter it took for "fish in the pan," gravies and white sauces, for crisp toast and light muffins, for the deep, hot, juicy pies which alter-nated with the molded jellies for dessert, for fresh vege-tables— Neal, it seemed, expected her to buy string beans and spinach straight through the winter! The grocery bill was heavy, too. He asked her eagerly if it were too late in the fall for preserving, and answering eagerly that it was not, Anne made apple jelly and grape jelly and quince mar-malade; sugar, sugar, sugar, white mountains of it, cool and high like the Alps, dissolved into the big kettles filled with sizzling, wine-colored juice, ranged closely together on her neat little gas stove.

Neal did not complain about the bills; and he praised her cooking, as he praised everything else she did. But once he drew money from the savings bank, where his account was already much depleted by her engagement and wedding presents from him, by the engraved invitations to their mar-riage and by their trip to Washington with all its delightful "extras," and once the bills were not paid when those of the following month came in, and then, were ugly little words —"account rendered"—at the top of the statements. It was then that Anne commenced to do her sad little sums.

She roused herself from them at last and began her day's work, for the first time, without joyousness. It was, as Neal had foretold, child's play for her after her long, hard, drudgery at the farm, as far as actual labor was concerned. She did all the washing and ironing, including Neal's shirts and the sheets, all her own cleaning. And still, by eleven o'clock in the morning, earlier than that sometimes, her work was finished for the day until it was time to prepare supper. Neal did not come home to dinner, taking a light lunch, which she put up, to his office with him, and she easily fell into the way of eating a very light lunch herself, which did not take her five minutes to prepare—a cup of tea, a slice of bread and butter, apple-sauce or prunes; then she changed her dress, and did the mending. She slipped out of bed in the morning while Neal was still asleep, put the clothes to soak, swept and dusted, chilled his orange juice, steamed his cereal, percolated his coffee. At first he remonstrated with her; he liked to find her there beside him to kiss when he woke up—besides there was no need of it. But gradually the mental satisfaction and deep physical comfort of rising in a warm, tidy house, to a waiting breakfast perfectly cooked and served, overcame his remonstrances. In the evening he came home to the same shining order, the same complete refreshment. There was never a towel out of place, or a crumpled one, in the tiny tiled bathroom, which Anne scrubbed every day. There was never cool soup or luke-warm salad; and half an hour after they had finished supper, the dishes had been put away, the gas stove was cold, the kitchen dark, and she was curled up against his shoulder in the big Morris chair that was so hideous, but which held them both so luxuriously.

"One thing I'll never fling in your face," Neal chuckled more than once when they were thus comfortably settled, "'the bread that mother used to make.' Why, you can give mother cards and spades in housekeeping right now!"

It was true. Neither Mrs. Conrad nor Harriet excelled in the domestic arts, which they considered beneath them. The "flat wash" went out to a little steam laundry, whence it returned grimy and torn; the more personal things were entrusted to a lady of color who lived in an adjacent alley, and who had the habit of procrastinating and pilfering. She also came in once a week to do a little alleged cleaning, which never seemed to reach the back stairs or the more remote corners. Nominally, the elder Conrads also kept a "general maid"; actually, they were oftener without one; and during the intervals, they "managed." This management was nothing to brag about. At first, it had been suggested that Neal and Anne should dine with them every Sunday after church; but during one of the periods of "management," Anne asked her family-in-law if they would not like to reverse this arrangement, for once, and they accepted, with condescending reluctance. The dinner which she set before them was neither elaborate nor original—tomato bisque soup; roast chicken, mashed potatoes, onions and string beans, accompanied by light rolls, and her new grape jelly; fruit salad; vanilla ice cream with chocolate sauce, sponge cake, and coffee; but it was a better one than she had ever eaten, as to seasoning and serving, in her mother-in-law's house, and both were well aware of the fact. The temporary reversal of plan became a permanent one. Then the Thanksgiving feast took place at the younger Conrads', and it was a feast, for Anne outdid herself. It looked as if the Christmas one might take place there too. Then they began to ask in Neal's friends, young lawyers and their wives who had been swift to offer hospitality to the bride and groom; the mayor and his sister, the minister and his two married daughters. This meant shaded candles on the table, salted nuts, chilled celery and olives, more elaborate courses. It meant extra work, too. Still the labor was nothing, absolutely nothing. Anne laughed at that.

But those bills! The figures began to dance before her eyes. Anne, who was never sick, began to realize that their horrible cavorting, their sinister leaping, were giving her a headache. She continued, mechanically, until she had finished everything she needed to do, then she lay down on the davenport in the living-room so as not to rumple the clean white spread on the brass bed, and thought matters over. That night, when supper was over, instead of curling up in Neal's arms, she faced him with grave determination.

"Neal," she said soberly, "I've been thinking things over. Our expenses. We've got to make them less."

"Can't," replied Neal comfortably. "Come here."

"We've got to. It makes me unhappy not to have bills paid promptly."

"All right. I'll draw some more money out of the bank."

"That makes me unhappy, too."

"Goodness, Anne! You're probably the unhappiest woman in Hinsboro."

"Besides," she continued relentlessly, and without noticing his levity, "you can't keep on, much longer, drawing money out of the bank, can you? I mean, there isn't such an awful lot left."

"Look here, Anne, what's set you worrying about money? I earn it, don't I? I earn more and more all the time. And I haven't kicked at its going. I'm just as proud as I can be—"

"I want to pay cash for everything. I have plenty of time to go out and get things myself instead of having them delivered. The 'cash and carry' shops are much cheaper than the ones we're dealing with now; and Hamburg steaks, and stews, and roast pork are cheaper than porterhouse, and chicken and chops, and just as nourishing. It's possible even to have nice suppers without any meat at all— I've been studying food values. Macaroni and cheese and cocoa and grapefruit make a very nourishing meal."

"Good Lord!" exclaimed Neal.

"Besides," went on Anne, "we're feeding too many people. I never saw any one with such an appetite as Arthur. That Sunday dinner for your family costs as much as everything we eat, the entire week, by ourselves. And if we must 'pay back' every time your friends ask us to their houses, we'll have to stop going."

"Why, Anne! I never guessed you were so inhospitable."

"I'm not inhospitable, but I'm honest. It isn't honest to feed one group of people with food for which we haven't paid another group of people."

Neal did not answer.

"I want you," said Anne, "to give me thirty dollars, the first of every month, the rest of this winter. I'll do the best I can with it. If I can save out of it in one month, we'll have company the next. If I can't, we won't. In the spring, if you've earned enough to put back all you've taken out of the bank, and have enough left over to increase my allowance say to forty dollars, we can have company every week, if you want to—first your family, then some of your friends. But of every increase you give me, I want you to put the same amount back into the bank."

"Anne, I've been mistaken in your character. I see you're a cold, calculating woman."

"Oh, Neal, *darling!* Don't say that, even in fun!"

"How can I help it, when you propose to starve me?"

"I don't propose to starve you. You'll hardly know the difference."

The tears were very near her lashes, her lips were trembling; but she stood her ground, even through Neal's onslaught.

"It's a good investment for me to appear prosperous. Instead of talking about economizing, we ought to be talking about new clothes, and a new car and a new house. I need all that, building up my future."

"We can have all that in the future, if we're careful now. But your future won't amount to much, if you found it on debt."

Finally, without having given her a definite answer, he absolutely refused to discuss the question any further. She could see that he, as well as herself, was hurt. He was generous to a fault, and he could not bear to see his generosity curtailed. Besides, what right had she to call him overconfident or question his judgment, when his self-confidence and his judgment had always been justified? Perhaps she was making a mistake. She was nothing but an ignorant, inexperienced little country girl, presuming to dictate to him. Perhaps she was making a mistake. Yet instinctively she felt, though she did not know, that she was right.

The next morning, without comment, Neal gathered up the offending bills, and a day later, they came back to her, receipted. On Friday evening he asked her, casually, if she had telephoned his mother asking her for Sunday dinner.

"I telephoned her that we couldn't have any Sunday dinners for the present because I've accepted an offer to sing in the choir of the First Congregational Church," said Anne calmly. "I'll have to sing twice on Sunday and go to at least one rehearsal during the week. Mrs. Simmons told me while we were hanging out our clothes that a soprano was needed badly. So I went and offered. The minister is awfully grateful to me; he thinks the favor is all on my side. I'm going to be paid two dollars a week."

Mrs. Simmons was their landlady, who lived on the ground floor of the little story-and-a-half house.

"She told me about a little boy, too," Anne went on, inwardly quaking but outwardly collected, "Jimmie Scott. He's been sick and fell behind in school work. His mother's been trying to find some one who would come to him late every morning for an hour and tutor him. I went to see Mrs. Scott this morning, and she was lovely to me. And Jimmie is a darling—eight years old, but he doesn't look it. I'm going to begin teaching him on Monday. Mrs. Scott says, if he does well with me, and is happy, she may not put him back in school at all this winter. He's going to do well. And he's going to be happy. And I'm going to get a dollar a day. You said you didn't want me to teach *school*, but you never said anything about *one* child, and I thought perhaps . . ."

"That was quite a wash you hung out, wasn't it?" Neal asked dryly.

He was angry, terribly angry, she was sure of it. She, who

would gladly have let herself be chopped to pieces—small pieces—to save him a pain in his little finger, had made him angry. It was almost too much to endure. Almost, but not quite. The streak of hardness in Anne saved her now. She faced him, somehow, without flinching. And then, suddenly, his expression changed, and he pulled her towards him, joyously, laughingly, wrapping his long, lean arms about her in a bear hug.

"You precious kid! You got the better of me after all, didn't you? Well, go to it! But stick your money in the bank. I'll give you the thirty dollars for housekeeping the first of every month."

CHAPTER NINE

November, December, January, February, March, April, May— Twenty-five dollars a month for rent, including heat and light, thirty dollars a month for food, another thirty for incidentals—ice, telephone, gasoline, contributions in church, cigarettes for Neal, a new pair of shoes for Anne, small dentist's bills for both of them. They were spending no more, on all their living expenses, than Neal was giving his family, and yet how much more they got for the money! Though they would have been perfectly contented to stay at home, occasionally they attended a concert, or the movies, and there were frequent subscription dances in Hinsboro, at moderate cost, to which they went, Anne wearing alternately the pink frilly dress and the white *crêpe de chine* in which she had been married—there was, after all, no chance to "save" it, she found with smothered regret. At Mrs. Simmons' instigation they joined a small musical club, the Bach and Beethoven Society, to which she and her sons, Fred and Frank, belonged. This club met on alternate Saturday evenings at the homes of its various members, when a short "program," also supplied by the members, was followed by light refreshments. Several of the same young women who belonged to this club played bridge together every Wednesday afternoon, and Anne, without much difficulty, mastered the rudiments of the game, and the art of serving tea after it. And, gaining courage, when her mother-in-law entertained the Hinsboro Chapter of the Daughters of the American Revolution, Anne offered her services for the day.

"It's very kind of you, my dear. I should have asked you

of course, in any case, but I thought you might feel it embarrassing to attend, when you are not eligible to the organization."

"I am eligible," said Anne carelessly. "Mother has belonged for years, though she seldom goes to the meetings—we don't think much of it at home, because we're all descended from Revolutionary heroes there. Hamstead has a Chapter that's been active for years. Mother joined through the Colonial Governor, Ephraim Wadsworth, afterwards General Wadsworth. And my father's great-grandfather, Moses Chamberlain, who was one of the first settlers in the upper Connecticut Valley, was a Lieutenant Colonel in the Revolution. I could of course go in through both those men, and I believe several others, but I've never bothered."

Anne was continually taking the wind out of her mother-in-law's sails. Mrs. Conrad had difficulty in suppressing her righteous indignation.

"Neal never told me you belonged to *those* Chamberlains—"

"I don't believe Neal knows it. We've never discussed it."

"And the Wadsworths—why, Anne, you could belong to the Colonial Dames too—as far as your ancestry is concerned. But of course you have to be formally invited to that."

"I *have* been formally invited," said Anne, still carelessly, "Mrs. Scott, Jimmie's mother, asked me. But I'm considering whether I can afford the dues."

"I should be delighted to pay your dues."

Anne, who by this time was well aware of Neal's contribution to the Conrad family, felt that this offer had its humorous aspect. But she did not say so. She dipped her white *crêpe de chine* carefully in gasoline, hung it on the clothes-line which she shared with Mrs. Simmons to dry, and made individual golden cakes frosted with White Mountain cream for her mother-in-law's party.

When spring came, Neal took out the horseless carriage, which had been stored in Mrs. Simmons' shed through the

colder winter months, and every Sunday afternoon they went
out for a drive. Sometimes Neal reached home early enough
for one on a week day, too; but he was staying later and
later at his office, as the volume of his work steadily increased.
When Jimmie Scott went away to the seashore, and the
soprano whose place Anne had filled at the First Congregational Church returned, Neal tried to extract a promise from
his wife that she would embark on no more wage-earning
ventures without consulting him.

"We're really ahead of the game now. Everything's back
in the savings bank that we took out, and more too; and if
I don't take any vacation this summer, not even for a few
days, but plug right ahead—"

"Oh, of course, that's what you ought to do—"

"But wouldn't *you* like to go home for a little while?"

"This is home."

"I meant to Hamstead. It gets terribly hot in Hinsboro."

"And leave you?"

She would not hear of it. She insisted that she did not mind
the heat at all, that the outings which they would take together in the horseless carriage would furnish her with all
the fresh air she needed. Those, and working in the little
garden which she had planted in Mrs. Simmons' back yard.
That garden was going to save them a great deal, in vegetables.

She did mind the heat, however, much more than she had
expected, much more than she ever confessed. The low-
ceilinged rooms, close up under the eaves, which had been
so cozy and comfortable in winter were hideously hot by
the first of July. At the end of September they were still
hideously hot. Neal was out of them from half-past eight
in the morning until six in the evening; then, after a supper
served on the tiny back porch—iced tea, crisp salad, cold
meat sliced thin, a light cake—he was out in the horseless
carriage until bedtime. Sometimes he took Anne with him;
sometimes he did not; there were "men to see"—"certain mat-

ters had come up—" He was gone more and more, became more and more preoccupied—and more and more he prospered. He bought her an electric fan, and then another. She put them in the bedroom which she kept closed and dark all day, and when he entered at night, he never found it unendurably warm. But her work never seemed to give her any respite from the heat. If she went into the garden early, she had to wash and bake in the middle of the day. If she did her household tasks first, the noonday sun was streaming down on her plants and vines by the time she was bending over them. She "put up" quarts and quarts of string beans, peas, corn, tomatoes—all they could possibly need through the following winter. The vegetables simmered and boiled on the little gas stove, the thermometer in the kitchen mounted higher and higher. But so did that account in the savings bank, which she had seen at first almost destroyed and then restored, bit by bit. Neal bought her a sewing machine, the best on the market, and paid cash for it. With this in her possession, she began to replenish their wardrobes, which were both becoming depleted. Materials were marked down, in the summer sales, and she bought remnants and mill-ends for a song that went into neatly tailored pajamas and shirts for Neal, dresses and aprons and underwear for herself. The bureau drawers, which had been growing empty, were refilled with fresh piles of clothing.

Suddenly the heat broke, there was an unseasonable "cold snap." Anne, who had gone out in the horseless carriage for a short ride without a wrap, came home chilled to the marrow of her bones. The next morning she was too ill to get up.

She did get up, nevertheless, her head throbbing, her limbs alternately quivering with cold and burning with fever. She ached all over. Her feet felt like lumps of lead, which, however heavy, she must drag after her. Neal, reading the morning paper, drinking his coffee, eating his cereal, noticed nothing the matter with her. When he had gone for the day, she lay down on the unmade bed, her breakfast dishes un-

washed, her bread unbaked. Towards noon she roused herself, telephoned for the supplies which she could not go out
and get, and forced herself to put the flat in order before she
succumbed again. Mrs. Simmons had "gone to the beach" for
a vacation, with Fred and Frank, who had arranged to get
"time off" together by going late, or she would have appealed
to her kindly landlady to help her. At five in the afternoon
she staggered to her feet, having eaten nothing all day, made
herself a cup of strong tea, peeled potatoes and dropped them
in cold water, opened a jar of string beans, molded Hamburg
steak into little balls. Just before six the telephone rang. It
was Neal.

"Hello, honey. How are you?"

"All right."

"Would you mind very much if I didn't come home to
supper? There's a Mr. Dawson, of Belford, here, who wants
to go over some matters with me, and he's asked me to take
dinner with him at the hotel. I think I better, perhaps—"

"Why, of course, Neal—"

"I won't be late. Good-by."

But he was late. Anne put the half-prepared food into the
refrigerator, and crept supperless back to bed. She lay there
for hours, too miserably uncomfortable to sleep, too stupid
and dizzy to read, counting the moments until he should
come and comfort her. At last she heard his key turning in
the latch. He bounded into the bedroom and sat down beside
her, bubbling over with excitement.

"Anne—Anne—are you asleep? What do you think has happened? Mr. Dawson and a few other men have been talking
to me, and they want me to run for state legislator. The
candidate from this district—Mr. Sooker, you know—has died,
and they think I'd never have a better chance to try my
luck. There are only three weeks before election, and of
course that means a whirlwind campaign, but I bet I can
make it, though of course I'd have to be gone from home a
lot. But you wouldn't mind that, would you? It's what we've

both hoped for, come sooner than we dared to hope. And, thanks to you, there's plenty of money saved up for the necessary expenses. Oh, Anne, do say you're glad!"

She said so, of course, dizzily, her voice sounding a long way off to her. She *was* glad—thankful—overjoyed. Only—why didn't she feel so? Why did she merely feel wretchedly ill, dreadfully lonely, and so much like a tired child who wanted to cry out her troubles against some kind, strong shoulder, instead of like a woman sharing exultantly in her husband's triumph. And why—oh, why—couldn't Neal—Neal, who had always been so thoughtful, so solicitous before, in the light of this new conquest, even see, how sick she was without being told?

CHAPTER TEN

He had not seen, the next morning when, earlier than usual, he left for his office. He still had not seen, three weeks later, when the duly registered voters of the district signified at the polls their willingness to have him represent them in the legislature at Belford that winter, and he came home, in the gray dawn following election day, to tell her so.

During the intervening time, struggling, striving to keep on her feet, and do her work, Anne had waited, at first hopefully, then despairingly, for the confidences which she had expected he would pour into her ear, the advice which he would seek from her "womanly intuition." She was sure there must be principles at stake, great principles by which he must either stand or fall. Instead, she heard, when he had time to talk to her at all, about rallies, about advertising space in newspapers, about quantities of cigars and dozens of bottles of whiskey. He was constantly telephoning that he wouldn't be home for supper, that he was in an awful rush just at that moment, but later he would tell her all about how things were going—pretty well, on the whole, he thought, though the only time to guess was after the votes were counted! And then later, when he did get home, some one would telephone him, and he would dash out again, without having exchanged a dozen words with her. He bought a new automobile—a "motor car" he called it now—a lower built model, with a top and windshield and acetylene lights, "turning in" the horseless carriage without a pang, though Anne watched it as it was being backed out of the shed for the last time with quivering lips. He bought a new overcoat, two new suits, quantities of new ties. Anne had hoped for a silk dress that fall, for she had patched and mended her navy-blue taffeta until it cracked away from her careful fingers with every stitch she took; but that, she knew, would be out of the question now. Sick as she felt, she longed to have him ask her to go with him to some of the public meetings, but he never did. Harriet went, making disturbances at several with her raucous pleas of "Votes for Women" and Neal was very angry. He spoke his opinion loudly about women who "meddled in things they didn't understand and never would," and Anne saw that it would only annoy him if she expressed an interest even dimly resembling Harriet's in the affairs of the nation. He had a secretary at his office now, Miss Lillie Letts, who chewed gum and wore transparent, flesh-colored shirtwaists; but she was efficient, she did everything for Neal that Anne had pictured herself doing some day. His mail went to the office, not to the little flat; Miss Letts opened it, answered it, filed it. He received his political visitors at the office, ushered in by Miss Letts. He rented an extra room, and invested in an Axminster rug, and a new center-table, mahogany veneered. Miss Letts selected them. He had no time for the Bach and Beethoven Society, for church, or the movies. Anne sat at home, coughing her head off—for her cold had settled in her chest—and aching all over, mentally as well as physically. There were no evenings together in the Morris chair, her head on his shoulder, his arms about her. She tried to wait up for him, night after night, but she was so tired, and he was so late—nearly always after midnight. She read the newspaper, cutting out every reference made to Neal, disregarding all mention of such minor candidates as Governor and Senator, then she went to bed. She was never asleep when he came in, but whether he hesitated to risk disturbing her, or whether he was too tired himself to crave for her companionship—Anne never knew which it was—he tumbled into bed beside her without a sign that he was aware of her presence. In the morning he never wakened

until she shook him gently, telling him that he had over-
slept, or the telephone bell jangled across his blurred senses.
Then he bolted his breakfast, and was gone.

Then finally he came to her and told her that he had
won. . . .

So that was what a campaign was like.

The Legislature met in January, still two months away. In
the meantime, Neal felt that he must, as far as possible, catch
up with his neglected profession. It had been neglected, of
course; but it had not suffered. He had gained prestige as a
successful candidate, and new cases poured in upon him. He
decided to keep the extra room, and Miss Letts. He really
needed both. At last, he talked to Anne about his plans for
going to Belford.

"I shall have to be there at least from Monday to Thursday
every week. Sometimes from Monday to Friday, though I
hope not often, for it's going to be hard, managing the office
work with only two days here. I'll have to keep it open Saturday afternoon, and maybe sometimes Sundays. Miss Letts
is willing. Of course I've raised her salary."

There seemed to be no answer expected of Anne. She made
none.

"So I'll be going back and forth, all the time. And it seems
to me that it would be better for you to stay right on here.
You're comfortably settled, and it would be a nuisance for
you to pull up stakes just for two or three months—the sessions will be over in April. Of course it isn't as if you were in
a house all alone. I know Mrs. Simmons is right here, and
you can call on her, if you need anything."

This time, had any reply been expected of her, Anne
could not have made it. He meant to leave her behind! The
idea had never occurred to her, and here it was all mapped
out, in orderly fashion, in his mind. He would miss her so
little, with his new interests, that he could face with resigna-
tion—with approval—the thought of being separated from her
more than half the time for several months. And she would

not have left him, for any known bribe, to spend a few days
during the torrid summer among the mountains that were so
dear to her. She had slaved for his comfort, for his well being,
and she had insured both, at the cost of her own radiant
health, for try as she might, she could not seem to pull herself
up physically. But the rest, the change, the excitement to
which she had been looking forward would, she had not had
the slightest doubt, do that. And now she was to have no
rest, no change, no excitement.

"It'll be much cheaper that way, too," Neal was saying. "Of
course the rent here has got to go on, for office and flat both,
and I can get a single room, without a bath, for two dollars a
day at the Talmage Tavern. A double room is at least a dollar
more, and the food would be twice of course what it would
for me alone. I spent a good deal of money during those three
weeks of the campaign. Concentrating that way, it cost more.
I know you'll get all those debts cleaned up quickly."

Mercifully, she did not doubt either his love or his sincerity,
as indeed, she had no reason to do. He was looking at the
situation in the reasonable, logical way, the way he always
looked at everything, the way that enabled him to get ahead
so fast. When the arrangement became known, every one
seemed to regard it as eminently sensible and suitable. Mrs.
Conrad thought so; Mrs. Simmons thought so; Miss Letts
thought so. Anne was ashamed at not sharing their enthusiasm more wholeheartedly, but at least she did not let them
guess that she did not do so. She longed to suggest having
Sol and Sam spend the winter months with her, going to
school in Hinsboro; but she recalled the size of their appetites,
the expense that would be entailed in food and suitable clothing, if she had them both; and either one would be lonely
without the other, lonelier than she would be all by herself.
She gave up the idea without even mentioning it. Neal, she
supposed, would hardly object if she occupied herself by taking a pupil or two, provided she could find any. Jimmie Scott

had, inconsiderately, recovered. But she did not feel well enough to attempt the undertaking.

In the flush of his victory, Neal's dormant passion for her awakened again and burned more hotly than ever before. But it had a different quality. If it was more intense, it was less tender. He seemed suddenly aware, not that he had neglected her, but that he had been deprived of her; and, looking ahead, was aware that his impending absence would deprive him of her still further. He sought to possess her the more completely in the present because the past had dispossessed him, and because the future was about to do so, fiercely resentful of a condition for which he had only himself to blame. There was a lack of spontaneity, a weariness, in Anne's response, which changed it from an answering flame to a mere affectionate and dutiful acquiescence; still, she never failed to respond. And Neal noticed the change in her far less than she noticed the change in him.

The holidays brought a flash of gayety. Neal had whipped his affairs into shape, and was ready enough to join in a few festivities before his departure. They entertained the Bach and Beethoven Society, went to a subscription dance at Odd Fellows' Hall, to an oyster supper at the First Congregational Church and to Sunday dinner at the Mayor's. Somewhat tardily, he became aware that Anne's trousseau had grown very shabby, and that neither she—nor he—had suggested that she might like to have some new clothes. Penitently, he bethought himself of the long-forgotten Mrs. Maple, and dictated a note for Miss Letts to send to her. The plump and prosperous modiste responded with a boxful of the latest fashions; but this time Anne caught sight of the price-tickets, and resolutely sent everything back. Neal gave her two dress-lengths—a black satin and a green voile—instead, and she made them up herself, on the superior sewing-machine, and insisted that they would do just as well. He knew they would not; and, after he reached Boston bought a long, fur-trimmed coat, with hat to match, at an excellent department store directly opposite the State House—where he could not very well help seeing it—and sent them to her.

He never knew how seldom she wore them. His days in Hinsboro, which dwindled to one, or at the most two, a week, were spent in feverish activities at the office. He gave up all pretense of getting home to supper, not even telephoning any more to say that he could not do so. From Belford he wrote her hurried little notes on scratch paper every day—well, nearly every day. "1 A.M. Tues. Dearest: Just home from the leg. dead tired, stormy session but very interesting. Tell you all about it when I see you, Neal." . . . "8 A.M. Thurs. Am just rushing out to breakfast with Dawson, darling Anne, as this is my only chance of seeing him to-day, so excuse a brief line. Yrs. ever, N." (Undated) "Afraid the Gov. is going to veto the tax bill. Have an appointment to see him at 11, in haste, N." It did not surprise him that her letters were not much longer, and not much more communicative than his own. He did not dream that day after day when he was not at home—and indeed often when, nominally, he was, she did not get up at all, or very little. The cold had vanished at last, leaving her weak and listless; but uncontrollable nausea had taken its place.

She hated the very smell of food, she could not bear the sight of it. All day long she revolted against the thought of it, and then, at night, dreamed of it. Resolutely she tried one form of nourishment after another, in the hope of finding something which she could retain, but one thing after another became loathsome to her. Milk—coffee—tea—dry toast—gruel—fruit juice—Mrs. Conrad and Mrs. Simmons both came to see her and offered advice. Unfortunately, their advice was not the same, and only puzzled their victim.

"You should lie very still, not make the slightest effort—the quieter you keep, until you get over the nausea, the better. I'll dust and carpet-sweep and wipe up the bathroom for you—nonsense, I'm glad to do it. If you'll promise me you won't stir. And take something *hot*. A cup of beef extract. I believe you'll find that very tasty."

"Exercise, my dear Anne, exercise is the main thing. Even if you don't feel like it, move about. I'd offer to come over and do your housework for you—not that I'm *accustomed* to doing anything of the sort—if I didn't know how much better it was for you to do it yourself. And try a little solid food. Often that sets better than liquids. No, don't say you can't, because of course you *can*."

Anne did not say she couldn't. Bewildered, but willing, she tried to do as she was told,—and grew steadily worse, while the tiny flat in which she had taken such pride and which she had kept so sweet and shining was left to neglect and disorder. And still Neal didn't guess, didn't notice— Of course he loved her, loved her dearly, but—was he *blind?*

March came in like a lion, roaring lustily. Anne lay in bed, listening to the wind howling, to the icy tapping of sleet against the window panes. It was nearly dark by four in the afternoon. She had not tried to get up at all, since it made her faint with dizziness even to cross the room to her bureau, and, after all, what was there to get up for? She had not brushed her hair, or washed her face, or made her bed. She wondered, vaguely, if she would ever feel like doing any of those things again, and drew the tumbled sheet up about her head to shut out the sound of the storm. As she did so, the doorbell rang.

At first she paid no attention. It rang once more, insistently. It rang again and again, the sound reverberating through the gloomy little rooms. At last she staggered to her feet, thrust them into her bed-slippers, and threw her soiled kimono about her shoulders. When she reached the front door, some one was pounding on it.

Leaning against the wall, she turned the lock. Before her stood Mr. Goldenburg, his kind, round face beaming with joy at the surprise he had given her. She sprang towards him with a cry of happiness. The next instant she had fainted away.

CHAPTER ELEVEN

"Now, my tear lidel frient, tell old Abie all apoud it."

"Oh, Mr. Goldenburg, *I am* so glad to see you! I never was so glad to see any one in all my life."

"Vel, vel—you must yust lie still a minute, an' holt my hant. I ain't goner run away. You'll feel petter bretty soon, *hein?*"

He had carried her back to bed, still unconscious, put a hot-water bottle at her feet, and dashed cold water over her white face. When she came to herself, she was crying bitterly, and clinging to him as if she would never let him go.

"Hey, listen, Anne—haf you any aromatic ammonia?"

"No—but it wouldn't matter if I had. I—I throw up everything I swallow, even water."

"So—so. Where is Neal?"

"In Belford. From Monday to Friday every week. And from Friday to Monday he's in his office."

"So—so."

"He doesn't know. He hasn't noticed. Oh, Mr. Goldenburg, I've read in books about young wives whispering 'their sweet secret' to their husbands blushing divinely, and both rejoicing, and the husbands surrounding the wives with 'the tenderest care.' And all that. I never read a word about this awful nausea, and feeling as if you'd rather die than live, and being lonely and forlorn. If I did tell Neal he'd probably just say, 'Oh—I'm in an awful hurry just now, but I'll be glad to hear about it next time I come home.'"

"Now den, Anne. You know dat ain't fair to Neal."

"Well, has he been fair to *me* I'd like to know?—I wouldn't have known myself what *was* the matter with me, if Mrs.

Conrad hadn't told me. She told me in such a dreadful way—
I'll never forget it or forgive her— She acts as if it were all
my fault—you'd think Neal had nothing to do with it at all
—and as if it were some dreadful crime. She had three children herself, didn't she? 'Don't you realize, Anne,' she said
severely, 'that you can't *afford* to have a baby?' And then
she said something about self-control. Self-control—she never
talked to her son about self-control! And we could afford a
baby every year on the money Neal turns over to her! And
she won't come and take care of me because she thinks I
ought to get up and take exercise! Exercise!"

"Now, den, Anne, you know it ain't respectful to speak so
of your moder-in-law. I'm sure she's a very nice lady." Mr.
Goldenburg tried to speak firmly, but the tones of his voice
did not carry conviction, which was hardly surprising, considering that, at the moment, he was thinking boiling in oil
too good for the elder Mrs. Conrad. "Vere is your landlady?
She lives downstairs, *hein?*"

"Yes, but she won't come because once when she had told
me to lie still I got up and made some biscuits for Neal's
supper. She doesn't believe in exercise."

"Haf you seen a doctor?"

"No, Mrs. Conrad said that wasn't necessary. She said it
would be a 'needless expense.' That this—this awful feeling
had to 'run its course' no matter what you did. So I thought—"

Mr. Goldenburg, disengaging his hand, walked over to the
telephone. "There *is* a doctor in Hinsboro, I suppose, *hein?*"
he asked sarcastically. "Dr. Pratt? So—led me see vat is his
number—seven-thirty-five— Yes, yes."

Dr. Pratt was in, he would be over, he said, right away.
And, in the scant half hour that elapsed before his appearance, Mr. Goldenburg proceeded to "tidy things up" with
a dexterity and a swiftness remarkable in so plump and placid
a person. He found a rag and a can of Dutch Cleanser, and
scrubbed the bathroom basin; he hung clean towels beside
it. He changed Anne's pillow cases and bureau scarf, and

laid her tumbled toilet articles in a neat row—hairbrush, mirror, nail-file, buttonhook. He ran the carpet-sweeper over the Axminster rug in the living-room, and dusted the flat surfaces of the mission furniture, wound the clock, watered the plants, threw away the rubbishy collection of old newspapers and magazines, lighted the gas stove and put the kettle on to boil. Then with complete composure he admitted the surprised physician, still wearing one of Anne's aprons firmly tied about his waist.

Dr. Pratt was not long in rendering his verdict. There must be regular care and skilled treatment without delay. Anne's condition was not dangerous, but he could not venture to describe it as otherwise than serious. She was very weak, had apparently been badly run down before—yes, yes, a heavy bronchial cold, also neglected. Well, would she rather be moved to a hospital, or have a nurse and maid installed? And of course her husband must be advised at once. It was useless for Anne to protest; Dr. Pratt spoke, brusquely, about the danger to the baby when she tried to do so. Appealingly, she turned to Mr. Goldenburg.

"Do you suppose, if you telegraphed Mabel, she would come and stay with me? I wouldn't know where to get a maid, or what to do with her afterwards. But Mabel—Mabel is my best friend," she explained to the doctor, "except Mr. and Mrs. Goldenburg. We've often planned that she should come and visit me, but somehow—"

"Why not telephone? Then she could get here sooner."

Mr. Goldenburg was already in action again. Without much difficulty, he located Mabel, and Mabel said that she would be delighted to come, that she would be there in the morning. The doctor departed, promising to send around a nurse at once; and, within an hour, the nurse materialized. And leaving her to bathe the patient and make her bed, Mr. Goldenburg sought out first Mrs. Simmons, next Mrs. Conrad, and finally—catching the last train to Belford—Neal.

Anne never knew exactly what he said to any of them; she

was, in fact, too ill to inquire, or to care, for several weeks. But, as those weeks dragged their slow course through, she became vaguely and comfortably conscious, sick as she was, that she was happier than she had been in a long, long time. Mabel arrived, and barely allowing time to change from her travel dress to an all-enveloping apron, scrubbed and scoured the flat from end to end, and kept it, from then on, in a state of matchless cleanliness. Miss Keep, the nurse, waited on her by inches. Her hair was not tangled and matted any more, there was ice at the back of her neck, a hot-water bottle at her feet, she was gently rubbed—her back, her arms, her forehead—with bay rum. If it was given to her when she was drowsy, she soon found that she could retain a little food—only a spoonful or so, at first, and it had to be either very hot or very cold, but gradually the temperature did not matter so much, and she could take more and more. Neal came home looking very much cowed, badly frightened—all the gay self-confidence, the driving energy, wiped from his face. He brought her flowers—the first he had given her since her honeymoon, and sat down beside her on the bed, his shoulders sagging, and tried to talk to her, but couldn't because his voice shook so. At first, that is—afterwards he collected himself and spoke better. But not until she had seen how shaken he was, how sorry and, forgiving him, forgot there was anything to forgive.

By the first of April, Anne was sufficiently better so that Miss Keep could leave, Mabel caring for her—since now she did not need so much care—and doing the housework, too. By the first of May she was up for a little while each day. The session of the legislature was over, and Neal was home again for good, home, that is, until another election at least—he had decided to run for office again then, this time for the State Senate. He was very kind to her, very thoughtful, and though he was very busy, and usually brought work home with him, he seldom stayed in the office during evening or on Sundays—once in a while, of course, but not very often. Soon she was able to play for him on the new piano with which he had surprised her, the first time she walked out to the living-room, and to go for short, easy rides with him in the automobile. The first of June, Mabel went home, leaving them alone again, and they were very happy. They were grateful to Mabel, grateful beyond expression, but they would only have a few more months alone. Anne did quantities of sewing, sitting on the little porch; she trimmed a bassinet with pink silk and white dotted muslin and lace which the Goldenburgs sent her, she lined a little wicker chest of drawers with scented pads, she feather-stitched tiny flannel petticoats and hemstitched tiny muslin dresses. Mrs. Simmons did her washing and ironing and the cleaning, and Neal took care of the garden; but except for this help, Anne did her own work again. Dr. Pratt made no objection to her working now that she felt all right, provided she did not overdo. In fact, it was much better that she should, he said, since she had always been used to activity, and idleness would be bad for her. When he delivered himself of this opinion, Mrs. Conrad announced with satisfaction, that this was what she had kept saying, right along.

Anne's baby was born in the Hinsboro hospital on a torrid night near the end of August. She was in labor for thirty-six hours, and, at the end of that time, the child was taken from her with instruments. At first she fought her hard battle uncomplainingly and bravely, submitting to everything she was told to do, and everything that was done to her, calmly and patiently. But as the agony increased and became unbearable, quite suddenly, she lost her self-control, shrieking and sobbing for mercy. When the doctor began to give her whiffs of ether to take off the sharp edge of the pains, Neal, who had stayed with her up to that time, became deathly sick from the smell of it, and left her. She felt herself abandoned to a bottomless pit of torture. When Dr. Pratt finally held the ether cone to her face, telling her to breathe as much as she wanted of it, she snatched it from him, and pulled it down over her mouth and nose, tightly, tightly, oblivion the only mercy she sought—if it could last forever, if it only could, her last conscious prayer.

Her consciousness returned in waves. She babbled, telling secrets she did not mean to divulge, and yet unable to be silent. She felt bruised and beaten, she longed to be left to die in peace—and still they kept doing things to her, things that disturbed her, things that hurt her. If they would only go away! She cried, weakly, the tears dropping down from her cheeks to the pillow, and yet she could not move to wipe them off, and no one else seemed to notice them.

Then suddenly, Neal was there beside her, kissing the tears away; and between them on the bed, lay their little son.

CHAPTER TWELVE

In the next eight years, Neal built up his law practice, which
continued to grow, not indeed by leaps and bounds, but
steadily and satisfactorily. He also served four terms in the
state legislature, the third as Speaker of the House, the fourth
as chairman of the most important committee in the Senate;
and, during all this time, he commuted back and forth between Belford and Hinsboro, bringing his laundry with him
to save expense, and occupying his two-dollar room at the
Talmage Tavern.

During the same eight years, Anne, smothering again and
again her disappointment at taking no tangible part in her
husband's campaigns, and at being left behind when he went
to Belford, washed, cooked, cleaned, sewed, and took care
of Junior; presented that husky youngster, when he was three
years old, with a little sister, Nancy; took care of them both;
washed, cooked, cleaned and sewed some more.

When the second baby was imminent, it became apparent
that the little flat, in which they had continued to live up
to this time, would not suffice for the family needs any longer.
They had not saved up enough money to carry out their
treasured plan of building, unless they built a house which
would be merely another temporary makeshift. So they moved
to a six-room cottage, which they were able to rent cheaply,
and which was sorely in need of paint, paper, and plumbing.
By degrees they persuaded a reluctant landlord to make it
more comfortable and attractive. With two more rooms in
their possession than they had had since their marriage, they
converted one into a nursery, and one into a den, and the

wide, though dilapidated veranda which encircled the house, usually much cluttered with a sand box, a kiddy coop, a never-emptied basket of mending, and a miscellaneous collection of shabby toys, gave them, in mild weather, an extra living-room; while the large yard provided the children with a space in which to range, and Anne a space in which to plant and cultivate both a flower and a vegetable garden.

But, though they were glad to be free of Mrs. Simmons' flat, they missed Mrs. Simmons herself. She had been willing enough to help with the heavier housework and to "listen" for the baby when Neal and Anne went out together as long as they remained under her roof, but she felt it beneath her to "hire out"—the "out" being taken literally. Mabel came and spent a month with them when Anne left the hospital after Nancy's birth, a complacent Mabel, engaged to George, who had become more and more prosperous and who now had the largest farm and the finest barns in Hamstead. She was most helpful and kind; but she was unwilling to prolong her visit, as she had done before. After she left, Anne was unable to go motoring with Neal, or attend the meetings of the Bach and Beethoven Society, or entertain her little bridge club. Worse than this, her close confinement to the house, and the never-ending drudgery of her work began to tell on her heavily. She not only grew very thin herself, but the baby stopped gaining, became fretful, and turned blue under her eyes. Alarmed, Anne consulted Dr. Pratt, and he told her that unless she had regular help and equally regular recreation, she would have to wean Nancy.

"And that," he added, meaningly, "you should not, of course, consider in this warm weather."

Anne's dread of the "servant problem" rose from a deeper source than the horrible stories she had heard from her mother-in-law about the depravity of all domestic workers, and the fact that she felt she could ill-afford to feed and pay a maid; it rose also from her very sincere sense of her own probable incompetence in directing, rather than doing, work, and her unwillingness to entrust the care of the children to any one else. But to her infinite surprise and relief, Dora King, the first applicant in response to the advertisement which Anne inserted in the *Hinsboro Times*, came when she said she would, contentedly took possession of the attic, and seemed perfectly satisfied to remain. She was not a skilled servant; indeed, she had never had a "place" before. She was, like Anne herself, a farmer's daughter, who had drifted to a little city, and who had not enjoyed "clerking" as much as she expected. She was willing to learn; and Anne, far from resenting her ignorance, marveled at the quickness with which she overcame it.

But, even with Dora's help, her working hours were long and hard, and though she managed to nurse the baby through the summer, she was obliged to wean her with the coming of cool weather, a process which proved trying for them both. Indeed, as time went on, Anne became more and more appalled at the number of things that could happen to children, normal, reasonably healthy children. They had croup, and kept her awake all night; they had colic, and kept her distracted all day; they had measles and mumps and whooping-cough and chicken pox; they had nasty little sniffling colds, and deep frightening coughs and after a certain number of these, Dr. Pratt insisted that they must have their tonsils and adenoids removed. Junior fell out of a tree and broke his leg; Nancy upset a kettle of hot water on herself and scalded her arm. They outgrew their rompers as fast as Anne could make them; tore them as fast as she could mend them; soiled them as fast as she could change and wash them. Their faces were continually becoming smeared with mud or egg. They clamored for drinks of water after they had gone to bed, for sugar cookies as soon as they had been sent outdoors to play. They swarmed over her the minute she put on a fresh dress, and they scattered disreputable toys all over the living-room ten minutes after she had whipped it into perfect order.

But they adored her. She was to them far more important,

far more precious than their father. They loved him, of course; but he did not figure largely in their field of life, not nearly as largely as she did, not even as largely as Dora. He was away from home a great deal, and they learned to take this as a matter of course. They were glad to see him when he returned, but they did not miss him when he was away. They were not dependent on him—in a manner which they recognized—for food and comfort. Neither did he read them stories at night, or sing gay little songs with them in the morning, sitting down with them at the piano directly after breakfast to do so. He did not dress dolls, or stuff depleted teddy-bears, or cause limping railroad trains to leap forward again, or build cathedrals out of stone blocks. He was BUSY.

So, in the adoration of her children and of Dora—for she attained that also—Anne found, for a long time, all the beauty and romance which her life contained. She was not unhappy; she felt fewer and fewer pangs because Neal seemed to need her so little, in her overwhelming consciousness that Junior and Nancy needed her so much. If she had no talents towards directing political destiny, she at least had undeniable gifts as a homemaker. The dingy little cottage became gradually more and more lovely. She experimented with hangings, with rugs, with furniture, reading omnivorously and far into the night every authority she could find on such subjects, buying cautiously and cannily, on her rare trips to Belford, where she studied the shops as carefully as if they had been equations in algebra, and on her rarer trips to Hamstead where antiques were still to be found in sheltered attics. And her housekeeping became so locally renowned that the elder Mrs. Conrad was much annoyed. She "put up" more fruits and vegetables than any woman in Hinsboro. She kept hens, and supplied not only her own family and her mother-in-law's with eggs and poultry, but sold some of both besides, until Neal put a stop to that; then canned her extra chickens, and stowed away her extra eggs in waterglass. Her angel cakes, her lemon pies, her Parker House rolls were in demand for every church supper and harvest festival. She continued to make all her own clothes, to make Neal's shirts and pajamas; she began to make the children's clothes, too, and Dora's.

And so the seasons sped past, filled to overflowing, with hardly a landmark to show their passing. She had been married five years, six, seven; Junior was five years old and starting in Kindergarten; she had been married eight years, nine, ten; Nancy was five years old and starting in Kindergarten. She was not so busy any more, and the house was empty, terribly so. Then war was declared, and suddenly, she was busier than ever. She knitted innumerable sweaters, she joined a class in surgical dressings, she sold Liberty bonds from house to house, she fed her family on "substitutes" so successfully that they saw "meatless, sweetless, and wheatless" days go by without a murmur. She was spurred to supreme efforts in "conservation" because Neal had been appointed Food Administrator for the state. He filled the position with the greatest brilliance and thoroughness. He organized and promoted his department with consummate success; he went into every county, making patriotic speeches, presiding at rallies, attending conferences. Twice he was actually "called to Washington" by wire, and on one of these occasions, he went to the White House and talked earnestly to the President for five minutes. His picture surmounted the charts of instructions which conscious housewives—not only of Hinsboro and Belford, where he was well known already, but of the entire state, where he was less well known—hung in their kitchens. The press of the state, which, up to this time, had paid him scant attention, began first to notice and then to "feature" him. It was rumored that the governor, a rather shy, retiring man, was jealous of him. He gave substantial contributions to all patriotic causes—a thousand dollars here, two thousand dollars there. He did not consult Anne beforehand in making these donations and when she heard them publicly announced, she could hardly believe her ears.

"How can you give a thousand dollars to the Fund for French Wounded when you haven't *got* it?" she demanded aghast.

"I've *got* to have it . . . well, if you must know, I've borrowed a little . . . I meant to suggest that you should come to Washington with me the next time I get a wire—the President intimated he would want to see me again before long—but I guess, from the way you talk you wouldn't think the expense of the trip was justified—"

"No, I wouldn't," she answered quietly. She was terribly wounded at the sarcasm with which he had spoken, terribly hurt by her renewed consciousness of her own unimportance. She rose, half blinded with tears, and going out to the kitchen, began to put together a cake-batter which contained neither butter nor white flour and only one egg. Mixed with melted chocolate, and eaten very fresh, it was not really bad at all. As she stirred, she lifted her eyes to the chart surmounted by Neal's picture and read, for the hundredth time, his stirring proclamation. Slowly her vision cleared, and she felt serene and proud once more.

By the time the Armistice was signed, there was no doubt that Neal had become the most conspicuous figure in his state. Emboldened by this progress, he ran the following fall for Lieutenant-Governor. He had been confident, glowingly confident, of victory. And, by one of those strange turns of fortune which make gambling a safe and sure sport compared to politics, he had been overwhelmingly defeated. The blow was the more bitter because Low, the man running for Governor on the same ticket, was elected by a substantial majority.

Neal was not a good loser; he had been silent in his success —that is, at home—seldom discussing his progress with Anne; now he became complainingly loquacious.

"Low sold me out; it was money that defeated me, money and crooked politics."

"You have always spent quite a little yourself, in your campaigns."

"Are you accusing me of being a crook?" he almost shouted at her.

"Of course not; quite the contrary. I'm saying that I don't believe your opponent was either, or Mr. Low. It stands to reason that Mr. Low would rather have you for Lieutenant-Governor than a man of the opposite party."

She did not again fall into the error of expressing such an opinion. Neal could not bear to have her, or any one else, think that he himself was to blame for his defeat. He actually swore at her, he was so angry. He apologized, after a time, for his language, but in the meanwhile he went sullenly about the house, or shut himself up in his office, declining to come home to his meals. This was not the worst of it; sometimes when Anne telephoned the office he did not answer, and she had no idea where to find him. She had hard work to keep from crying—then hard work to keep him from seeing that she had been crying. If his political success had been difficult for her to bear, his political failure was doubly so. Through her tears she saw in remembrance the man she had married—so gay, so kind, so loving and tender. Through her tears she saw too, in reality, the man to whom she was married—somber, selfish, indifferent, curt. If she had loved him less, it would have been easier for her. But to her he was still as he had been on the day when he first held her in his arms, the most wonderful being in the world.

She had the wisdom, greater than might reasonably be expected, to neither reproach nor nag him; and, after a few weeks, he pulled himself together, and flung himself into his law-practice with renewed vigor. He was making money now, real money, and if he kept his nose to the grindstone, and closed his ears to the humming of the political bee for all time, he could become—well, very comfortably fixed financially. On Christmas day he gave Anne the deeds for a large lot on the outskirts of the city which she had long admired, and suggested to her, a little gruffly, that he thought the time had come when they could build if she would still like to, and that he would tell an architect who was said to know his business to start drawing plans whenever she said the word. They could amuse themselves going over blueprints, these long winter evenings. By the time the ground had thawed out enough to start excavating, they could probably have decided what they wanted. She knew that this was his way of seeking to make amends, and responded with delight. With the plans spread out before them, their heads touching, they came closer together, mentally and spiritually as well as physically, than they had been in a long time; and, with the coming of spring they spent every spare moment in supervising the building. This took longer than they had expected —almost a year—which annoyed Neal; and it cost more than they expected—by several thousands—which troubled Anne. But they had found a common interest, a common enthusiasm again, and both were happy.

The new house, when it was finally done, was extremely comfortable, and very attractive. It was white-painted and green-shuttered, a "simple Colonial model" with a flower garden in front, a vegetable garden behind, a neat garage at one side, and a glassed-in sun parlor at the other, wide lawns all about it. Downstairs there were a broad hall, a large living-room with a big, friendly fireplace, a small den for Neal, a good-sized dining-room and a kitchen with light on two sides, and every possible appliance to make cooking easy and pleasant. Upstairs were a sewing-room and five bedrooms, one for Neal and Anne, one for Junior, one for Nancy, one for Dora, and a spare-room; and three bathrooms. Overall there was a spacious attic, and under all a spacious cellar. The most modern type of furnace was installed; so were all imaginable electrical devices—a vacuum cleaner, a washing machine, a mangle, a stove. And there was Colonial furniture upstairs and down, Persian rugs on the ground floor, simple ornaments scattered here and there, open bookcases well filled, a few good prints and water colors. They bought no new car that year, though theirs was several seasons old already, and Anne pared her housekeeping expenses almost as closely as in the first days of her marriage. But no reasonable expense was spared on the house, and it stood in her name, unmortgaged and fully paid for. They had built for all time, and built well.

CHAPTER THIRTEEN

Their first guest, after they were duly installed in the new house, was Clarence Hathaway.

He appeared in the wake of a telegram stating that he was passing through Hinsboro on his way back to Washington after a vacation in Canada, and would like to "spend the weekend if they could put him up." And Anne felt a stirred excitement, even greater than Neal's surprise, when the message reached them.

"Good old Clare—he doesn't forget his friends, does he? He's first Secretary now, you know, in Paris—getting on the way he planned all right, and look at me—"

"You're getting on all right too, aren't you? *I* think so! Oh, Neal—what shall I wear?"

Neal burst out laughing. "That's the first question any woman asks, under any circumstances, I guess," he jeered gently. Then after a moment's silence, he added, "I suppose it does matter. Couldn't you run up to Belford and get something?"

"There isn't time."

"Well, you look all right to me whatever Hathaway may think, and that ought to go as big with you as it does with me when you say *you* think I'm getting on all right whatever—"

"It *does* go big with me, darling. Only—"

She realized how big the "only" was with the first casual glance which Hathaway cast in her direction after the mutual greetings had been exchanged. The house was quite all right; Anne felt sure of that; she hoped especially that he had

noticed the guest-towels and bed linen in his room, which
she had embroidered herself. And Dora was all right. She
carried off her unaccustomed but wholly correct black uniform and spotless frilly apron with pleased pride, and served
tea without a visible tremor. The tea was brought into the
living-room on a silver tray, steaming in a silver pot, flanked
with thick cream and hot water in smaller silver pots and
lemon sliced thin on a little crystal dish, and fragile flowered
teacups; and it was accompanied by lettuce sandwiches, and
hot biscuits stuffed with marmalade, and frosted cakes set
out on a mahogany muffin-stand. The children were all right
too. They came in for just the proper moment, Nancy, in
smocked China silk, curtseying, Junior, in a blue serge coat
and white trousers, shaking hands, neither shy nor forward,
neither silent nor chattering. Anne saw them go out of the
room, her heart swelling with satisfaction. And of course Neal
was all right; his old charm, his old buoyancy, had come to
the surface and bubbled over again at the sight of his friend.
Hathaway himself, for all his elegance, had no more distinction, no more magnetism. But she—

There had been so much else to do in preparation for the
great visit that she had found herself with only fifteen minutes
left in which to dress; so she had washed hastily, and hastily
twisted her curls into a knot on the top of her head. Neither
her hair nor her skin had ever had any care, and beautiful
as they still were, they had begun to suffer from neglect; she
had not been to the dentist's since Nancy was a baby—at Dr.
Pratt's insistence she had gone then; while her hands, inevitably, had suffered most of all. They were rough, enlarged,
reddened. Her "best dress" was nearly a year old, and she
had made it herself, as she did all her dresses; it was a brown
taffeta, many seasons behind the style, too long, too full, over-
trimmed. She had thought it pretty once; now she hated it.
And when Hathaway gave her that casual look, she felt that
she could gladly tear it off and throw it into the scrap basket.

That was, indeed, exactly what she did do with it, several

hours later, when, the perfect dinner served, the children in bed and asleep, she left the two men to "talk over old times together" and went to her room. Exhausted, from emotion as much as fatigue, she flung herself down on her bed without undressing. Then, jerking herself upright with a swift, ungraceful movement, she ripped the offending garment from neckband to hem, and stamped on it.

"No wonder he thought you were a perfect fright," she sobbed aloud, "I'll never own another dress like that as long as I live. I'll take the first train to New York after he goes and buy myself some clothes. No, I won't either; I'll go to that nice Mrs. Maple in Washington. I guess I can go there and shop, if I can't go for—for any other reason! I can leave the children with Dora perfectly well, and I don't need to scrimp and save any more. Why have I been such an awful fool as to keep on doing it, and on, and on! I'll have my hands taken care of too; they're as rough as nutmeg graters! And my face massaged and my hair treated. I—I am probably the most hideous looking woman in all the world."

Meanwhile, downstairs, the conversation had taken a turn which she was very far from guessing.

The discussion of "old times" did not last long, and the "dear old college days" supposed to form the sole topic of conversation between classmates meeting after a long separation, received no more than a passing mention. Hathaway talked of himself for a while, of his satisfactory advancement, his delightful post in Paris, his hopes for an even more notable appointment; easily and quietly, without arrogance, without even a too apparent complacence. And it was he who finally began to talk of Neal.

"But you'll get terribly fed up if I go on like this— How about yourself? Doing well, aren't you?"

"Financially, yes. It was hard sledding at first, but this year I've earned close to fifteen thousand. I give both Anne's family and mine a regular allowance, and she has two brothers whom

I'm helping to educate. But even so, we'll be pretty comfortable, if I can keep on going ahead, and I think I can. I've never run into debt, or even spent all my income—Anne's seen to that," he added ungrudgingly. "I have a few good investments, and I carry life insurance. We all have savings bank accounts—the children too. And of course now we have this house."

"Not startling, but pretty solid, I should say. But why do you stress the word 'financially'? Don't you feel you're doing well every way?"

"I was thinking that I hadn't done as well politically as I'd hoped."

"Because of one trivial defeat!"

"It didn't seem trivial to me. I expected to be Governor of this state by now."

"Well, yes. I rather thought that was your plan. But after all—"

Hathaway tapped the arm of his chair with his fingers, gazing into the open fire as he did so. Then he asked a most astonishing question.

"How about your wife? Was she interested in politics too?"

"Anne?" Neal's surprise was apparent in his voice. "Why, Anne would be interested, I guess, in anything I wanted to do. She—she's devoted to me."

"Yes, of course, I saw that. But I mean—has she been helping you actively and directly as well as passively and indirectly?"

"She's gone without everything," Neal answered, coming swiftly to Anne's defense, under the impression that she was being attacked. "Good times, and pretty clothes, and trips and friends. I never would have been able to go into politics if she hadn't. And she's been a perfect wife and mother. The children adore her, and so do I, though I guess I don't show it as much as I might. I've got a devilish one-track mind, and when I get started on a lawsuit or a campaign, I almost forget I have a family—sometimes. Just the way I forgot everything else in the world when I saw Anne, and made up my mind I'd got to have her. It would be hell if I didn't know she was still there, in the background, too. Once I thought I was going to lose her—I'd neglected her terribly, and she was going to have a baby, which made it all the worse—and I nearly went wild when I realized what I'd done."

"But after you'd had a chance to forget about that bad time, you neglected her again?"

"I suppose I did—do. But—there's never been another woman."

"Good God! I should say not! What do you want—the Capitoline Venus?"

"No," roared Neal, angrily, "what are you driving at, anyway?"

"My dear fellow, please don't think I'm venturing to criticize your conduct. And as for criticizing your wife—well, I thought ten years ago she was one of the loveliest, as well as one of the most remarkable girls, I'd ever met in my life. I've remembered her, pretty vividly, all this time. That's a little unusual for me. And I confess that seeing her to-night has been an acute disappointment."

"Well, I'm not disappointed in her. She suits me."

"Just wait a minute, can't you? I still think she's beautiful—and remarkable. Even more remarkable than I'd guessed. But I think she's tragic."

"Tragic!"

"Yes. How old is she? Under thirty? I thought so. Well, she looks over forty. She has a good mind, hasn't she? Taught school before you married her, was awfully keen on educating herself better? How long is it since she's read anything but nursery rhymes? She's stagnating, mentally as well as physically. Kept in the background! I should think she had! She's submerged herself in your personality, and your career and your children until she's nothing but a washed-out drudge without a particle of individuality left. She's done it voluntarily, because she loved you—loves you. But she must know, even if you don't know, that she was capable of something a good deal bigger. And she must have passed some pretty bitter hours when she first realized you didn't intend to give her a chance to fulfill her destiny. For God's sake, why haven't you tried putting her in the *foreground?* With her looks, and her mind, and her natural gifts as a hostess— Neal, you utter fool."

"Even if you are my guest, and an old friend, I think you've gone about far enough in discussing my wife."

"Then suppose we discuss mine for a change."

"Yours! I didn't know you were married!"

"I'm not. But I was."

"You mean you lost her? Clare—I'm darned sorry, I hadn't heard—"

"Yes, I lost her. But she didn't die. She found out she cared for some one else more than she did for me. I found it out, too."

"Oh—"

"Yes. Exactly. She was a poor girl when I married her, almost as poor as Anne. And she came from a home that wasn't much better. But she was pretty, devilishly pretty and ambitious—for herself. I was much the best bet that her hand had ever held. I fell for her, hard—and fast. I ought to have known better— Lord knows I've had experience enough—but I married her. She began by almost ruining me financially. There was absolutely no limit to what she wanted. And she ended by almost ruining me diplomatically. Cæsar's wife had nothing on that of a rising young secretary. I left that post in Rome, which I enjoyed so much, because I was given an indefinite leave of absence. When I went to Paris, I went without her."

Slangily, casually, without a trace of his usual careful elegance, Hathaway had told his story. But Neal found himself clearing his throat, more moved than he could have imagined. And not only moved—enlightened. Clare—had made no comparisons—aloud. But Neal saw those that he had made mentally, as clearly as if they had been engraved in flaming letters. Saw, too, how he had injured Anne; and since he could, perhaps, never be entirely selfless, how he had, in injuring her, injured himself as well. Before he succeeded in framing an answer, Hathaway spoke again.

"So that's that. And seeing Anne—you don't mind if I call her Anne, do you?—here to-night brought it all back to me—because she's—she's so different. And you're so lucky—and playing against your luck!"

"What," Neal managed to ask, "would you do, if you were I?"

Hathaway balanced the question. "Would anything very dreadful happen," he asked at length, "if you left those two corking kids with that pretty maid—she'd look after them all right, wouldn't she?—and took Anne on a vacation? You could do with a little change yourself—you'd find that one-track mind of yours developing into a transcontinental trunk-line when you got back. You're stale, man! I'm sailing next week on the *France*—why don't you see if you could get a stateroom on the same boat? And—and spend the summer in Paris—and let me help give you both a good time!"

CHAPTER FOURTEEN

Neal had come down with a heavy cold which kept him confined to the hotel, but he insisted, since he was not really sick, and since there was so little time left, that Anne should not stay in with him, but should go, as they had both planned to do, and have tea with Clare at the Château de Madrid.

She did not answer at once when he made this suggestion, or even turn towards him. She was standing by one of the long windows of their *salon*, looking out on the courtyard of the hotel,—the green grass plot, the tall feathery tree that shaded their bedroom, the prim little iron chairs standing stiffly about. The open doors of the dining-room beyond revealed it to be empty, as befitted the time half-way between luncheon and dinner. But there were bright crowded nosegays on the white-covered table, and, beyond, the cheerful clatter of silver and glass being put away. Now and then an aproned *garçon* flicking a napkin, passed into view and disappeared again.

It was very warm, for Paris, and Anne's beautifully dressed hair, shining like burnished gold, escaped from its net about the white nape of her neck and her white brow, and curled in little soft moist tendrils. She was flushed, too, with the heat, a little languid; her cheeks were very pink, and her long lashes drooped over them as if it were an effort for her to keep her eyes open. Her diaphanous *négligé*, pale orchid-color, had slipped away from one white, rounded shoulder, and she raised a slim white hand and pulled it into place. The *négligé* was cut in a deep V, and when she had adjusted it over her shoulder, she also tightened the ribbon on the sheer lace-edged slip beneath it, to raise it over her breast.

"I shan't be disappointed," she said at length, "if I don't go. There are some letters I ought to write and—"

"Nonsense!"

"And I shall have to dress."

"Since when," teased Neal, "has that been a burden to you? . . . though I must say you look very nice the way you are."

She flushed, deliciously. "I meant—it is so very warm."

"That new powder-blue crêpe has just come in from Lucien Lelong."

"Yes—I know—and the powder-blue hat from Camille . . . I suppose that Clare might think it unappreciative if we both went back on him."

She disappeared, into the bedroom, and a moment later Neal heard the sound of running water from the bathroom beyond. He smiled. There would be scented salts in that bath, he knew, and scented powder, showered from a great ball-like puff, after it, and just a touch of liquid scent besides, *jasmine de corse* that cost four dollars for a tiny bottle and came from a famous perfumer. Then fresh lingerie pulled from a deep drawer, another lace-edged slip, silk stockings as fine as gossamer. Last of all, that powder-blue frock, as perfect of cut as it was of color, with a wide hat and narrow slippers to match the frock. Then Anne would reappear, smiling almost shyly, waiting for his exclamation of approval.

How happy she had been all summer! It was nearly four months now since they had stood beside the gang-plank, watching it lifted, waving good-by to Dora and Junior and Nancy, to Mr. and Mrs. Goldenburg and George and Mabel, who had all come to see them off, for it was a great day for these old friends as well as for themselves when Neal and Anne actually "went to Europe." Neither of them was seasick a single minute, and every inch of the ship, from their own tiny cabin, to the great *salon* where they played bridge and danced, and drank strange new refreshing drinks, was a source of delight to them. Then came the landing at Havre, with the choppy blue waves beneath them and the scarless blue sky above them, and the hurrying porters in their blue blouses chattering French, and the funny train with seats facing each other across the car in the little compartment. Then the garden-like country side, the stone cottages, red tiled roofs, high walls, smug fields; and finally—Paris, the lights streaming in the Place de la Concorde as they crossed it for the first time, the quaint hotel on the Rue St. Honoré where Clare had engaged rooms for them, and the Bois de Boulogne beckoning them for their first evening drive.

The very morning after their arrival, while they were still laughing over their breakfast of *café au lait* and long hard rolls, served in their little *salon*, and wondering how they were ever to "hold out" until lunch time on such meager fare, Clare, who had not left them until nearly midnight, reappeared, and mapped out their program. Before they did a single thing, before they even went to see the Louvre and Notre Dame, before they had lunch at Ciro's or dinner at the Café de la Paix, Anne must be reclothed. He would accompany them to a dressmaker's—a *petite maison* not too expensive but very *recherchée*, and worthy of being entrusted with this task.

"And I expect," he said frankly, "that the job will have to be done from the skin up. You don't look to me as if you had on the right things underneath. Nobody has waistlines any more; on the contrary, every one has legs."

"You don't expect *me* to go with Anne to the dressmaker's?" protested Neal, aghast.

"Of course. Both of us. Husband and interested friend. They'd think she didn't have any male relatives to pay the bills if she went alone."

And Clare was right about this as he was about everything else—Neal found himself welcomed with open arms at the *petite maison*, and in course of time at several *grandes maisons* as well. He actually enjoyed the welcome—at the first three or four establishments—then it began to pall on him, and he suggested that Clare and Anne should go without him, while he went around to the American Express to see if, by any chance, any one from Belford had registered there. But he paid the bills without a murmur, in a glow of satisfaction, as he saw Anne transformed, almost before his eyes. This was not entirely due to the dressmakers. There also was a *coiffeur*, Antoine, in whom Clare had great and well-deserved confidence; and under his direction a course in beauty culture was begun which in a few weeks produced astonishing results. Presently Anne looked no more than her age again; then she began to look a good deal less than her age. Clare dropped in occasionally, to watch Antoine's skillful ministrations, to suggest that the shining hair which glittered like gold when it had just been washed, should be massed a little higher on the erect little head, that the small pink nails followed the shape of the fingers better when they were curved than when they were pointed, that not even a suggestion of rouge should be dusted over cheeks so softly rosy. The color deepened in Anne's face at the tribute implied. It was still deep when, immaculate and demure, she went back to Neal.

As soon as she had the proper toilette, Anne, still acting under the direction of Clare, who had spoken a word for his friends to his chief, left her own card and Neal's at the Embassy. And shortly after these cards had been returned, Clare gave a luncheon in his apartment to which the Ambassador and the Ambassadress came as "honor guests," though it was really in honor of Neal and Anne. Thus launched, they found themselves approaching the *Grande Semaine* with a new circle of delightful acquaintances. They went to the races, Neal showing himself, from the very beginning, to have a real *flair* for betting. He won a great deal of money, which Anne tried hard to feel was not ethical; but when he announced that they could prolong their holiday on the strength of his ill-gotten gains, she forgot all about their source; and her costume for the Opera Ball, which Clare designed and Neal paid for, took a prize.

Left to their own devices, they would probably have fallen into the error common to their country folk, of trying to see all Europe in this one brief visit; but when Clare caught them looking at circulars and timetables, he drew these away, and laughingly threw them into the scrap basket. Enough to see in Paris, this time, he insisted. There was more there than they could discover in three years, let alone three months. And how was Anne to keep up with her French lessons with the shabby but brilliant little old *professeur* if they went dashing off to Switzerland or Italy? He relented, later on, to the extent of advising them to accept certain very attractive weekend invitations to big French country houses, which were the result of the *entrée* he had secured for them—invitations in which he also was always included. And, in August, when *monsieur le professeur* took his meager *vacances*, they toured the château country and the battlefields in his motor car, and went, after that, to Chartres and Rouen in the same conveyance. But, for the most part, they limited their excursions to day-trips on the Seine boats, or long afternoons in the forest of Fontainebleau and the gardens of Versailles. Anne learned to ride—Clare had two horses so there was always one at her disposal. She learned to drive Clare's Mercedes. Neal had never thought she "would be able to manage" the Dodge, but now he saw that he had been mistaken. Watching her development, he realized that Clare had not said half that might be said about her possibilities. Well, he would never make the old mistakes again. They were going home now, very soon, and when they did . . .

Anne came into the room, dressed as he had foreseen, waiting for his praise. A violent fit of sneezing interrupted him as he tried to express it.

"I don't dare kiss you, darling," he mumbled, behind his enveloping handkerchief. "Sure to give this darned cold to you— Clare's sent up word he's waiting for you. Have a good time."

She found Clare leaning against the boxlike desk of the *concierge,* chatting with that functionary. The *ménage* was devoted to him.

"Neal has a cold," she said as they shook hands, "he couldn't risk going out, of course. But he insisted that I should come, just the same."

"Naturally. I should never have forgiven you if you hadn't. But how on earth could he catch a cold in such weather?"

"Absurd, isn't it? *Mais le voilà, tout de même!*"

"My word, Anne, how you are coming along! You ripple that off as if you'd lived here all your life. What are you reading now?"

"Balzac—trying to anyway. '*La Femme de Trente Ans.*'"

"A wonderful story, and a wonderful study in psychology. You ought to find it especially interesting."

"Why?"

"You're just turning thirty yourself, aren't you?"

Something in the way he asked the question made her flush. They were skimming out towards the Champs-Elysées now and Clare was driving himself—it was a long time, Anne realized, since she had seen his discreet little chauffeur.

"I'm not in the least like Julie," she protested.

"No? Well, don't be discouraged. You're progressing wonderfully."

"I didn't mean it that way. Of course I don't *wish* to be in the least like Julie."

"Why not? She's immortal, you know."

Slightly troubled at his tone, she did not answer. He changed the subject swiftly.

"And so—you're really leaving Tuesday?"

"I suppose so."

"You sound as if you were sorry."

"Oh, Clare—how could any one help being sorry to leave Paris for Hinsboro?"

There was real grief in her voice; but the next instant she tried to catch back the words.

"Of course I'm counting the days until I see Junior and Nancy. If I could only have had them here too, it would have been quite perfect."

"Like most women, you like to have your cake and eat it too, don't you, Anne? . . . Well, I can understand that the sort of existence you were leading when I came to your house last spring might pall a good deal now."

"And if it hadn't been for you," she said with eager gratitude, "I never would have had a glimpse, perhaps, of any other kind of existence! The minute you looked at me, I saw how shabby and provincial I really was. I went upstairs—and —and cried, Clare. And all the time I was crying, you were persuading Neal to give me this wonderful chance. I can't ever thank you enough."

"Don't try," he said lightly, "it hasn't been a dull summer for me either you know. Riding with you at dawn, driving with you at dusk, lunching with you at Neuilly, dining with you at Chartres, and then that afternoon at Reims, those week-ends in the country. Ah—here we are."

He helped her out of the motor, and they passed through the arched entrance of the Château de Madrid. In the courtyard the little multicolored lights were already twinkling, and their table which they had occupied so many times before, was reserved for them, the solicitous headwaiter pulling out their seats. In a moment, a *garçon* who had waited on them before, and whose flashing smile gave them welcome, began bringing in tea and little cakes. The orchestra was playing, most unusually, a slow and ancient waltz. Clare rose, pushed back his chair, and bowed. He had never, Anne thought, looked handsomer, his slim elegance set off by his perfect clothes, his smile entrancing, his manner even more charming than usual.

"Shall we dance?" he asked.

She nodded, and rising, laid her arm lightly on his sleeve,

as they walked over to the parquet. Then she slipped into his arms. He was a remarkably fine dancer, and, closely held, she followed his sure and graceful lead for a few moments without speaking. Then suddenly, she raised her head.

"Isn't that 'The Beautiful Blue Danube' they're playing?"

"Yes. The best waltz ever written, probably."

"Would—would you mind very much if we didn't finish it? If—if we didn't finish our tea?"

"Aren't you well, Anne?"

"Yes. But I—I feel a little faint. I think I had better go home."

"Too bad—but never mind! I'll drive you back through the Bois. You'll feel better moving about in the air. It *is* frightfully hot. And heat always seems so much worse, out of season."

He made no objections, expressed no surprise. In fact, he said nothing at all until they had reached the little lake where so many happy bourgeois lovers hire boats and row placidly about. Then he stopped the car.

"We may as well have this out now, Anne," he said, quietly, "I'd prefer to take you to my apartment, but of course you'd refuse to go. We can sit on that bank. None of those people will notice us. They're all too much occupied with their own affairs."

He spread out a light wrap she had brought with her, and motioned to her to sit down. It was characteristic, that even in as tense a moment as this, he did not forget to protect the Lucien Lelong frock.

"Well," he questioned, still lightly, when looking a protest but uttering none, she had settled herself, "Have you actually realized at last that I am in love with you?"

She nodded, her eyes filling with tears.

"Don't cry, Anne. There'll be nothing to cry about, you'll see. . . . And you feel sure Neal doesn't suspect at all?"

"How could he?" she asked simply.

"You mean, it would never occur to him that his best friend would try to approach—his wife?"

A more meaning word had been on the tip of his tongue. He had softened it just in time.

"Of course it wouldn't occur to him. He would never do such a thing himself."

"You're probably right. Neal, with all his faults, is intrinsically honest. Also, he is not oversexed. Which makes it the easier for him to be honest."

"You shan't speak of Neal like that!" flashed Anne, "as if it were ridiculous to be honest and—and decent!"

"It isn't ridiculous. But it's sometimes inadequate."

"Listen, Anne," he went on, as she stared at him, apparently too stunned to answer, "I must ask you to believe that I haven't gone about this—with malice and forethought, so to speak. When I came to your house last spring, I pitied you, and admired you, and I wanted you to have a good time. That was the reason I persuaded Neal to bring you here, and the only reason. I hope very, very much that you will believe this."

"I do believe it," said Anne.

"But I was very lonely. I'd been through a dreadful domestic experience—"

"And now you want me to do the same thing to Neal that your wife did to you?"

She had scored. But, after a moment's hesitation, he went on, still speaking calmly. "Since you put it so crudely, I suppose I do now. But I never dreamed it was going to come to that. You had haunted me, in a way, ever since that dinner at the Shoreham so long ago, and I knew you'd interest me, and amuse me. But, to be perfectly frank, I didn't think you had it in you to attract me, in the sense of making me—want you. Well, I was mistaken. But even so, I don't believe matters would have gone as far as this if I hadn't begun to see that —I attracted you, too."

"You don't," cried Anne. "Oh, how can you say such dread-

ful things! I never loved any one but Neal, never in all my
life! Why, I wouldn't even finish that dance with you because
I suddenly remembered that the 'Beautiful Blue Danube' was
the very first waltz Neal and I ever had together. . . . I *hated*
your talking that way about 'The Woman of Thirty'—insin-
uating that you—that I . . . I very nearly didn't come out
with you to-day at all. I hesitated a long time. If Neal hadn't
insisted . . ."

"Exactly. If you weren't in love with me you wouldn't be
self-conscious about motoring with me or joking with me, or
having me close to you in a dance. You wouldn't give it a
second thought. What's more, you wouldn't be here *listening
to me now*. Anne . . ."

In the deepening twilight he leaned suddenly towards her,
and flung his arms about her. Then, abandoning all restraint,
he kissed her, over and over again, on the mouth. The passion
and violence of the embrace, without preliminary caress,
struck her like a blow. But with a sickening sense of self-horror
she realized that she had made no determined effort to escape
from it; that she had, for a moment, actually responded to it;
realized also that Clare, still holding her, was speaking to her
in a voice vibrant with triumph.

"You see,"—he whispered. "Anne, darling, won't you admit
—for you do see that you love me. You wouldn't have kissed
back if you didn't. I'll make everything very easy for you,
about the children and all that. Neal wouldn't take them
from you. He'll either find, when he gets home, that he's dead
politically once and for all, as I rather suspect, or he'll throw
himself into his career again, and forget about you, as he's
done before. In either case, you'll be left to face that awful
isolation and drudgery, and you know you can't do that. You
know you want to stay here with me, in this beautiful, bright
city, where you've really begun to live for the first time. We'd
have to be careful for a while, of course, to avoid scandal. But
once we were married, every one would forget all about it,

if we behaved ourselves. Why, the ambassadress has been divorced herself."

Somehow Anne wrenched herself free. She was trembling now, violently, but her eyes were quite dry. Indeed, she felt as if she would never know the healing of tears again. She could hardly speak. Her lips were shaking, as well as her body; nevertheless there was an inner force about her which compelled him to listen to her.

"I don't love you," she reiterated, brokenly but persistently. "I've been grateful to you and I always shall be, in—in spite of what's happened. I believe someday you'll be as sorry that it happened as I am. And you're right. I have been—been attracted by you. Perhaps that's what made me—for the moment—kiss back—something restless and reckless and primitive. Women are primitive sometimes as well as men. I wish more people would recognize that. But I don't love you. It's Neal I love. I'd rather go back to Hinsboro, to all that drudgery and isolation as you call it—to being neglected and forgotten by him as you've hinted, as *long as I can be with him than to stay here* in Paris—and all that it means—with you. Not just because I never could look the children in the face again if I didn't; not just because I'd give his family the chance they've always been looking for to prove how unworthy I'd been of him if I did; not just because I'd be an unchaste woman, seduced—seduced—" she brought out clearly the word over which he had stumbled—"by a dishonorable man. But because I love him. Because I know he belongs to me, no matter what he does or doesn't do. Because I belong to him. If he fails, I'm willing to fail with him. And if he succeeds, in the end, I'm going to be there to see it, even if I can't share it." She stopped, overwhelmed by her own vehemence—that, by itself, would have counted for nothing with Clare; but he quailed before the depth and beauty of her sincerity. For one vibrant moment of silence they faced each other—then he bent his head, stricken by the consciousness that he had been very close to violating a shrine—

"From the bottom of my heart," he said, "I ask your forgiveness."

.　　.　　.　　.　　.　　.

Groping her way down the dark, winding little corridor that led to her rooms, Anne was suddenly confronted with a large lozenge of light. Neal had heard her approaching footsteps,—he must have been listening for them—and had flung the door of their little *salon*, with its welcoming radiance, wide open. And dashing out to meet her, he almost smothered her in a bear hug.

"Oh, Anne, where have you been so long? I thought you'd never come! Do hurry! You can't imagine what's happened. Anne—Anne—read that cablegram—"

She snatched at the flimsy bit of blue paper which he was waving in her face. She had barely regained her composure; and now, glimpsing the typewritten message, she began to tremble again.

It was signed by Low, the Governor of their state. And it read:

"SHELTON, JUNIOR SENATOR, DIED THIS MORNING. HOPE YOU WILL ACCEPT APPOINTMENT FROM ME HIS SEAT UNITED STATES SENATE."

PART THREE

Weaving the Pattern

CHAPTER FIFTEEN

To the day of her death Anne Conrad will remember her first winter in Washington as a Senator's wife with driving insistence.

She and Neal discussed the question of a temporary home all the way over on the boat coming back from Paris, and finally decided, on account of the children, that a small house would be preferable to an apartment. Dora brought Nancy and Junior to meet them in New York; and after a brief and unsatisfactory glimpse of her small son and daughter, for whom she had begun to actually hunger, Anne sent them back to Hinsboro in care of the faithful maid, who could be trusted with the preliminaries of closing the house there—the house into which she had put so much loving effort, so much Spartan self-sacrifice, and which she would now hardly see for years to come. She herself went on at once to Washington with Neal to begin her search for a dwelling-place.

She began it confidently. It should not, she thought, be very hard to find exactly what they wanted—their needs were not extensive nor their standards exacting; and she urged Neal to follow his impatient desire to begin "getting settled" in his quarters at the Senate Office Building. These certainly left nothing to be desired. Though he was a newcomer, and therefore not entitled to the most convenient and luxurious apartments, his large private office, handsomely furnished in mahogany, and opening from the smaller room which his private secretary, stenographers and page were to occupy, seemed to both him and Anne the last word in distinction and elegance. Neal felt himself swelling with national impor-

tance from the first moment that he sat down in front of the
blank polished surface of his enormous desk, the warm autumn sunshine falling full across it from the high window near
by, and pushed the little bell which summoned Miss Letts to
come and take dictation from him. A cable had informed Miss
Letts of the impending change in her sphere of usefulness,
and she had preceded the Conrads to Washington. By way
of preparation for her rising fortunes, she had attained a bob
and a permanent wave, and a complexion as brilliantly hued
as her varied wardrobe. Anne, secure now in her own simple
and correct elegance, thought that the little secretary's skirts
were too short and her blouses too sheer, and she knew that
there was very little underneath them; but she had the wisdom to do her thinking silently. She recognized the compe-
tence of Miss Letts and was grateful for it, because it made
everything so much easier for Neal. The offices had been
cleaned, and the framed pictures of the Mayor of Hinsboro
with his council—when Neal had been a member of it—and
the grouped legislature—all the years that Neal had been a
member of it—his diploma from Harvard College and the
Harvard law school and the "enlargement" of Anne with the
children were already hanging on the walls. They had been
transferred without trouble to Neal from his office in Hinsboro. The ormolu clock on the mantelpiece was going, and it
was correct to a second; there were fresh yellow candles in
the "sidepieces" that matched the clock. Laid out where he
could not fail to see them instantly were a brand-new copy of
the Congressional Directory, a seating-plan of the Senate
Chamber, and numerous blocks of "scratch paper"—the large
thin ones white, the small fat ones pink, with the heading—
"United States Senate" imposingly printed upon them. His
personal stationery had been tentatively ordered, and as soon
as an impression of his signature had been obtained—for this
would appear on every envelope he used, thus insuring the
franking privilege—the order would go through. There was a
scrap basket of ample proportions, there was a scrap book

full of flattering comments about his appointment. And of course there was the appointment itself. Miss Letts had not had it framed, because she wanted to consult his taste, but she had samples of several suitable frames, waiting to submit to him, that he might make his choice between them.

So the beginning of Neal's "settling" was made comparatively easy for him, by Miss Letts, and soon there was a complete office force to make the continuance of it easier still. But Anne agreed with him perfectly when he told her that everything was in terrible confusion, and that he did not see how he was ever going to get straightened out and adjusted. So she went out to look for houses by herself. The real-estate agent to whom she had applied assured her enthusiastically that he had the very thing she wanted. He led her to several untenanted marble palaces, hung with mangy tapestries and furnished in rickety gilt, and to a long succession of tall narrow edifices made of bright red brick, with one tin bath, and gloomy "back-parlors." She regarded these docilely at first; then she began to object mildly.

"But this isn't at all the sort of house I described to you. You said you understood perfectly what I wanted."

"Indeed, Mrs. Conrad, I do. Nothing could be more suitable for a Senatorial establishment than these residences. You will wish to entertain extensively, of course. The Argentine Ambassador occupied this house we have just been in, for several years. His dinners were famous. You noticed, of course, the advantages of the dining-room."

"I noticed its disadvantages," replied Anne, the trace of hardness which was sometimes apparent coming in her voice; "it isn't on the same floor with the kitchen. And the pantry has no windows in it."

"But most houses, I assure you, are built that way. And the rent is so very reasonable—only six hundred dollars a month."

"Almost exactly my husband's entire monthly salary. Now will you please show me what I asked you for in the beginning: small houses, with about eight rooms, conveniently arranged, and at a reasonable rental. Unless it is clear to you now what I want, I think I had better go to another agent. Several have written and telephoned that they would be glad to show me houses."

The agent was grieved. It had not occurred to him that such a young, pretty, and gentle lady would be so unamenable to his blandishments. Allowing her to see that his feelings were hurt, first by coming for her in a dilapidated open car, instead of the stately limousine he had hitherto affected, and next by maintaining a lofty and dignified silence, he led her from one small dingy dwelling to another. They were all dirty beyond description, and in most of them both plumbing and heating plants were antiquated and inadequate; the maid's room, generally without a bath, was built in a dark corner of the basement. Anne went back to the Willard, late in the afternoon, dizzy with discouragement, and Neal expressed surprise at her lack of success.

"You don't mean to say you haven't found anything *yet?* I hate to keep talking about money, but it's darned expensive here, as you know, more for this one small room than our two big ones cost in Paris, while the restaurant charges are three times as high. Aren't you a little too fussy? We ought to be getting settled, you know, and having Dora and the children come down. They'll be late starting school as it is, and that's always a disadvantage. Surely you must be able to get *something*. I'd take a day off and help you hunt, but things are so terribly piled up at the office—"

"I know, Neal, I'll try again. But honestly, it's awfully hard. I think I'll write Dora to start the children in at school in Hinsboro."

"Good heavens! Is it as hopeless as *that?*"

"Well—I'm afraid it is."

But the next morning she began again. This time the houses she saw were somewhat newer and cleaner. But they were either built with basement entrances, which she knew would multiply the cares of housekeeping, on account of the number of stairs to be climbed, or else they were flimsily constructed in boxlike blocks on unattractive and inaccessible streets.

At last she dismissed the agent, declined the doubtfully useful services of several others, and started out by herself on foot, stopping before every house that displayed in its window a sign of "For sale or to let." The bewildering aspect of the city, in which a hovel and a palace often stand side by side, so that it is difficult for an outsider to recognize a "desirable" neighborhood, and the prevalence of "squares" and "circles" which constantly caused her to lose her way, made her task more difficult. But at last she discovered tucked away between two handsome brownstone "residences" a small house of yellow-painted brick. It was only two stories high; its location was excellent; and a notice so large that it completely filled the modest bay window in which this was placed, proclaimed that it was seeking a tenant. Tremblingly, Anne sought out the agent, one of whom she had not previously heard. He catered to so small and select a clientele that he never advertised, and considered solicitation beneath his standards; but he received her with condescending cordiality. Yes, he would be glad to show her the house, which had just come on the market—Mrs. Harrison, its owner, had suddenly decided to go to Europe, for the winter, perhaps for longer. It proved to contain a small but sunny drawing-room opening into a dark little dining-room whose one window overlooked a diminutive back yard, and a kitchen in the ell; on the second story two large bedrooms and one small one, and a bathroom; in the basement, under the drawing-room, a storeroom which might conceivably be used as a playroom. The furniture was shabby, and Anne was amazed that any woman could leave her house so far from clean. But she felt, at last, that she had found something which offered possibilities, at least. She asked the amount of the rent.

"Two hundred and fifty dollars a month, without heat or light, linen and silver, of course. Very reasonable. And the telephone hasn't been disconnected. You won't have the inconvenience and delay of waiting to have one installed."

Anne was aghast. But she was also desperate.

"I'll let you know to-morrow. I think probably I'll take it."

"I'm sure you couldn't do better, Mrs. Conrad."

It was because Anne was so miserably sure of this herself that she painted the little house in brighter colors than it deserved to Neal that evening. And, even with this effort at *couleur-de-rose* he was not enthusiastic.

"That's a terrible price. Why, we wouldn't have any more room than we did in the cottage—not as much, really—and you know what that cost! There's no family living-room except the one that will have to be a parlor, too, no place for me to work. Dora would have to use the same bathroom we did —imagine, all five of us, mornings—and Nancy would have to sleep with her. And there's no garage."

"I know all that. But we *could* manage. And it's the first place I've seen where we could."

It was on the tip of her tongue to urge him to go out and hunt himself if he felt he could do better. But she managed to restrain herself, remarking only, "I wish you'd come and look at it in the morning."

"I really ought to get to the office in good season. You see—"

"Yes, I know; but it will take only a few minutes."

Somewhat grudgingly, Neal consented to accompany her; and equally grudgingly he signed the lease a few days later, conveying the impression, though he did not actually say so, that he could have done much better himself if the affairs of the nation had not weighed so heavily upon him. Then Anne, with a regretful look at her pretty hands, which she had hoped were to be kept looking that way always now, bought herself some cheap gingham dresses, a supply of scrubbing brushes, cleansing powders and soft cloths, and began the process of cleaning house from top to bottom.

It was backbreaking work; and her muscles were soft after her summer of physical inactivity. But she did not know where to seek for a scrubwoman; and she already saw, very plainly, that she would have to begin to save pennies again. She left the Willard directly after breakfast, carrying a cold lunch with her, and worked until dinner time. By evening she was so tired that once she actually went to sleep while Neal was telling her about the exciting events of his day, and he was offended.

She did not even have the satisfaction of doing her house-cleaning in uninterrupted peace. The telephone rang constantly; she began to feel that the "inconvenience and delay of having it installed" might have had its advantages. At first she answered it conscientiously, believing that its peals might portend tidings of importance to Neal. It usually proved, however, to be a photographer, who had—miraculously, as it seemed to her—discovered that she was in town, and wished her to have her picture taken. She would not have guessed that a city the size of Washington could contain so many photographers, or that a new Senator's wife could seem so desirable a victim to any of them. She answered their suggestions with increasing vagueness and decreasing courtesy. No, she was afraid she couldn't set a time for an appointment just yet; no, really, it wouldn't do any good to mail her a card reminding her that she would be in the studio at noon on Monday; no, she couldn't say that she would prefer home portraiture. When the same firm called her three times in twenty-four hours she hung up the receiver with a bang, and answered the telephone no more. Then, of course, a magnate from Belford who had only a day in the city called and received the report that "they didn't answer." It did not seem to occur to him that he could call up the Senate Office Building. He went home to Belford and wrote Neal an indignant letter, and spread the news among his neighbors that "Conrad was getting a swelled head already." Neal was very angry about it, and Anne felt that he had a right to be.

At the hands of the newspapers she fared even worse. The society editors, like the photographers, had telephoned her;

like the photographers, she had put them off. She could not bear the thought of giving interviews. But if a man is known by the company he keeps, so is the journalist known by the interviews which he—or she—secures. Miss Sharp, of the *Evening Inquirer* decided to present herself at the new Senator's residence, and take her chances on being rebuffed, even though she went without an appointment. Her ring at the doorbell remained unanswered; and she turned for help to a young woman, her head enveloped in a mobcap, who was vigorously washing windows.

"Can you tell me whether Mrs. Conrad is at home?" she asked.

The window-washer wrung out her cloth from the pail of steaming suds by her side, and turned her head halfway around.

"I am Mrs. Conrad," she replied calmly, and went on washing windows.

Miss Sharp fled; but as she fled, she thought, and thought rapidly. There are some things, of course, which it is not proper for the society department to cover, but there is nothing in its code of ethics to prevent it from helping some other department to cover the same things. Before the sun had gone down, Anne had been surreptitiously photographed in the act of washing her last window; and the following evening, this distorted likeness of herself, together with the heavy headline, "SENATOR'S WIFE ACTS AS OWN SCRUBWOMAN" surmounted two columns, more conspicuous for their imagination than their accuracy, on the front page of the *Inquirer*. This was such good "copy" that it was, of course, copied— from one end of the United States to the other. Reporters were sent to Hamstead and to Hinsboro, to dig up forgotten or unknown facts or fancies about the new Senator's wife. Photographs of "Pupper and Mummer" with Sol and Sam on the front porch between them adorned the Sunday supplements, with the schoolhouse where Anne had taught in a "circle" above at the left, and the little house with a cross marking "the honey-moon flat" in a "box" below at the right. Anne was delineated bending over the washtub and milking the family cow. Had Neal been a candidate for the presidency no sort of publicity could have been more helpful; since he was instead an appointee to the Senate, none could have been more disastrous. Anne knew it, without his comments on the subject, and without her mother-in-law's letters. Nevertheless, she was spared neither of these.

By the time the nine days' excitement had subsided somewhat, the housecleaning was finished, groceries and coal had been installed, and Anne had gone to Hinsboro to help Dora finish closing the house there, and bring the maid and the children back with her to Washington. The beauty and comfort of her own home, even in its dismantled state, affected her poignantly; and as she walked through her little garden, set in stark order for the winter, she was very close to crying. A cold autumn wind was blowing through the bare branches, and she tried to persuade herself that it was this which brought the quick color to her cheeks and the tears to her eyes. But that night, on the train, in the drawing-room which she had taken in an unusual fit of extravagance, she told her troubles to Dora and wept on that comfortable shoulder, as they sat side by side on the hard little sofa that was to be Dora's bed, after Junior had been tucked away in the upper berth, and Nancy in the lower berth which she was to share with her mother.

"A shame I call it!" Dora kept saying, patting Anne's shoulder gently. "A lovely lady like you! Inventing such stories!"

"But they're not invented—not all of them," sobbed Anne. "You know I never had any one to work for me before you came. I *did* teach school and do the washing—though I never milked a cow! And that house in Washington was so dirty. I couldn't bring the children into it until it was cleaned—they'd have caught typhoid fever or whatever it is you do catch when things are dirty."

"I ought to have been there to help you," began Dora regretfully, but Anne interrupted her.

"How could you? There was the other house on your hands, wasn't there? And the children? Did Mrs. Conrad offer to help you at all? No, of course not!"

"Well, anyway, we'll manage better from now on."

But the managing when they reached Washington did not prove to be any too easy. After an early breakfast, Anne walked over to the garage—the nearest one they had been able to find was several blocks away—and got the car, while Neal read the morning paper, for it was, of course, important that he should keep himself thoroughly informed about current events. By the time she had taken the children to school he was, however, ready to have her take him to the Senate Office Building; and after she had left him there, she did the marketing, for the "cash and carry" stores were much cheaper than the ones that "delivered." Back at the little yellow brick house, the chamberwork awaited her, for Dora had agreed to take care of the furnace if Anne would do this; and the maid, in addition to looking after the fires, with the trips back and forth to the basement which this involved, had also cooked, served and cleared away breakfast, cleaned the living-room, and answered the doorbell and telephone. She struggled through the heavy washings, too, with none of the conveniences or space that had made these comparatively easy for her in Hinsboro; and Anne helped with the ironing and did the mending. In no time, the hands of the clock were pointing to the hour at which she must go and get the children; steer them through their luncheon, plan for their afternoon outing. She usually took them with her when she went to get their father, his labors for the day over, and they skipped home on either side of her after she had left the car at the garage for the night. Then there were the simple home lessons with which they needed help, preparation for Sunday-school on Saturday night, dancing-school to dress them for and take them to Saturday morning. There was supper to get for all of them on Dora's night out—a hearty supper, for Neal had quickly fallen into the way of taking a very light lunch, and came home hungry.

"Just a piece of pie and a bit of cheese," he assured her, "or cracker and milk. That's all most of the men take at noon— plenty, too, when you're getting no exercise— Yes, another piece of steak, please, dear, a thick one, with lots of gravy." (Neal's senatorial importance had not cured him of his taste for "fish in the pan.") "What have you got for dessert?"

Anne found herself standing beside her bed at night press- ing her hands against her throbbing temples, as if by this pressure she could push back the pressing duties which drove her forward. She was tired all the time, tired as she had not been since the days when Nancy was a delicate baby and Junior an exacting three-year-old and she had been obliged, at the doctor's orders, to engage Dora and cease doing all her own work. She began to dust every other day, instead of every day, to overlook the smaller holes and less important buttons when she did her mending, to shorten the bedtime stories and songs which had always given her the most precious hours of association with her children. But still she was continually hurried and hurried; her driving weariness threatened to an- nihilate her. For, as she soon discovered, the demands made upon her time and strength by her home and family were as nothing compared to the outside demands made upon her in her official position as a Senator's wife.

CHAPTER SIXTEEN

Anne's experiences with photographers and reporters should have given her a glimmering of what lay before her, should have brought home to her the fact that she was no longer a private individual whose life, however full, was at least her own, to regulate and arrange as she chose. But the first task of finding and fitting and running her home had been so heavy, that she had allowed herself to overlook this fact. The oversight was, however, of short duration.

She had settled herself with an overflowing mending-basket before the living-room fire one rainy afternoon, comfortably conscious that she had an hour or more to herself before it would be time to go for Neal—though after that there would still be supper to get, for this was Dora's day out. The children were playing contentedly enough in the basement nursery. (Was it going to be too damp for them down there? She must assure herself that it wasn't, and yet, if it *was*—good heavens, where else *could* they play?) She had on a rather shabby little serge house-dress, because she found it easier, with running the car so much, to slip a big coat over such a dress, than to keep changing all the time to her smart Parisian *tailleur*. She knew, of course she knew, that she ought to put on something more suitable for afternoon, but it hardly seemed worth while, when she must go out again so soon in that driving rain. The side curtains of the car leaked, and she suspected that the top was not above reproach. Decidedly, it was not worth while . . . Her shoes, too, she realized, glancing down at them, were getting shabby with all this driving, and she hadn't blacked them the night before, she had been so terribly tired. She

mustn't let herself get careless, get shoddy again, after all she
had learned in Paris. But—oh, well—she picked up her fourth
sock.

The doorbell rang. She started up, dropping the contents of
her basket on the floor as she did so. Before she could restore
thimble, scissors, spools and stockings to their proper place, it
rang again, more insistently. She ran to the front door and
flung it open.

Two very elegant ladies confronted her. They had on dark
velvet dresses, rich furs and white gloves, and their satin slippers were smooth and narrow. Behind them, at the curb,
stood a shiny limousine with a man in livery at the wheel.

"Is Mrs. Conrad receiving to-day?" they asked simultaneously, in shrill, high voices. And as they did so, they each
extended three cards, two little ones and one large one,
neatly folded into triangles at the upper right hand corner.

Mechanically, Anne reached behind her for the silver card
tray that reposed on the hall table, and set it down again, the
cards fluttering over its edge, before she answered. Then, in
spite of her bewilderment, she spoke cordially.

"Won't you come in? I'm Mrs. Conrad. . . . I think you'll
find these chairs, here by the fire, comfortable."

"Oh, *thank you*. We didn't know whether you'd have begun your Thursdays yet or not, it's so *early* in the season. And
it's early in the afternoon, too, of course we *know* that. But
we're going to the concert—we *never* miss it—so we have to
start early. If we don't get started on our calls we *never* could
get around, it's such a *problem*, isn't it? But perhaps you
weren't quite *ready* to begin receiving, Mrs. Conrad? You
must excuse us, but we've been so *anxious* to meet the new
Senator's wife. I'm Mrs. Roper and this is my friend Mrs.
Ranger. We always make our calls together, we're such
friends."

Anne's head was whirling. Her Thursdays? Mrs. Roper and
Mrs. Ranger? She groped towards a light which she could not
find, and her visitors were instantly aware of the fact.

"Of course you *knew*, Mrs. Conrad, that Senators' wives receive on Thursdays? The Supreme Court ladies on Mondays, the Congressional ladies on Tuesdays, the Cabinet ladies on Wednesdays, the Senatorial ladies on Thursdays, the Diplomatic ladies on Fridays—that leaves Saturdays and Sundays for the resident society, the *cave-dwellers*, you know. But *of course* I don't need to tell you all this! How are you getting on with your own visits?"

"My own visits?" gasped Anne, thinking of the windows she had washed and the floors she had scrubbed and all the other pushing, daily duties which made her press her hands against her temples at night, they harried her so. Visits indeed!

"*Of course* you've called promptly on all your superiors in rank—it's so important to do that *at once*. It creates quite a wrong impression if you don't. And if you don't *return* the calls we poor *inferiors* make upon you, we'll think you're *snobbish*, you know. So many Senators' wives *are*. Well, next week we shall expect to see you, dear Mrs. Conrad. We always receive together, we're such *friends*. Of course you've heard how *intimate* we are."

They rose, shook hands, and hurried away with staccato exclamations about ten more calls to make before "the" concert began. The front door closed behind them, but Anne could hear them talking as they went down the steps.

"My dear, did you *ever?* I do believe all those stories about the cow and the washtub and everything are true, don't *you?* No tea and no one to open the door, and those shabby clothes, what did she do in Paris, do you suppose, go to *art-galleries?* And it's evident she doesn't know a *thing* about what's expected of her. Where do you think we better go *next?* What do you say to Mrs. Stone's, everything is so *lovely* there, and she and the huge crowd she always has on her Thursdays will so enjoy hearing all about this *freak* . . . Oh, Madame Estavi, are you coming to call on Mrs. Conrad, too? Yes, we've just *been*. Yes, she's *in*."

Another caller was coming up the steps, and it was plain

that those who were leaving were refraining with difficulty from telling her how inadequate her reception was going to be. Anne saw, with relief, that the new visitor was of a different type—was indeed herself timid and ill at ease, in spite of her pretty clothes and air of unmistakable good breeding. But this relief was shortlived. Madame Estavi, the wife of the Third Secretary of the Peruvian Embassy, was herself a newcomer embarking on her first round of calls, and finding it an ordeal to explain her identity and purpose in a foreign language with which her acquaintance was of the slightest, and amidst strange surroundings which still appalled and bewildered her. She accepted the place by the fire so recently vacated, and sat holding herself very erect, with painful pauses, which Anne did not know how to fill in, between her civil, stilted little sentences. In the midst of one of these pauses, a fearful shriek rent the air; and an instant later, Nancy, with Junior in hot pursuit, tore wildly into the room, tripped over the rug, and fell sprawling on the floor between the two ladies.

"He hit me."—"I didn't either."—"Well, he took my rabbit, and said he was going to vi-vi-sect it, and the stuffing all came out, and so I knocked him over the head with my shovel."—"And then you bet I hit her. Wouldn't you?"

The last remark was addressed to the astonished caller by Junior, who had picked himself up, and was confronting her accusingly. She rose, looking very much startled. Anne had visions of little Peruvian children, beautifully behaved always, in charge of a competent and devoted nursery governess who never, under any circumstances, left their side. "I'm dreadfully sorry," she said wretchedly. "Really, they don't often act like this. Junior, go upstairs and wash that—that—whatever it is—off your face and hands. And stay there until I send for you." The "send" was sheer bravado. Anne had, as she realized all too well, no one to send. "Please, Madame Estavi"—But Madame Estavi had quietly and effectively vanished, and there were more callers coming up the

steps. Before the riotous and untidy children could be elim-
inated, these callers were upon Anne. One of them was a bluff
and hearty naval officer who sat down in an antique chair
which promptly broke beneath him. (Anne had already discovered that much of the furniture in her furnished house
was not reliable, but this was the first disaster she had faced
because of it.)

The naval officer, who had lumbago, as he explained in detail to her, appeared less bluff and hearty after his accident,
and tried to signal to his wife that his back hurt him, and
that he felt they had better move along. But his wife was
stone deaf and she did not catch his meaning. She thought he
was trying to call her attention to the picture over the mantelpiece.

The dreadful afternoon wore on. Anne, nervously keeping
her eyes from the clock, was nevertheless aware that Neal
would be expecting her, would be waiting for her, and yet
she could not escape and go to him. At last the telephone
rang sharply.

"Neal, dear," she whispered into the transmitter, "I can't
come for you, I'm sorry. No, I can't speak any louder, there
are people here, they'll hear me. No, I can't explain. No, I'm
not sick. No, the children aren't either."

She returned to the drawing-room certain that she had
been overheard. Well, that was bad enough, but at least it
meant that these intruding strangers would go—would leave
her in peace. But it did not. Sensing that something was
amiss, and eager to know what it was, they lingered to find
out.

Neal let himself in with his latchkey, banging the door after
him, and shouted to her from the hall.

"Why didn't you *tell* me you were going to have company?"
he roared, "I waited, and waited . . ."

Neither of them ever referred again to the next few minutes. He strode into the little parlor, halted, and became
dumb. Introductions were mumbled, but afterwards the si-

lence deepened. One by one, disappointed, the callers departed. As the last one vanished from sight and hearing, Anne turned on her husband with a rage such as he had seldom seen her display.

"Don't you ever dare speak to me that way again!" she cried. "You ought to have realized I was in some difficulty and helped me out instead of making things ten times worse than they were already! You ought to have known that Senators' wives have to receive on Thursdays and make hundreds and thousands of calls themselves other days, dropping little dog-eared cards from one end of Washington to the other. To-morrow I'm going to get all this straightened out by some one who *does* know and will tell me all about it. I'll find out what I've got to do, and do it well. But in the meantime, I'm going upstairs and I'm going to bed. You can get your own supper and the children's and hear their home work and see that they take their baths. If any of you come near me this evening, I warn you that I'll have hysterics."

"Why, Anne," said Neal gently, "I'm awfully sorry. I didn't think . . ." His own annoyance had vanished into thin air at the sight of her distress, which he did not minimize. He spoke with unaccustomed and unexpected tenderness. "Darling, it's all right. You'll get the hang of all this in no time. Anne—don't cry."

CHAPTER SEVENTEEN

At nine o'clock the next morning, Anne called up the Vice-President's house, and asked for Mrs. Hammel.

She thought that the man who answered her gasped slightly. But she was not sure. He only said, "I will connect you with Mrs. Hammel's secretary, Madam," and after a short succession of clicks she heard a smooth, purring voice that sounded somehow, in spite of its smoothness, as if it might, upon occasion, grow dreadfully hard. "Miss Butters speaking."

"This is Mrs. Neal Conrad, Senator Conrad's wife. I asked for Mrs. Hammel."

"Oh—but you see Mrs. Hammel never goes to the telephone, Mrs. Conrad. Couldn't you give me the message? I am her secretary, you know. I take all her messages. Every one who wishes to get in touch with Mrs. Hammel does so through me."

Again reproved, again convicted of ignorance! Anne felt herself flushing, alone in the little dark entry where her telephone hung. But she gritted her teeth.

"I wonder if she would let me come and see her? To-day?"

"To-day? Really, Mrs. Conrad, I doubt whether that would be possible. Mrs. Hammel would be delighted to see you of course, but she is very much engaged. Perhaps next week I could give you an appointment."

"Won't you *ask* her whether she would see me? It's really urgent."

"In that case . . . What is your telephone number, Mrs. Conrad? I will try to call you back a little later. But of course

I can't promise. Mrs. Hammel always gives up her mornings to her correspondence, we try not to let anything disturb her. There are so many demands upon her, you see."

Anne hung up the receiver, already regretting her sudden impulse to appeal to the Vice-President's wife. As she lay in bed the evening before, miserably wakeful, she had remembered a "feature story" that she had read about Mrs. Hammel in the *Inquirer* the Sunday before. This article had praised the "Second Lady of the Land" in no uncertain terms, her tact, her sweetness, her sympathetic graciousness. It was accompanied by a picture of her huge white marble residence, that looked like a great block of vanilla ice-cream, ornamented with whipped cream that had been forced through a tube into all kinds of festoons; also by a picture of the lady herself, smiling, plump, bejeweled and bewaved. But there was a look of real human kindness in the gentle eyes and soft mouth, and withal a look of mild shrewdness, which even the artificial pose of the photographer could not destroy; and there was a paragraph in the article which had arrested Anne's attention especially, and which seemed burned on her memory.

"Mrs. Hammel before her marriage was a Miss Sarah Gown, a school teacher in the great Western state which her distinguished husband has so rapidly 'put on the map.' When they first met he was a cattle herder. The early days of their marriage were spent on a ranch, sixty miles from the nearest village. Mrs. Hammel of course did all her own work, and, in the evenings, taught her husband, who had had fewer educational opportunities than herself, from the shabby text books which she had taken away with her from the mountain schools. She lost her first baby, a little daughter, and came near losing her own life, because no doctor could penetrate to the ranch through the snow drifts which covered the rough trails to the ranch in winter. Mrs. Hammel's second daughter is now the Duchess of Nebalini, her husband being the cousin of the King of Italy."

There were other paragraphs after that, describing the rise in the Hammel fortunes, both political and financial. But they did not matter so much. What mattered was that Mrs. Hammel had once been a little country school teacher, like Anne herself, had suffered far more in her bridal days, and she had married a man who possessed far fewer advantages, of every kind, than Neal. And she had won through. She lived in an ice-cream palace, she had an English butler and a private secretary, and that dreadful Miss Sharp wrote complimentary articles about her. She was so remote that no one could speak to her on the telephone, and of course she always, always, did the right thing—now. But she must have had to learn, too; and perhaps, perhaps, she remembered how bitterly hard that learning was. . . .

The telephone rang. Miss Butters was speaking again, her voice even smoother and more purring than before.

"Oh, Mrs. Conrad . . . I gave Mrs. Hammel your message, and she will be pleased to see you at eleven. She is of course very much pressed, very much occupied, so I am sure you will understand and make your call brief. At eleven then—"

"It was Miss Butters," Anne said to herself as she buttoned on her little blue *tailleur* and jammed her small, perky blue hat down over her curls, "who made up the last part of that message. Mrs. Hammel never said it at all. If she hadn't meant to be kind, she wouldn't have said she'd see me."

Anne was right. Mrs. Hammel did mean to be kind. She looked to the bewildered newcomer like a comfortable, middle-aged angel, her wings concealed by her perfect Worth gown of gray *crêpe de chine*, but her halo almost distinguishable above the smooth ripples of her permanent wave. A single string of beautiful creamy pearls quivered slightly over the ample bosom which was so trimly confined by the smoothly fitting undergarment that lay beneath the insidiously simple, costly gown, a single great emerald glittered on her plump right hand, three great diamonds above the narrow platinum band on her left. There were steel buckles on the gray suède shoes. But there was something very homey about her, in spite of the fact that she might have served as the personification of "What the Well-Dressed Woman (with unlimited means) Will Wear"; she almost patted Anne's hand as she shook it; and an uncanny degree of intelligence shone from the beams of her kindly eyes.

"So you're the wife of the new appointee to the Senate? Bless me, how young you look—I shouldn't wonder if you're the Senatorial baby. And pretty as a picture. I always tell women when I think they're pretty, and I never apologize for it, either. I know they really like it. Your husband's young, too, isn't he? Mr. Hammel's been watching his career with interest—he believes there's a big future ahead of him yet. And ahead of you, too, of course. I'm pleased you wanted to run in and see me like this. Was there something special—? Tell me while we have some nice hot chocolate with lots of whipped cream on top—terribly fattening, but you don't need to worry about that, and I'm past worrying—now then—"

Anne went straight to the point. She told her story quickly, and she told it well. In a few brief sentences she had outlined her background, upbringing, and previous experience. Then, with slightly more detail, she related the events of the afternoon before. Mrs. Hammel listened attentively, drinking cup after cup of hot chocolate, each one sweetened with three lumps of sugar and smothered with whipped cream. Once or twice the corners of her mouth twitched, and when Anne had finished she coughed a little behind a fine cambric handkerchief which she extracted from a small silver mesh bag. There was an agreeable aroma of French perfume about the handkerchief.

"Well, well," she said, "I don't know when I've been so much interested. And you thought of coming straight to me —which I'm very glad you did—on account of that article in the *Inquirer*. Are you on good terms with the press yourself?"

"I'm afraid not. You see—" Anne plunged into that story too. This time Mrs. Hammel laughed outright.

"Yes, I've read some of these articles, and of course I realized they weren't overaccurate, but I didn't know just what lay behind them. Well, my dear, the first thing for you to do is to get a picture taken of yourself that does you justice—several of them—and then ring up Miss Sharp and ask her to come and have tea and a little chat with you."

Mrs. Hammel stirred her fourth cup of chocolate reminiscently.

"When I first came here," she said, "I thought I didn't want to have anything to do with the newspaper women. Miss Sharp wrote *me* and asked me for an interview and I declined to give it to her. Her reply, which she sent me by special delivery, was a masterpiece. I've kept it ever since—some-day I'll show it to you. She told me that her bread and butter depended on getting something about me, but that, after all, was beyond the point. If her newspaper couldn't secure a real interview with me, it would fake one. If she didn't write that article—false or true—some one else would. If I would coöperate with the newspaper women, give them what they had a recognized right to ask of me as Vice-President's wife, I'd never regret it. If I told them anything in confidence, that confidence would be respected. If I admitted that I was going to a certain place, or was on the point of doing a certain thing, but that for reasons of my own I wished this kept quiet, no word about it would ever appear in print. In short, that they were prepared to help me in every way they could if I would only let them. If I wouldn't, all sorts of false and sensational reports would inevitably appear about me. I sent for Miss Sharp and had a frank talk with her. We've been the best of friends ever since. And she's kept her word—absolutely."

"Oh, thanks," began Anne, "I'll—" Mrs. Hammel interrupted.

"She belongs to a rather interesting organization—the Woman's National Press Club. All the society editors do, besides a number of other reporters and advertisers and a few magazine writers. About forty of them in all. I'm going to one of their Monday luncheons—jolly, informal affairs—as guest of honor next week. I wonder—would you like to come with me? It could be very easily arranged. You'd have a good time, and—well, I think it would be a good plan all around."

Anne's quick gratitude was so real that Mrs. Hammel was more touched than she betrayed. Her capacity for chocolate being at last exhausted, she began to turn the great emerald around on her carefully manicured finger, not with any indication of nervousness, but as if she frankly enjoyed its gleaming gorgeousness.

"And of course you must start right in making calls. To-day. Diplomatic day. Ordinarily the wife of the senior senator from your state would go with you, to help you at the beginning. But Senator Brown hasn't any wife. He's a widower. Many of them are. You won't wonder at that, when you've lived here a little while—it's a killing pace for a woman in official life. Many a poor lady should be buried with the inscription, 'She died of making too many calls.' And other Senators are bachelors. That's not to be wondered at either. They pay attention—marked attention—to a girl for a season or two, and she's flattered and all that, but she gets to thinking it over, how many Senators are widowers I mean, and she decides— You'll find them all labeled in the Congressional Directory. 'The star designates those whose wives accompany them; the parallel lines designate those having other ladies with them.' Well, the first time I saw that, I wondered who those 'other ladies' were. It sounded suspiciously vague, as if—ahem! But, bless you, Senators don't have any time for little diversions like that. Those parallel lines only mean that a wife having perished, or not having been attained at all, because the hours at hard labor look too long for her, a sister, or a mother or some one like that has been pressed into service."

Anne, shaking with laughter, had begun to realize that she was going to like Mrs. Hammel very, very much.

"But to get back to the calls you must make to-day. You'll find a list of the embassies in your copy of the Congressional

Directory. If your husband hasn't brought yours up from the office he's been very remiss. Every Senator's wife has one, with her name stamped neatly in the lower right-hand corner. 'Mrs. Neal Conrad' will look very nice, you'll see. Only the Ambassadresses, remember. The Ministers' wives come first to you. They don't like it, because that distinction isn't made in other capitals, but it's made here. And return Madame Estavi's call, of course. She's really a dear, though very shy. You don't need to be afraid of *her*. Then go through the cards that were left you yesterday, and return the calls of any 'cave dwellers' who may be receiving Saturday and Sunday. Monday go to all the Supreme Court ladies—there are only nine of those, you know; you can gallop right through them in an afternoon, easily. Tuesday of course you'll go to the Congressional ladies if any have called on you. No? Well, then, that's easy. Wednesday—now there's a moot question. Most of the Senators' wives feel that the Cabinet ladies should call first— the Senate confirms the appointment of Cabinet officers, you see. But the Cabinet officers and their wives always take precedence at dinners—I think, if I were you, I'd stretch a point, and go at least to see Mrs. Standish, the wife of the Secretary of State. She's a perfect dear, and you'll have such a good time at her house; you may not get much farther anyway. Then next Thursday, if I were you, I should receive again myself. And—er—do it right. After that, you ought to receive and make calls on alternate Thursdays, till you've been the rounds. But this time, I'd—er— Mrs. Roper and Mrs. Ranger will tell every one they see, of course, about yesterday, and next Thursday your house will be packed with people who've come to see if they were told the truth. And my, what a disappointment they'll get." Once more Mrs. Hammel gave vent to hearty laughter. "I'd like to be there myself, my dear, to see the fun. If I can possibly make it, I shall be."

She rose, gathered up her silver mesh bag and other small effects, and kissed Anne on the cheek.

"Run along now, and get to work, my dear," she said. "I've lots of confidence in you."

This confidence was not misplaced. Doggedly, even as she had scrubbed floors and taught school doggedly, Anne set to work to pay her official calls. She drove her own car, changing her gloves before entering a house, and again after she left it, and finding her own parking spaces. But Neal came home on the street cars from the Senate Office Building, and the children walked home from school, so that she would not have to go for them. And Dora announced beforehand that she could not dream of going out the next Thursday, and by Tuesday had begun on even more substantial plans for helping Anne. It was barely half-past three when, as Mrs. Hammel had predicted, Anne's callers began to come. The polite Ambassadresses instantly returning their official visits. The Supreme Court ladies, whose program was not yet very full. Mrs. Standish, always sweet, efficient and poised, to whom, moreover, Mrs. Hammel had been able to murmur a few words about Anne, as they drove home together from the informal monthly tea to which the President's wife always invited the ladies of her "official family." The excitement eaters and curiosity seekers regaled by Mrs. Roper and Mrs. Ranger. Miss Sharp and several other members of the Woman's National Press Club, who had been most agreeably impressed by Anne when she had come, with Mrs. Hammel, to their Monday luncheon. The "professional callers" who are the bane of every woman in official life, and who go from house to house either because they are utterly idle, or because they are actually hungry, supplying themselves, in the latter case, with unlimited sandwiches and cakes. A large contingent from a girls' school, which made a point of advertising that its pupils would be "conducted to see the wives of the great men who are forming the destiny of our nation." Numerous young secretaries and *attachés*, who had heard rumors that Mrs. Conrad was—really—extremely pretty, and who thought it quite likely that she might often like to go to Charity Balls during the season when Neal would be either unwilling or unable to accompany her. A scattering of tourists' and government workers from the Conrads' own state. Ministers, Colonels, a judge or two, with their wives. In short, the kaleidoscopic fragment of Washington life which confronts the official hostess on her day at home.

The door was opened for these callers by a wholly correct butler from Rauschers' who was in great demand for "at homes"; near him, at the drawing-room door, stood a smiling little boy, his face very rosy and clean above his Eton collar, his hair slicked back from his moist part. The fame which Junior's smile has since enjoyed, and which is well merited, may be traced from that day. It was frank, sweet, intelligent, and withal, just a shade wistful. It was arresting and disarming. Nine times out of ten, the callers' first remark to Anne was, "Is that *your* little boy who welcomed me so politely? What beautiful manners he has! And what a LOVELY SMILE." Anne smiled herself in appreciation of this greeting, and Anne too had a smile which was nothing to be ashamed of. She stood in front of a bright little fire, which glowed under a mantel banked with flowers, to receive her guests, her golden hair wound like a coronet above the curls which framed her rosy face, her slim figure supple and graceful under its sheath of rose-colored satin. Neal, scintillating with cordiality, sartorially perfect in gray trousers and cutaway, stood beside her. Stood beside her, that is, most of the time; now and then he wandered about a little, to chat with a group which seemed a trifle silent, or hasten the progress of a guest who looked a little hungry into the dining-room. Here an immaculate maid, the stiff, embroidered *bretelles* of her apron snowy against her black silk uniform, was hovering over a tea table, on which silver dishes containing tomato-jelly sandwiches, angel food, tiny frosted cakes, and tinier biscuits stuffed with chicken salad, were scattered over an embroidered tablecloth. The maid was being assisted by a beautiful little girl, whose angelic gaze as she held out a plate or a cup seemed

to supplicate the further consumption of delicacies. ("I don't
need to ask if that's your little girl," the callers said, nine
times out of ten, as they took their departure. "She looks *exactly* like you! Why, she's perfectly *lovely!*") And, pouring
the tea, bland, and benign above the silver service, sat Mrs.
Hammel, dressed in mauve velvet, orchids fastened to her
bodice, plumes nodding from her brocade toque . . .

The "leader" in the society section of the *Inquirer* on the
following Sunday was written by Miss Sharp. A picture of
Anne, with Junior and Nancy as they had appeared at her
second At Home—smiling and seraphic as they gazed over
their mother's shoulder—surmounted it. This picture left
nothing to be desired; neither did the headline "Vice-President's wife pours for Mrs. Conrad." Neither did the text which
accompanied these.

"Mrs. Neal Conrad, whose husband's recent appointment
to the Senate has been a matter of national interest, made
her bow to official society in Washington last Thursday, at a
delightful reception which she gave in the charming residence on New Hampshire Avenue which she and Senator
Conrad have leased for the winter. Mrs. Conrad was assisted in receiving by the Senator, who forsook the cares
and responsibilities of office for the afternoon, and who,
like his wife, will quite evidently be a great addition to
the senatorial circle. Mrs. Conrad was charmingly gowned in
a Lanvin confection of pink, one of the many beautiful dresses
which she brought home with her from Paris, where she and
Senator Conrad spent the summer as guests of Mr. Clarence
Hathaway, First Secretary of the American Embassy, a
close friend of Senator Conrad's ever since the days when
they were classmates at Harvard. Mrs. Hammel, who has been
one of the first to welcome Mrs. Conrad, with whom she has
many tastes in common, to Washington, presided at the
perfectly appointed tea table, coming directly from the luncheon given in her honor by Madame Marceau, the wife of the
French Ambassador, who also called on Mrs. Conrad during

the course of the afternoon. Among the many distinguished guests were noticed . . ."

There was more, a great deal more. But that was all that mattered. The first hard weeks had been lived through, the first dreadful mistakes lived down, the "features" about the washtub and the cow forgotten. Anne had begun to "arrive."

CHAPTER EIGHTEEN

"I do solemnly swear that I will support and defend the Constitution of the United States against all enemies, foreign and domestic; that I will bear true faith and allegiance to the same; that I take this obligation freely, without any mental reservation or purpose of evasion; and that I will well and faithfully discharge the duties of the office in which I am about to enter—so help me God."

Neal, facing the Vice-President, with his back to the Senate Chamber, stood beside Senator Brown, repeating the words, a phrase at a time, after Mr. Hammel. Anne, sitting in the Senators' gallery, her cold hands clenched tightly in her lap, colder chills of excitement creeping up and down her spine and stabbing swiftly at her heart, looked down at him with misty eyes. The mist blurred her vision so that she could hardly see him as the Vice-President shook hands with him, and he turned, signed his name in the large book held open by a clerk, and walking with his head held high, to a desk at the rear of the room, slid sidewise into the chair behind the desk.

It was the opening day of Congress, and Neal had repeated the oath of office administered to a new Senator, and then, literally, had taken his seat.

Anne had not been to the Capitol since she had visited it, years before, on her honeymoon-journey to Washington. Driving down to it now, she found it surrounded by police; and a friendly officer helped her to locate a parking-space. Another policeman, standing beside the revolving door at the entrance to the Senate wing, noticed her hesitation as she

paused between the crowded elevator on her left and the
empty one at her right marked "For Senators Only."

"Does that mean their wives, too?" she asked shyly, but
smiling.

The policeman grinned and pushed the bell for her himself. "Sure does," he answered reassuringly. "Get right in, Mrs.
Conrad. . . . I read that piece about you in last Sunday's paper, and reggernized you by the pickshur. You sure have got
some cute kids— Gallery floor, you want."

Elated by this evidence of her dawning prominence, Anne
confronted the doorman of the Senators' gallery without
qualms. But he apparently did not read the papers; and he
was struggling with a persistent mob which was striving to
get past him, and which even his massive bulk and grim
manner could not entirely stem. He could hardly be expected
to look with favor upon another contestant for space.

"Mrs. Conrad?" he snarled, peering at her with suspicious,
bulging eyes. "Lord! why don't they give out cards to this
opening?—No, you don't neither. Can't tell, but it's against
the rules— Senator Conrad's wife? Say, that don't go down
any more. He's got three wives in there already."

There was a titter of derision about her, and Anne felt her
cheeks growing hot.

"I will try to get some one to identify me," she said with
a composure which she was very far from feeling.

"That won't be very hard," a merry voice boomed behind
her; and turning suddenly, she almost bumped into Mrs.
Hammel. "Come and sit with me, my dear. Delighted to have
you. You know Mrs. Hastings, don't you—the Speaker's wife?
—You and Mrs. Standish are friends already, of course. Now
then—right down there on the left—no, not in the front row.
Those are the seats reserved for Mrs. Shaw. But the ones directly behind."

Panting, but placid, Mrs. Hammel wove her way into the
gallery. Anne, with a withering glance at the now obsequious
doorkeeper, squeezed behind her and her two distinguished

companions, and edged down the crowded steps to the designated places. There was the slight, pleasant confusion of removing wraps. Mrs. Hastings dropped her white kid gloves, and Anne quickly bent and picked them up. Mrs. Standish's sable cape stuck a little at the shoulders, and Anne helped to pull it free from her velvet dress; then, murmuring her appreciation of her rescue, she loosened her own coat, and settled down to look about her.

The Senators' gallery was already packed to the last row, except for the unoccupied seats which were roped off for Mrs. Shaw, the President's wife. There was a shining brass plate on the balcony-railing, she noticed, requesting visitors not to lean their elbows or place small personal possessions upon it; and she wondered why so trivial a thing should have caught her attention. All the galleries were crowded, and the one above the clock back of the rostrum was seething. Mrs. Standish caught her questioning gaze at this, and answered her.

"The press-gallery," she said in a voice that was unusually distinct, in spite of its softness, "full to-day, of course, because this is the opening session. You'll learn to watch that gallery —it's always the best gauge of the importance of what's happening here. If it's empty, you'll know there's nothing special going on. If it's teeming, even if you haven't heard that there's anything afoot, don't leave your seat, for something *is* afoot." Then, as the journalists suddenly began to clap, she smiled and added, "They've caught sight of Mrs. Hammel. She's marvelously popular. Applause is forbidden in the Senate— though the House lives on it—but these sporadic outbursts will occur."

Mrs. Hammel rose, bowed, smiled; almost imperceptibly, she flicked her handkerchief. She could not actually be said to wave to her admirers, but the gesture almost amounted to that. They clapped with renewed vigor.

The Senate Chamber, Anne thought, as she resumed her contemplation of it, was strangely unimpressive for so important an apartment. It was drab, dingy, close. Certainly the

Senators could not derive much inspiration from their surroundings, wherever else they might gather it. They were
beginning to come in now—not very impressive, either! Anne
was disappointed. She did not know exactly what she had
expected, but certainly not this. Many of them were bald;
nearly all of them were gray; some were very lean or badly
overweight. Little pompous groups, clad in shabby morning-
clothes, were greeting each other ceremoniously, as they met
for the first time that season. Others, more rough and ready
as to both dress and manner, reached out welcoming hands,
and slapped their colleagues on the back. One Senator, tall,
thin, and harassed of expression, sat adding up columns of
figures, apparently oblivious of the confusion around him. Another, a broad expanse of white linen waistcoat covering the
front of his ample person, seemed all ready to deliver a spell-
binding speech, although nobody appeared ready to listen. A
third, dressed with faultless informality, a dark carnation in
his buttonhole, was, quite superfluously, striking attitudes.
His roving eyes caught Anne's, and rested for a moment on
her face; then he bowed slightly. She felt quite sure she had
not met him, but she returned the salutation, angry at herself
for blushing, and conscious that Mrs. Standish, whom nothing
seemed to escape, was watching her.

"Senator Lassiter," this lady remarked, her sweet voice a
trifle dry, "the Beau Brummell of the Senate. Also—ah—the
Lovelace. I believe you know Clarence Hathaway? Well,
something the same type."

Anne was grateful for the rap of the Vice-President's gavel.
He had entered, on the stroke of twelve, so unobtrusively
that she had not seen him. The Chaplain offered prayer—a
very long and all-inclusive sort of a prayer. Senator Brown
delivered a short eulogy on the late Senator Shelton, to which
nobody paid much attention. There was, actually, more of a
stir followed by a deeper silence when Brown, his address
finished, turned towards Neal and waited for the younger
man to join him. Neal had made a fine record in his own

state, and there was genuine interest in his appointment. But Anne, watching him, was experiencing a deeper emotion than interest; she was remembering, poignantly, the day she had joined the church, the testimony to her faith that she had given before the assembled congregation in the bare little building with its slender spire pointing towards the green hills behind it. This oath that Neal was taking seemed to her no less solemn, no less sacred—did he, she wondered, feel the same way about it? She hoped, prayerfully, that he did.

At all events, he had not forgotten her in this great and pregnant moment of his life. He had hardly taken his seat when he turned, swept the gallery with his keen eyes, and smiled as he found her and saw the expression of love and emotion on her face. For a moment they looked full at each other; Anne felt her composure returning, her vision clearing. She was able to return his smile. Then, apparently satisfied, he nodded, and looked away again, giving his undivided attention to the business of the day.

This did not last long. Several brief resolutions were submitted, considered by unanimous consent, and agreed to.— "Resolved, that a committee consisting of two Senators be appointed to join such committee as may be appointed by the House of Representatives to wait upon the President of the United States and inform him that a quorum of each House is assembled, and that the Congress is ready to receive any communication he may be pleased to make."—"Resolved, that the Secretary inform the House of Representatives that a quorum of the Senate is assembled and that the Senate is ready to proceed to business."—"Resolved, that the hour of daily meeting of the Senate be twelve o'clock meridian until otherwise ordered."—The Vice-President's gavel descended again. The crowd began to stream out. Anne was conscious that Mrs. Hammel was speaking to her.

"You'll come to the House, to-morrow, of course, and hear the President read his message?"

"Oh, of course! I wouldn't miss it for anything!"

As a matter of fact, she had not intended to do anything of the sort; her interest in public affairs was still bounded by Neal's participation in them; and Neal, who had been a figure of importance to-day, would have no part in the morrow's proceedings. Moreover, being extremely sensitive, she dreaded the possibility of another rebuff such as she had received at the hands of the ruthless doorman; no occasion, she felt, could be worth a repetition of that. But it was evident that Mrs. Hammel expected her to return to the Capitol the next day; and she had made the gallant resolve that Mrs. Hammel should never be disappointed in her.

Her determination was rewarded. When Neal came home that night, he gave her a beautifully engraved little card, upon the back of which she discovered the number, row and section of a reserved seat. Armed with this, she penetrated to the House of Representatives without difficulty; and, having found her appointed place, she saw that Mrs. Hammel, Mrs. Hastings, and several other women whom she knew were all near her, and all in welcoming mood; and when Mrs. Shaw, accompanied by a military aide, came in and sat down immediately in front of her, she experienced an unexpected thrill in being presented to the First Lady of the Land. And, after that, one thrill followed another in swift succession: The House, which had struck her at first as being as disorderly as the Senate was drab, subsided quietly on one side of the great hall, in order to make room for the members of the Diplomatic Corps, of the Supreme Court, of the Cabinet and of the Senate, who filed impressively down the aisle. The quiet Vice-President took his place beside the genial Speaker. The President, with his escort of Senators and Representatives, advanced slowly, and mounted the rostrum, dignity and power emanating from his presence. It was *all* thrilling, so thrilling that Anne caught her breath with excitement. When the President began to speak her sense of stimulation increased— She listened with rapt attention to his recommendations, even though she did not understand all of them very

well. There were, it seemed, many matters to which he felt
Congress should give immediate attention. Appropriations
for the army, navy, farm relief, a ship subsidy, a maternity
bill. Anne recognized her ignorance on these subjects, and
resolved to study them, in order to be able to follow intelligently any action that might be taken on them as the season
progressed.

Suddenly she realized that her attention had begun to wander, perhaps because she was hungry. The hands of the clock
over the rostrum were pointing to one, and she was relieved
when the President, now somewhat hoarse, stopped reading
and inclined his head to acknowledge the applause of his
listeners. Mrs. Shaw, bowing graciously in every direction,
was preparing to leave the gallery; and Mrs. Hammel, touching Anne's arm, was asking her a question.

"You are coming over to the luncheon, of course?"

"The luncheon?"

"Yes—the Senate Ladies' luncheon. Don't tell me there is
another thing you haven't heard about! Well, I will explain
as we go over in the subway. We will say good-by to Mrs.
Standish and Mrs. Hastings here. They don't come with us."

Breathlessly, Anne followed Mrs. Hammel through the
crowd to the basement of the Capitol, around several corners,
and into a small open electric car with seats running side-
ways and facing in both directions, which was waiting, drawn
up beside a concrete platform. It was full already, but Mrs.
Hammel, bowing right and left, was immediately afforded
space for herself and Anne. A bell clanged, with a sharp, tiny
report; then the little car leapt forward, and they bounded
noisily away. By raising her voice, Mrs. Hammel succeeded
in making Anne hear her above the clatter.

"Every Tuesday. Marble room in the Senate Office Building. Take turns acting as hostesses. Six at a time. Cold meat,
salad, rolls, coffee, cake, no more allowed. Can't have com-
petition in menus. Make feeling. I'm the President. Great fun.
You'll see. Here we are. Get out."

The marble room, reached by marble stairs, draped with red velvet and glittering with chandeliers, proved a most imposing apartment. Down its wide length ran a long narrow table, covered with a white cloth. Thermos bottles, plates of rolls and jelly, and large heavily frosted cakes were placed upon this at regular intervals; and several well-dressed women were fluttering about it, pouring water and straightening silverware. Another group was clustered about a smaller table in a remote corner, almost concealing the platters of cold meat and salad with which they were occupied. Mrs. Hammel, interrupting herself with frequent greetings, continued her explanation to the still bewildered Anne.

"The waiters from the Senate restaurant come over and set the table for us and clear away afterwards. But the hostesses for the day act as waitresses. They are chosen in alphabetical order—your turn will come next time since your name begins with a 'C.' The chairman—whoever is chosen—will tell you what to bring. . . . Oh, good morning, Mrs. Churchill. How are you? Nice to see you back. . . . All Senators' hostesses are eligible for membership—you must sign your name and pay your dollar for yearly dues to-day. The rules are simple. . . . Hello, Mrs. Farnham! . . . But mind you never bring a guest with you who is a resident of Washington—that *will* get you into trouble! Mrs. Lee, I want you to take Mrs. Conrad under your wing to-day, and see that she meets everybody and has a good time."

Mrs. Lee, thus announced, shook hands with Anne and led her to a seat at the long table introducing her to the other women who had already taken their places near her. Then she sat down on Anne's left, and reached for a thermos bottle. It contained piping hot coffee, and she filled Anne's cup and her own before sending it down the line. The hostesses were already beginning to pass the great platters of cold meat and salad. There was a good deal of informal merriment—a much pleasanter medium for getting acquainted, Anne reflected, this luncheon, than those stiff brief calls. A few of the women she had met already, though not many, as only two Thursdays had elapsed since the memorable one when she had involuntarily held her first "At Home." Those she did know welcomed her cordially and presented her to others. When the rich, moist cakes had been eaten—from the same dishes on which the meat and salad had been served—Mrs. Hammel rose in her place at the end of the long table, and called the attention of the Ladies of the Senate to the fact that one of their members, Mrs. Long, was ill. It was voted to send her flowers. Then a note of appreciation which had come from Mrs. Shelton was read acknowledging a letter of condolence which had been written by the secretary. Afterwards, as there was no further business Mrs. Hammel announced the names of the hostesses for the following week—Mrs. Bean, Mrs. Brainard, Miss Bullard, Mrs. Clay, Mrs. Conrad—with Miss Bullard appointed as chairman. Anne found herself carried off for a conference. A salad, it was decided, was to be her contribution—and would she please plan to be a little early, the following Thursday, to help with preparations? The hostesses usually *did*.

The merry little party was already breaking up when the deliberations of the committee were finished. Mrs. Hammel had vanished. Anne found herself approaching the elevator with Mrs. Lee and Mrs. Stone—the same Mrs. Stone, she instinctively felt, to whom her first callers had gone from her house on that fatal Thursday to relate her short-comings. At all events, Mrs. Stone, a tall, grimly handsome woman, had seemed less cordial to her than to any of the others, and she now felt the chill of the elder woman's cold, critical gaze.

The elevator man slid open the door of his cage and the three ladies prepared to enter.

"Up or down?" he asked.

"Up," said Mrs. Lee who had an errand to do in her husband's office.

"Down," said Anne, who was intent on getting home to relate the exciting events of the day to Dora.

The elevator slid down. Unconscious of wrongdoing, Anne alighted, nodding good-by to Mrs. Lee as she ascended out of sight and turned to find Mrs. Stone standing balefully beside her.

"Don't you know any better than that?" she demanded angrily.

Anne cringed, inwardly but not outwardly. The fabric of her happiness was rent, but she did not allow this disturber of the peace to guess that she was hurt.

"Know any better than what?" she asked.

"Than to tell the elevator man to go down when Mrs. Lee had told him to go up. Her husband has been in the Senate for eighteen years. She takes precedence over *all* of us. And all of the rest of us take precedence over *you*."

"Oh," said Anne shortly, with no indication of being impressed. Mrs. Stone became more and more indignant.

"The matter of precedence is one of *extreme* importance," she declaimed, "and those who do not recognize this only show their ignorance and ill-breeding. A hostess who does not seat her guests according to rank offends irretrievably. I myself have *left* three luncheons because I was not properly placed."

"And was that," inquired Anne, "well-bred?"

Mrs. Stone, who was a very important person—especially in her own estimation—stared speechlessly. No one had ever been so impudent to her before. Anne gathered courage.

"People don't ask you to their homes to insult you," she said, in contemptuous tones. "I am sure the people in my state would think I had 'offended irretrievably' if I treated a hostess like that. And I am confident Mrs. Lee knew I didn't mean to be rude—she looks like a very understanding sort of person. But I won't forget," Anne added with significance, "about precedence—that *you* always take precedence over *me*."

She walked down the steps of the Senate Office Building without a backward glance, and over to the place where she had parked her car. She was conscious that she had scored a victory. She was also conscious that she had made an enemy.

CHAPTER NINETEEN

The morning after the Senate Ladies' Luncheon, Mrs. Lee called Anne on the telephone, and asked if she might not stop and take her to the Congressional Club reception on Friday.

"You have had an invitation to join, of course?"

"Yes—but you see I have been so busy making diplomatic calls—"

"I know—it is hard to wedge both the calls and the clubs in the same afternoon. But everything is over at the Club a little after five, and that leaves almost another hour for calls afterwards. If you are pretty well caught up couldn't you manage somehow?"

"I believe I could; especially as I would love to go to the Club with you," Anne said frankly.

"I am so glad, for I would love to take you," responded Mrs. Lee cordially. "Promptly at 2:45 then."

In her eagerness to be prompt, Anne was standing on the steps of her house, watching the street in both directions, when Mrs. Lee drove up; and as she took her place beside the older lady in the big limousine, Mrs. Lee regarded her with covert but thorough approbation. Anne had on a dress and coat of sapphire blue velvet, with close-fitting collar and cuffs of ermine; and her sapphire blue velvet hat was faced with white satin. Nothing could have been more becoming; she had "matched her eyes" as the *grandes couturières* are so fond of charging their customers to do. Moreover, her white gloves, her suède shoes, and the beaded bag which she carried were all perfectly in keeping. More than one woman stopped to look at her, almost enviously, as she and Mrs. Lee were leaving their wraps in the reception hall of the Congressional Club, which was temporarily transformed into a cloak room.

"Wouldn't you like to come in and see the library where we hold our board meetings before we go upstairs?" Mrs. Lee asked, "being third vice-president, I have to spend every Wednesday morning there, and I would like to show it to you. The secretary's little cubby-hole is cunning too—but we won't delay too long. The reception has begun already."

Mrs. Lee steered Anne gently in the direction of the broad carved staircase, banked with ferns and palms, and separated half way up into two branches. It was crowded—as every place in Washington seemed to be crowded!—and because of the confusion they were obliged to stop for a moment beside the statue of the Winged Victory that stood on the landing.

"Usually we have a program on Friday afternoons," Mrs. Lee explained during this enforced pause, "a concert or a lecture, or something like that; then a short reception afterwards. But as this is our first gathering of the season, the afternoon is *entirely* given over to the reception—it is so pleasant, isn't it, to have this meeting place for seeing our friends! The Congressional Club fulfills a much wider purpose than the Ladies of the Senate, since the wives of both Houses of Congress are members, and daughters may come in too as associate members if they wish. There—I believe we can squeeze ahead an inch or two now!"

The crowd suddenly surged forward, bearing Mrs. Lee and Anne with it up the stairs, and into the great oval room at the top. This room was hung from end to end with feathery southern smilax, and above the smilax floated the flags of every state in the union. The wide white mantel was banked with pink flowers; and above it hung a fine oil painting beautifully illuminated. Near the pillars at the entrance, in front of a little alcove cushioned in green velvet, the president of the Club, Mrs. Gray, and the two first vice-presidents, Mrs. Gorham and Mrs. Bean were standing to receive the guests

—Mrs. Gray in beige lace, Mrs. Gorham in mauve crêpe, Mrs.
Bean in black satin. At the front end of the room, the Marine
Band, gorgeous in the scarlet, gold and blue of full dress uniform, was playing. About a dozen ladies were "floating"
through the crowd making themselves especially agreeable
to newcomers or those who seemed to be alone; and in the
little dining-room beyond, an enormous basket of American
beauty roses towered between two silver candelabra, on a
table spread with a lace cloth and covered with delicacies.
Mrs. Hastings sat at one end pouring tea and Mrs. Lassiter
at the other pouring coffee; they both greeted Anne cordially,
and Mrs. Lassiter detained her for a moment.

"My son and I were sorry to miss you when we called yesterday," she said. "Of course you can't stay in every Thursday, but Blythe very seldom accompanies me on my rounds
and he was really disappointed. Have you and Senator Conrad, by any miracle, a free evening next week or the week
after? We would like so much to have you dine with us—"

"We would be glad to come any evening," said Anne with
her accustomed frankness. "You are the first person who has
asked us to dinner."

"What a neglect of opportunity!" murmured Mrs. Lassiter,
"but it won't last long. Next winter we will have to speak
for you months ahead. Meanwhile, I will get in touch with
you again very shortly, Mrs. Conrad."

Mrs. Lee seemed as pleased as Anne herself at the invitation, and she told Anne something about the Lassiters as they
drove away. Mrs. Lassiter was a very wealthy widow, it
seemed, and acted as hostess for her son, who was unmarried, and the greatest "catch" in the "Senatorial Circle."—
"Only, no one has been able to catch him yet," laughed Mrs.
Lee; "he is elusive—and just a bit delusive—but he'll give you
a good time. You made quite an impression on him at the
opening of Congress. He asked who you were immediately
after he saw you in the gallery, and has told several people
he thought you were the prettiest woman there."

The promised dinner invitation was delivered by hand before Neal and Anne had finished their own supper that night. It was surmounted by a gold crest, over which was written in ink "In honor of the French Ambassador and Madame Marceau." Underneath, partly engraved and partly written, appeared the words

Mrs. Lassiter
requests the pleasure of
Senator and Mrs. Conrad's
company at dinner
on Wednesday evening, December the 14th
at eight o'clock.

2141 Massachusetts Avenue.

"Less than a week off!" exclaimed Anne. "Oh, Neal, what shall I wear?"

Neal laughed. "What a question for a woman who has just got back from Paris! Your clothes are lovely, Anne, you know they are,—and you mustn't try to save them. When the ones you have now begin to get shabby you must have some more. I think that white velvet with the glittery trimming—rhinestone do you call it?—is about the best—and I guess you better *wear* the best." He turned the invitation over thoughtfully. "They must have been going to have this dinner anyway; they've added us to their other guests, or asked us in place of some one who couldn't accept. But that doesn't matter. It's really a compliment— The card wasn't mailed; perhaps you better not mail your acceptance either."

"I can run over with it right after supper," Dora, who had been listening with shared excitement broke in eagerly, "it's just a step and I need a breath of air."

"Thanks, Dora—it is going to be hard, Neal, driving a car in evening clothes."

"I know—I do wish we could afford more help. Dora must

stop doing the washing, that's certain. You must send it out, Anne, or get a woman to come in and help with it and to get supper the nights Dora goes out."

"We can't afford it," Anne objected. But her objection was rather weak. It was all too obvious that neither she nor Dora could continue to work as hard as they had been doing without breaking down, if so many outside demands were to be made upon them.

"We have got to afford it," Neal retorted resolutely. "Thank goodness this is a short season! I'll be back in Hinsboro the fifth of March, digging away for dear life! No vacation for me this summer! My poor old clients will have to cough up enough for us to live on decently here, since the Government won't, and next winter we will be doing things *right*. In the meantime, we will have to find some kind of a temporary solution."

The solution presented itself in an unexpected, not to say startling, manner. When Anne returned from her round of calls the following afternoon ("Will I *ever*," she was saying to herself, "do anything in the afternoon again but call, *call*, CALL!") she drew back in alarm before a huddled figure which was crouched on her front steps, in an attitude of the deepest dejection. At her startled exclamation, the figure unfolded itself and stood up—a gaunt, unkempt man, young but haggard, dressed in a shabby uniform.

"Good-evenin', marm," he said awkwardly, taking off his frayed cap, "sorry if ah frightened you. Don't need a man, do you?"

"Good gracious," exclaimed Anne, "I don't know. What kind of a man? What do you mean?"

"Well, ah meant my kind of a man," the intruder explained hopefully. "Ah ben lookin' for work quite a spell. But ah can't seem to find none. 'Pears like the fellers that stayed to home while we-all was to war collared all the jobs. Leastwise ah can't find none. No, marm, not in Washington. Ah come up here to try to fix ma claim at the Veterans' Bureau and ah ain't got ma claim and ah ain't got no money to go home with neither. Ah'm plumb broke. And ah got so dead beat, walkin' the streets, lookin' for somethin' to do, that ah finally set down here on your stoop. Your house ain't so grand as most. Ah thought maybe some one lived here wasn't real rich, mat be glad to get a few odd jobs done cheap. Ah ain't askin' for much . . . your hired girl wouldn't let me in. But she said ah could wait outside till you-all come home."

"Can you drive a car?" asked Anne without circumlocution. The haggard veteran grinned.

"Well, ah hain't had much experience with Rolls-Royces and them, lady, but a Dodge or the like of that—"

"It *is* a Dodge," said Anne with surprising suddenness. "Are you willing to wash windows and tend a furnace and put on a white coat and open the door?"

"Ah'm willing to do anythin'," said the man with pathetic eagerness.

"Are you—are you white? It is so dark I can't see. I've had my maid a long time and I don't know how she would feel about a colored man in the house," said Anne with slight confusion.

"That's all right, marm, ah don't mind you askin'. Yes, ah'm white all right. 'Pore white trash' you'd call me ah reckon. Ah come from the mountings, Kentucky—ah seen your hired girl. She's powerful pert lookin'. Ah'd be pleased to help her any ways ah could. Ah can cook a meal, too, real good."

"What's your name?" demanded Anne.

"Delancy."

"Good gracious," said Anne, for the second time, "is that your first name or last name?"

"Mah first name's Hod—Horace."

"Well, Horace Delancy, if I get you the clothes you need and feed you, will you come to me for—thirty dollars a month? Until you have proved you are worth more? There's a little bit of a dark room in the rear of the basement. I'm ashamed to ask any one to sleep in it, but if you—"

"Oh, marm," exclaimed Horace Delancy, "oh, lady!"

He pitched suddenly forward. Anne caught him, supported him, reached for the doorbell. Before Dora could answer it Neal swung suddenly into sight around the corner of the street and ran towards the house. Anne turned to him, cutting short his startled exclamation.

"This is our new chauffeur," said Anne calmly, "an answer to prayer. He just fainted away because, I expect—it's some time since he had a square meal; but he is going to be another household treasure just like Dora."

CHAPTER TWENTY

Horace Delancy, warm, fed, bathed, shaved, and clad in neat whipcord, drove Anne and Neal to their dinner at the Lassiters the following Wednesday evening.

It was—of course—a crazy thing to take a man off the street like that into one's house. Both Anne and Neal admitted it. But somehow, neither of them hesitated to do the crazy thing just the same; and Dora's harsh and suspicious comments were nullified by her kind and charitable actions. She scrubbed, scoured, and set in order the little basement room; she placed heaped dishes of steaming food before the derelict at frequent and regular intervals; she lengthened the sleeves of the chauffeur's uniform and the white duck house coats that Anne bought. And she was repaid in kind. Horace Delancy had scarcely recovered from his faint when he assumed control of the furnace. The following morning he drove the children to school, Neal to the Senate Office Building, and Anne to the Central Market; and before evening he had washed every window in the house. It was not until Sunday, however, that his supreme opportunity came. Dora went out then, and he served his astonished benefactors, not the cold "pick-up" supper which is usually associated with a religious observance of the Sabbath, but a meal in which fried chicken, corn fritters, beaten biscuit, fruit salad, and Lady Baltimore cake were a few of the more substantial offerings. Afterwards Anne confronted him accusingly.

"I don't believe you are 'poor white trash' at all!" she remonstrated.

Horace Delancy grinned his disarming smile.

"Ah never said ah was. Ah said likely you'd *call* me that. Mah maw's a good cook. She's got a right nice little place of her own. Widow woman. It was her learned me to cook when ah was a young 'un. Mis' Conrad, marm, Dora says you-all is figurin' on gettin' you a wash-lady. Ah kin wring out clothes real good and hang 'em up. Maw she learned me that too. Ah reckon me and Dora can handle that there wash between us *right*."

Her release from the pressure of domestic duties immediately gave Anne an increased freedom of both action and spirit. On the eventful evening of the dinner she sang as she put the studs in Neal's dress shirt and laid it on the bed beside the white velvet dress with the "glittery" trimming. When Neal came home she had already bathed and was sitting clad in her silk slip before her dressing table, her hair hanging like a cloud of gold about her.

"Lorelei!" he whispered, laughing, and rested his cheek, still cold from the December wind, against her smooth warm face. Then suddenly his arms slid down around her slim, pliant body, and tightened there. He lifted her up, and sat down himself, holding her closely to him. "Darling Anne! I do love you so! I don't say so often, I know, or show it as much as I might, and sometimes I know I seem preoccupied —indifferent—neglectful even but—" He did not try to go on. Indeed there was no necessity that he should. Anne understood, and made her understanding sweetly clear. When at last he set her on her feet again, he began to fumble a little weakly, a little shamefacedly, in his pocket.

"While we were discussing Horace the other night," he said, "you remarked that we needn't worry about his stealing, because there was nothing in the house he could possibly *want* to steal except your engagement ring and that you wore that all the time. Well—of course I don't want to put a premium on crime, but you set me thinking. It is a long time since I have given you a present—would this be pretty, do you think, with the 'glittery' dress?"

"This" when taken out of the satin box with a little spring that clicked, and unwound from layers of flat cotton and twisted tissue paper, proved to be a diamond pendant, hung on a slender platinum chain finished with a diamond clasp. Anne lifted it out breathlessly, starry eyed.

"Oh, Neal! Oh, how lovely! Oh—"

"You can't afford it!" finished Neal mockingly, "of course I can! A man can't afford *not* to give presents to his wife every now and then. Besides, you're not to worry, it is all paid for. I had an unexpected check to-day—an account long overdue paid up. I'd given up hope of realizing anything on it. But I attended to all our monthly bills, bang up, just like *that!* And still I had enough left over for this too!"

The pendant *was* pretty with the "glittery" dress. In fact it was perfect. And as Anne, followed by Neal, swept into the Lassiter drawing-room while the butler beside the silk portièred entrance announced, "Senator and Mrs. Conrad" in tones charged with suppressed importance, both were swiftly conscious of the fact that Anne was unsurpassed in elegance by any other woman present, though nearly a dozen, superbly dressed, were already gathered in the great apartment hung with tapestries and furnished with delicate chairs and sofas surmounted with the monogram of Marie Antoinette. Senator Lassiter, who was talking with the French Ambassadress, detached himself immediately from her side, and hastened forward; while his mother, with less *empressement* but with equal cordiality, turned to greet them also.

"We are so very happy to have you with us—now let me see. I wish to be sure you meet every one here to-night—you know the Marceaus—and have you also met the Italian Ambassador and Donna Martinelli? Ah, I thought so, for I know you have been most punctilious about making your diplomatic calls! Madame Estavi is also a friend already, I am sure—the Speaker of the House and Mrs. Hastings, Senator and Mrs. Lee, Senator and Mrs. Stone."

The even, cultured voice flowed on. Two more servants in

purple livery entered, bearing silver trays, laden with frosty
cocktails, and tiny savory sandwiches. Senator Lassiter offered his arm to the Ambassadress, and advanced, with her
beside him, at the head of the procession which wound its
way to the strains of music from an unseen organ through a
second great drawing-room, across a galleried hall, and into
a long, paneled dining-room flanked with great carved side-
boards. The table was covered with a lace cloth; golden vases
filled with poinsettias alternated with golden *épergnes* filled
with smooth, glowing fruit, down its stately length; at each
place was a golden service plate, golden knives and forks,
thin stemmed goblets of fine Venetian glass. The liveried men
servants—six of them in evidence now—were offering caviar,
resting in the carved hollows of great blocks of ice. This was
followed by a clear green turtle soup, lobster Newburg in
"horns of plenty" made of fluffy pastry, a saddle of mutton
with multitudinous vegetables, a molded gelatine salad accompanied by cheese soufflé, white balls of ice cream, rolled
in shredded coconut and resting on illuminated spun sugar,
tiny candy-like cakes. There was sherry to drink, claret,
sauterne and champagne, though Anne touched none of it,
and after the ladies had returned to the drawing-room, there
was coffee, dark brandy, colorless cointreau and emerald-
colored crème de menthe poured slowly from bulky bottles
into infinitesimal glasses.

Anne, feeling as if she had been suddenly transported to
one of Monte Cristo's banquets, hoped that she was successfully concealing the swimming sensation which almost overcame her as she seated herself between Senator Stone and
Señor Estavi at the very end of the table. To her, a "company
dinner," achieved after hours of hard labor on the part of
both Dora and herself, had consisted of fruit cocktail, tomato bisque soup, roast chicken, a sweet salad smothered in
mayonnaise, vanilla ice cream with chocolate sauce, and
angel cake. She must, it seemed, reorganize her ideas about
entertaining as completely as she had reorganized them

about dress. But she resolved to do so swiftly and competently; and rousing herself, she heard the small black-bearded man with indefinable charm and distinction who was placed at her left asking hopefully, "*Vous parlez français, Madame?*"

"*Mais oui,*" she answered breathlessly, her head clearing instantly, and launching into her newly acquired but fluent French she began to chatter pleasantly with the agreeable little Peruvian. He was delighted at this unexpected display of linguistic accomplishment. It was very rare, he explained, that he encountered "*une Americaine du Nord*" who could summon more than a few broken phrases of a foreign language to her command in an emergency; he would, of course, have learned English himself if he had had any idea that he might have the honor of being sent to Washington, but his appointment had been wholly unexpected. He had, however, a fair knowledge of French, German, Italian, and Portuguese besides his native Spanish; and in a month, if the pleasure of escorting her into dinner occurred again he would address her in her own tongue. (This promise, it may be noted in passing, he faithfully kept, astonishing her by the mastery of grammar, idiom and vocabulary which he acquired in so short a time.) So far, his positions had been in Central America and the Orient. Salvador—really a little Paris. Peking, the wonder city of the world. Anne, entranced, almost forgot the rather sullen, silent figure on her other side; then accusing herself mentally of being prejudiced against him for no better reason than because he was the husband of a woman who had been rude to her, she made a definite effort to seem sweet and gracious. Her attempts met with little response, however. Senator Stone seemed either unaware of conversational obligations or indifferent to them. He was brusque and biting in his speech; and Anne, feeling ill repaid for her pains, was tempted to turn again to Señor Estavi and the magic lands to which he had transported her in fancy. The streak of stubbornness in her nature, however, rather than any social intuition, prevented her from following this path of least resistance; and she struggled bravely through course after course undeterred by sarcastic or monosyllabic replies and an attitude of critical indifference. In the end she had her reward. For Senator Lassiter, appearing at her side apparently from nowhere in an incredibly short time after she had finished her coffee, assured her that she would be much more comfortable on a deep brocaded sofa at the front end of the room than in the small high chair on which she was then sitting; and shepherded her suavely and inconspicuously to a place a little apart from the other guests.

"How I wish," he murmured, throwing his handsome head back a little and speaking through half-closed lips, "that once, just once, I could take a young and pretty woman out to dinner! But it is always my fate to have middle-aged, not to say elderly, Ambassadresses at my side—estimable ladies who have begun to put on weight and who hold their double chins high—it is unthinkable that any man should indulge in airy persiflage with dowagers of rank!"

"Because they would resent it as an impertinence? or because they offer no inducement to levity and indiscretion?" asked Anne, who was beginning to enjoy herself again.

"Both, my dear lady. You have no idea how virtuous I am when there is nothing about to tempt me. But in the presence of lovely young matrons with perfect complexions and a gift of repartee I sometimes forget myself."

"But they, I suppose, always jog your memory?" said Anne demurely.

"Oh, no—not always. Sometimes they are forgetful too— How's your memory?" he inquired with a slight drawl.

"Excellent," said Anne, with emphasis.

But Senator Lassiter did not seem to be daunted; and when a little later she told him that she thought perhaps she and Neal should be leaving, he informed her, with even more of

a drawl, that they could not go until after the guests of honor
had departed.

"But they will go," he said, "exactly on the tick of ten-thirty.
That is the law of the Medes and Persians. Even if she were
in the middle of a sentence, the Ambassadress would rise on
the stroke of the clock, collect her husband with one well-
directed glance, thank my mother and myself for the delightful evening we had given her, smile graciously upon the rest
of you and disappear. The worst of it is, that after that you
will be free to go too; you will no doubt take advantage of
your freedom; and I do not feel at all sure when I shall see
you again."

"Neal and I have been asked to another dinner," said Anne.

"Not really! Two in the same winter!" mocked Lassiter
lightly.

"Yes, really. In honor of the Hammels. The Standishes are
giving it. I think it is most awfully kind of them to invite us.
But what I started to say was—perhaps you will be there and
I might meet you then."

"I see," said Lassiter, suddenly grave. "Thank you. I shall
be there."

Anne had the sudden, uncomfortable feeling that she had
made an appointment with him. With his usual intuition he
guessed this, and with his usual smooth skillfulness restored
her composure.

"And at many other festivities which you will attend," he
said casually. "We are certain to move in interlocking circles,
if not actually the same one, as I rather suspect may be the
case. I hope you dance? I shall permit myself to look for you
at the Children's Hospital Ball."

He bowed slightly, in kind and superficial tribute. Near
them a gilt clock, surmounted by Cupids, and standing on a
high carved mantel between two vases filled with Annuncia-
tion lilies, chimed softly and struck the half hour. The Ambassadress, who was favoring Neal with a few formal remarks,

instantly extended her hand in farewell, and sought the Ambassador with her eye.

"What did I tell you!" laughed Lassiter softly. "Good-by —dear Lady Delight."

CHAPTER TWENTY-ONE

Luncheons, teas, dinners, calls. Official receptions, charity balls, evening musicals, calls. Tuesday noons at the Senate Office Building, Friday afternoons at the Congressional Club. Calls. Calls. Calls.

Anne had been swept breathlessly into the swing of it, almost before she realized what had happened. In January came a week when she did not lunch at home, in February a week when she and Neal did not once dine at home, in early March a week when she was out for both luncheon and dinner every day. She grew very thin and she slept badly, feeling restless and "edgy" for some time after she went to bed, and tossing about so that she feared she might disturb Neal, and finally asked him, rather shyly, if he would not like to have her get twin beds for their room.

"No," he said shortly, "not at all." And laughed, drawing her to him. "Not trying to slip gradually away from me, with that as the first step, are you, Anne, now that you have all sorts of celebrities at your feet?"

"Of course not," she protested; and did not repeat her suggestion. Her beauty took on a slightly haggard quality, and there were dark circles under her eyes, fainter color in her cheeks; but what she lost in freshness she gained, subtly, in sophistication and distinction.

And she loved it all: the over-lapping engagements, the stiff, square, creased envelopes delivered by hand, the clanging telephone, the long cardboard flower boxes with their contents shrouded in moist oiled paper and tiny cards tucked in their corners, the cool home-comings when she left a heated ballroom just before dawn and felt the fresh breeze in her face as Horace drove her swiftly up New Hampshire Avenue, the warm, scented air of flower-decked drawing-rooms, the slamming of limousine doors, the little stir of welcome as she approached a group of friends, the merry approbation of Mrs. Hammel, the semi-serious attentions of Senator Lassiter, the evident pride with which Neal watched her rapid ascent from rung to rung of the social ladder—

For Anne was progressing with a rapidity which was sufficiently rare to be remarkable even in that capacity where so many others have been tested, and have proven beyond any possible question the fine adaptability of the fine American woman.

Nothing perhaps was more indicative of her advance in *savoir-faire* than the difference in the degree of composure with which she approached the White House. When she first drove under its white-pillared *porte-cochère* to deposit her card and Neal's on the small silver salver extended to her by the manservant in livery who emerged from the imposing doorway before her car had actually come to a stop, her fingers trembled so that she could hardly lay down the neatly folded bits of cardboard. The deference which doth "hedge in a king" and which—deny it though we may—seems to many of us to hedge in a president also, rose before her in all its grandeur, terrifying her with its significance. It did not matter that the policemen on duty took her arrival calmly, and as a matter of course, that they actually motioned her on her way with a smile; and that the manservant closed the door of the motor, after he had taken her cards, with the manner of one who is proud to serve a welcomed and honored guest. Her sense of awe persisted all the afternoon; and when Mrs. Hammel told her she should follow up this ceremony of card leaving, after a little interval, with a note to Miss Hopkinson, Mrs. Shaw's secretary, requesting to be received by the President's wife, her reluctance to take this bold step was as evident in her face as it was in her voice.

"Why, Mrs. Hammel, I *couldn't!* Ask Mrs. Shaw to receive *me!* Surely I ought to wait for her to make the suggestion, if such a suggestion is ever to be made!"

"Certainly you ought not! Do you imagine that Mrs. Shaw spends her leisure moments glancing through the cards that are showered upon her and deciding whom to favor with an invitation? She never sees those cards. She *has* no leisure moments. But Miss Hopkinson, the grim old dragon—and a pretty good sort, too, when you get to know her!—has you all neatly docketed and knows whether you have done right by our Nell, and all that. So run along home, Goldilocks, and get your note written!"

Anne used up sheet after sheet of her new monogrammed paper before she achieved a letter that pleased her; but finally it was written and dispatched. When no answer was immediately forthcoming she experienced a sensation of shame—surely she ought never to have written that note! She was being snubbed for her temerity! In the daytime she managed to forget the fancied reproof, but at night she cringed under the sheets at the thought of it. Then, when she had resolutely dismissed the matter from her mind, Dora came to her one morning, wreathed in smiles, and extended a small square envelope engraved on one corner with the magic words "The White House" in small gold block letters.

"This just came, Mis' Conrad. I thought mebbe you'd like it right away."

The flap crackled under Anne's eager hands. A neat card, surmounted by a gilt eagle was disclosed. Anne read:

> *Mrs. Shaw*
> *will be glad to receive*
> *Mrs. Conrad*
> *on Wednesday, January seventh*
> *at five o'clock.*

"There!" said Dora triumphantly; for Dora had been told, of course, all about the note to Miss Hopkinson.

But Anne did not feel triumphant. She felt frightened. And when, at quarter before five on Wednesday, January seventh, she went down her front steps dressed in the sapphire velvet, she grew hot and cold by turns. But she walked steadily across the White House *porte-cochère,* bowed slightly and serenely to the man who opened the door for her, and regarded the tall formally dressed man whom she encountered just inside the entrance with composure.

"This is Mrs. Conrad, Senator Conrad's wife. I have an appointment to see Mrs. Shaw at five."

"Yes, Mrs. Conrad. Mrs. Shaw is expecting you. Would you like to leave your wraps here?—Now if you will come with me into the Blue Room Mrs. Shaw will be there in just a minute."

"How nice he is!" The tall figure had vanished and, relaxing a little, she looked about the circular apartment with its long draped windows giving glimpses of the garden beyond and the white flowers massed about the gilt clock on the mantelpiece. The parquet floor shone like a mirror, and the stiffly beautiful chairs and sofa upholstered in smooth azure damask were grouped around the edges of the room.

"There must be some place more homelike than this where they can sit in the evening!" said Anne to herself, and thought with amusement of Neal's insistence that no man could be comfortable in a room that did not look as if he could put his feet up somewhere in it. She tried to visualize the President putting his feet on one of the blue damask sofas and failed. But the idea brought a smile to her lips. She was still smiling when the door at her left clicked and opened, and the tall spare formally dressed man came into the room again.

"Mrs. Shaw," he said in an impressive whisper.

Mrs. Shaw extended her hand. She sat down herself and asked Anne to do so; and then pleasantly, casually, and fluently she began to talk. Anne, answering at first almost in monosyllables, found herself, at the end of five minutes, talking pleasantly, casually, and fluently also. For the President's wife—amiable, composed, unpretentious, at once put her visitor completely at ease. Her flat crêpe dress of dull purple, with smooth, scalloped flounces and long, tight-fitting sleeves was simplicity itself; her dark hair touched with gray was skillfully but almost severely arranged; and she wore no ornaments except a glittering buckle which fastened the narrow, purple, velvet band around her throat and the glittering buckles on her narrow suède shoes. If she lacked something of Mrs. Hammel's merry charm she gave a greater sense of security and repose. Anne liked her, immediately and immensely. She forgot all about everything deferential. She remembered that this woman, sitting beside her—the First Lady of the Land—had in her youth worked her way through college, taught school, gone to Europe as the paid chaperon for a group of young "society girls," and married an impecunious young storekeeper whom she had endeavored to inculcate with her ideas of culture. Anne began to realize something of the struggle—both for him and his wife—that must have preceded his ascent to the position of a prosperous cosmopolitan merchant—of a Cabinet member—of President of the United States. She visualized the grief—both for him and his wife—which must have bowed them to earth when both their children had died within a week of each other, of scarlet fever, and there had never been any more—

"Just a minute, Mr. Cooper," Mrs. Shaw was saying calmly. Anne turned and saw that the tall formally dressed figure was standing in the doorway, bowing. "Mr. Cooper has come to let us know that our fifteen minutes together are over, Mrs. Conrad. I am so sorry. But I hope to see you very soon again. You will come to the Congressional reception, of course?"

Anne had not intended to do anything of the sort. She had been secretly relieved that Neal had had a sore throat on the night of the Diplomatic Reception, with which the official season had opened and that therefore they had not attended it. But now she answered eagerly.

"Yes, of course! I am looking forward to it ever so much!"

She found that she really meant this; and during the next week her viewpoint did not change. There was no dread merged with her anticipation. The following Thursday she was athrill with excitement as she put on the "glittery" dress and her new pendant; she hummed a gay little air as she folded her evening coat around her, and she seized Neal's arm with an exclamation of pure rapture as their car marked with its "blue card" swung into the slow line of shining limousines advancing, a few feet at a time, down West Executive Avenue, and she caught sight of the effulgent globes of light glowing above the wings of the White House, like orange-colored flowers against the black velvet darkness. They passed through the grilled entrance gate with an easy turn, and stopped at the south entrance just behind Senator and Mrs. Lee. The two men lifted tall silk hats, and drew back for their wives to precede them through the revolving doors; then, as the ladies went into the cloak room to remove their wraps, Mrs. Lee linked her arm cordially inside Anne's elbow.

"Stay with us, won't you? We know the ropes, we'll show you just what to do and where to go so you will see the most—"

They went swiftly past a little room with its many paneled cupboards containing the china of former administrations, through the long corridor where the portraits of the wives of former presidents smiled serenely down from their golden frames, into the little elevator at the left. Then Mrs. Lee with a smothered exclamation that they were "just in time" led them part way across the great hall, and motioned them to take their places beside a tasseled silken cord which was placed across it. In the space beyond they could see the scarlet-coated Marine Band grouped near the front door. Suddenly the selection which the band was rendering came to an abrupt end, and there was a moment of poignant silence. Then the strains of "Hail to the Chief" rang out, and a brilliant procession turned from the broad stairway near the East Room and advanced slowly toward the center of the hall: six aides, gorgeous in gold-braided uniforms; two marines, one bearing the Stars and Stripes, the other the President's flag; the President with Mrs. Shaw on his arm— Mrs. Shaw carrying a small sparkling bag in her white-gloved hands, her long brocaded train flowing from her shoulders like a golden banner; the Secretary of State and Mrs. Standish, who was regal in purple velvet and rose point lace; the other Members of the Cabinet and their wives. Anne was so close to them that she could have touched them as they passed on into the Blue Room; and the Secretary of Commerce, a hearty, jovial sort of person, leaned across the silken rope and shook hands with her as he passed. Mr. Goldenburg greeting her after a long separation would have welcomed her in much the same manner—

But there was no time to stand still, making happy comparisons. The instant that the presidential party had disappeared Mrs. Lee whisked Neal and Anne away into the stately dining-room, where they took their places in line with members of both Houses and their wives who were already gathered there. Mrs. Roper and Mrs. Ranger with their submerged spouses were just ahead.

"This is your very *first* reception, isn't it?" exclaimed Mrs. Roper, thrusting her head back to speak to Anne. "We missed you so much the night of the Diplomats. But of course you did not realize that is the most *brilliant* of all! This is *tame* by comparison."

"It doesn't seem tame to me," said Anne with honest enthusiasm.

"Oh, well, of course! But when you have been here as long as we have, you will hardly ever bother to attend, will she, Mrs. Ranger? We wouldn't have come to-night if it hadn't been for the pleasure of coming *together*, we're such friends."

"Single file, please."

The crisp voice of the aide standing at the door of the Red Room suddenly hushed them. Neal stopped behind Anne, who watched the two great friends gushing as they paused before an unresponsive President. Then she gave her name and Neal's to the aide who bent to hear them.

"Senator and Mrs. Conrad." She was shaking hands with the President, whose tired face did not relax for an instant from its lines of dark fatigue. But there was something personal and cordial in Mrs. Shaw's welcome although she would be obliged, before the evening was over, to speak to hundreds of men and women.

"So you did come!" she said pleasantly to Anne, recognizing her instantly. "I am very glad."

"Is she always so nice?" Anne asked Mrs. Lee as, the brief instant of contact over, they were swept along into the Green Room.

"Oh, always! She knows the President isn't well, that all this is an effort for him, and so she tries to make up for his unresponsiveness. She is naturally friendly, and she has a wonderful memory, which is a huge help to her of course! Shall we go inside 'behind the line' here and get back to the Blue Room where we can mingle with the Members of the Cabinet, or shall we join the *hoi polloi* in the East Room?"

"The Blue Room—no, I think the East Room—oh, I want to do both! I want to do everything!" Anne exclaimed joyously.

Neal teased her about it afterwards. He insisted that theirs was the very last motor to leave the White House that night; and though this was not strictly so, it was true that not until long after the presidential procession had wound its slow and stately way up the great stone stairs again would Anne hear of going home. No, she didn't mind the noise; no, she rather enjoyed the crowd; no, she didn't think they had seen everybody there was to see and done everything there was to do yet. She kept running into pleasant women with whom she was apparently on the best of terms and presenting Neal to them with an eagerness that revealed her immense pride in both her friends and her husband. And when the dancing began, she was swept swiftly away from Neal by Senator Lassiter, who though he had not previously been in evidence, was discovered standing beside Anne before any one else could claim her, and who, though he surrendered her suavely to Senator Lee when his colleague had the temerity to cut in, hovered on the near horizon, and cut in himself soon and repeatedly.

"I didn't have a chance at you myself at all," Neal grumbled when at last they were on their way home again, and rolling slowly past the orange-colored globes of light.

"I know it! Wasn't it wonderful that I should be so—well, so really popular! It seems too good to be true."

He could not feel even a trifle resentful in the face of her glowing happiness. He put his arm around her and drew her closer to him.

"It is wonderful perhaps but it isn't strange," he whispered. "I'm glad you've recovered from your stage fright about the White House. You fit in there wonderfully. You'd do just as well at the job as Mrs. Shaw herself!"

"Neal!" Anne exclaimed, "how can you?" But there was no reproach in her voice.

CHAPTER TWENTY-TWO

By early spring, Neal was frankly tired of the social strain and said so.

"Another dinner," he would exclaim, twitching open the envelope Anne offered him almost resentfully. Then he would read the invitation aloud, as if informing her of its contents for the first time. "'In honor of the Secretary of State and Mrs. Standish—Mr. and Mrs. Brown request the pleasure of Senator and Mrs. Conrad's company'—well, I suppose you think we ought to go to that one."

"Yes," Anne would answer evenly. She always did think they ought to go to "that" one. And when the acceptance had been irrevocably sent she was apt to announce that there was a musical or reception the same evening to which they had better "go on afterwards."

"Well, you needn't stay long on my account," was Neal's invariable comment when they were on their way. "Should we have Horace come back at eleven-thirty, Anne? That will give us three-quarters of an hour."

"Not quite. It is nearly eleven now. So I really think midnight will be better. I know that there are to be singers from the Metropolitan and the program may be a long one."

"And after the 'program' there will be dancing and supper—when we have just had that enormous dinner—and then more dancing— Gosh! Midnight! I suppose I may as well face the fact that it will be nearly two before we get away."

"You might leave before I do. I could come home with friends."

"No, I'll stick it out," Neal would growl under his breath, "but next week isn't quite so full, is it?"

"Not quite," Anne always replied tactfully. But when the next week came, it was even fuller.

He had taken it for granted that they would all leave for Hinsboro immediately after the adjournment of Congress and had looked forward to their home-coming; but as Anne pointed out, the children had their school year to finish, and she could not very well leave them; besides, it would be almost impossible to open their own house, turning on the water and so on, until warmer weather came. There was no use in having delusions about Hinsboro weather in March.

"Well, what do you propose to do?" asked Neal almost angrily. "I can't sit around here until June twiddling my thumbs. I have got to get back and tend to my practice. It has been neglected too long already."

"Yes," said Anne tactfully. She looked very pretty sitting in the little bay window of their bedroom, wrapped in a rose-colored *négligé,* with the morning sunshine falling on her loosened hair. It was a Sunday morning and they had slept late; for with the arrival of Horace Delancy, he had insisted that "quality" ought not to be roused early every day in the week. With him to help, Dora could see the children through their breakfast and he would take Junior and Miss Nancy to Sunday School. But the Senator and Mrs. Conrad should have orange juice and percolated coffee with thick cream, and crisp toast made on an electric heater taken upstairs to them. Gladly acting upon his suggestion, Anne and Neal dozed half the morning, secure in the consciousness that the children were well cared for and happy, and, after breakfasting in bed, lounged comfortably about, reading the papers, talking with each other, and sometimes even settling down for another nap, until it was time for them to dress for their one-thirty dinner.

"I hardly dare say what I am going to," she ventured slowly, flashing a swift glance toward Neal to be sure that she had interpreted his mood correctly and that it was a propitious time to plunge, "when you don't take kindly to the idea of twin beds or even to the thought of having me stay on to a party without you. But I think we ought to— to be separated for a time, just as we had to be when you went to Belford."

"Just what do you mean?" inquired Neal grimly.

"I think I should stay on here through the spring with the children and I think you should go back to Hinsboro and earn all the money you can in your practice. Because we are going to need it. You can stay with Mrs. Simmons. I have written her and she will be glad to have you."

"Oh, so you have written Mrs. Simmons, already?" asked Neal without marked approval. "You seem to have this all figured out without consulting me at all! I think I might have something to say about it myself."

"I didn't, when you went to Belford without me," said Anne serenely.

"And why this sudden greed for filthy lucre?" asked Neal, deciding that it was perhaps well to change the subject. "You have always been terribly keen about saving, but I never knew you to make a point of spending money before!"

"Because, when the time came that we really *needed* to spend I wanted to be able to do it. And I think the time *has* come."

"I see," said Neal a little ironically. "Am I permitted to ask just how these vast sums are to be squandered, since I am to earn them?"

"Neal, darling, don't talk about it in that tone! You know how hard it was to find even this crowded little house that we could rent, and you know how uncomfortable we've been in it all winter! You know how difficult it is to entertain here, even in the simplest way. On my days at home, the walls fairly bulge, and it's impossible to squeeze more than eight persons into the dining-room for a meal. I want you to let

me begin hunting now for a house that we can live in suit-
ably—next winter—and buy it."

"In other words," he said dryly, "I suppose you have got
your eye on one already!" And as Anne colored and gave a
little laugh he laughed too and sat down beside her. "All
right. I know you are right. Sorry if I was cross, dear. Tell
me about it."

"It is in Georgetown," Anne breathed excitedly, "an old
house, rather badly out of repair—"

"Georgetown!" interrupted Neal contemptuously. "Why
that's full of shacks and niggers! What on earth do you want
to go there for?"

"Because the best values in real-estate are there," said
Anne proudly, "it used to be 'the court end of town' and
was a metropolis before Washington even existed! Now the
lovely colonial houses are being snapped up again and soon
there won't be any left, people are moving out there so fast.
This house I like is a big square brick one, on a corner lot,
and it's a great bargain. Of course it needs a lot done to it,
but—"

"But you could supervise the improvements this spring
while I am leading a celibate life slaving away in Hinsboro—
well—how much would it cost all told?"

"The house is only five thousand dollars, if we pay cash
for it. I should have to spend at least that much more on
repairs. And then of course I should have to furnish it."

"I see. You want at least fifteen thousand dollars then."

"I want more than that. I might as well tell you so, all
at once."

"How much?"

"The clothes I bought in Paris are just about gone, they
have had such hard wear this winter. I'll have to get new
ones; I've made a list of what I need, and a thousand dollars
is a conservative estimate of the cost. Then the Dodge is
actually falling to pieces. We've got to have a new motor,
and I think it ought to be a bigger one this time. More of a

town car. And I want to put the children in private schools next fall—both of them—and meantime"—Anne drew her breath and went on—"I want to take them to Europe during their vacation. I'll have the work on the house all organized by then, and I'll be as careful about expenses as I possibly can. We don't need to go on a big expensive ship like the *France*. We can cross on a cabin boat, quite comfortably, and then we could go straight to Fontainebleau and stay there nearly all summer. The children can study French and I can go on with mine. And I want to take up my music again. I don't think it's too late to get back the little I knew and have lost, and even learn some more. It—it means a lot to me—music—and I have—neglected it."

"I know you have, dear," said Neal.

"And I thought we might have some horses and ride in the forest. Of course if you could only come too it would be perfect. But I suppose you couldn't."

"No," said Neal steadily, "of course not. I'll have to work all summer. But I do want you and the children to go. I can see just how much it will mean to us—all of us—in the end if you do. Too bad Clare isn't in Paris any longer to smooth the path for you, that's all."

"I do not need any paths smoothed," said Anne crisply, "by any one but you. I think myself it was fine that Clarence got the appointment to Siam. He is very young to be a full-fledged Minister."

"And you think it is better to be first in a little Iberian village than second in Rome, do you?" quoted Neal gayly. "Well, perhaps you are right, though I imagine Clarence suffered some pretty bitter pangs when he left Paris behind him and started for the center of Asia."

"A few pangs won't hurt Clarence," said Anne still crisply. "He may get rid of that sleek look I have always hated in Siam— I'll book our passage right off, if you're willing, it's so hard to get reservations in late June, especially on the cheaper ships—and now about the house? Could you go with me this afternoon and look it over? It isn't occupied and I have the key."

They went, immediately after dinner.

The distance from the Capitol seemed to Neal a distinct disadvantage and the neighborhood so undesirable that he had to take Anne's word that it was not. Moreover, the fine old house was in a sad state of dilapidation. But he had discernment enough to see that it *was* fine, to notice the chaste elegance of the entrance, the exquisite carving on the mantels and above the windows, the grace of the curving stairway. The arrangement of the ground floor was adaptable both for family life and for entertaining—a long drawing-room on one side of the front door, a square library and a square dining-room on the other. All these rooms had fire-places, and so did the four spacious chambers above; and though there was only one battered bathroom it was easy to see that others could be wedged in. The service quarters in the ell were adequate, with plenty of space not only for Dora and Horace, but for extra servants if they should eventually need them; the attic and cellar were both ample, and in the rear were wide long "galleries," while beyond the neglected lawns and gardens was a long stable. The house which he and Anne had built in Hinsboro was a comfortable, nondescript, middle-class home; this, properly repaired and furnished would become a residence of individual charm and distinction—the suitable setting for a rising statesman, the dignified background for his wife.

"Suppose we drive back and get the kids and Dora and Horace?" he suggested. "If they all like it as much as we do, I guess we may just as well consider the question settled."

CHAPTER TWENTY-THREE

The day after the adjournment of Congress Neal left alone for Hinsboro, facing the fact that as Anne had once stayed there without him, saving money that he might spend it, so he must now stay there without her, saving money that she might spend it. If he faced it rather grimly; if he found but little joy in his work; if his days at the office were monotonous, and his nights in the little room under the eaves in Mrs. Simmons's cottage, which had been his bridal chamber, were lonely; if he missed the variety and amusement of his political occupations, the crowded color of his life in Washington, the companionship of his wife and children almost unutterably; still, the fact remained that he accomplished what he set out to do, and more, that his reputation as a lawyer of national and international note dated from that summer. True, he already had wide experience and a large practice upon which to build; the foundations for his fame were laid; but it was only now that he began the brilliant super-structure which was to bring him fame and fortune. The money that Anne needed for her house and her trip was forthcoming before she asked for it, and in larger sums than she either expected or required; nor was this situation confined to the summer of their separation; never again were they confronted with "straitened circumstances." They were, quite definitely, on the way to wealth.

In June he permitted himself the brief luxury of going to Washington to see how the improvements on the house were advancing and to accompany his family from there to New York when they sailed on the *De Grasse*. He did not leave

Hinsboro again until he returned to New York three months
later, to welcome them back again. During the interval, since
the little house on New Hampshire Avenue was closed when
Anne left for Europe, he was able to live in his own home
in Hinsboro; and Dora and Horace, whose wages had been
raised, ministered capably and faithfully to his material
needs. In the fall he returned uncomplainingly to Mrs. Simmons's cottage, the two servants accompanying Anne and
Nancy and the new French maids to Georgetown. Junior, un-
believably changed, considering the brevity of his absence
from his native shores—better mannered, better groomed,
more mature—entered Groton, beginning his six years of preparation for Harvard. As Anne did not approve of boarding
school for girls, there was no question of sending Nancy away.
She was to go to Holton Arms in Washington.

Just before Congress opened again Neal rejoined his family. Anne had done her work well; and the place in Georgetown, in its completely repaired and renovated condition,
surpassed his every expectation. It was comfortable, it was
charming, it was distinguished. The uncrowded drawing-
room with its two or three fine pictures, its crystal-shaded
lights, its rose brocade hangings and upholstery, its carefully
chosen antique furniture, was a real achievement in selective
taste and arrangement. The Colonial fashion in mahogany
and silver had been scrupulously observed in furnishing the
white-paneled dining-room, where one rare old sporting print
surmounted the mantel; the library, which gave a greater
sense of relaxation, had deep chairs and sofas of Cordova
leather, with small, convenient tables placed beside each one,
walls lined with built-in book cases, and an abundance of current literature scattered about. The bedrooms, with their
carved four-posters, low-boys and high-boys and braided
rugs, were equally successful; the glassed-in galleries, the
tiled bathrooms, the glittering kitchen, the immaculate basement—all were perfect. And in the remodeled stables two

saddle horses and two automobiles—a roadster for Neal and a limousine for Anne—were already installed.

As they sat before the library fire the evening of their reunion, after their delicious and beautifully served dinner, Anne commenced outlining her plans for the winter.

"I am going to start my days at home right away," she said, "that will give me time to get in three before Christmas, and I think this year we had better have an occasional Sunday tea as well. Now as to dinners—I thought I would ask the Hammels to set a day first and after that the Marceaus—and so on. The new cook is so wonderful—"

"I'll say she is!" interrupted Neal, still replete with dinner.

"Yes,—really when it comes to the three C's—cooking, clothes, and culture—we must admit the supremacy of France, no matter how patriotic we feel. Well, with Dora and Horace reënforced by Alphonsine and Madeleine, I see no reason why we should hesitate to ask *any one* here. There is just one hitch—I had a letter from Harriet saying now that we have a guest room, she feels sure we would like to have a long visit from her."

"The Hell we would!" said Neal with vehemence.

"And that she thinks she ought to do her best towards influencing Congress prohibiting the sale of tobacco in any form and limiting the sale of tea and coffee. She believes they are all harmful and she wants to lobby against them with this as a center."

"Good God!" ejaculated Neal with still greater vehemence.

"Well, what can I do? I can't decline to allow your own—and your only—sister to come to our house, can I?"

"No-o-o-o, I suppose not, but she will be a terrible nuisance, and as you infer, she would not fit in very well with your scheme of entertaining. Better have her come at once and get her visit over with. You can postpone your parties until after she is gone."

Anne sighed. "That may mean I can't wedge them in at all. You know how congested everything gets later in the season.

The Hammels won't have a free evening. But my problems don't end with Harriet—my mother has written too. She says now that we have a spare room, she is sure that we would be glad to have Sol and Sam come and stay with us and go to George Washington University."

"Great Heavens, Anne! You can't put Sol and Sam and Harriet all in the same guest room!"

"No, but Harriet doesn't think of Sol and Sam and mother doesn't think of Harriet. And I suppose they all have equal claims upon us. Of course Junior won't need his room except during the holidays—I could crowd the three boys all in there, but I hate to—I want him to have that for his very own—I have taken such pride in fixing it for him. I hoped I was through with remodeling for a while, but I think I will have to have a room finished off in the attic. There is space enough for a fairly good one and for a shower bath."

"But if they start in a college course they will have to be here four years," said Neal, aghast.

"Of course. But as far as that goes, we do not know that the legislation Harriet is interested in will be disposed of this season."

"That's true too—well, we will just have to live in hopes. It's too bad, honey, just when you thought you had everything so nicely organized, but I guess it can't be helped."

His coöperative and helpful attitude made it easier for Anne to stifle her disappointment. She wrote to her mother saying that she would have a room ready for Sol and Sam by the first of January; and she wrote to Harriet to come at once, hoping that this aggressive lady would, by some miracle, prove sufficiently adaptable to her surroundings to be at least partially assimilated by them.

Her hopes were groundless. Harriet arrived in the middle of Anne's first "At Home." The day was stormy, and she wore a "serviceable hat," large black rubbers and a dingy brown mackintosh. Relieved of these, and of her dripping umbrella, she was disclosed clad in a high-necked, white cotton "shirt-

waist," and a gray whipcord skirt, which was cut in multitudinous "gores" and finished around the bottom with braid.

Anne had left her guests for a moment to see Harriet comfortably installed in the precious guest room. She was conscientiously cordial but she faltered a little.

"I thought you might like to pour tea for me a little while,"
she said hesitatingly; "you could relieve Mme. Estavi at five.
That will give you plenty of time to change your dress."

"I shall not take time to change," Harriet assured her
briskly. "I shall come down at once. I see there are a number
of people here and I certainly shall not lose this opportunity
to talk about the evils of smoking, tea and coffee."

"Wouldn't it be better to wait and do that at some meeting?" suggested Anne. "At strictly social affairs like this, we
don't bring up debatable questions."

"That shows you are not really interested in great causes,"
said Harriet, brushing her hair back flatly from her high forehead. "I shall have no such scruples. I am conscious of the
frivolity into which you have led Neal, but I shall try to
counteract such an influence. As to meetings, I shall attend
those too, of course. In fact, I shall hold some here. I can see
there is plenty of room for them in this large house which
you have so extravagantly purchased, regardless of the fact
that you already had a beautiful home in Hinsboro."

The first person whom Harriet approached on the subject
near to her heart coming down stairs chanced to be the Brazil-
ian Ambassador, who had inherited numerous coffee *fazendas*,
the revenue from which permitted him to pursue his career
unhampered by financial worries. Accosted by this strange-
looking female, whose relationship to Neal he did not grasp,
he leapt to the conclusion that he had fallen into the clutches
of one of those "professional callers" whose presence is such
a nightmare to both hosts and guests at many Washington
functions, who wander about uninvited in search of warmth
and food and amusement, and who are often very poor and
very peculiar. Expecting that at any moment she might begin

to remove fruit from the silver *épergne* on the sideboard, or stuff sandwiches into a paper bag, he tried to guide her gently toward the front door and expedite her departure. Anne, catching sight of them just in time, and guessing the worst, whispered desperately to Senator Lassiter who, as usual, had sprung up from nowhere and was standing near her, and begged him to go to the rescue. Immensely amused, he shepherded Harriet skillfully to the sun-parlor and encouraged her to talk, conveying the impression that he agreed perfectly with everything she had to say. When, late in the afternoon, he was relieved by Neal, he left her with the happy idea that she had made a convert. The misleading philanderer, however, wandered off in search of Anne, laughing softly and claiming a reward.

"What thanks do I get for helping you out?" he asked, drawing up an easy chair and offering her a cup of steaming tea and a cigarette.

Anne, who was extremely tired after receiving nearly three hundred persons, accepted his ministrations gratefully.

"No end of thanks," she said with a smile, as she leaned back and blew little rings of smoke into the air.

"Ah—but I would like something concrete. Would you ride with me to-morrow morning or let me take you to a concert in the afternoon?"

"Neither. You know we went all over that thoroughly last spring, Blythe, after Neal went away. I won't play with fire."

"Oh, but this is such a tiny little spark! and you are going to need my help with that Tartar all winter."

Anne deliberated. In her determination that there should be no semblance of a repetition of the episode in Paris she had leaned over backward in her observance of the proprieties. But after all Lassiter was extremely useful to her and she had perhaps been unnecessarily prudish.

"The concert, then," she conceded; "we are dining out and dancing afterward, and with all that, on top of all this, I will be tired and sleeping late. I don't pretend to come down to breakfast any more and the best time for riding is early in the morning. Neal and Nancy get in a canter together then."

Harriet felt aggrieved that Neal and Anne were leaving her alone on the very night of her arrival. It was impossible to make her understand that in a city where dinner lists were compiled weeks beforehand, they could not ask to bring an extra and unexpected guest with them to a formal dinner, and when she caught sight of Anne's evening dress, flaming red and fresh from Paris, her mounting disapproval burst all bounds.

"I never wore a sleeveless gown in my life or one cut below the collar bone," she began. Nancy unfortunately interrupted her.

"Perhaps you would if you had a lovely neck and arms like mother, instead of being scrawny," she suggested.

Harriet glared at the child. "Are you bringing up your daughter to be as fast as yourself?" she asked Anne. "I notice that you permit her to see you smoke. And I was horrified to observe that you seem to have contracted the habit. I am sure that nice Senator Lassiter must have been deeply shocked."

"Oh, no, he isn't. He gives mother most of her cigarettes," Nancy hastened to explain. "He says she doesn't know good kinds from bad, so he has to help her out."

"You mean to tell me that you, a married woman, presumably respectable—"

But Anne had disappeared. She felt she could not listen to another word from Harriet that evening. The next morning, however, her sister-in-law invaded the room where Anne, with nothing more substantial over her shoulders than the wisp of lace which served as a nightgown yoke, sat up in bed reading her mail and drinking her coffee.

"How do you expect your household to be properly managed if you don't get up in good season and supervise it?" demanded Harriet.

"Well, it is managed," answered Anne patiently. "I don't know of one where there is so little friction or where the serv-

ants do so much and do it pleasantly besides. Do be reasonable, Harriet; I worked hard for years; but my days of
manual labor are over now. Alphonsine attends to the marketing herself—French cooks always do. The rest of the machin-
ery I wind up just like a clock and I see that it does not run
down. Beyond that I do not need to do anything."

The telephone beside her bed tingled. Anne picked it up.

"Oh, good morning, Blythe— No, I haven't forgotten. I'll
wedge in a few calls first; if you are going to the Martinellis'
we might start together from there—why, that's very kind of
you. She is right here, I'll ask her—Harriet, Senator Lassiter
says that he and his mother would like very much to have you
lunch with them, informally, on Sunday. He says Madam
Lassiter is interested in your views."

"I feel it my duty to go," Harriet replied, "though I do not
approve of Sunday entertaining on general principles. But if
it will help the cause—by the way, Anne, I should like a
branch telephone installed in my own room. It will be extremely useful in mapping out my arrangements."

Thankful that her mind had been diverted, Anne gave the
necessary order, and Harriet, placated for the moment, hurried off to map out her plan of campaign for the improvement
of the nation. Before noon, it had been disclosed that she
intended to use Horace and the limousine to facilitate her
calls on all the members of both Houses of Congress, as she
expected to influence these legislators in the right direction;
that she had invited twenty zealots from the National Anti-
Tobacco League to tea in order that they might arrange for a
series of "parlor meetings" to be held every Monday morning
in Anne's drawing-room; and that she had instructed Madeleine to fashion her a costume "symbolic of purity, peace and
progress" from a bolt of white satin which she had found in
the bottom bureau drawer and which the bewildered maid
had already been instructed to make into "sleeps" for Madame.

Feeling that no amount of "supervision" would restore good

feeling in her disordered ménage, Anne rose, poured oil on the troubled waters, and resolved to abandon all plans of her own for entertaining until a more opportune season.

By Christmas time, the entire family was thoroughly submerged by Harriet's domination. Without consulting Anne she had suggested to her parents and her brother, Arthur, that they should join her for the holidays; and the house, which had seemed so pleasantly spacious before the arrival of the correct and critical Conrads, had become so crowded that there was no breathing space in it either figuratively or literally. Anne welcomed the impending appearance of Sol and Sam as an excuse for clearing it out.

Harriet was too firmly entrenched to dislodge, but the others, with veiled comments on Anne's lack of true hospitality, departed on the same day that the boys arrived. But her brothers brought no solace with them. It was immediately apparent that they would have to be completely outfitted with clothes, that they would have to be brushed and bathed and barbered, before they could even present themselves as applicants for entrance to the university. They were so acutely unhappy themselves, in the alien atmosphere into which they had suddenly been plunged, that Anne's heart ached for them. She could not bear to listen to Harriet's sneers at "country bumpkins," or witness Neal's impatience with the "uncouth cubs." A dozen times a day she climbed to the attic chamber, to which they slunk away as much as possible, and coached them gently but firmly in matters of dress and deportment. They were so docile and tractable that it was pathetic, but she knew they were homesick for the ramshackle old house at West Hamstead, that they hungered for coarse accustomed food, that they would have been more comfortable in overalls than broadcloth, that they were stifled without the air of their native mountains. First Sam and then Sol came down with the "flu," and Anne, caring for them tenderly lest they should be more miserable than ever if abandoned to the mercies of a strange nurse, caught it herself;

then it swept through the household like wildfire. Nancy, Neal, the servants, each was felled in turn. Alphonsine, the peerless cook, threatened to leave if a murderous American doctor entered her room again ordering her to open her window and admit the poison of the night air. Madeleine, the peerless chambermaid, contended that it was not her work to carry trays, that Dora must do that, even though poor Dora, at the moment this verdict was issued, lay prostrate on a bed of pain. Chaos and confusion reigned supreme in the stately house which Neal and Anne had felt so sure was to be the seat of culture and well-ordered living.

At length the invalids recovered, the situation shook itself into shape. Alphonsine and Madeleine forgot their grievances and redoubled their efforts to please; the boys began to adjust their difficulties and to enjoy life at the university. Harriet departed for Hinsboro well pleased with her winter's work, and assuring her brother and sister-in-law that she would be on hand the following season to "carry it further." Senator Lassiter saw her off at the station, and then swung back to Georgetown intent on taking Anne for a spin in his roadster with no one to observe just how long they were gone. He found her huddled over the library fire, looking utterly desolate.

"How do you manage to have so much spare time on your hands, Blythe?" she asked listlessly. "Don't you ever spend an hour in the Senate Chamber or attend a committee meeting or dictate a letter? Neal is so busy this season that he hardly has time to breathe—not that it would matter if you had all the leisure in the world, I haven't any, so I couldn't go to ride with you. I've got to prepare for more company. I've just had a wire. A Mrs. Griffin and her son, Roy, who live in Wallacetown, are arriving on the Colonial. They are old friends of Neal's and pretty important constituents. Now that we have this house, we have plenty of room—"

Blythe Lassiter shrugged his shoulders. "You will be a wreck if you don't watch out," he predicted. "Really, Lady

Anne, you look frightfully seedy. The air will do you good."

"I don't need air. I need a little peace and quiet."

He left her reluctantly. It was several weeks before he found her alone again. Mrs. Griffin and Roy were not interested in "causes" and they were not seeking an education; but they had never been to Washington before and they did not know when they could come again. Therefore they desired to see it thoroughly. Their ambition was not limited by daylight or dark. The Lincoln Memorial at dawn, the lighted dome of the capitol at night, appealed to them equally. They had somehow assumed that the cherry blossoms were already blooming; and since these were not in flower, they thought perhaps it would be well to linger on. If they did this, Mrs. Griffin could attend the sessions of the Continental Congress of the Daughters of the American Revolution. Meanwhile they took it for granted that they would have cards for the gallery at the Senate Chamber and House of Representatives, a letter to the Librarian of Congress, a permit to see the Bureau of Engraving and Printing; that they would be received at the White House. Mrs. Griffin wrote home to Mabel Hildreth how kind Anne was to them and what a lovely large house she had and hinted that perhaps George and Mabel and one or two of their children might be coming to Washington that spring, too; a hint upon which they promptly acted. Neither Neal nor Anne had forgotten how good Mabel had been to them that first year of their marriage when Anne was so sick. This was, obviously, the time to repay the obligation. Besides, George had become one of the leading farmers of the state; he had tremendous influence with the agricultural vote; he was not only an old friend— he was a constituent with whom to reckon. Then Governor Low, to whom Neal owed his appointment to the Senate, stopped off on his way north from a conference of Governors which he had been attending in South Carolina, and Mrs. Low joined him. Anne and Neal gave a large official dinner in their honor—the first one, in spite of all their plans, which they had given that winter—followed by a still larger reception. The morning of these functions, Anne found in her mail a letter which she tossed to Neal with a little hysterical laugh.

"Just look at that," she exclaimed; "if it were not down in black and white I should not believe it—in spite of everything we have had to go through this winter—that any one would have the effrontery to write such a thing!"

Neal glanced at the offending sheet. "Dear Mrs. Conrad" —he read—"I do not know you personally, but I have always felt a deep interest in your state because my great-grand-mother came from there; so I should like to attend the reception which you are giving in honor of Governor and Mrs. Low this evening. However, I see by the papers that you are not planning to begin receiving until half-past ten, which is rather late for one of my advanced years to start out for a party; so I hope you won't mind if I come at half-past nine instead."

"At which hour we will still be at the dinner table," said Anne still more hysterically. Suddenly she began to cry. Neal regarded her with alarm.

"Look here," he said. "Your nerves are all shot to pieces. It's this hellish winter you have had. You shall never let yourself in for another like it again. Family, or no family, constituents or no constituents, I won't have you landing in a sanitarium."

"I am not going to land in a sanitarium," sobbed Anne, "I am going to land in the nursery again. Of course I am desperately tired, and that does make me nervous, but one reason I am so silly and uncontrolled is that I am—I am just deathly sick besides— Oh, Neal, I am almost certain that I am going to have another baby!"

But she did not. The pleasant physician who had seen them safely through the "flu" and whom Neal summoned the day after the big dinner—which was such a tremendous success that it was long remembered as one of the outstanding events of the winter—confirmed her suspicions as to her condition;

but when, after chatting merrily and casually with her for a few minutes, he went downstairs with Neal, he closed the library door and spoke frankly.

"There is no doubt that she is pregnant. Normally I should expect her to be confined about the end of October, but—I don't think things *are* quite normal. I will have another man in to look at her too, if you don't mind."

"If I don't mind!" Neal shouted. "You must do everything for her, *everything*, do you hear?"

"Don't take it so hard," said Dr. Harrison gently, "of course everything will be done for her."

Anne herself had no misgivings. After the first few weeks she was less troubled with nausea than she had been when Junior and Nancy were on their way; and when she had had a fortnight of complete rest, she was up and about almost as usual except that she was careful—or tried to be careful— about getting over-tired. She shopped happily for the prettiest baby-clothes she could find, remembering with a slight pang how much simpler and scantier the layettes for the other children had been. She refurnished the guest room as a nursery—"and we will never have another guest room," she laughed, "as long as we live in Washington!" She jested about the "little Benjamin" they were to have so long after they had supposed that their family was complete; she acquiesced uncomplainingly to spending the summer in Washington where Dr. Harrison could watch over her. But, late in August, she was taken acutely and suddenly ill; and when she finally groped her way back from the Valley of the Shadow and stretched out her arms across the bed to touch the little bundle that she expected to find beside her, there was only empty space.

For "little Benjamin" had come too soon; and he had been stillborn.

CHAPTER TWENTY-FOUR

Anne was very slow in recovering her strength. She had drawn so heavily upon her reserve that she had none left; and the debilitating heat and humidity of Washington in mid-summer served to retard her recovery still more. Dr. Harrison spoke frequently of the advisability of getting to a more bracing climate as soon as she was well enough to travel. But it was late September before she was able to leave her room; and by this time Nancy's school had opened and Sol and Sam had returned to college. So Anne would not hear of going away.

"I'll spend next summer in Hinsboro," she assured her long-suffering physician, "very quietly. The climate is bracing enough there, I assure you."

"The climate may be all right. In fact I have no doubt that it is, but I do not believe you will rest very much. Your husband comes up for election next fall, doesn't he?"

"Y-e-e-s, if he decides to run. I don't believe he has fully yet. But naturally he would like to. Having been appointed to the Senate I think he would like to prove that he could be elected."

"Quite so—and you would like to have him, I suppose?"

Anne flushed a little. "Yes, I would like to have him," she said quietly. "I am very proud of what he has done already. If he can do more, I shall be prouder still."

"And you wish to do everything you can to help him?"

"Of course."

"Then you had better begin by getting yourself in good physical condition."

Anne finally promised that she would talk to Neal about going away; but Neal, like most men, and especially like most husbands, while deeply concerned over acute illness, did not regard convalescence as a serious matter. As long as he felt that her condition was grave, as long as he could see that she was suffering, there was no medical suggestion which could have been made that he would not have insisted upon following. But now that she was up and dressed, now that she went out for a short ride in the motor every day, now that he saw her supervising Nancy's fall wardrobe with interest and shepherding her brothers into the social field, now that he heard her discussing dinners with Alphonsine, he assumed that she was "perfectly all right," and said so.

"Doctors always like to make mountains out of mole hills and drag cases out as much as possible," he announced, a little sententiously. "All this talk about 'nerves' and 'rest cures' and 'lowered vitality' sounds awfully important but personally I don't think it amounts to much. When you think of the families women used to raise and the amount of work they used to do—! Well, of course if you want another trip, I have nothing to say, but—"

Usually when Neal volunteered the information that he had nothing to say, this was preliminary to a lengthy argument. Anne, who didn't feel equal to arguing, cut him short politely but firmly.

"*I* don't want another trip, but I promised Dr. Harrison—"

"Well, I guess we can settle this ourselves without Dr. Harrison."

He spoke smugly. But in the succeeding weeks he watched her with secret anxiety. She was—he was reluctantly forced to admit to himself—very thin, very white and very listless. He tried to find satisfactory explanations for this: of course the loss of the baby had been a shock to her; but she would recover from that. Of course she had suffered a good deal of pain; but after all, her constitution was good, she ought to have excellent powers of recuperation. But did she? It began to look as if she did not. About the middle of November, quite as if it were his own idea advanced for the first time, he said a little gravely he thought it would be a good plan for her to have a change of air.

"It's nice and cool in Quebec," he told Anne, rather as if he were the discoverer of Canada's climate.

"It's nice and cool in Washington now," retorted Anne.

"Well, you could have gone away sooner if you had wanted to, couldn't you?" he asked almost angrily. "You said you didn't care—"

"I didn't and I don't unless you could come too—"

"Just before the opening of Congress? My dear girl, you know that is impossible. I am so driven at this time of the year I hardly know which way to turn. Besides . . ."

"Besides, you feel that this year, if you went away at all, you ought to go to Hinsboro?"

Neal hesitated, then drew in his breath and spoke with the air of one who was preparing for a deep plunge.

"Yes," he said at length, "I do. I have decided to run for the Senate. I would never be satisfied if I didn't and that means a real fight. I ought to have got started at it sooner. Of course the man that's in has certain advantages, but Fletcher, who is almost certain to oppose me, has millions behind him where I have thousands, and he owns the biggest newspaper in the state—whereas I haven't any contacts with the press worth mentioning, and even if I win the nomination —a very different proposition with the direct primaries than it used to be in the old convention days—the election won't be any walk-over this year. Business is bad. A good many mills are running on half time and others are closed, and the farm situation is really serious. Brown and all his bunch will play that up for what it is worth. He's a dangerous demagogue but he poses as the working-man's friend in the Senate."

"Aren't you their friend?"

"I've tried to be. But, according to Brown, I'm bound, tied

and delivered to the 'interests.' The machine has ground out
all my human qualities. Wall Street owns me body and soul.
You would not recognize your husband, Anne, in Stetson's
speeches—or on the front page of Fletcher's *Evening Inquirer*, as far as that goes. I don't suppose you keep up with
the home papers, but if you did . . ."

"I do mean to, and I used to regularly. Lately . . ."

"Well, I am not complaining but I do think, Anne, you
sometimes overlook the importance of keeping in touch with
state affairs in your desire not to miss anything here. You
are kind to every one who comes to Washington but you're
not at home a great deal. Now if you could get to Hinsboro
early this spring . . ."

"I can. I will."

"And make up your mind for a heavy summer—exert yourself. Don't act like a high-brow. I am not sure these trips to
Europe and the private schools and all these servants are
useful—politically speaking, I mean. A little of that stuff you
tried to hush up—teaching school, living in a tenement and
doing your own washing—has its points."

"I know. I'll try very hard, Neal, to do just what you would
like and just the way you'd like it done."

"Well, if you feel like that, is there any reason why you
should make a point of being rude to Mrs. Stone?"

"It was Mrs. Stone who made a point of being rude to
me! The first day I met her, Neal—why, I told you about
it!—and she has never lost a chance to snub me, insult me
almost ever since. I can't think why she should hate me so
when most people—well, most people like me. But anyway
I can't accept her attitude lying down."

"You can't? Well, you better if you want me to stay in
the Senate. It happens that Stone and Fletcher are thick
as thieves. They roomed together in college. And Fletcher
is making capital out of Mrs. Stone's dislike for you all over
the state. You are pictured as an impudent, aggressive,
ignorant little climber. The stories are terribly distorted, I

know, but there is a grain of truth in them, and they are not doing me any good."

Anne sat very still. "An ignorant, impudent, aggressive little climber—" So that was the way she appeared to her enemies and Neal's. The perseverance, the patience, the self-sacrifice, which had enabled her to grow from a raw little country girl into a well-developed, self-assured woman were ignoble rather than admirable qualities when viewed with unfriendly eyes. She felt as if something cold and sharp had penetrated to her heart and coiled around it. But Neal, unconscious that she was stricken, went on talking.

"You say most people like you—well, it's never a good thing to bank on popularity, but I think you *are* popular—too popular. I don't want to hurt your feelings, Anne, and of course I know you don't mean to be indiscreet, but—well . . . Lassiter was here a good deal last winter. Harriet called my attention to it first."

"She would," Anne breathed between tight lips.

"And father and mother noticed it too. Probably the servants did, and other people. It was rumored around that you— that he—anyway when the baby was born, there was a paragraph in *City Chatter*—Miss Letts showed it to me—not that I believe a word of the scurrilous stuff or that she did—you know that, of course. You know that I love you and trust you, but I thought you ought to know . . ."

Feeling that he had perhaps said enough, Neal bent over the evening paper. The front page was printed with headlines about the tariff—that new bill over which he was working so hard. It was half an hour before he looked up and when he did, he noticed that Anne had left the room. He supposed that she must have gone to bed, as she often did now that she was so far from strong, but when he reached the Colonial chamber which she had made so beautiful, she was not there either. Well, then she must be helping Sol and Sam with their French. She often did that too—astonishing how she had mastered it. He couldn't get a can of hot water himself if the steward who happened to wait on him didn't speak English—clever, Anne was—and better looking every year—a great credit to him. He never would have got where he had without her. Complacently, he went to sleep.

In the morning when he woke she lay, as usual, beside him, her curls tumbled over the pillow, one slim bare arm thrust under her head. He never guessed that she had spent most of the night walking blindly beside the Potomac River, regarded with an anxious curiosity by an occasional watchful policeman and with covetous misunderstanding by an occasional night-prowler. But there was something about her that kept both from approaching her—something almost unearthly—something wholly tragic. The slimy serpent of slander had crossed her path as it crosses the path of almost every man and woman of destiny. And in the first hour of her agony—it seemed to her that her feet would never touch clean earth again.

CHAPTER TWENTY-FIVE

"Yes, this is Mrs. Conrad speaking— No, Senator Conrad cannot come to the telephone. Oh, thank you, Mr. Baker, I'll take the figures—yes, I have it right, I think—Conrad thirty-two, Fletcher seventeen."

Anne hung up the receiver and went swiftly from the library to the shadowy hall. Neal, who cherished certain pet economies, insisted that all the lights did not need to be turned on at once. Anne, in the dimness could barely see him standing near the door, his white face strained and tense. She walked over to him and put her hand on his arm.

"Mr. Baker has just telephoned from Bakerfield," she said gently, "he said he wished to be the first to congratulate you. The result there is very encouraging."

"Bakerfield is only a small, unimportant place," Neal interrupted vehemently.

"I know. But perhaps the figures are an indication of what we may expect elsewhere. The vote is thirty-two for you and seventeen for Fletcher."

A harsh sound, something like a smothered growl arose from Neal's throat. As he had foreseen, the campaign had been a bitterly hard one. He had borne the brunt of it bravely, almost buoyantly, but on election night he had suddenly collapsed and, leaving his headquarters, had come home, refusing to see any one or even to speak with any one but Anne. Not that he seemed to derive much comfort from her presence. He sat crumpled in a heap or strode back and forth like a caged animal, and when he spoke at all it was savagely and despairingly. If the telephone had been

a coiled rattlesnake ready to strike at him, he could not have
manifested a greater horror at the suggestion of touching it.
So taking her place beside it, Anne sat through the endless
length of the dark afternoon, waiting for the tidings which
sooner or later would come. Good tidings, evil tidings. Tidings of victory, tidings of defeat. She had no way of guessing
which they were to be. She only knew that she must be there
when they came. That until then she must comfort, cheer,
cajole, caress—

In the gathering dusk, her hands clasped tightly in her
lap, she reviewed the months that had passed since that
night of desperation, when, bruised and bleeding, she had
walked slowly along the Speedway confessing herself beaten,
vowing that since she had tried so hard and failed, she would
never try any more; and then suddenly, miraculously, finding the strength to vow that she had only just begun to
fight. Turning from the gray Potomac, she had walked beside
the still pool in which the columns of the Lincoln Memorial
lay reflected in the ghastly light. There was peace there—
peace not to be found in the rushing river. She sat down
on the bank and clasped her hands over her eyes. Slowly,
surely her sanity seemed to return—her balance to be restored. Let Maud Stone send her back to Hinsboro, humbled
and humiliated, with Neal's career involved! Never, never,
never! The hard bitter woman should be cheated of her
triumph. Confess that a filthy periodical had the power to
challenge her good name? Her dead baby seemed to rise
from his grave forbidding her. Stretching out her hand she
almost seemed to touch him. . . . Behind the slender shaft
of the Washington Monument the sky grew vaguely rosy
with impending dawn. She shook the tears from her eyes,
threw back her head, and walked towards home. . . .

"State Headquarters? Yes, Mrs. Conrad speaking for Senator Conrad—two wards in Belford have gone for Fletcher
by a large majority. Thank you. Yes."

Out in the hall again. Neal seized her arm and spoke before she could do so. "I heard you. The first two wards they have heard from! If I lose Belford *I* am lost."

"You haven't lost it! What do two wards amount to in a city? Nothing, nothing at all . . ."

Back to the telephone. Back, in memory to Washington—to Mrs. Stone. The suavity of her greeting the next time she met her enemy:

"'Speak of angels and you hear their wings!' Miss Sharp has just been talking with me about you. She somehow conveyed the idea that I had the privilege of being intimate with you and she asked if I would not try to persuade you to let her publish a really *vivid* story about you."

"A vivid story?" said Mrs. Stone sharply, "about *me?*"

"Yes, I think they are so thrilling—those adventures of yours in Vaudeville, and your meeting with Senator Stone after you had been so unhappily married to the ventriloquist."

Mrs. Stone gasped. How Anne had unearthed these details of her early life, she didn't stop to inquire. She had taken every precaution, and she believed them to be known to not a soul in Washington. The capital, she felt sure, had supposed her "to the manner born." Her rigid insistence upon the rules of precedence, her arrogance in dealing with her inferiors in rank, the exclusiveness of her visiting list—Mrs. Stone, who had never heard of "Noblesse Oblige"—imagined that she had made of these an impregnable fortress for her social standing.

"Miss Sharp cannot write such a story!" she exclaimed with vehemence.

"It is written," said Anne calmly, "and she has had an offer for it from a very important syndicate. It ought to sweep the country! Of course she has been very careful to check up on the accuracy of the details. The champagne supper, for instance, in Senator Stone's suite the night you met him . . ."

Mrs. Stone's fortress was crumbling about her. She trembled. "How," she asked herself wildly, "could she have been foolhardy enough to offer attack when she herself was so vulnerable." Her lips shook as she spoke to Anne.

"I know that you and Miss Sharp are very good friends. I have heard her say there is no woman in the official set whom she admires so much. If you can persuade her not to publish this story . . ."

"I never could understand," Neal often said to Anne that summer, "how Stone happened to withdraw his support from Fletcher. If he had not, the situation would have been very different, but as it is my troubles have been cut about in half . . ."

"Yes—Mrs. Conrad speaking. Oh, the report from the third ward—two hundred eighty-six to ninety-five in favor of my husband? Yes—I will tell him— Neal, did you hear that? You have carried the third ward in Belford almost three to one."

"Well, until I hear from the north of the state, that won't reassure me much . . ."

"And could you," she heard herself asking Clarence Hathaway again—Clare who was back from Stockholm on leave—a sparkling winter day when Washington was enfolded in one of its rare snows, "manage to be—well, a good deal in evidence this winter?"

"Of course, Anne, but just why?" She told him. Briefly, almost boldly. He whitened a little.

"It's a comedy of errors, isn't it, Anne? You don't care a rap about Lassiter, never thought of him except in the most casual way. And yet this ugly story gets started and you ask *me* to act as a foil when . . ."

"When I do care several raps about you. When I might have cared a good deal if I had not always loved Neal—if I wouldn't always love him until it *hurts*."

"Yes, I know—well, I will do my best, my dear. One may, I suppose, venture to seal a bargain by kissing your hand?"

"No, Clare, not even that."

"Well, then, not even that."

And Clare had played his part. Played it with such consummate skill that the "ugly story" was buried past any resurrection. Anne did not appear to avoid Lassiter in the least. Clare would not have permitted her to make such a mistake. She saw him as much as ever; but somehow he did not stand out, overshadowed as he was by Clare—the perfect pattern of all that a husband's best friend ought to be. Every one in Washington not only said so but thought so. Reports of his perfection reached Hinsboro and Hinsboro too was impressed by Neal's good fortune.

"Headquarters calling. Figures from Chaselford, Summerdale, Medfield—just about a wash-out, Mrs. Conrad. Would you care for the exact figures?"

"Oh, no, thank you."

This time Neal was standing above her, his weight heavy against her weary shoulder.

"Bad news again? I knew it!"

"You're holding your own."

"Holding my own! Good God, I've got to do more than that!"

"You will, darling, you will. Would you not like a cup of cocoa or something?"

"No— No—don't leave that telephone. It may ring again at any moment."

But it didn't. The silence, like the darkness, grew oppressively heavy— Dora came in and suggested that it was past dinner time. Anne shook her head and Dora went out again. . . .

Roy Griffin, who knew so many lawyers; George Hildreth, who was State Master of the Grange; Mr. Goldenburg, whose one small shop had grown into a great chain with links all over the state; Low, who had appointed Neal to the Senate, and who had political wires running in every direction from his gubernatorial seat; would they all do their share? And, if they did, would it counterbalance Stetson's strength with the labor vote, where Neal had no strength? The *Wallace-town Bugle* and the other weeklies—a great many of them— if they were all friendly to Neal, would that make up for those two big papers of Fletcher's, which were hurling denunciatory editorials at Neal's head?

Spring came, glad and golden, magnolia-scented, to Washington, and Anne, asking herself these troubled questions, shook the beauty that was all about her impatiently from her consciousness, and strained with eagerness to reach Hinsboro, raw and wind-swept, and bleak as it was. But this was the year of the "Long Session," and Neal would not be at liberty to go home early in March. He would have to stay in the Senate through April, through May, through June. It was actually mid-July before adjournment came, at two o'clock one torrid morning when ugly feelings had been unleashed by fatigue and ugly words spoken by lips which were merely the mouth pieces for overwrought nerves. Neal, who had been steering a filibuster lost his temper that night and said unforgivable things to men who had been his friends for years. These unforgivable things were printed in the *Record*, and circulated through the country. Were they unforgettable too?

"Anne? Clare speaking from New York—how are things going?"

"Oh, Clare, I don't know. Not too well, I am afraid. Neal seems to be leading by a narrow margin in the country, but the city returns are slow in coming in, and those we have aren't very favorable."

"The later ones will be better. I'll call up again, say at midnight. Would that be convenient?"

"It will be a God-send. It's such a comfort, Clare, just to hear your voice."

"My boat sails at seven in the morning, but I've purposely not gone on board to-night. I want to hear that Neal's come through before I leave. Though, of course I know he is going to."

Junior wanted to go to a camp in the Yellowstone. Mme. Estavi was taking her little family to Europe for the summer and had invited Nancy to accompany them. But both children were kept at home. They added immeasurably to the picture—Junior's more and more famous smile; Nancy's sweeter and sweeter manners, made an indelibly favorable impression on wavering constituents who came to the house and so much had to be jammed into such a short time that not a single consideration could be overlooked. Neal's enemies had been at work all the time he was chained to his chair in the Senate. And now only August, September and October were left in which to tear down what they had built. No one man, even if he were super-human, could achieve as much as Neal was expected to achieve—as much as he would *have* to achieve if he were to win. Of course the children must do their share, even though it was a tiny one. Anne must make them see—must never let them forget—how much that share might mean to their father. And she must do her share too. Must shield Neal, spare him, save him. But how, *How*, HOW?

She kept open house. This was hard on the servants, who could never be sure of a day off, and who, in spite of their faithfulness, became disgruntled and snappy; but it was harder on Anne. Should she provide for twenty at lunch, or two? The supply lists which she made out every morning covered several sheets of paper. And yet the refrigerator, the pantry, and the store closet were continually empty.

"That last case of ginger ale was used up yesterday—ten loaves of bread I'll need for sandwiches, and if you *could* help, Ma'am, and buy a part of the cake this time, we would appreciate it— Well, three dozen chops might go 'round, but the last time the Mayor and his Council were here, you remember we didn't have so much as a bone left on the platter."

These were the echoes which reverberated from the kitchen. She listened to them and tried to heed them. But she did not feel she was always successful.

She went everywhere that she was asked, even when she was faint with fatigue. She picked up threads of her old association, with her church, her historical societies, her pupils; she wore clothes that were spotlessly fresh, delusively simple. The Conrads thought she had too many, and told her so, but she did not dare try to do with less. She was gracious, cordial, democratic, dignified, tireless, decorative. What did it all amount to? If she had been an illiterate, ignorant slattern would it really have made any difference? How much "influence," after all, did a wife have in this frantic, powerful, hideous struggle of politics? Probably very little. Perhaps none at all. Still, she had done her best, and if only Neal did not feel she had failed him, it would not matter what any one else thought. But how *would* he feel towards her if he were not elected? She remembered the hard months after his campaign for the Lieutenant-Governorship, when he had been defeated. Was it going to be like that again? . . .

"Hello— Hello— Senator Conrad's house? The polls have just closed here in Weatherby. Allen, First Selectman, speaking—yes—two to one for Neal. We are banking on him, Mrs. Conrad, to come through in Belford yet. . . ."

Would defeat in the long run be such a calamity? She saw herself living in Hinsboro again, in the house she loved so much and into the building of which her very soul had gone—comfortable, happy, unworried—no more calls to make; no more "appearances" to keep up; no more "admirers" to contend with; time for her children, her music, her real friends. There was that little hedge she had always wanted to plant in the garden, the "Rose of Sharon" counterpane which she had always wanted to quilt, the breakfast nook she had wanted to build out of the pantry that had proved too large. How much simple satisfaction—how much real joy —she was denied because she could never "find time" for these things. Would she not be happier, no longer deprived of these homely pleasures?

And yet, even as she asked herself the question, she knew that she would miss the insidious charm, the fascinating excitement of political life as much as Neal. She could bear that philosophically, but because of her own feeling, she could gauge his. He must, he must go on.

She slipped to her knees. With the same simplicity, with the same ardor, that she had prayed on her wedding night, she prayed again now. For Neal—for Neal—for Neal. . . .

Still on her knees she reached for the telephone.

"Headquarters calling again, Mrs. Conrad. We've heard from the last five wards in Belford—["Oh, God—let him win —let him win!"]—you must get your husband to the telephone."

She spoke to him. Her voice sounded strange and distant, like that of a foreign woman calling from some far shore.

"You will have to answer, Neal, this time." ("Oh, God— let him win—let him win—let him win!")

She pressed the receiver into Neal's hand, threw her arm around him. From the wire she could hear the crackle of laughter—the tumult of triumph—and staccato sharp the words that were being spoken:

"You old crape hanger you! What in Hell's the matter with you? You have the handsomest margin—"

"What do you *call* a 'handsome margin'?" Neal shouted through the receiver, clutching at Anne's shoulder.

"Well, if fifty thousand doesn't look handsome to you— Come on down here, you old Son of a Gun, and celebrate . . . ! ! !"

CHAPTER TWENTY-SIX

With Neal Conrad's senatorial career every reader of any daily paper is familiar. There is the tariff, which bears his name; there is his speech on the British Debt Funding plan, which is used as a model in "elocution" for every school boy; there is his unshakable stand on the League of Nations which sent him, at the head of a special senatorial committee, to Geneva. All this, and much more, is so well known that it needs no further comment. Besides, this is not the story of Neal Conrad to which numerous famous biographers have already failed to do justice. It is the story of his wife.

And of his wife as the only hostess to achieve a real "Salon" in Washington; as the only American woman whose dress drew forth royal commendation at Buckingham Palace; as the only this and that in various conspicuous capacities, enough has also been said. Her dresses and her dinners have been described a thousand times. Why, therefore, attempt to describe them again? It is neither the Beauty nor the Belle with whom we are primarily concerned—it is the woman . . . The woman who, on a certain hot afternoon in mid-June, boarded the Congressional Express with her husband, bound for the great National Convention in New York.

The lobby of the Waldorf Astoria, as they entered it, weary after their warm and dusty journey, was so jammed that they could hardly wedge their way through it to register. With every step that they advanced, some acquaintance stopped and seized them, shouting at them excitedly. With every turn they took, placards and posters of rival candidates—most of whom had their headquarters in the hotel—crackled above their heads. Scurrying bell-boys, distracted room clerks, help-less assistant managers, strove in vain to perform their nor-mal functions. Laden elevators sank and rose in the hopeless, endless endeavor to convey the mass of humanity which bounded into them like a phalanx from one floor to another. It was nearly an hour before they reached their suite; and Neal, mopping his brow and snatching up a glass of ice water, muttered as he drank, that he was "infernally late for the cursed committee meeting" and that he must be off at once.

"Committee meeting? *To-night?*" Anne asked in astonish-ment. "Why, it's after ten now."

"Probably shan't get in before three," he informed her hastily. "Well, goo'-by. Better order yourself an orangeade and a chicken sandwich and have Dora see you unpacked and settled before she goes to bed. Try to get some sleep. You'll have a hard day to-morrow."

Refreshed by a bath and a cooling drink, Anne slipped into the lacy nightgown which Dora had spread out for her, and settled herself for slumber. Her hopes for repose were, however, entirely unfounded; a party of men who were occupying the next room, and who had apparently met in secret conclave, were either unaware or unconcerned of the fact that they could be overheard, and that they were dis-turbing the public peace. Their voices reverberated through the thin wall. Their lack of harmony rent the air. They were —it appeared—delegates from Chicago, in revolt against their "boss" and violently distrustful of each other. When Neal returned, haggard and hollow eyed, about five, he found Anne sitting up in bed, taut with nervousness.

"Neal, dear, just listen to that racket! It hasn't stopped for a single instant. I can't stand it! We'll have to go to some hotel where it's more quiet."

"Quiet! At a National Convention! Good God, Anne, you don't know what you're talking about. There *isn't* any quiet. Those fellows aren't really objectionable. They're just having a little friendly argument. You should have heard *our* committee. Turn over, old lady, and go to sleep."

"I can't sleep."

"Well, stay awake then, but I shan't."

Flinging his clothes hastily in every direction, Neal sank down beside her and was instantly dead to the world. Two hours later he was abruptly aroused by a heavy pounding on the door and staggered to his feet still drunk with slumber.

"Yeah,"—Anne, who had not closed her eyes heard him saying through a gingerly opened crack—"I guess so. All right, I'll be there right away." He closed and locked the door again and began to gather up his garments from the floor, and put them on.

"I hoped I'd have time for a shave and a shower," he muttered, "but I'm needed right away. You can get to Madison Square Garden all right alone, Anne, can't you? I've left your ticket on the mantelpiece. Don't lose it, whatever you do. And hang on to it when you show it. It might be snatched right out of your hand. Well, goo'-by."

It was only a little after seven and he was gone again. The hubbub in the next room had worn itself out. Anne began to grow drowsy but, almost immediately, she was shaken into consciousness by a band which, from the noise it made, appeared to be passing directly beyond the foot of her bed.

It was, of course, in the street outside. She went to the window and watched it go by, a glitter of braid and brass. Then resigning herself to the impossibility of resting, she rang for coffee and Dora.

At ten, clutching her precious ticket, she left her room, waited fifteen minutes for an elevator not already too crowded to take her in, threaded her way breathlessly through the crowd in the lobby, even denser than it had been the night before, and after another long wait secured a taxi. The driver turned at a most perilous crossing to transfix her with a piercing glance:

"You gonna woik fer our candidate, lady?" he queried;

and giving his wheel a sharp twist, added, "You better—we're gonna keep you here 'til ya' do."

He set her down at an entrance which was apparently impenetrable and flanked with eight policemen. The officers of the law seemed to regard her contemptuously. One of them spoke to her.

"Where's your button?" he asked abruptly.

Thinking she had misunderstood, Anne showed him her ticket, but, mindful of Neal's injunction, without relaxing her grasp on it.

"Naw—I don't mean that—ain't you got a button with a certain pitcher on it?" Anne shook her head a little bewildered. "Well, before you come back next time, get yourself one. But go along in now."

She found herself in the basement. There was a clatter of typewriters rising from a string of crowded press rooms, a clicking of telegraph instruments, messengers darting to and fro, a blondined young woman presiding over a cigar stand, delegates almost covered with badges and ribbons, more clusters of policemen. Beside large black letters, painted on squares of stiff cardboard, proclaiming themselves as guides to certain sections, steep staircases led to vague upper regions. Anne was so confused that it took her some time to find her own rabbit-warren. But at last, flushed and triumphant, she emerged on the platform and looked around.

The great oval of the huge structure rose about her, fluttering with flags—big flags, middle-sized flags, little flags, flags infinitesimally small. Out beyond her on the floor, the standards of the states, like giant markers on a flower bed, rose in the aisles beside the seated delegations. Alaska and the Canal Zone were, so to speak, blowing hot and cold together. So were Vermont and Texas; the Middle West was flanked, aggressive and immovable, by the solid South. The packed galleries towered tier upon tier, above the seething crowd beneath them; the boxes encircled the building like a crown; the press sections, stretching out in two white-washed divisions, made her think of a great pale bird with its wings spread. Close beside her a radio announcer was broadcasting with the earnestness and enthusiasm that revealed the closeness of his contact with his unseen audience. Near the rostrum a group of men, who looked as if they had been up all night, were talking with their heads close together; the members of the National Committee, bristling with self-importance, were securely seated in the most desirable places; back of them on the platform rows of women, in light summer dresses, fanned themselves and chatted with each other. A band, very spritely and smart, was playing "Three O'clock in the Morning."

Without further difficulties Anne found her seat, an excellent one between Mrs. Lassiter and Mrs. Lee. They greeted her cordially, and as she shook hands with them, she felt herself being playfully tapped on the shoulder and, turning, she was confronted with Mrs. Ranger and Mrs. Roper.

"My dear, isn't this too *thrilling!* Of course, we two were certain to be together. You know we're *never* separated. We're such *friends.* But I actually see the hand of Heaven in the rest of the arrangement. We simply *adore* National Conventions, don't you?"

"I have never been to one before," said Anne, who, for all her sophistication had never outgrown the habit of truthfulness.

"My *dear!* How quaint! Why, we haven't missed one since 1908, though none of them have been quite so *harrowing* as this is going to be. But I am sure our *dear* candidate will be victorious in the end, aren't you? Though these terrible New Yorkers will stop at nothing to prevent his nomination, *absolutely nothing*— I have it on the best authority."

A gavel thudded suddenly down. A Bishop began to pray, the national anthem sounded, Kleig lights blazed. A small, neat man with glasses balanced so precariously on his nose that he was forced to keep pushing them back toward his short-sighted eyes, read resolutions, figures and statistics. The

Chairman of the National Committee introduced the Temporary Chairman, and this gentleman made an impassioned plea to God and the Convention to deliver him from the party in power. His fervor amounted to frenzy. He mopped his brow, and threw out his arms. But his audience remained calm. Anne saw several men looking at their watches, and in the press gallery, some bored looking reporters sauntered away from their seats. Anne, her own attention wandering, noticed the very fine sapphire that Mrs. Lassiter was wearing and realized that she was hungry. She had expected, of course, that Neal would come and take her out to lunch. But when the welcome adjournment came, she had still seen nothing of him, and Mrs. Roper and Mrs. Ranger bore her triumphantly away between them. The afternoon session came and went. The Permanent Chairman, efficient and belligerent, assumed control of the Convention with a few volcanic remarks. The Committees on Membership and Rules made their reports. The band played. The policemen clustered. The broadcaster continued to speak earnestly and enthusiastically into his machine. At last, genuinely worried, Anne approached Senator Lee, who had joined his wife, and asked if he thought "anything could have happened to Neal."

He laughed reassuringly. "My dear lady, your husband is one of the 'key' men. He can't be spared for window-dressing like this. He has to work."

"But isn't the work being done here at the Convention?"

Senator Lee laughed again. "Certainly not. What made you think it was? Because we sang the 'Star-Spangled Banner' and shed tears about Shaw's administration? There is a bitter fight over the platform and a bitterer one over the candidate. Those are the real issues."

He appeared to be about to say something more along the same line but checked himself at the sight of Anne's clouded face.

"Don't worry, Mrs. Conrad," he added gently, "and be as patient with your husband as you can if he seems to neglect you; and—by the way— I wouldn't plan on getting away from here this week if I were you."

"But the convention is to end Friday!" said Anne, growing more and more bewildered.

"A week from Friday, perhaps, if we are lucky. But we probably shan't be lucky."

Senator Lee's prayer for patience was needed. Neal, not having appeared for lunch, did not appear for dinner either; having spent one night at a committee meeting, he spent two more in the same way. He did not go with Anne to the Mayor's Garden Party at Washington Square or the Governor's dinner at the Ritz. He did not go with her to the Convention. He burst into their suite at extraordinary hours for brief moments, searching for clean collars and clamoring for ice water. Anne, consumed with curiosity and excitement, hungered for conversation and explanations. But she hungered in vain. Neal seemed hardly more aware of her than he was of the mantelpiece. It was there and she was there. That was all.

The bitterness of the fight on the platform became increasingly evident. The papers carried huge black headlines about it. The band played familiar tunes that were becoming to sound tiresome and silly, to fill in gaps in the program; a famous humorist cracked jokes that permeated from the press section to the rostrum; the Permanent Chairman bristled more and more. At last it was announced that no agreement having been reached, a majority and a minority report would both be submitted. There was a day of oratory and eloquence and hysteria; of plays to the gallery and appeals to sectionalism. It ended as it had begun, in confusion and hard feeling, and dramatic instability.

Anne, going back to the hotel after it was over, with a violent headache, found Neal sitting beside the marble-topped "center table" of their "parlor," with a sandwich in one hand and a pencil with which he was scribbling illegible characters on a plump pink Senate block in the other. There were dark circles under his eyes, and tired lines of fatigue about his mouth. But he was newly shaved and looked clean and cool in a light fresh suit. And as she entered he looked up with a smile.

"Hello," he said cheerfully, "the worst is over. I am a human being again. And I might say in passing, you have been a brick—as usual—during these last few days while I *haven't* been like a human being. Are you pretty tired?"

"Rather. It's all been so futile and ugly. I believe I won't go to the evening session."

"I'm sorry—I thought we might go together. The fact is—I am going to make a speech. There seems to be a sort of feeling that—well, that if I did I could straighten out this platform tangle."

"Oh, Neal, really? Then, of course, I'm going."

"Good! I hoped you would, and I thought we might have dinner—a real dinner—on the roof first. I hear it's cool and pleasant up there. Snap into a tub and out again and you'll feel better."

As she moved away, slipping her crushed dress over her shoulder, she had the curious impression which she had had a few days before when Senator Lee was talking to her, that Neal had intended to say something else and then decided against it. She turned and found that he was looking after her fixedly and suddenly she thought there were tears in his eyes. She went back to him.

"You are sure," she asked softly, "that nothing is the matter?"

"No, dear, nothing," he answered, and began to scribble again on the block of paper.

CHAPTER TWENTY-SEVEN

The speech which Neal Conrad made before the great National Convention in Madison Square Garden—clear, convincing, courageous, charming and incomparably dramatic, awoke the torpid delegates, soothed the angry alternates, and stirred the restive galleries in an applause that rocked the very foundations of the mammoth structure. Incidentally it also resulted in the immediate adoption of the majority report of the platform committee.

The following morning Senator Lassiter sought Anne out, an enormous bundle of newspapers under his arm—"I thought you might have slept late this morning," he said, smiling, "and so have had no time for these before you came over. It might interest you to look at them. Not only at the front pages, but at the editorial pages."

He nodded and left her. Anne unfolded the crackling sheets to be confronted with Neal's picture and heavy headlines which, in sharp staccato sentences, made it clear even to an unobservant public, how significantly he had scored. He had not only captured the right-hand column on the front page, he had also—she discovered upon following Senator Lassiter's advice—captured the "leader" on the editorial page; and not in one newspaper, but in all of them. She began to read avidly, flushed with pride.

Her attention was diverted by a stir among the delegates. The Permanent Chairman was announcing briskly that the names of the candidates for the office of President would be put in nomination, and that the roll of the states would be called by the Secretary of the Convention. This individual advanced to the front of the stage, and cried out, "A-l-a-b-a-m-a" as if he were challenging the South to mortal combat. A gentleman with a goatee and an expansive, immaculate waistcoat arose from the midst of the Alabama delegation, and replied, as if he were answering the challenge, "Alabama yields to California."

Pandemonium broke loose. The band, blaring its loudest, was completely drowned out by tin whistles, horns and rattles. States' standards waved, flags fluttered from the galleries, the Chairman thumped and thudded in vain, and shouted to the ushers to clear the aisles. The portly gentleman who had appeared beside him with a manuscript half an inch thick, in one hand, raised the other hand with a gesture of impatience because he could not make himself heard. But for a quarter of an hour he was quite powerless to do so. When at last the din had partially subsided, he bellowed forth the opening sentences of his address three times.

"The man who I am about to name," he shouted over and over again. But he did not name him. He talked for nearly three-quarters of an hour, and still, as far as he was concerned, his audience was left in the dark as to whom he was describing. At last, with a crescendo of enthusiasm he revealed his secret. The uproar began again. Some of the delegates commenced to parade. Others, conspicuously silent even in the midst of the noise, sat stubbornly in their seats, resisting all efforts to drag them forth. The march continued without them until the most fervid enthusiasts had shouted themselves hoarse and sank down again exhausted. When this happened, the Chairman, who had been looking tensely on, as if prepared to spring from the platform at any moment, snapped his eyes in the direction of the secretary, and the secretary took up his challenge again.

"Arizona!" he shouted. Arizona, it appeared, was also in a yielding mood, and again pandemonium broke loose. Again a would-be nominator, clasping a bulky manuscript, stood impatiently beside the Chairman, endeavoring to make himself heard. Again, when his chance finally came, he failed to take the Convention into his confidence concerning the identity of his candidate. Again, his final pronouncement was drowned by the whistles, the band, the sound of marching feet. This time it was the men and women who had sat still before who were parading, the ones who had been silent before who were shouting. The personnel was different; but the process was just the same.

By the time the fifth candidate had been placed in nomination Anne had resumed her reading; and when, exhausted by a tumult which, like the waves of a rough lake, seemed to be rising and falling without going anywhere, she decided that she might as well "see the thing through" since it must in any case be over very soon now, she realized that, when all possible names had been mentioned for the presidency, there still remained all possible—and impossible—names to mention for the Vice-Presidency.

Mornings of it—afternoons of it—evenings of it. The great principles of our party. The corruption of the unscrupulous politicians now in power. The leaders who, though dead, guide us with their sterling statesmanship. The country which our forefathers fought, bled and died to save. The Stars and Stripes, rippled by a gentle breeze, floating forever over a united country with no north, no south, no east, no west. On the Banks of the Wabash Far Away. The Sidewalks of New York. Way Down Upon the Swanee River. Ioway, Ioway, That's Where the Tall Corn Grows. Dixie. My Old Kentucky Home. The Man Who.

She had the terrible feeling which she had sometimes experienced on a long uncomfortable journey, that it was never going to end. She said so, dizzily, to Senator Lee.

He laughed. "The balloting will begin to-morrow, but we are a long way from the end of the Convention yet. Neither of the leading candidates can get two-thirds of the vote. There will be a dead-lock."

"And what will happen then?"

"One of them may withdraw, but I doubt that. It's more likely we'll have a compromise candidate."

"Have you any one specially in mind?" she asked, without much real interest.

Afterwards she remembered that Senator Lee had given her no direct answer, and wondered why. But with the first excitement of the balloting she forgot all about it. There was an indescribable thrill for her in hearing the chairman of a delegation announce that his state cast twenty-four votes for a certain well-loved candidate. At least there was a thrill the first time she heard it. Even the second and third and the fourth. But finally . . .

For as Senator Lee had predicted, the balloting went on and on and on. She wondered how she could ever have thought the nominating interminable. It was this, instead, that was endless. One week stretched into another and many of the delegates, whose funds were limited, deserted their hotels and betook themselves to lodging houses and cafeterias. The heat folded down over the city like some thick impenetrable blanket. A spirit of weariness, of hopelessness, of hate, began to permeate the heavy atmosphere. And still the band played. And the Chairman rapped with his gavel. And the balloting went on.

CHAPTER TWENTY-EIGHT

"Darling Anne."

She had been drowned in sleep, the profound, prolonged oblivion of utter exhaustion; but Neal's voice, calling to her, brought her back in dizzy waves of memory to the consciousness of her surroundings. The brass bed with the picture of "still life" hanging over it. The pitcher of ice water on the mantelpiece. The faded flowers beside the riddled pincushion. Her bedroom at the Waldorf Astoria. The National Convention. The balloting. The Man Who.

"Anne," said Neal again. And again, "Darling." Her head was still heavy with slumber. But through it flashed the love-laden thought that he needed her. She sat up, pulling at a shoulder strap that had slipped away from her white shoulder, and pushing back the soft masses of her hair.

"What is it?" she asked.

"I wanted to tell you—how much I love you."

She laughed comfortably and stretched out her arms.

"Is that all?" she said lightly, "not that it isn't enough—worth more than anything else in the world! But you don't wake me up in the middle of the night usually to tell me so! You expect me to take it for granted!" Then with sudden apprehension clutching at her heart, "Neal," she cried, "there isn't anything wrong, is there? You haven't had bad news from the children?"

"No, no," he said soothingly. "The children are all right. It's just—" He broke off, and sitting down beside her on the bed, put his arms around her. "I think I haven't told you often enough perhaps—what you mean to me. I *have* let you take it for granted. I have taken *you* for granted—or seemed to. I haven't really. I wouldn't have amounted to—to much of anything, without you. No one realizes that better than I. You've had all the qualities I've lacked—courage and endurance and talent and faith and vision. I've known all that, Anne, from the first moment I saw you, and I've loved you from that moment too. I've never stopped trying since that night we stood in the meadow and pledged our lives to each other—to give you what I promised you then—lace to wear instead of calico. Real lace. The lace—of a Queen."

"What are you trying to tell me, Neal?" she breathed.

"That the Convention is over, that the dead-lock is broken." His voice failed him suddenly, and he trembled violently, but he collected himself and went on. "When you told me you thought you wouldn't go to Madison Square Garden again, I didn't urge you because—well, I still couldn't be sure, though from the very beginning I have hoped—I have thought—I have had such good loyal friends working for me—I have known how events were shaping—" Realizing that he was becoming incoherent, he checked himself again, and again went on. "On the ninety-seventh ballot some one—a Southerner—voted for me. Then there were several scattered votes from New England. A whole Western delegation. When the count was ready I had nearly a hundred. On the next ballot there were over three hundred and then—and then—Oh, Anne, I'll never forget those banners—those marching feet—those lifted voices singing—cheering—shouting. They got me up on the platform and I—spoke to them. And afterwards they wanted me to go away with them. But I—came home to you—to tell you that I had been nominated President of the United States."

In the carpeted corridor beyond men and women passed, calling to each other excitedly. Porters wheeling trucks that squeaked, banged baggage hastily out of rooms that had suddenly been vacated and carted it away. The roar of the city lifted from the streets suddenly rushed through the dim

room. The shrill voice of newsboys rose screaming above the
blare of bands and the confusion of traffic.

"Extra—extra!"—"Dark Horse wins!"—"Conrad nominated
for President!" "Extra! Extra!"

"But I," repeated Neal, "came home—to you."